LOVE CHILD

Also by Irene Carr

MARY'S CHILD
CHRISSIE'S CHILDREN
LOVERS MEETING

LOVE
CHILD

Irene Carr

Hodder & Stoughton

First published in Great Britain in 1998
by Hodder and Stoughton
A division of Hodder Headline PLC

British Library Cataloguing in Publication Data
A CIP catalogue record for this title is available
from the British Library

ISBN 0 340 68951 X

Typeset by
Phoenix Typesetting, Ilkley, West Yorkshire
Printed and bound in Great Britain by
Mackays of Chatham plc, Chatham, Kent

Hodder and Stoughton
A division of Hodder Headline PLC
338 Euston Road
London NW1 3BH

LOVE CHILD

Chapter One

DECEMBER 1890. MONKWEARMOUTH IN SUNDERLAND.

'That's something for you to remember me by!' Her husband's drunken bawling followed Amy Campbell as she ran down the stairs. His jeering laughter echoed in the bare passage, uncarpeted and unlit, that led to the open front door. Amy passed through it and plunged blindly into the night and the storm, the rain that fell in torrents. She left behind her the marital home, the single room with just a bed, a pair of upright chairs and a table, all paid for by her.

Although his laughter followed her, Josh Campbell did not. The laughter faded and was lost altogether as thunder cracked overhead. The gaslamps were mere globules of dim yellow light in the rain, leaving the streets in darkness. At the bottom end of the street the cranes in Buchanan's shipyard towered over the terraced houses which crowded around the yard like barracks. The cranes were still now, and all the yards up and down both banks of the river were silent. This was the biggest shipbuilding town in the world, but the day's work was long over.

Amy saw nothing anyway, wrapped in her pain and misery. She was nineteen years old and had been married just a month. Josh Campbell, red-haired, florid, stockily muscular, had been on his best behaviour when he courted her. He drank but all sailors did and she never saw him drunk. That – and the violence – came after the wedding. Amy shuddered. The wind coming in from the sea was icy cold and smelt of salt and coal smoke, but was not the cause of the tears that ran with the rain down Amy's face.

She passed St Peter's church, lit briefly by a sheet of lightning, and climbed up Church Street. As she crossed Roker Avenue a tram came rattling through the driving rain, water spraying up from under its wheels, the horses pulling it with their heads down, coats glistening. Amy ran in front of it, unseeing and deaf to the clatter of hooves and the driver's bellow of 'Look out, there!' and hurried on, trying hopelessly to outrun her shock and heartbreak.

The junction where six roads met at the Wheatsheaf public house was still busy with people, despite the rain. They splashed through the puddles under umbrellas, or peered out from the windows of the trams. Few had time to note the slender girl, face white and blue eyes wide, in just a dress, her blonde hair hanging in rats' tails.

Soon the town was left behind her, and she was out on the road to Newcastle, walking in country. The darkness was total and she was alone on a road only a shade lighter than the black hedges on either side. Amy knew this road a little, having travelled it once before, when her husband brought her from Newcastle to Sunderland, but it was a strange place in the night. However, she could not go back — not yet. She shuddered at the thought and wandered on, wearying now as her initial stark fear ebbed away.

The storm that had rumbled away inland now returned, the lightning laying bare the road ahead for an instant, the thunder shaking her. The rain fell more heavily, and Amy was soaked to her skin.

She heard the beat of the horse's hooves first of all. Turning to peer back along the road she saw the swaying bulk of the horse — and a cart? No, a trap, marked by a coachlamp on each side. As it rolled up the light from the lamps washed over her. She stepped aside, but was too late to avoid the muddy water spurting up from under the trap's iron-shod wheels, forcing her to cry out.

The trap stopped with a clattering of hooves a few yards ahead of her. A man sat at the front holding the reins, his head turned to look back over his shoulder at Amy. He bulked large, seen against the light, and now he said, concerned, 'Are you all right? I didn't see you until I was on top of you.' He looped up the reins, threw aside the tarpaulin over his knees and got down from the trap, unshipping one of the coachlamps as he did so. He strode back to Amy with the lamp held high. He saw her face, huge-eyed and pale in the night, and caught his breath. He thought she was lovely. Then his gaze moved from her wet features to her upright figure. 'Good God!' He peered at her, shocked. 'You're soaking, girl!'

Amy shivered from reaction and cold. She was a simple, gentle girl, alone and frightened now, wanting only a kind word. The man wore a caped raincoat that glistened oily in the rain, and a cap with the peak tugged down to shield his eyes. Peering up at him, and into the light, she could see only that he was young.

The young man reached out a hand to feel the stuff of her dress and found it sodden, although it was obviously a lady's dress, expensive, not that of a working girl. But no lady would be tramping the roads on a night like this. The dress had been given to Amy before her marriage when she was in service. It had belonged to the daughter of the house where Amy had worked, who had passed it on scarcely worn. Amy had put it on in a desperate attempt to please Josh Campbell. It had failed miserably. Now she stood and let this young stranger finger it.

He let it go and said, 'You can't wander in the rain like this. I'll take you home.' He spoke as a man used to taking decisions, giving orders. 'I'm staying at the Buchanan place just up the road. I'm Lucien Hawkins and Andrew Buchanan is a friend of mine.'

Amy was awed. Andrew Buchanan owned the shipyard at the end of the street where she lived. She had seen him, once or twice, riding into the yard in his carriage drawn by two high-stepping greys.

Now Lucien pulled off the raincoat he wore and wrapped

it around Amy, urging her towards the trap.

She let him lead her until she stood at its step. 'I've no home to go to,' she said suddenly. She realised that now. She had fled from Josh Campbell and would not return, and her parents would not make her welcome because a young woman without work was just another mouth to feed. Her place in the house where she had been in service would be taken. Besides, she had her pride. She would be ashamed to admit she had run in fear from her husband of only a few weeks. Now she stood in the road with the rain falling on her mane of blonde hair, the young man staring down at her.

For a moment he was at a loss, then he said, 'Well, you can't stay here. Let's get you dry first.' With his hands on her slim waist he lifted her up into the trap and sat her down, tucking the stiff folds of the tarpaulin around her legs. He shook the reins, and the pony broke into a trot. Lucien gave Amy a brief smile. 'It isn't far now.'

In less than a mile they came to a pair of wrought-iron gates set wide. He swung the trap in at the gates. 'This is the Buchanan house.' He went on, suspecting something of the girl's distress and trying to put her at her ease. 'Andrew shut it up after his wife left him – a sad business.' He shook his head. 'He took his son to London and the servants went with them.' Amy had heard talk that Andrew Buchanan's wife had 'gone off wi' another feller'.

Lucien went on, 'When he heard I was coming up to this part of the world for a week or so he insisted I use his place. He intended the gatekeeper and his wife to look after me – he'd left them to care for the house – but they went off to see to the gate-keeper's sick mother.' He pointed with his whip at the lodge, its windows shuttered. The trap started up a gravel drive, and the whip swung to point again: 'But there's the house.'

At first Amy saw only a faint orange glow in the night, which she realised came from an uncurtained window and the fire within. Soon she made out the outline of the house against the night sky. It sprawled wide before her, the wings on either side

of the front door spread like welcoming arms, and the glow beto-
kened a warm welcome. Her spirits lifted at sight of it.

The young man wheeled the trap to a halt in front of the steps
leading up to the front door. He jumped down and handed Amy
down, then led her up the steps. Taking a key from his pocket he
opened the door and ushered Amy ahead of him and into the hall.
They trod on a carpet laid on a gleaming wooden floor and there
was a smell of furniture polish. Sheeted furniture stood like
ghosts in the gloom.

Lucien said, 'There are plenty of lamps and candles. I'll light
some shortly.'

Amy accepted this as normal. The house in which she had
worked had been in the country, without gas or electricity, its
light provided by oil lamps and candles. She felt no fear, was sure
there was nothing here to harm her.

A hand in her back thrust her gently onward through a
doorway leading off the hall into a drawing room. Here the furniture was not sheeted. The big fire in the hearth had been banked
up that morning to last the day and was now burning through.
By its light Amy saw a big chesterfield on either side of the fireplace, while numerous armchairs, and small tables covered with
pictures and ornaments, were spaced about the room. On one of
the chesterfields lay a stack of neatly folded blankets. Lucien
gestured at these.

'As I said, I'm alone in the place and I've been camping out in
just this one room.' He grinned disarmingly. 'I'm used to hard
lying at sea sometimes and I'm not much of a housekeeper, I'm
afraid.'

Amy saw he stood a head taller than she, with wide shoulders.
He had a thatch of thick, black hair, a straight nose and wide
mouth set firm. It was a good face, though not handsome. They
smiled at each other, uncertainly, but there was an electricity
between them. Now he seized a poker and stirred the fire into
flaming life so their shadows danced on wall and ceiling.

A kettle stood in the hearth and he jammed this on to the

coals. Then he brought from a sideboard a tray that held a jug, several glasses and a decanter. He poured whisky from the decanter into the jug and said, 'There you are. Top it up from the kettle when that boils and help yourself. It'll warm you inside. I must go and stable the pony.' He left her standing by the fire. Amy heard the clump of his boots as he passed through the hall, then the front door closing.

Her mind was functioning again by now, although only on a primary level. She recoiled from the memory of Josh Campbell and what he had done to her, tried to wipe it from her mind. Again, she felt she was safe here.

The fire was throwing out heat, but Amy still shivered in the wet clothes that clung to her body. She fetched one of the blankets, and felt its soft texture. She drew the thick curtains across the tall windows and hesitated a moment, nervous, wondering if he would be back soon. But then she told herself that he would be some time seeing to the pony, and she was *cold*. She stripped to the skin and wrapped the blanket around her, like a tent that covered her from head to foot, then hung up her clothes on the backs of several chairs for them to dry. By that time the kettle was singing and she poured the hot water on to the whisky, filled a glass with the mixture and sipped it. As Lucien Hawkins had promised, it warmed her through.

Amy was sitting on the rug before the fire when he returned, her legs curled under her. She had taken the pins from her blonde hair and let it down to dry, and it hung like a silken curtain around her face. She started to get to her feet — she had never been seated in a room like this before, she had always stood and taken orders — but Lucien said quickly, 'No, don't get up.' As she subsided he asked, 'You're feeling more comfortable now?'

'Yes, thank you, sir.' Amy was remembering her manners and her training now.

For some reason he could not identify, this made Lucien feel awkward. He had guessed she was a working girl despite the dress, and now that was confirmed by the way she addressed him.

It was the way of a servant. And he did not think of her as such. He went to pour himself a glass of toddy, stepping around Amy where she sat cocooned and shapeless in the blanket, only her head showing. He had seen much more shoulders and bosom on many a society beauty, but this was . . . different. He stood at a distance of some feet, leaning against a corner of the mantelpiece as he talked.

'I met Andrew Buchanan in the Navy. He held a commission until he inherited the estate and the yard. He was senior to me, older, a commander while I was only a lieutenant, but we were firm friends. We served in a cruiser and went on leave together. Wait . . .' He searched among a score of framed photographs crowded on a table and returned with one, holding it out to her. 'There you are. That's Andrew and myself when we went walking in Austria a couple of summers back.'

Amy saw two young men in tweeds, heavy boots and deer-stalker hats. One was Lucien, and the other was equally tall and dark, but with fuller features. She recognised Andrew Buchanan. She also realised that Lucien's head was now close to hers as he knelt at her side. She turned and smiled at him.

He returned the smile, eased back to sit on the edge of the chesterfield but was still within touching distance. Amy felt the warmth of this house wrapping her round, and from that moment she knew she loved him. It may have been akin to the affection of a kicked dog for a new, kinder master, but there was no denying the strength of the emotion. Amy lifted her face to him.

Lucien had always been contemptuous of those men who 'took advantage' of the girls in their service, but now he kissed her because she wanted him to – and he could not help it. As he did so he reached out to hold her. Amy was conscious of the blanket slipping as she raised her hands to clasp them behind his neck, but she did not care and let it fall.

He was gentle with her and she responded passionately. When that first ardour was spent, there was tenderness while the fires built in them again and there was more passion . . . So they passed the night until the flames in the hearth died to embers, and sleep overcame their bodies entwined under the blankets.

Amy woke in the pale dawn to cold reality. The facts she had been unable to face the previous night, that she had shrunk from thinking about, now forced themselves on her. She knew that this young man whose naked body pressed against her own belonged in this house, houses like this, and she did not, except as a servant. She knew she had a husband, who would be at sea now as his ship had been due to sail an hour after she parted from him. He had treated her brutally and she was sure he would do so again, but she had given her vows. She had made her bed – and it was not this one.

Amy slid out of the blankets. Lucien stirred but did not waken. Her clothes were crumpled but dry and she dressed quickly before taking one last swift glance around the room to make sure she had left nothing. She saw the photograph of the two young men where Lucien had stood it on the mantelpiece, and took it, clutching it tightly as she closed the front door quietly behind her.

The rain had stopped and a pale winter sun, all light without heat, was climbing out of the mist that clung to the earth. Amy paused at the gatekeeper's lodge to look back. Now, in the light of day, she could see that the Buchanan house was built of warm red brick which seemed to glow in the sunlight that glinted from the windows. It promised comfort and shelter, refuge.

Amy's upbringing and her simple soul told her that she had sinned here. She had committed adultery. She turned from the promise of the Buchanan house and walked away.

Lucien woke an hour after she had left him. He could not believe that she had gone, and he went running through the house at first, calling for her. She had not told him her name, so he could only cry, 'Hello! Where are you?' When he realised she was not in the house he ran round to the stable and harnessed the pony in the trap then set off after her. He kept the pony to a fast trot, but never encountered the girl. The town had swallowed her up.

There was a week to go before he had to travel to Portsmouth to commission the torpedo boat that would be his first independent command. He spent that week searching the town for the girl and at the end of it departed in despair. He could not believe that the love he had so incredibly won he had so quickly lost.

For some years from then on, if he was not serving abroad, he returned to spend a week or more in Sunderland, wandering through the streets, his eyes scanning the faces that passed him. He made the excuse that, as a naval man, he was interested in the shipbuilding that went on there. However, eventually memory faded, and when he met and married Olivia, the visits ceased, although he still recalled the girl he had loved on a night of storm.

Amy returned to the first-floor room in Monkwearmouth that she shared with Josh Campbell. Its window looked out on the back yard, while the other two rooms on that top floor faced on to the street and were rented by another couple. A third family lived in the two rooms below. All the houses in the long terraces built beside the shipyards were split up and let similarly.

As Amy had expected, Josh was not there, having joined his ship the night before. He had left the signs of his occupation in spilt food and empty bottles. The fire was cold and dead. Amy took the galvanised iron bucket downstairs to the coalhouse in the backyard and filled it with coal. She used an old axe to chop some firewood then carried all that load up the stairs and lit the fire.

She spent the rest of that day cleaning the room and washing her clothes and those Josh had left scattered about the floor. In the evening she walked down to St Peter's church and prayed for forgiveness of her sin. She took the photograph of the two young men out of its frame, which she threw away. The cover of her large Bible had come loose at the back, and she loosened it further to make a pocket and slid the photograph in there. Josh Campbell would never look in her Bible.

The child was born in August and Amy called her Lucy. She knew Josh Campbell was not the father. When he had tried to take her that night before he sailed, he had failed, being impotent with drink, and to mask that failure he had beaten her. He was gone for almost a year. When he returned and saw the baby girl he viewed her with some pride.

'She looks a bit like me. Her hair's a lot darker, though.' It was almost black, not like his red poll.

'That's from my father's side,' put in Amy. 'His brothers are all dark.' It was an explanation she would give again and again as Lucy grew up.

'Ah!' Josh had seen enough. 'Have you got a drink in the house?'

He gave her some money – he had not been able to spend it on the long run home from China – but the rest he squandered on drink. When it was gone he signed on for another cruise. And so began the pattern of their lives, with Amy struggling to make and keep a home while Josh was mostly at sea. And as her child grew, Amy saw Lucien Hawkins in those dark eyes.

Chapter Two

SUMMER 1896

'Do you know where it is, Mam?' five-year-old Lucy asked, face turned up and dark eyes solemn as she trotted at her mother's side.

'Aye, I know it,' answered Amy.

They were walking out along the Newcastle road on an early morning of bright sunlight. Amy Campbell pushed the battered old perambulator carrying her other three children, seated one behind the other. Tommy was two, Rose three and Billy just a year old. They all wore dresses down to their knees, boys and girls alike, with long socks and button boots on their feet. Rose was blonde like her mother, but the boys had their father's red hair.

'Have you been there before?' Lucy pressed.

'Never you mind. Now hold your tongue and save your breath for walking.' Amy had told no one of her first visit to the Buchanan house and was not going to start now.

Lucy tried again. 'Is it far now, Mam? My legs are tired.'

Amy halted and sighed. 'All right.' She lifted Lucy and balanced her on the edge of the pram so she was facing her mother, and folded her small fists around its handle. 'Hold on so you don't fall off.' She started pushing again.

Amy was on her way to the Buchanan house. Old Mrs Harris, who lived only two doors away from the Campbells and had done washing at the house for nearly ten years, had told Amy only the evening before, 'They're wanting some help up at the Buchanan place.' Amy could find work near her home, cleaning and such-like, but Mrs Harris had told her the money was better at the Buchanan house.

Amy had hesitated, remembering with guilt that it was in the Buchanan house that she had become an adultress. There was further guilt because it was a memory that clung to her – or that she clung to. Then again, there was the reputation of the house now, the scandal she had heard. However, needs must when the devil drives, and Amy lived with the devil. There were four children to feed, and although Josh Campbell was at home, he had spent what pay he had saved from his last cruise and was now looking for another ship. Amy knew she would get nothing from him.

Now she said, 'Here we are.' They had been following a high wall that ran by the side of the road, and now this was broken by a wide gateway. The two wrought-iron gates stood open, but as Amy turned the pram in from the road she was challenged by the gatekeeper.

'Now then, missus, what's your business?' But it was said with a cheerful grin. He stood in the doorway of his lodge, a man well into his forties. Amy remembered that six years ago he had been away, seeing to his sick mother.

Amy answered, 'I heard from Mrs Harris that there was help needed with the washing.'

'Ah! Mrs Harris. Aye. Well, you follow the path that goes round to the back. The washhouse is round there.'

'Thank you, sir.'

'Not "sir",' he corrected her, the grin widening. 'Call me Fred like everybody else does, short for Fred Wilson.'

'Thank you. I'm Amy Campbell.'

She leaned forward to push the pram again, and Lucy, head twisted to see the way they were going, breathed, 'Ooh, Mam! It's lovely.' Amy stared at the parkland fringed with trees, the carriage drive running through it, and the house at the end of it. She caught her breath. It was as she had seen it last, with the morning sun lighting the warm red brick. She could understand Lucy's admiration. The child had known nothing like this, only the three meagrely furnished rooms, one of them just big enough for a bed, in the terraced street where she had been born and raised. Amy had scrimped and saved and pleaded with Josh to accomplish the move from a single room to the three needed by her brood. After a moment her smile faded as she remembered again that this was the place where she had fallen. She shoved the pram forward. She wondered, at once both afraid and eager, if she would meet Lucien Hawkins. She knew both hope and apprehension – and guilt. But she need not have worried because Lucien was at sea off the coast of Africa. Now she tried to put him out of her mind, as a memory of one episode best forgotten.

The path led around the house through the trees, so that while they still caught glimpses of the house, the people inside would not see them, or any other servant or tradesman calling.

The washhouse stood at the back of the house, with its boiler and tubs, poss-sticks, scrubbing brushes and steamy heat. Amy wasted no time in getting to work with the other women there, who were washing the clothes of the Buchanans and their guests and servants. She set the three younger children down from the pram and told Lucy, 'Now mind you watch them. Don't let them wander off. I'll just be in there if you want me.' She disappeared into the washhouse but tried to find work that would keep her near the door so she could look out frequently to see that her children were safe and behaving themselves.

Lucy settled down to playing with Tommy and Rose and acting as sheepdog to the crawling Billy. Lucy had expected to have this duty, indeed she knew her mother had kept her off school for the purpose, and she was happy enough, still savouring that first sight of the house. She found a patch of grass and earth, sheltered by a crescent of bushes, and showed Tommy and Rose how to build huts out of twigs. Later she fetched water in a tin from where it ran from a washhouse outlet and they made castles out of mud. Billy was determined to crawl, in a constant effort to escape, and Lucy kept bringing him back.

Besides her duties there was plenty to interest and intrigue her. The stables were nearby, and two or three grooms worked at mucking out or grooming the horses while another polished a carriage. When she turned her head she could see through a back window into the kitchen. The cook and her kitchenmaids and scullerymaids were busily washing up after breakfast and preparing for lunch. Lucy licked her lips. She had eaten only a slice of bread with a scrape of dripping that morning, washed down with tea.

The women in the washhouse gossiped as they laboured in the heat, of death and illness, birth and marriage, the ships being built in the river and the shipyards that were the key to the town's prosperity. And, looking over their shoulders to be sure they weren't overheard, 'Housekeeper, she's *supposed* to be.' After the giggles subsided, 'Well, that's what he calls her.'

'What about the lad, then?'

'That's his son by his wife that ran off. And she'd had a few men afore that one!'

The voices called from all around the washhouse, lifting above the din of scrubbing and the pounding of the poss-sticks in the tubs. 'It's a bloody wonder that housekeeper hasn't had any bairns by him. She's been in his bed every night for the last three years.'

'Ah! But they know what they're doing, those two. It'll be bad luck or intended if she ever falls for one.'

'Not intended by Andrew Buchanan. He's got his son, who'll inherit whatever Andrew leaves, so he'll want no more bairns.'

'He can enjoy hissel' going through the motions, though.' That brought more ribald laughter.

Lucy peeped through the open door and saw her mother feeding wet clothes between the wooden rollers of a mangle. Amy did not laugh with the others, but had a forced smile. She did not like this talk. Lucy did not know the smile was put on, but did sense her mother was unhappy. She turned back from the door and hauled little Billy back from crawling off into the bushes that grew close to the washhouse. Lucy did not understand the drift of the conversation at all, except that Andrew Buchanan had a son and did not want any more children. She had heard of him before. The Buchanan shipyard was only a hundred yards from where she lived, so his name was often mentioned. At five years old she barely comprehended what a shipyard was or how an owner fitted into her world. She was soon to be given a lesson.

An hour later Billy crawled off again, and when Lucy dashed to fetch him back she found herself facing a boy who knelt in the bushes. 'Hello,' he said.

Lucy turned Billy around and smacked his behind. 'Get back.' To the boy she said, 'Hello.'

'How old are you?' he asked.

'Five.'

'I'm eight.' That was said with satisfaction, his seniority established. He scrambled out of the bushes and stood up. He wore a white shirt and grey flannel shorts which came down below his knees. The socks below had slid down over his ankles to show grubby shins. He was burned brown by the sun and his hair was black and tangled with a curl to it. 'What's your name?'

'Lucy Campbell.'

He grinned down at her, teasing. 'Little Lucy Campbell! I'm Nick Buchanan. Don't you go to school?'

She resented that 'little Lucy', but answered, 'Aye, but my mam kept me off to look after the bairns.' Lucy dashed after Rose this time, as the toddler tried to get into the washhouse.

Nick followed her, accompanying her as she brought Rose back to the little patch of grass where the others played. Nick said, eyes scanning the house, 'I'm hiding from the curate. He comes in to give me lessons, but this morning it's Latin and it bores me stiff.'

Lucy did not know what Latin was and could not understand

why this boy should be taught by a curate, whatever that was. 'Do you live in the house?' That earned her respect. To live in a place like this . . .

'Yes.' Nick replied in staccato sentences, absorbed in watching for the curate. 'My uncle is my guardian. My parents died in India. Daddy was in the Army there. He was Uncle Andrew's younger brother.'

Lucy was interested, though still not understanding. This was different from all the other children she knew, whose fathers worked in the shipyards – or went to sea and came home rarely and, in the case of Josh Campbell, drunk.

Nick chuckled. 'He went into a cupboard – the curate, I mean – and I locked the door. I wonder if he's still in there?' He crouched then, as footsteps approached, ducking back towards the bushes, then straightened. 'It's only Murdoch.' His wide grin slipped away and now he was scowling.

Another boy had come around a corner of the house and was wandering towards the stables. Lucy asked, 'Is he your brother?'

'No, my cousin. Uncle Andrew's boy.'

'Is the curate looking for him?'

'No. The curate doesn't teach him. He goes to school.'

'Why isn't he at school, then?'

The other boy had seen Nick and now he called, 'Why aren't you at your lessons?'

Nick said, 'That's Murdoch, poking his nose in and trying to give me orders.'

In the washhouse, the woman who was in charge called, 'I need some help down here for a few minutes, Amy. Come over, pet.' Amy left her place near the door and hurried to the far end of the washhouse.

Murdoch was two or three years older than Nick and several inches taller, a burly boy with a fleshy face, and dark like Nick. He stopped in front of Nick and demanded again, 'Why aren't you in the schoolroom?'

Nick shrugged. 'I didn't feel like it.'

Murdoch lectured him, 'Father pays the curate to teach you, so you're wasting his money.'

Nick snapped back, 'I didn't ask him to spend it.'

'He hasn't any choice. You're an orphan and his ward and you haven't any money so he has to keep you. You should be grateful. If it wasn't for Father you would be begging or in an orphanage.'

Nick was pale, his mouth clamped tight shut. His lips barely parted as he warned, 'You'd better shut up, Murdoch.'

Lucy was still puzzling over the question she had tried to ask earlier. Now she repeated it, asking Murdoch, 'Why aren't you at school?'

He was startled for a moment, not expecting any interruption from this small girl with the solemn face. Still sneering at Nick he answered, 'Because our school has different holidays to the ones you common people have in the town.'

Lucy did not take offence because she knew nothing of boarding schools. She asked, 'What's common people?'

'Ones that don't wash,' replied Murdoch. 'People like you. You're dirty.' He pointed an accusing finger.

Lucy understood that. She objected, 'That's just where I helped Tommy to build the castle.'

Murdoch jeered, 'That? That's not a castle! That's just a heap of muck!' And he stepped forward and kicked it to pieces.

Lucy cried, 'What did you do that for?'

'Because it was mucky and because I wanted to. This is my father's house and I can do as I like.' Murdoch turned back to Nick and rubbed it in. 'And you'd better run back to the curate before I tell Father and have you kicked out.'

Tommy and Rose stared at the destruction and began to wail. A second later little Billy joined in out of sympathy. Nick, goaded beyond endurance, charged at Murdoch, his fists flailing. The bigger boy held him off, laughing at first. The outraged Lucy hurled herself at Murdoch and wrapped her arms around his legs. Then she reverted to the failing Amy had trained out of her – and sank her teeth into his thigh.

Murdoch's laughter was cut short and he yelled with pain. He reached down to try to prise Lucy away but Nick seized the opportunity and pummelled him about the head, then locked the fingers of one hand in Murdoch's hair while he continued to punch with the other.

The three of them spun in a slow, shuffling circle, silent except for Murdoch's yelling. Nick was furiously aiming blows to land on Murdoch. Lucy could not speak because she had her teeth set in his leg and clung to it with her eyes closed. She had somehow swung around so she was behind him. He could only reach her with one hand so was unable to pry her loose. He began to shriek and weep with the pain of it.

'What the *hell* is going on here?' The bellow sounded above their heads. The horseman wore shirt, breeches and gleaming boots and sat on a tall hunter. He was in his fifties, seen to be tall as he leaped down from his mount, brown faced and dark eyed with black hair that the riding had left windblown in tousled waves. He demanded, 'Stop it! All of you!' His big hands on the collars of Murdoch and Nick yanked them apart and he held them at the stretch of his arms. He stared down at the small girl who peered up at him and ordered her, 'Leave it.' It was the order he would have given to a dog, but then he reflected, grinning, that the circumstances were similar to a dogfight.

Lucy sat back on her heels, then stood up and shuffled backwards to join her siblings. She cuddled little Billy and his wails ceased, but too late.

Amy had returned to her place near the door of the washhouse and so heard the man's bellow and Billy's weeping. She came hurrying out anxiously to see what trouble her brood might have got into, and halted with a hand to her mouth. A boy stood with his hand pressed to his leg and big tears rolling down his cheeks. He was bruised about the face. Another boy, smaller and equally bruised was licking his knuckles but not crying. And between them was – Amy caught her breath – Andrew Buchanan.

Amy had no doubt who he was. She still had the photograph of Andrew and Lucien Hawkins as young men, and he had changed little over the years.

Grooms were now running from the stables and touching their caps. A woman had accompanied Andrew, riding sidesaddle in a habit. One of the grooms held her mount while she dismounted, and Amy saw she was tall, blonde, and slender but full breasted. This would be the notorious Nell Jarman, Andrew Buchanan's 'housekeeper'.

Now Nell spoke, voice soft and good humoured. 'It was only a childish squabble, Andrew, though it sounded like murder!'

'True. But I want to know who is responsible.' Andrew demanded, 'Who started this?'

Nick said nothing, but Murdoch began, 'They set on me—'

'*Ooh!* We never!' Lucy put in, outraged. 'You said he should be doing his lessons because he hadn't any money, and I was dirty, and—'

'*Sshh!*' Amy clapped a hand over Lucy's mouth and said quickly, fearing she might lose her job, 'I'm sorry, sir, but she's only young and she's got excited.'

Andrew said flatly, 'Yes.' He exchanged glances with Nell Jarman and said heavily, 'I think I see.' He propelled Murdoch towards the house with a shove of his hand. 'Get that leg seen to and then go to your room. I'll talk to you later.' The suppressed anger in his voice was clear and it silenced Murdoch. Andrew watched Murdoch limp off then turned on Nick and asked, 'Why aren't you at your lessons?'

Nick, quiet now, answered, 'Latin bores me.'

Andrew said drily, 'I feel some sympathy for you there, but you're not only learning Latin, there's obedience as well. And where's the curate?' When Nick could not meet his eye, Andrew demanded, 'What have you done with him?'

Nick answered, voice low, 'I locked him in the cupboard.'

Nell Jarman coughed – it may have been a cough – with a hand lifted to cover her mouth, or hide her face. From behind it she murmured, 'Discipline is not the reverend gentleman's strong point.'

Andrew's lips twitched and he said, 'That I know. But I will not have the boys taking advantage of it. Go and let him out, Nick, and tell him I would be grateful if he would join me in the drawing room for some refreshment. Then you, too, can go to your room and I'll deal with you later.' As Nick walked away, Andrew called after him, 'And remember you are my brother's son and always welcome in this house.'

As Nick passed Lucy he grinned at her and one of his eyes closed in a wink. Then he walked on.

Andrew now turned towards Lucy and the other children. To her he said, smiling, 'I see you were trying to eat my son.'

Amy put in quickly, still afraid she would lose her day's work, 'I thought I'd broken her of that habit, Mr Buchanan, but she must have been frightened. She's not a misbehaving child as a rule.'

Lucy complained, 'He knocked the castle down, Mam. I'd helped Tommy and Rose to make it and that boy kicked it down.'

'Ssh!' Amy hissed at her again.

Andrew sighed and said, 'So I understand.' But he smiled at Lucy. 'Never mind. Go on with your play. No doubt you'll find plenty of mud to make another castle.'

Now Nell Jarman addressed Amy: 'You've come to help with the washing?'

'Aye, ma'am. Mrs Harris – she lives two doors away from me – she said you were wanting help today.'

'I know Mrs Harris.' Nell's attention shifted and she asked, 'And these are your children?' Her gaze roamed over them, seeing the patched, well-worn and well-washed clothes, and thought, No money but they're the bairns of a decent woman by the looks of them.

Amy now looked properly at her children for the first time since she had run from the washhouse. It was obvious that they had been playing with mud. The dresses she had washed and ironed so diligently the day before were daubed with huge patches of the muck. She moaned. 'Oh, look at the state of them and all clean on this morning.'

Nell laughed, 'Bairns are the same the world over.'

Andrew pulled out his watch from the fob pocket of his breeches, and glanced at it. The grooms were harnessing the two greys to the carriage. Andrew would be driven down to the yard as soon as he had drunk a cup of coffee with the released curate. He started towards the house.

Nell began to turn away to accompany him but called back to Amy, 'Leave your name and address so I can send you a post-card if I have work for you again.'

'Thank you, ma'am.' The possibility of more work cheered Amy, but as she returned to her labours now she warned Lucy, 'You keep out of trouble and don't get those bairns any dirtier than they are already.' However, she knew with a sinking heart that she would be washing their clothes again tomorrow.

The rest of the day passed peacefully, and when the work was done Amy set out for home, pushing the pram with the three younger children inside. Lucy walked, tired as they all were, but asking questions. 'Mam, what's a curate?' 'Mam, what's a guardian?' 'Mam, are there schools with different holidays to ours?' And when it was explained, 'They live in the school and only go home for holidays?' Amy replied as well as she could, though absently.

As they walked back along the path to the wrought-iron gates, the lights were being lit in the Buchanan house. Amy could see, through narrow gaps between the trees, the lit windows of the room where her little daughter had been conceived. That episode was now so distant it might have been a dream. But Amy knew it was not. Suppose she had not been married to Josh Campbell, had not been bound by her vows? But she had been, still was, would be till the end of her days.

'Mam, my legs are tired.'

Amy lifted Lucy up, balanced her on the pram and said

mechanically, 'Hold on to the handle now, so you don't fall.'

Lucy said drowsily, 'It's a lovely house, Mam. Can we go again?'

'We'll see.' If there was work Amy would have to go, even if every sight of the house broke her heart.

Josh Campbell was waiting for them when they got back to their three rooms. He stood at the top of the stairs and watched as Amy trudged wearily along the passage which ran through the house – like all the others – from front door to back yard. She struggled up the stairs with little Billy in one arm, towing the pram with the other, herding the three older children in front of her. Josh stood aside to let them pass into the kitchen and Amy smelt the drink on him. He asked thickly, 'How much did you get?'

Amy sank down into the one old armchair that a neighbour had given them. She was worn out from the day's labour in the steaming heat of the washhouse and her legs and back ached from pushing the heavily loaded pram. She answered weakly, 'A shilling.' Amy took it from the pocket of her apron to show him.

Josh grabbed it and stared at the coin disgustedly. 'Is that *all*? Only a bob for a whole bloody day's work?'

'There's plenty of others would do it if I didn't.' Then as Josh headed for the door and the stairs she pleaded, 'Don't take it all. The bairns want some supper.'

Josh threw over his shoulder, 'I'll bring something back.' Then he was gone.

Amy got out the second shilling she had been paid that day. Lying to Josh had become a necessity for survival. She instructed Lucy what to ask for and sent her off to the little shop on the corner with the shilling. Lucy returned with the bread, and the bacon pieces that were more fat than meat, and the change. They had a supper of bacon and fried bread, and went to bed.

Amy woke from an exhausted slumber to hear Josh falling drunkenly into the bed beside her. She lay still, tensed, but after a while was able to relax as she heard him snoring.

It was a long time before she could sleep again. She knew she was expecting yet another child.

Chapter Three

SPRING 1900

Lucy woke early in the bed she shared with Rose, and four-year-old Elsie, another redhead and the latest addition to the family. That had been a difficult birth and Amy had never fully recovered but she tried to hide this from the children. Lucy lay still for a moment, listening to the low drumming that came from the clatter of booted feet as the men streamed past her window in the street below, on their way to Buchanan's yard. The other girls still slept and there was no sound from Tommy or Billy, whose bed was on the other side of the curtain that divided the room in two.

Lucy crept out of the bed and over to the landing. The door to the small bedroom over the passage, which Josh and Amy shared, was closed. A cupboard opening off the landing held a china wash-basin and jug. Lucy used the jug to bail a little water out of the pail brought up by Amy from the yard the night before. Lucy washed in the bowl and then poured the soapy water into another bucket. When that was full it would be carried down the stairs and emptied into the sink in the yard.

She was already excited at the prospect of the day ahead, despite the rain that pattered on the windows, and she sang softly under her breath.

*

They were on the Newcastle road when Elsie squeaked from the pram, 'Are we going to that big house, Mam?' Rose, Billy and Tommy were all at school this day: Amy had arranged for old Mrs Harris to give them lunch, and had left sandwiches of bread and dripping for them.

'That's right,' Amy replied. Amy kept one eye on the sky where the black clouds scudded on the wind. There had been rain when they had started out from Monkwearmouth, and would likely be more before long. Down on the shore the big green rollers would be bursting in foam. On the river the gulls wheeled above the ships that were building in Buchanan's yard, and the others ranked along the banks of the Wear.

Nine-year-old Lucy trotted alongside as Amy pushed the pram as much for its support as for it carrying her youngest daughter – or her youngest so far, at any rate. Amy needed that support, because she was pregnant yet again and feeling worse this time than ever before.

The pram was now battered and rusty, and Lucy thought its wheels squeaked worse than Elsie did, but she did not complain and smiled happily as she kept pace with her mother. Amy had kept her home from school, as she always did when going to the Buchanan house to work, this time to watch over Elsie.

'I like that house.' Lucy skipped an extra step so she could turn and look up at her mother.

Amy smiled faintly. 'Aye. I know you do.'

Since that first time, she had received a postcard every two or three weeks from Nell Jarman, asking her to go to the Buchanan house to help with the washing. Amy had built up a reputation as a good worker, adept with the smoothing iron. She was glad of the work because the money it brought in helped to feed her family. Josh Campbell had not changed: he was away at sea for long periods and brought little of his earnings home.

Amy loved the Buchanan house, despite an aversion to it because of the memories it triggered. Every time she saw it was like reopening an old wound. But there it was, patches of warm red brick and glinting windows seen through the trees as they circled through the woodland to reach the back of the house. To Lucy it was like a fairytale palace after the crowded little houses in the long, drab streets.

Amy was glad to immerse herself in her work after telling Lucy, 'Don't let Elsie wander off too far and see she keeps clean,' and warning, 'Mind you behave yourself, our Elsie.'

Lucy listened patiently and politely but knew the instructions were automatic – and unnecessary. Elsie would not wander off nor misbehave. She would play at being a cook, as she always did, making imaginary meals for imaginary people with leaves and twigs as utensils. For Lucy, the only problem with Elsie would be boredom. In the pram was a boy's comic, which had passed through innumerable hands before reaching Tommy Campbell and so Lucy, but it offered sight of other worlds. Lucy settled down under a tree, where she could see Elsie simply by lifting her eyes from the page, and began to read.

Only minutes later, Nick said, 'Hello,' and sat down beside her.

Lucy asked, 'What are you doing here?' Nick had been at prep school for four years now. He wore long, grey flannel trousers and a white cricket shirt open at the neck.

'Some kid went down with spots so they sent the rest of us home a week early for the hols. I got back last night. How's little Lucy?'

'Don't call me "little Lucy",' she replied irritably. 'I'm not little.'

'Yes, you are!' He grinned at her as he always did when he baited her this way. He had another four years' growth now and was head and shoulders taller than Lucy. During those four years he had teased her relentlessly, but he had also told her what he could remember of his life in India, with an *ayah* and servants at his beck and call, and about his place in this house – and the jeers of Murdoch Buchanan.

Nick had once told her, 'Murdoch is cunning. He waits until there's only him and me before he tells me I'm poor and dependent on his father for everything.'

Lucy had asked, 'Why don't you tell his father? He's your – your guardian, isn't he?'

'Never!' Nick was determined about that. 'Uncle Andrew is all right, but I'm not going blubbing to him and telling tales.' And his jaw had set stubbornly.

However, he was grinning when he stood up now. 'I'm going to see if Helen is at home. I've got a secret to tell you later.'

'What secret?' asked Lucy warily, wondering if this was another of the jokes he played on her.

He would only say, 'I'll tell you when I get back,' and strode off around the corner of the house.

Lucy watched him go with regret. His teasing annoyed her, although he was good company, imaginative and cheerful. She went back to her comic but found it hard to concentrate, wondering what his secret was.

She became conscious of the rain when a big drop splashed on the page she was reading. She looked up and saw the sky had clouded over. Rain pattered on the leaves of the trees over her head. She called, 'Come on inside, Elsie!' Seizing her little sister by the hand she hauled her in through the washhouse door.

The washhouse was an echoing cavern smelling of soap and filled with steam that rose from boilers and poss-tubs. The damp heat made the women run with sweat as they turned the handles of the big cast-iron mangles or beat the clothes in the tubs with the heavy poss-sticks. Amy Campbell stood over a tub of soapy water, rubbing clothes on a scrubbing-board. She shouted above the noise of scrubbing, thumping poss-sticks and the singing of the women, 'What are you doing in here?'

'It's raining, Mam!' Lucy yelled back.

'Well, play there by the door. Don't get in anybody's way.' Amy went wearily back to her scrubbing. She was tired already and the day not half-over.

Elsie had snatched up some of the twigs and stones she had been using outside, and now carried on her game on the floor by the door. Lucy sat down there with her comic.

It was another ten minutes or so before Lucy looked up and saw Nick had returned. He stood under the tree, and Helen Whittaker was with him. She was of an age with Lucy but was blonde, blue eyed and beautiful. She was an only child and her mother had died when she was born. Her father had married late in life and was in his fifties now. He was a wealthy businessman who had moved into a large house, further down the road past the Buchanan place, a year or so ago. Nick had been a frequent visitor there when he was not at school, but Lucy had only seen the girl once or twice. Helen's father, because of his business interests, saw little of her and she was left in the care of a governess who let her do as she liked. She was dressed plainly but expensively in a light, knee-length dress with a high collar, black shoes and stockings.

Nick was looking about him and Lucy scrambled to her feet and leaned out of the door to call, 'I'm in here!'

Nick's head turned and Helen's finger pointed to where Lucy stood in the doorway. Nick beckoned but Lucy called, 'I'm looking after Elsie,' and she waved the comic to indicate her sister kneeling at play by the door.

Nick came over to her impatiently. 'It'll only take a minute or two.'

'What will?' Lucy questioned.

'The secret.'

'Why can't you tell me?'

'I can't just tell you. I have to *show you*.'

'You're having me on.'

'I'm *not!*' Nick retorted, exasperated.

Now Lucy was stubborn. 'Well, you'll have to tell me a bit

about it, or I stay here,' and she lifted the comic again.

'All *right!*' Nick approached Lucy, and as he did so saw her expression of triumph, and grinned. 'You win.' He stopped, Helen at his shoulder.

Helen peered past him into the washhouse and wrinkled her nose prettily at the steam and the heat and the smell of the soap. 'What an awful place.'

Lucy defended, 'No, it isn't. That's my mam in there, scrubbing.'

'Is it really your mother?' Helen peered through the steam at Amy, hunched over the scrubbing-board with strands of her hair hanging damply about her pale face. 'She doesn't look very well.'

Lucy argued, 'Yes, she does.'

Nick broke in, 'Look, do you two want to see this secret?'

'Yes, please,' said Helen politely. Lucy did not speak, but with Nick's eye on her, she nodded.

'You know I'm supposed to start at public school next term.' Nick waited for confirmation and they both nodded. He went on, 'Murdoch's been there for two years now. When I go he'll be on at me all the time. And I don't *want* to go to school. I want to go to sea.' He stopped.

The two girls waited a moment then Lucy said, 'You've told us all that before.'

'Ah! But not how I'm going to do it.'

Helen still waited politely, but Lucy pressed, 'Do what?'

'Go to sea, of course. Now I'll show you, if you'll come.' Nick paused expectantly.

Lucy hesitated and now Helen urged her, 'Oh, come on, Lucy. Your sister will be all right for a minute or two.'

Elsie was playing happily. Lucy glanced at her mother and saw Amy was working with her back to the door. 'Just a minute, then.'

So Nick led them into the trees until the washhouse was out of sight, and to a summer house. Lucy gaped at it, having never suspected its existence, hidden away among the trees. It was a wooden hut with big windows, and inside was an armchair and a cushioned couch. It appeared a cheerful, comfortable little house where a lady might sit to work on her embroidery when the sun was bright but the wind too chill for out of doors. Lucy pictured Nell Jarman thus – then realised the place had a neglected look, as if it had not been used for years.

Nick burrowed in a gap between the floor of the house and the earth on which it stood. He emerged with a bundle in his hands which he unwrapped. It proved to be an oilskin such as sailors wore, and inside was an old tobacco tin which Nick opened and showed to them. It was half-full of coins, mostly copper, but there were some sixpences and shillings and a solitary half-crown. He explained, 'I've been saving up nearly all the money I was given when I was at home. And the oilskin is my bad-weather kit.' He paused for effect, then finished, 'I'm going to run away to sea.'

They were silent for a moment, then Helen said practically, 'Don't be silly.'

'I'm not being silly!' Nick was indignant. 'When I'm ready I'll slip out when they think I'm asleep and creep aboard a ship. Then I'll stay hidden until she's out at sea.'

'Oh.' Helen was impressed.

Lucy was not, however, and asked, 'How do you know which ship?' When Nick stared, she explained, 'My dad's always talking about ships and when they might be sailing and where to. He's a sailor. Some ships come in for a boilerclean and don't go out for days. And there's other ships get laid up for weeks or months when trade is slack.' The phrases, gleaned from listening to Josh Campbell talking to her mother, tripped glibly off her tongue.

Helen asked, 'Why do they need their boilers cleaned?'

'I know that,' Nick claimed, trying to reassert his superiority. 'They get furred up inside after steaming a long way.' He was impressed by Lucy by now, and muttered, 'I don't want to be sitting in the hold of some ship for days before she sails. Can you find out when there's one sailing?'

Lucy admitted, 'I don't know.' Now she regretted showing off her knowledge.

'You could ask your father.'

'No, I couldn't.' Lucy did not intend to question Josh Campbell. She was more than likely to get a slap for her trouble.

'Oh, go on!' Nick urged. 'When will you be here again?'

'I don't know that, either.'

Nick looked at Helen, but she shook her head. 'I can't find out that sort of thing. I'm sorry.'

Nick sighed and his shoulders slumped, and that wrung out of Lucy the promise, 'I'll try.'

Nick brightened. 'You will? Good! Now we only need to find out when you're here again.'

Lucy told him, 'Come round to the washhouse when they finish work in there tonight.' She remembered Elsie and ran back to see to her, while Helen and Nick wandered off into the house. Lucy glimpsed them occasionally as they passed a window.

In the afternoon a bored Lucy begged her mother, 'Can I take Elsie for a walk, Mam?'

Amy wiped sweat from her forehead with the back of her hand and said tiredly, 'Mind you stay inside the grounds. And not in front of the house where they can see you.' The servants and tradesmen had to keep to the back of the house.

So she led Elsie by the hand, strolling through the trees until the gatekeeper's lodge and the carriage drive were in sight. Fred Wilson was working in his garden, digging with his fork, jacket and waistcoat discarded and his braces dangling. Andrew Buchanan, in an old hacking jacket and moleskin trousers, sat on a canvas-seated stool in the shade of the trees. An easel stood before him and he was dabbing at a canvas with a brush. Lucy was curious. She knew she should not, but stepped closer, then stood on tiptoe and leaned to one side, to try to see what he was painting. She could only make out a block of red below a blue wash. She was very quiet but then Andrew swore, 'Damn it to hell!'

'Ooh!' said Elsie.

Andrew twisted round on the stool, dark eyes glaring, and Lucy bobbed a curtsy as her mother had told her and said nervously, 'Sorry, sir.' Now she could see he had a smudge of red paint on his nose. 'I was just — looking.' It was a feeble excuse and Andrew still glared. She added desperately, 'It's very good.'

The glare faded but he was still straight faced when he asked, 'Know a bit about art, do you? Can you see what it's supposed to be?'

Lucy edged forward, and it was quite clear now she could see it properly. 'It's the house.' It was all there, windows and roof and red walls, the surrounding trees.

Andrew muttered, 'Well, at least you can recognise it. Thank God for that.' He was frowning now as he stared at the painting. 'But there's something wrong with the damn thing.'

Lucy breathed, 'I think it's lovely!'

'I'm glad you think so.' Andrew rubbed at his jaw and left another smudge of paint there. 'But do you see what's *wrong* with it? Because it *is* wrong and I'm damned if I can see where.'

Lucy said meekly, 'I think the house is warmer than the picture.'

Andrew studied the painting, then, surprised and curious, he looked at Lucy. 'You're right. Who are you and where d'you come from?'

'Lucy Campbell, sir. And me mam is helping in the washhouse today.'

'You'd better get back to her, then.' He took the painting from the easel and asked, 'D'you want this? Because I don't. I'll keep the one I get right.'

Lucy took the canvas and asked, disbelieving, 'To keep?'

'Or burn it if you like. It's yours.'

'Thank you, sir.' Elsie reached out a hand to touch the painting and Lucy smacked it away. 'Leave it alone! And come on.' She grabbed Elsie's hand then led her away, turning to say once more, 'Thank you, sir.' Andrew only grunted in reply as he packed up easel and stool then set off towards the house.

When Amy finished work for the day, Lucy showed her the picture and explained to a shocked Amy how she came to have it. 'He wasn't angry, didn't tell me off! Honest, Mam! "You can keep it or burn it," he said, "I don't want it."'

'Well, as he said you could . . .' Amy, mollified and too tired to argue, accepted, but she warned, 'don't let your father see it.'

'No, Mam.' Lucy knew he would burn it or sell it. She hid it in the hollow compartment in the bottom of the pram.

Before Amy had finished for the day, Nell Jarman came to the washhouse and asked her, 'Can you come a week today, Mrs Campbell?'

'Yes, ma'am, thank you.' Amy was cheered by the thought of another day's work.

Lucy was able to sidle over to where Nick and Helen waited in the trees and tell him, 'We're coming next week.'

'Good! Find out a ship for me, little Lucy.'

'Little Lucy!' She nearly retorted, 'Find out yourself!' but he was grinning at her so she only shook her small fist at him and ran off, leaving him laughing.

As she trudged home with her mother that night she remembered Helen's comment and looked up at Amy. She realised that her mother was pallid and drawn. She had never really looked at her before, had always taken her presence and care for granted. Now she was frightened.

Lucy was also afraid she would let Nick down, as she had no idea how to find out the times of sailings of ships. Could she wait at the dock gates and ask the sailors when they came out? She could tell them her father was looking for a ship — that was true enough because his money was spent. So she tried, only to be told to 'Clear off!' by the watchman on the dock gates. She worried over the problem for the next week to the point of despair, then found there was no need.

On the morning they were to go to the Buchanan house again,

her mother asked Josh Campbell, who was still in bed after the previous night's drinking, 'What ship are you on and when is she sailing?' Amy always went down to the dock with the children to see their father off. After all the hard years, she still tried to maintain a family relationship. She also needed to know the ship's name for when she went to the shipping office to draw whatever part of his pay Josh had granted her.

Josh bawled thickly, 'She's the *Scintilla*, a rotten old tub, and she's sailing out o' the North Dock at half past ten tonight. But I won't be on her. Now, shurrup and let me sleep!'

Lucy knew he was not joining his ship because he had won some money backing horses. She also knew it must have been a substantial win, as he had given five shillings to Amy. That meant he would be drunk for a week at least. Lucy had learned a great deal in her nine years.

Amy had kept Lucy off school to look after Elsie, but the little girl was poorly. Amy didn't want to leave her in Lucy's care when Josh was drinking, so she asked Mrs Harris to take Elsie for the day, which meant Lucy could go to school. However, some instinct told Amy to take her eldest daughter with her, and Lucy was only too ready to go.

Nick was waiting in the trees at the back of the Buchanan house when Lucy told him, 'There's a ship sailing from the North Dock at half past ten tonight. She's called the *Scintilla*.'

'Well done, little Lucy!' Nick seized her shoulders and kissed her.

Lucy shrieked, 'No! Don't be daft!' although she was pleased by his praise.

'Lucy!' The voice called weakly, and she turned to see her mother standing in the washhouse doorway and holding on to the frame. Amy beckoned. 'Come here.' Lucy ran over, and her mother said, 'I feel badly. Come on in and do this scrubbing for me.' So Lucy scrubbed the clothes while her mother sat with eyes closed on a stool by the door, where she was sheltered but still had some fresh air.

Later Lucy fed clothes through the rollers of a big old mangle and stood on another stool to pound the washing in a tub with a wooden poss-stick. It was no new experience for her, having often helped her mother at home. The other women in the washhouse helped and encouraged her: 'There's a good little lass!'

In the afternoon Amy recovered a little, but the women told her, 'You stay there and rest. You're still a bad colour.' She was pale, her dark eyes huge in her thin face, so at the end of the day it was Lucy who was wielding the smoothing iron, and there Nell Jarman found her.

Nell smiled at Lucy. 'You're a young recruit.'

Amy struggled to her feet. 'I was just letting her have a go while I had a rest, ma'am.'

Nell saw the pallor, and knew there was more to it than that. 'I think you should go home and see a doctor.'

'Yes, ma'am, I will.' Amy was afraid she would lose her work at the Buchanan house. 'But I'll be fine in a day or two. I'm just a bit off colour.'

'Yes, I'm sure you will,' Nell agreed in a soothing tone. She turned back to the ironing and told Lucy, 'You've done very well.'

'Thank you, ma'am.' Lucy asked boldly, 'Could I have a job in the house when I leave school, please, ma'am?'

Nell laughed. 'You're making your claim early! Well, come and see me when you finish with school.' And to Amy: 'Will you come next week, Mrs Campbell? But only if you're well enough.'

'Yes, ma'am, I'm sure I will be.'

Amy was not sure about Lucy working at the Buchanan house, afraid that the house might be bad luck for her and her family, but she was too ill to care now and Lucy would not leave school for another four years. That would be time enough to worry, and the bairn would probably change her mind before then.

Amy dragged her aching body the weary walk home, staggered up the stairs and fell on to the bed. Josh Campbell was not in the house, so a frightened Lucy ran to tell Mrs Harris, who sent Lucy running for the doctor. When the doctor arrived, Mrs Harris took all five of Amy's children to her own two rooms to be out of the way. Dr Galloway, greying and twenty years in that practice, came in his trap. He bit his lip over Amy's condition, although she was not the first such case he had attended, and he knew with bitter certainty that she was unlikely to be his last.

He did what he could for her, but Amy lost the child. Afterwards he tried to break the news gently to the worn and exhausted young woman. 'I'm afraid there must be no more children. You would not survive another pregnancy.' However, with Josh he was more direct, eyed him coldly and told him, 'It will require some self-discipline on your part, but another pregnancy will kill your wife. Do you understand what I am saying?'

He waited until Josh muttered, 'Aye. I'll leave her alone.'

'Don't forget what I've told you.' The doctor picked up his bag, and warned, '*I* won't.'

When Lucy returned with the other children, she found her mother sleeping, her face as white as the sheet drawn up to her chin. Lucy stared at her and knew that her father was to blame. Josh Campbell sat hunched on a cracket by the fire. Seated on the low stool, his eyes were on a level with hers, and for the first time she looked at him with anger not caution.

Josh saw her look and muttered defensively, 'She's going to be all right in a day or two.' But he saw no forgiveness in Lucy's bitter stare, and turned away. 'Get yourself off to bed.' Then half to himself, 'I should ha' got that ship tonight. I'll look for another tomorrow.'

Lucy knew he was running away. She went to her bed with the other two girls, but she could still picture her mother lying in the other bed only feet away on the other side of the wall. After a long time she cried herself to sleep.

✳

Nick stole out of the Buchanan house under cover of darkness, avoiding the gatekeeper's lodge by throwing the bundle of his clothes and oilskin over the wall and then climbing after it. He tramped the road into Sunderland and down to the North Dock. The gates were still open, and he slipped past the watchman while he was busy tending to the stove in his little hut.

Nick found the *Scintilla* tied up to the quay, and climbed the gangplank to her deck on tiptoe. A hand reached out of the darkness to seize his collar and a voice said deeply, 'Now then, young feller, where d'ye think you're going?'

The seaman who had been standing watch at the head of the gangplank handed Nick over to a policeman, and an hour or so later Nick stood in Andrew Buchanan's study, his bundle at his feet and a sullen scowl on his face.

Andrew stood before the fire, his hands behind his back. Nell Jarman sat on one side, working on a piece of embroidery.

Andrew said, 'It seems you are quite determined.'

Nick said, 'I'm not going back to school.'

Andrew sighed. 'You know very well that there are schools where I could send you from which you would not escape, but I don't see the point of that. At the same time, I don't want to see you condemned to the life of a cabin boy. It's hard, and not as glamorous as it's made out to be. Moreover, the opportunities for promotion are limited. That would be a waste, because your reports show, despite your reluctance to continue with school, that you are intelligent and a good scholar. So, while I still think you will find the sea a hard career, as that is what you want, then I will look for a place for you as a cadet or apprentice. Will that do?'

Nick stared up at him. 'Will you?' And when Andrew nodded, 'Oh, thank you.'

'Very well, then. Off you go to bed.' As the boy reached the door Andrew added, 'Was your decision influenced by Murdoch at all?'

Nick paused, thinking it over, then he said slowly, 'No, I would want to go to sea anyway.'

When he had gone, Andrew sighed. 'As I thought: "Anyway". So he prefers the company of seamen to that of Murdoch.' He appealed to Nell, 'Do you think that son of mine will improve as he grows older?'

'I'm sure he will,' she smiled and lied, not wanting to hurt him with an honest reply.

So Nick soon went to sea and passed out of Lucy's life. She had always been annoyed by his teasing and calling her 'little Lucy', but she missed his mocking grin and his laugh.

The day after Amy's miscarriage, when Josh Campbell was out drinking, Lucy recovered the painting from the bottom of the pram and hung it in a cradle made of string under the bed she shared with the other two girls. It was safe there, and when in rare moments she was alone she could take it out and look at it – and dream.

Dreaming was necessary, because Amy never returned to the Buchanan house. The doctor had made it clear that laundry work was too heavy for her and forbade it. She found some light work locally, but the pay was less, and had to take money from Josh's pocket. Sometimes he found her out and beat her, but she kept on because she had to. Amy did not even have dreams to sustain her.

As the years passed Lucy grew into a young woman, and waited for the day her dream would become reality.

Chapter Four

'Where are my bloody boots?' Josh Campbell's cursing in the kitchen came through to Lucy where she lay in bed in the front room. She had been awake a long time, before even her mother had risen. Excitement had kept her from sleep the night before and had woken her now.

Amy's voice came more softly, 'They're in the fireplace where I always put them.'

'Give us them here and get my breakfast.' Josh swore again. Lucy heard the clump of the boots and knew he was seated on the cracket and pulling them on. Josh had given up the sea for a while and got a job as a labourer at Buchanan's yard. He now had no bad-tempered ship's mate to bawl him out of his bunk, as he had at sea, and he needed urging every day to get him out to work.

'Your breakfast's ready,' said Amy. She got up before he did each day, to have his breakfast made when it was time to wake him. Every night she set his boots in the hearth so they would be ready for him.

Now Josh ate bacon and bread and sucked tea from a big china mug, until the yard's hooter sounded, seeming to shake the windows in their frames. Josh stood up and pulled on the ragged jacket he wore to work. Amy said, 'Here's your tea.' She handed him the tin can that held the dry tea, sugar and a spoonful of

condensed milk for his morning break. There were also sandwiches tied up in a red and white spotted handkerchief. Josh
grabbed them and tramped down the stairs into the street,
where he joined the river of men flowing down to Buchanan's
yard.

Now Lucy got out of bed, dressed quickly and washed in the
bowl in the cupboard on the landing. Amy sighed. 'I still wish
you'd just take that job in the shop.' She had found a position in
one of the High Street shops for her daughter, but Lucy had
refused it. Amy pressed her, 'Promise me you'll take it if they
don't give you a job up at the Buchanan house.'

'All right,' Lucy agreed, but she went on confidently, 'They
will, though. That Mrs Jarman said I had to see her when I left
school.'

'That was four years ago!' Amy warned, 'People like that,
gentry, they'll not remember what they said to a little lass after all
that time. And you're still a little lass, really.' She stroked Lucy's
brown hair fondly. Her daughter was not among the taller girls
of her class at school and she was slightly built, but already
showing the promise of the attractive woman she would be one
day, dark-haired and dark-eyed. She stood out from her brothers
and sisters and Amy knew she took after Lucien Hawkins. There
was a self possession and pride about Lucy, that the others lacked.
Amy saw it with natural pride but also shame at her own guilt.
'These big houses, they don't like girls too young or too small,
because they reckon they can't do the work of a grown woman.
So they wait and take them on when they're older.'

Lucy said stubbornly, 'You've never wanted me to work there.
Why not? You worked in a place like that.'

'Aye, but I was older than you are now. I was sixteen when
they decided I was big enough and strong enough.' Amy hesitated.
She was reluctant for Lucy to go to the Buchanan house, because
she could not wipe the guilty memory of a tall young man from
her mind. Might Lucy meet her real father there? It was possible.
He had said he was a friend of Andrew Buchanan so it was likely

he would visit the house again. But would he or Lucy see any resemblance in the other? Amy doubted it. He had probably forgotten the affair — and her. Now she looked at her daughter, whose mouth was turned down at the corners, and gave way. 'But I hope they take you on. Good luck.' She kissed Lucy and stood on the narrow landing to watch her run down the stairs, along the passage and out of the house.

Lucy walked the long miles out to the Buchanan house, skipping now and then with excitement, swallowing with nervousness. Would Mrs Jarman take her on? She almost ran the last stretch of road and was flushed and catching her breath when she told Fred Wilson at the gates, 'I've come to see Mrs Jarman about a job.'

He pursed his lips doubtfully. 'Nobody's said anything to me about you. Does she know you're coming?'

'She might not remember, but years back I came here with my mam, that's Amy Campbell, she was working in the washhouse. Mrs Jarman told me that I was to come and see her when I left school.' Lucy stumbled through the jumbled explanation and smiled up at him.

Now Fred looked at her again with his head on one side. 'Aye. I remember you. Your mam used to push a pram wi' the bairns in and you alongside. So you've come looking for a job.' His lips pursed again. 'Well, you've grown into a bonny lass, and a fine looking woman you'll be one o' these days, but that's not yet. You're young and a bit on the small side.' He saw the smile slip away and went on quickly, 'But you go up and see Mrs Jarman. Best o' luck!'

Lucy went on her way, but slowly now. Being told again that she was too young and too small had sapped her confidence, until she lifted her downcast eyes from the path, and there was the house. It was unchanged, redly warm and holding out its arms, windows twinkling at her. It cheered her and she told herself she was not giving up, not by a long chalk. By the time she had walked around the path to the kitchen door, her back was straight again and she rapped on the panel firmly.

A maid in black dress, white cap and apron opened to her. She was tall and her small waist emphasised her bosom. She looked down her nose at Lucy and asked, 'Yes?'

Lucy answered, 'I've come to see Mrs Jarman.'

A woman's voice called from the kitchen, 'Who is it, Jinny?'

Jinny called over her shoulder, 'A little lass come to see Mrs Jarman, Cook.'

The voice demanded, 'Is she expected?'

Lucy guessed that if she gave a negative answer she would be turned away. She swallowed and gambled, 'Yes, I am.'

'You'd better take her up, then,' said the voice.

So Jinny led the way through the kitchen. The bustling kitchenmaids and scullerymaids glanced her way, all curiously, some with a smile. Mrs Yates, the cook, broad and buxom and fat arms floured to the elbows, watched her passing and said, 'You're not very big, lass.' Lucy gulped and scurried after her guide.

Nell Jarman sat in a straight-backed chair in the breakfast room. Its walls were crowded with pictures, its sideboard with silver dishes holding porridge, bacon, sausages, eggs. Lucy's eyes widened. She had never seen anything like it. Opposite Nell sat Andrew Buchanan, just a pair of big hands holding a copy of *The Times* spread wide that hid the rest of him. Lucy stood several feet from the table and Nell, facing her.

Jinny announced, 'This is Lucy Campbell, ma'am. She says you are expecting her.'

Nell peered at Lucy. 'Not that I recall.'

Lucy said hastily, 'Four years ago, ma'am. You said I was to come to you for a place when I left school.'

'Oh.' Nell's lips twitched. 'When you were asked if you were expected, it meant did you have an appointment to see me today.'

Now Lucy said, 'Oh!'

Nell saw Jinny waiting and listening and knew she was

committing the conversation to memory to be recited in the servants' hall over lunch. Nell said, 'Very well, Jinny, you may go.' When the maid had flounced out and the door closed behind her, Nell turned back to Lucy. 'You say I said you should come here for a job?'

'I used to come here with my mam, that's Amy Campbell. She helped out in the washhouse but had to give it up because she was poorly.'

Nell nodded. 'I remember now.'

Andrew Buchanan said, 'Damn! Need my glasses.' He dropped his newspaper and walked to the door. As he passed Nell he said shortly, 'Too small.' Then he was gone out of the room.

So Lucy was braced for Nell's next comment. And it came, albeit gently: 'You're not very tall,' said Nell. 'How old are you?'

'Thirteen.' Lucy added quickly, 'And a half, ma'am. And my mam says I'm growing very fast.'

'I daresay,' said Nell unhappily, remembering her promise and seeing the anxiety on the girl's face, 'but I do think it might be better if you waited until you had more experience and were a bit bigger before you came here.'

Lucy pleaded desperately, 'But I've had a lot of ex-experience! I've helped my mam. I can do any job you like, cooking, ironing – do you remember I did that ironing for you when my mam was taken ill? I was only little then, a lot littler than I am now!'

Her voice had risen and now Andrew Buchanan came back into the room with a pair of reading glasses in his hand. He stared at Lucy irritably and demanded of Nell, 'What *is* going on?'

Nell answered, 'Lucy has asked for a position. I told her some years ago that she could come to me when she finished school, but I think she is still young and rather small, and she should wait for a while longer.'

'Very well.' Andrew sat down in his chair and picked up his newspaper again.

Lucy cried, 'But I've waited four years already! Ever since that time when you were making the painting of the house and you gave it to me!'

'Ssh!' Nell reached for the tasselled cord to ring the bell that would bring Jinny back to eject Lucy, but stayed her hand. 'You must not shout like that and you should speak when spoken to. Don't you know that?'

Lucy nodded, appalled now because she had ruined her chances of ever working in this house. She whispered, 'Yes, ma'am. I'm sorry.'

Andrew said, 'That's right. I remember now: the painting girl.' He peered at her over the reading glasses. 'You said the house looked warmer than I'd got it.' He eyed Lucy from top to toe and back again, then said reasonably, 'Well, you can't argue about it: you're small – and young.'

'Yes, sir,' Lucy agreed miserably.

He glanced across at Nell and she sensed his change of mood and put in, 'I understand she's growing very fast.'

Andrew said gravely, 'Ah! Is she now? I didn't know that.' He lifted *The Times* again. 'Well, you do as you think best.'

So Lucy was employed to work at the Buchanan house. And when Nell and Andrew were alone, she said, 'Thank you.' He peered at her round the side of *The Times*, quizzically, and she explained, 'I like that little girl, liked her as a child. I would have hated to send her away.'

Andrew grinned at her, 'That's what I thought.'

Lucy returned home that day for her clothes, and her mother provided a chest, the same one she had used when in service before she married. Some of the clothes had been bought by Lucy herself. She had saved whatever coppers she had earned and managed to keep to herself over the past four years. Her mother provided the rest. They spent the money and brought home the clothes while Josh was at work.

Lucy told Josh that night, 'I've got a job at the Buchanan house, Dad. I'm going there tomorrow.'

Josh sat at his tea and glowered at her. 'I thought your mother had got you fixed up at a shop in the High Street.'

'I didn't want to go there.'

Josh had wanted her to work in the shop, because he would have been able to get his hands on her wages. 'You didn't want to go there? You'll go where I say!'

Amy intervened. 'The job in the High Street went to some-body else.' She played on his meanness: 'If Lucy stays at home now we'll have her to keep.'

Josh glowered at Amy but saw the logic in that. His savage gaze shifted to Lucy and he said, 'All right. Get yourself out o' here tomorrow.' However, he had not finished with her and demanded, 'Let's see what money you've got.'

Lucy had been expecting that and had been primed by her mother. She took her little purse from the pocket of her apron and opened it. Josh snatched it from her and emptied its contents into his palm. He counted the coins with one dirty finger and scowled up at her. 'You've been keeping money for yourself while I've sweated my guts out to feed the lot o' you.'

He made to pocket the money, but Amy put in quickly, 'Ah, she's only a bairn still. You'll not send her out into the world without a penny. What would the neighbours say?'

That was a persuading argument: Josh already came in for criticism from the people living around the Campbells, and he did not relish his character being discussed loudly when he walked abroad. He could imagine the comments shouted across the street from one house to another: 'There goes that mean bugger Campbell!' So he grumbled but handed back a few of the coins to Lucy, before slapping her so her head rocked on her shoulders. 'Don't you cheat me again,' he warned.

Lucy put a hand to the weal on her face and lowered her head so he would not see the anger in her eyes. She put away what remained of her money and did not answer back. At Amy's suggestion she had taken some of her money out of her purse beforehand, so that Josh would never see it.

Lucy left the next day. Now she pushed the old pram with her box set on top of it and her mother walked beside her. The picture painted by Andrew Buchanan was inside the box. Lucy unloaded it at the kitchen door of the Buchanan house and her mother took over the pram. Amy put her arms around her daughter and hugged her. 'Look after yourself and be a good girl.'

'I will, Mam.'

'Come and see me sometimes.'

'Aye, Mam.' In spite of her excitement and relief at being away from Josh and starting work in the Buchanan house, Lucy found herself weeping with her mother.

It was Amy who eventually tore herself away and hurried off along the path around the house, pushing the pram. Lucy was left at the kitchen door, a forlorn little figure.

The door opened, and one of the scullerymaids helped her drag her box inside. Mrs Yates said, 'We'll just have to feed you up a bit.'

First Lucy was taken to see Nell Jarman. Jinny led her to the interview, saying, 'She's in the housekeeper's room.' Jinny giggled. 'Mind, there's many a night she doesn't sleep in it and she's in with the boss.' Lucy was only mildly shocked: she had become wise in some of the ways of the world.

The housekeeper's room was at the rear of the house, large and comfortably furnished with a couch and armchairs, table and chairs, a desk – and a bed. It was a home and office in one. Lucy took it in with a single awed, yearning glance and never forgot it. If only, one day, she could work her way up to this luxury. To live in a big house like this, with a room of her own, free from Josh Campbell and his like. She decided that would be her life's ambition.

Nell Jarman explained Lucy's duties and wished her well, then she was given a bed in a tiny room she shared with another scullery maid, for that was Lucy's position. She was on the lowest rung of the domestic ladder but was content because this was where she wanted to be. Nevertheless, on this first night she would not share a bed with her sisters, she undressed by the light of a candle then lay awake a long time and whimpered before she finally slept.

Chapter Five

SUMMER 1908

Lucy Campbell was passing through the hall when the front door bell rang. Jinny Unwin, the second housemaid, tall and willowy, exerted her rank and called, 'Will you see to that, Lucy!'

'Aye!' Lucy replied and Jinny went on with dusting the hall.

Lucy hurried to answer the continued jangling of the bell. She had passed four happy years in the Buchanan house. Now seventeen and an attractive young woman, dark, wide-eyed and lithe she moved gracefully with a whisk of skirts, not running but tripping lightly across the floor of the hall. She had progressed from scullerymaid to kitchenmaid and was now third housemaid. On this fine morning with the sunlight streaming through the windows of the Buchanan house she had already been at work for several hours. Her duties before breakfast were to empty all the grates and wash the steps outside. That was now done and breakfast behind her. Now she had to 'do' the rooms of Devereaux the butler, Sykes the footman and Nell Jarman, the housekeeper. First, however, there was this caller to see to, since Devereaux was still attending on Andrew Buchanan and Nell Jarman at breakfast.

On each side of the front door was a narrow, rectangular window, and looking through one of these Lucy could see a tall figure. She opened the door and began, 'Good morning, sir . . .'

The tall man had his back to her, but now he turned, stared at her for a second then broke into a smile of recognition. 'Good Lord!' said Nick Buchanan. 'It's little Lucy.'

She had not seen Nick since he had tried to run away to sea. After coming to work in the Buchanan house she had learned that Nick had gone to sea as an apprentice, and three years ago had taken up a berth in a ship trading between Far Eastern ports. Lucy needed no time to remember him, however, despite the fact that the twelve-year-old boy was now a twenty-year-old man several inches over six feet tall and wide in the shoulders. He wore a sea officer's uniform of navy blue with a thin gold ring around the cuff. His face was tanned and the smile had widened into the old familiar grin.

Lucy stammered, 'M-Mr Buchanan, sir. It's lovely to see you.'

'And you, Lucy. How long have you been working here?'

'About four years now, sir.' Lucy stood back, pulling the door wide to admit him, but Nick stepped aside with a flourish of one big hand, to usher in Helen Whittaker ahead of him. Lucy said, 'Good morning, miss.'

Helen was a frequent visitor at the Buchanan house, being a neighbour, albeit living a quarter-mile away. Her father had died suddenly two years ago when Helen was sixteen, and now her two maiden aunts, her father's elder sisters, lived with her as guardians. Lucy knew them, Binkie and Teddie, gentle old ladies out of another era. Helen had once said, 'Teddie is short for Edwina, but I don't know why Beatrice is called Binkie.' Helen and Lucy always exchanged friendly words because of their childhood memories, though those exchanges were somewhat stilted on account of the social gap between them.

Now Helen said happily, 'Hello, Lucy. I've left the pony and trap outside. Will you have someone see to her for me, please?'

Nick smiled down at Helen and explained to Lucy, 'I sent a telegram to Helen and she met me at the station with the trap — came without waiting for breakfast! There's devotion for you.' His tone was jocular but there was affection in his smile.

Helen returned the smile. Her earlier promise had been fulfilled and she had grown into a beauty. Now she was radiant. 'The cheek of this chap! In his last letter he said he would let me know when he was arriving and could I meet him. That was too late for my reply to reach him. By then he was on the way home!'

So they had been writing to each other over the years, Lucy noted, though it had nothing to do with her. 'Mr Buchanan and Mrs Jarman are in the breakfast room, sir.'

'Then we'll join them.' Nick took Helen's arm, urging her on, and they disappeared into the breakfast room. Lucy saw Andrew rising from his chair, a delighted smile spreading across his face. She heard Nick say, 'Good morning, Uncle, Mrs Jarman. Hello, Devereaux! D'you think you could find us some breakfast, please?' before the door closed behind him.

Lucy turned away, to find Jinny confronting her and asking, 'Here! Who was that you were talking to?'

Lucy explained, 'That's Mister Buchanan's nephew, Nick. He's just come back from sea. He's been out east, China and that way, for four or five years.'

Jinny had only come to the Buchanan house after Nick had gone abroad. She said, 'You were a bit familiar,' and smirked suggestively. 'Did you keep him company sometimes?' It was an open secret in the servants' hall that Jinny and Sykes, the footman, 'kept company'. He had been seen coming out of her room more than once.

Lucy flushed and retorted angrily, 'No, I didn't! And don't you dare put it about that I did! I've got a tongue in my head as well.'

'All right!' Jinny hastily lifted a hand in mock defence, but she knew that if word ever got to Mrs Jarman of her sleeping with Sykes they would both be seeking a new position. 'No harm intended. It was just, well, you seemed like old friends.'

Lucy, mollified, explained, 'When we were both bairns I used to come up here with my mother. She used to help with the washing. Nick sometimes came to talk to me, because he was often on his own with his cousin away at school – didn't like him, anyway. That Miss Whittaker was with Nick a lot of the time.'

Jinny smirked again. 'She seems to know him all right.'

Lucy guessed, 'I suppose they've been writing to each other.'

'There's more to it between him and her now, from what I saw,' said Jinny knowingly.

Lucy shrugged. 'I don't know anything about that.' And would not have told Jinny if she did know. 'I've got to fetch one of the grooms to feed and water her pony,' she said, and headed towards the stables.

From there she went on with her other duties. When she had set all in the housekeeper's room to rights Lucy looked over the comfortable furniture in its chintz coverings, as she did each day. Her ambition to have a room like this to herself one day was even stronger now. To be a housekeeper in a big establishment akin to the Buchanan house, to have the responsibility and the pride, the security and the lifestyle. She believed it was a realisable aspiration, knowing she was good at her work, well thought of by Mrs Jarman and Devereaux, the butler.

Lucy saw Nick again at lunch. Helen had stayed on for that and was sitting next to Nick. Lucy helped Sykes serve the dishes, supervised by Devereaux, who also dispensed the wine. It was a festive meal with a great deal of laughter. At one point Nick called to the butler, 'There'll be a cart coming from the station with a darned great trunk of mine this afternoon. I give you fair warning, it will take two of you to lift it.'

Devereaux inclined his head. 'I'll see one of the gardeners gives Sykes a hand, sir.'

There were times when Lucy became aware that Nick had glanced in her direction, but apart from that, as usual the family discussed their affairs as if the servants were not there.

Nick asked, 'Have you heard from Murdoch?'

At first Andrew did not answer, and Nell Jarman put in quickly, 'He's well.'

Andrew looked at her and her gaze shifted from him to the servants and back again. He acknowledged the reminder with a nod and said, 'You know he had a job in India, got it through his aunt Adelaide?'

Nick nodded. 'A pretty good job, too, I think.'

Andrew inclined his head. 'It was, but now he's inherited a lot of money from his maternal grandmother. In the last letter I had from Adelaide she said he'd thrown up the job to go travelling. That's all I know.' There was an uncomfortable silence and Andrew very obviously changed the subject. 'I have to go back to the yard this afternoon. What are you two doing?'

'I really ought to go home so Binkie and Teddie know I'm all right.' Helen looked sideways at Nick. 'I just told them I was fetching you from the station, and that was hours ago.'

Nick said, 'Then I'll come with you. And afterwards we could take a walk. I'd like to stretch my legs.' He sat back in his chair and looked around at them all. 'It's good to be home again.'

'I think I'll organise a tennis party later. Would you like that?' Helen said.

Nick grinned. 'I would. I'm a bit rusty, because you don't get a lot of tennis sailing between Calcutta, Shanghai and similar places. But it'll be fun getting into it again.'

Lucy had her day off on the following Saturday, and she walked into Monkwearmouth. It was a pilgrimage she made once a month to see her mother. Lucy found her alone in the house. Josh Campbell was working in Buchanan's yard and Rose in a shop in nearby Dundas Street. Tommy had left school at Easter and was working for a barber as a lather boy, rubbing the soapy lather well into the customers' cheeks before the barber shaved them, sweeping out the shop and running errands. The other two children were out at play. Elsie was in the street, involved in some intricate skipping game with a group of girls, two or three of them jumping into the rope at a time, all of them chanting. Lucy glimpsed Billy's red hair in a knot of boys round a marbles pitch in the cobbled back lane.

Amy looked gaunt and haggard. This worried Lucy, though it was no shock to her, having witnessed the steady decline in her mother's health over the past few months. She asked, 'How are you, Mam?'

Amy smiled at her from her chair by the empty grate, no fire being kept on in the summer weather. She answered wanly, 'I'm canny. What about you, lass?'

'Thriving, Mam, thriving.' Lucy saw that the range had been blackleaded, but the brass fireirons, poker, shovel and tongs were dull and needed polishing. There was dust lying thickly on the mantelpiece. That had not happened before.

Amy started to get up, saying, 'I'll make you a cup of tea.'

Lucy pressed her back into the chair. 'I'll do it. You sit still.' And she lit the gas ring in the hearth, filled the kettle and made tea for them.

'And what's been happening since I saw you last?' Amy asked. She looked forward to these visits of her daughter, enjoyed hearing of her doings and those of the others at the Buchanan house, so Lucy told her of all the little domestic crises and events, the dramas and the scandal.

'Mr Nicholas came home a few days back.'

'Nicholas?' Amy frowned, trying to remember. 'You haven't mentioned him before.'

'Well, he wasn't there.' Lucy explained how Nick had gone to sea and then to the Far East. 'But you'll recall Nick. He was just a boy when you worked there. We – that's him and me, when I was little – we got into a fight with Murdoch, that's Andrew Buchanan's son. *Now* you remember!' Amy had begun to laugh.

Lucy smiled, watching as her mother wiped the tears of mirth from her eyes.

Amy said, 'I can still see it, you two at him like a pair o' terriers and my daughter trying to chew the leg off him! Oh, our Lucy, I

thought I was going to lose me job that day on account o' you.'
Lucy felt happier now, seeing her mother smiling. Amy went on,
'And what's this lad like now?'

'I've not seen much of him because he's out of the house most
of the day with that Helen Whittaker. I've told you about her.'

'Oh, aye. Have they got an understanding, then?'

'Lord! How would I know? But I suppose they have. He's been
writing to her all these years he's been away.'

Amy persisted, 'But what is he like?'

'Tall, dark, broad. Not handsome exactly, but . . .' She could
picture Nick very well but found him hard to describe. 'Well, you
know. I would think a lot of girls would fall for him.'

Amy said worriedly, 'But not you.'

It was Lucy's turn to laugh. 'Not likely! Clem Nolan is more
my kind of lad.' Clem was the young lodger Amy had taken in
some months before to help balance her household budget. 'How
are you getting on with him?'

'He's a decent young feller,' said Amy. 'He likes a drink but
his money is a godsend and Josh has quietened down now there's
a stranger in the house.' Then she warned, half-joking, half-
serious, 'You behave yourself with him. I want no scandal talked
about this house.'

Lucy assured her, 'Don't worry. Clem's a nice lad but that's
all there is to it,' thinking, For now, anyway . . .

Amy nodded approvingly then asked, 'What about the other
chap, the one you were both fighting that time – Andrew
Buchanan's son? What's he doing?'

Lucy shrugged. 'They were talking about him the other day.
Didn't I tell you a while back that he had an aunt in India and he
got a job there through her before I started at the Buchanans'
place?' When Amy nodded, Lucy went on, 'It seems he came into
a pot o' money his grandmother left him not long ago and he's
travelling about the world. Best place for him, I think.'

'Now don't hold grudges,' Amy appealed to her. 'He's probably altogether different now. People change as they get older.'

Lucy laughed. 'Just to please you, I'll give him the benefit of the doubt.'

'Well, then,' said Amy, changing the subject, 'what else has been happening?'

So they talked the morning away.

Lucy helped her mother prepare the midday meal, for which the family assembled. Josh did not appear, but his absence was not commented on. It was accepted that he would be in the pub on the corner until he had drunk enough. Rose chattered away about the customers she had served and the other girls in the shop: '. . . and that Maisie didn't make the tea this morning when it was her turn so I told Mr Peterson, I said . . .'

Tommy groused, 'Sweeping up and lathering up and never a tip comes my way. Get this, Tommy. Fetch that, Tommy . . .'

Billy and Elsie raced up the stairs and he pulled her back with a hand on her skirt so that he won. Elsie complained, 'You're always cheating. And fighting. You picked on Ted Stobbart.'

Shock-headed Billy hotly refuted this: 'No, I didn't! *He* picked on Jackie Turner and Jackie isn't half his size. I don't cheat, either . . .'

They all squabbled throughout the meal and Amy sighed and shook her head wearily.

Clem Nolan came in from his work as a carpenter at Buchanan's yard. He had told Amy he had run away from his home in Newcastle because his father had been cruel to him. Not tall, but a few inches taller than Lucy, he was a handsome young man with curly yellow hair and a wide, confident smile. He greeted her: 'Hello, Lucy!'

'Hello, Clem.' Lucy was conscious as they ate that he was stealing glances at her, but this had been happening with young men for some time, and she could carry on eating with composure.

That was until her mother shook off her lethargy and said sharply, 'You can stop that, Rose!'

'I'm not doing anything,' Rose complained. She was fifteen now, blonde and blue eyed like her mother and pretty, but at that moment she was pouting sulkily.

'You know very well what I'm talking about.' Amy was obviously repeating an order given before.

Rose gave a jerk of her head and a sniff. 'You're always on at me.'

'Because I have to.' Amy clinched the argument with, 'Stop it or I'll tell your father.' That shut Rose's mouth: there was no knowing what temper Josh Campbell would be in when he came home, and he might seize on any excuse to be violent.

Afterwards, when Rose had gone back to her job in Dundas Street and the other three children were out, Clem Nolan offered, 'Will I get you a bucket o' water, Mrs Campbell?'

'Aye, it's nearly empty and we've got the washing up to do. Thank you, Clem.'

He lifted the enamel bucket and set off down the stairs to fill it from the tap in the yard.

Lucy asked, 'What was all that about with Rose when we were having our dinner?'

Amy sighed. 'She was making eyes at Clem. She's done it before and I've told her about it. She's a bonny lass and she knows it, but she's not much more than a bairn yet. She gets a few young lads running after her, as you might expect, but Clem's a grown man and I'll not have her putting temptation his way.' She was silent for a moment then went on, with a catch in her voice, 'She's growing up to be a proper little tart.'

Lucy tried to comfort her. 'It's just her age. Young lasses, you know. She'll grow out of it.'

Amy shook her head wearily. 'I'm just not able to control her and the others like I used to. I'm dead tired all the time. And Josh doesn't help. I threatened her with him, but one o' these days she'll defy me and I doubt if he'll do anything to correct her. I doubt if he cares.'

She might have cried again then, but Clem returned with the

bucket of water. Lucy helped Amy wash up and spent the after-noon with her before setting out to return to the Buchanan house. Amy kissed her and said, 'I'll see you next month.'

Clem offered with his wide smile, 'Can I walk a bit o' the road with you? Set you on your way? I'd like to get a breath o' fresh air.'

'Aye. Come on, then.' Lucy gave Amy a reassuring wink and Clem shrugged into his jacket then followed her down the stairs.

Walking along the street, Lucy asked, 'Are you settling in there all right, Clem?'

'Oh, aye. Your mother looks after me, feeds me well, puts up a good bait for me to take to work. It's great.'

As they climbed up the slope of Church Street they saw Josh Campbell lurching along on the opposite pavement. He stopped at the door of the Frigate, the pub on the corner, and stared owlishly across at them, then he grinned drunkenly and staggered in through the door.

Lucy asked, 'How are you getting along with him?'

'All right.' Clem hesitated, then went on, 'He's nowhere near as bad as my father. He used to belt me a lot when I was young. I think Josh might be different when I'm not there.'

Lucy said bitterly, 'I'm sure he is.' And when she saw his embarrassment, 'Don't worry, you can be frank with me about him. I know him too well. But you don't want to get involved in some other family's troubles. If he gets awkward you'll have to move on, I know that. I'd be grateful if you'd stay as long as you can, though, for my mother's sake.'

Clem assured her quickly, 'Oh, I will, Lucy,' adding confi-dently, 'You can rely on me.'

It was pleasant strolling in the early evening. The sky was a clear blue, without chimney smoke because there were few fires lit in the houses at that time of year, and the sun was still warm. He went with her as far as the Wheatsheaf corner, where the blacksmith's shop stood opposite the public house, and the road to Newcastle started. They parted then, with a wave and a smile, and Clem called, 'I'll be seeing you!'

*

Lucy went on alone. The sun was setting as she passed the Whittaker home. Helen's tennis party was just ending, and as Lucy trudged along the dusty road, she saw the players through gaps in the trees that surrounded the house. There were a dozen or more young men and girls, the men in white shirts and flannel trousers, the girls in white lawn sports dresses with skirts ending above their ankles. A few were still playing in the last of the light but most of them were relaxing, girls sitting in basket chairs, the men standing around them, while a maid served tea and glasses of lemonade. Lucy saw Nick's tall figure towering above the seated Helen and heard their laughter. Then they were left behind her as she went on to the Buchanan house. She had to rise early the next day to carry out her duties.

On another fine evening a week later, as Lucy was helping to serve the dinner under the watchful eye of Devereaux, Nick said, 'Helen wants to spend a week in London, to do some shopping and see a show or two. I thought I'd go with her. I've telegraphed to book rooms at the Dorchester and we're off tomorrow.'

Andrew emptied his wine glass, then as Devereaux came to refill it, said, 'That sounds like a good idea.'

Nick added, 'And I want to look around for another job while we're there.'

Nell Jarman complained, 'We're not going to lose you already!'

Nick grinned at her. 'Not likely! I'm in no hurry to go back to sea, but it does no harm to know what's on offer.'

Andrew said approvingly, 'It's good to have you at home for a while.'

Lucy left with a tray of dishes and was met in the hall by an excited Jinny Unwin, who snatched the tray from Lucy and told her, 'There's a young chap at the back door asking for you! Get out there quick and get rid of him before Devereaux finds out!'

The maids were not allowed to have 'followers', young men calling for them.

Lucy hurried back to the kitchen, wondering who it could be, and past the reproving stare of Mrs Yates, busy at the big, black stove, red faced and perspiring, who began querulously, 'You know you're not allowed . . .' But Lucy was out of the back door, the recriminations left behind her.

'Hello, Lucy,' Clem Nolan called. He stood behind the washhouse with only his head poked around the corner. He wore his usual broad smile and lifted one hand to whip off his cap and beckon to her. 'Can I talk to you for a minute?'

Lucy ran over to him and asked, 'What are you doing here?'

Clem's smile slipped for a moment and he complained petulantly, 'They told me – the cook and that other lass – to hide here so nobody in the house could see me hanging about.' Then something of the smile returned as he asked anxiously, 'I hope I'm not getting you into trouble?'

Lucy reassured him, 'Not so long as you keep out of sight. But what are you doing here?' And suddenly frightened, 'Is my mam all right?'

Clem reassured her hastily. 'Oh, aye. She asked me to tell you she's fine. No, what I came for was to tell you I'm going away for a bit. There's a few of us being sent down to a yard on the Tees to do a job there.' He smoothed a hand over his yellow hair and said shyly, 'I just came to say goodbye, because I'm off tomorrow.'

'You walked all this way just to tell me that?' Lucy was touched. 'That was thoughtful of you, Clem. But we'll be seeing you again?'

'Aye. Your mam has promised to keep a place for me. She won't take anybody else while I'm away.' He stood for a moment, his eyes on Lucy, admiring. Then he said, 'Well, I'd better get back.'

'Yes, you had. It'll be dark afore you reach Monkwearmouth. Come on.' Lucy led him around the house by the path through the trees. On the way she saw one of the gardeners still at work and persuaded him to let her have a bunch of flowers. She gave them to Clem as they stopped at the gate. 'Those are for me mam. Tell her I'm thriving.'

'I will.' He hesitated for a long second for one last look at her. She was slender, pretty and flushed under his stare. 'Cheerio for now, then.' He started to turn away reluctantly.

Lucy reached up to kiss his cheek then shoved him on his way with a hand in his back. 'Get on with you!'

He looked over his shoulder as he set off and saw her running lightly back along the path, seeming to fly in the shadows under the trees. Clem smiled to himself unpleasantly.

Nick left for London early the next day. Lucy had only just finished washing the steps at the front door when the Whittakers' gleaming black Humber, its 'cape cart' hood folded down and the chauffeur at the wheel, drifted to a halt beside her. Helen Whittaker jumped down from the rear. She wore a travelling costume of grey serge, the toes of neat black shoes peeping out from under its skirt. A wide-brimmed hat held her piled blonde hair in place with a wisp of a veil tied under her chin. Teddie Whittaker, the younger of her two guardian aunts, dumpy in a thick Ulster, remained in her seat, beaming benignly. Teddie was going to London as chaperone.

Helen called, 'Morning, Lucy.'

'Good morning, miss.'

Nick ran down the steps to greet Helen. 'Good morning. We've fine weather for the journey. Let's hope we have a week of it.' Helen laughed happily.

Lucy stood with her coarse canvas apron over her dress, the galvanised bucket in one hand, using the other in a vain attempt to tuck a loose tendril of hair back into place, and thought what a handsome couple they made.

Nick turned to look down at her. 'Goodbye, little Lucy.'

'Goodbye. Enjoy yourselves, sir – miss.'

'I'm sure we will. Ah! Thank you.' Sykes, the footman, handed Nick his suitcase, which he tossed into the back of the car, climbing in after it. The chauffeur closed the door, resumed his seat and set off down the drive. Nick waved, then they were gone.

Lucy's smile faded and she turned back to her work with a sigh. Life would be a duller place for the next week without Nick.

It was only two days later, in the evening, that the bell in the servants' hall jangled, indicating that someone stood at the front door. Dinner was over and Devereaux had retired to his sitting room, so Lucy called, 'I'll see to it!' She hurried along the passage from the servants' quarters to the front hall. The sun had set and the electric chandelier in the hall was lit, also the light outside the front door. Andrew Buchanan had bought a generator and had the house wired for electricity just a year ago. Lucy could see a tall figure through a side window, and assumed Nick had come back early.

She opened the door, pulling it wide, and smiled. For a split second she thought again that it was Nick – tall, dark, wide shouldered – but then realised it was not. The man facing her was not quite so tall or broad as Nick. In that first instant he was scowling, but a smile came quickly when he saw Lucy and he said, 'Good evening.'

'Good evening, sir.' Lucy bobbed a curtsy as he walked in, and she took the bowler hat and cane he handed her. She saw a cab drawn by a trotting horse disappearing down the drive and two suitcases stood at the foot of the steps.

The stranger said, 'I'm Murdoch Buchanan, Andrew's son. And you are?'

Lucy recognised the boy in the man, now, but how he had changed! The plumpness of body and feature had gone and there was a hard, handsome look about him. He was well dressed in tweeds, and his voice matched his smile, warm and attractive. She answered, stumbling because she was taken aback at his sudden reappearance after all these years, 'L-Lucy, sir. Lucy Campbell.'

He stared at her for a second, brows wrinkling as he cast about in his memory, but the smile unwavering. Suddenly he snapped his fingers. 'Of course! You used to be with your mother. She came to the house to help with the laundry.' The smile widened. 'I think I may still have the marks of your teeth in my leg!' He roared with laughter as Lucy blushed.

She said, 'I'll tell Mr Buchanan you're here, sir.'

Murdoch waved a hand. 'No need. I'll announce myself. In the drawing room, is he? Have someone bring in those cases and put them in my room. Is Sykes still here?'

'Yes, sir.'

'Good.' Murdoch fumbled in his waistcoat pocket and produced a key. 'Ask him to unpack them, please.' He tossed the key to her and Lucy caught it. Murdoch chuckled and walked on, but at the door to the drawing room he halted and looked back at her. 'Lucy Campbell. Well, well. What a grand welcome home.' He opened the door and passed through, and Lucy heard him say, 'Hello, Father – Mrs Jarman . . .' before the door closed behind him.

Lucy sought out Sykes and passed on Murdoch's orders. The footman grumbled, 'All very well but it's not my job. I'm not here to be a valet to anybody that comes to stay. That Nick looks after his own cases an' everything.'

Lucy pointed out, 'Well, you're not doing anything else now and you might as well make the chap feel welcome now he's come home.'

Sykes grumbled but took the key and went off for the cases.

Jinny asked eagerly, 'What's he like, then?'

Lucy answered guardedly, 'He's tall, dark.'

Jinny demanded impatiently, 'You know what I mean! Is he – you know?'

Lucy turned away to hide the blood rising to her face. 'He's – nice.'

'Nice! What d'you mean – nice?'

Mrs Yates put in severely, 'That'll be quite enough o' that, thank you, miss.' And eyeing Jinny, 'I know what *you* mean and you'll do well to keep your thoughts to yourself.' So Jinny shut her mouth, lips pressed tight, and bustled out of the room. Lucy was spared further questions, to her relief.

Next morning Sykes said, smirking, 'That Mr Murdoch is a real gent. He gave me a bob just for humping his cases upstairs and unpacking them.' He flipped the shilling into the air with his thumb and caught it in the palm of his hand. 'I'm ready to do anything for him.'

Jinny saw Mrs Yates could not overhear her and smirked, 'You're not the only one. I took in his hot water this morning.'

'Oh, aye?' said Sykes jealously, because he regarded Jinny as his property. 'What did you get off him?'

Jinny giggled. 'Nothing! Don't be silly.' She liked to keep Sykes on her string. 'It was just that he was polite and chummy, asked me how long I'd been here, did I like it — things like that.' She stopped, remembering, the smile still on her lips.

Sykes muttered, 'No need for you to go barmy over him.'

Lucy listened and kept silent. She wondered if she had 'gone barmy' over Murdoch, and pointlessly, because it seemed he favoured no one more than another.

This appeared to be confirmed as the day wore on. Everyone Murdoch came into contact with reported favourably. He even descended into the kitchen and thanked Mrs Yates for his lunch: 'It's good to be back eating your cooking.' That left her beaming approvingly. Even Fred Wilson, the gatekeeper, paying a visit to the servants' hall, declared, 'He's turned out a fine young feller. Wouldn't ha' thought it a few years back, but there y'are, people sometimes change as they grow up.'

Lucy held her tongue. She saw as much of Murdoch as any of the others, and maybe she saw a lot more of him, but her natural shyness prevented her from mentioning it, let alone boasting. However, it seemed that chance threw them together frequently during the next few days. At first their talk was formal on his side, monosyllabic on hers. She was a servant, who should speak when spoken to.

'How old are you, Lucy?' He had met her in the hall, which was deserted save for the two of them, and he smiled down at her.

'Seventeen, sir – just.'

Murdoch nodded. 'You're quite the young lady now.' Then he stepped aside, went on his way and let Lucy proceed on hers. However, she paused before the big mirror in the hall the next time she passed that way and stared at her reflection. No one had ever called her a young lady before. She started to blush again and hurried on.

They saw each other a score of times every day, and on two or three occasions each day they chanced to be alone and so could talk. Their conversations lengthened and Lucy's part in them grew with familiarity. When she was alone, Lucy realised uneasily that she was treading on dangerous ground, but she would forget that the next time she met Murdoch – or remembering, think weakly, Where's the harm?

At the end of a week, on an afternoon when Andrew and Nell Jarman had gone to Sunderland, Murdoch and Lucy stood close in the drawing room. They laughed together and he laid his hand on her arm. Lucy let it lie there and he stooped towards her.

They both heard the footsteps in the hall at the same time and Lucy shied away, suddenly flustered. They stared at each other, Murdoch with that faint smile on his lips. Above her beating heart, Lucy heard the front door opened and a familiar voice, the words indistinct. Then came Devereaux's outraged tone: 'You should make your enquiry at the servants' entrance! Go round to the back of the house.' The door closed.

Lucy ran out into the hall. In the room behind her Murdoch glared and cursed savagely. Lucy did not hear him but intercepted the returning Devereaux. He transferred his outrage to her and confirmed her suspicions: 'That was your father, Lucy. He came to the front door asking for you, if you please!'

'I'm sorry, Mr Devereaux.' Lucy asked anxiously, 'Did he say why he had come?'

'No, he did not. I suggest you get along to the back of the

73

house and meet him.' As Lucy ran, the butler called after her, 'He is not to enter the house! He smells of drink!'

Lucy found Josh Campbell outside the kitchen door, and the butler had not exaggerated: Josh had been boozing. He demanded, his voice slurred, 'Who was that stuck-up bugger that told me to come round the back?'

Lucy ignored that. 'What are you doing here? Is Mam all right?'

'Bloody gatekeeper said I was to come round the back an' all. He can go to hell.' Josh hiccuped. 'No, she isn't. I've had the doctor to her. She's bad.'

'I'll get my coat and ask Mr Devereaux for a day off.' Lucy started to turn away but Josh grabbed her sleeve.

'Never mind a day off.' He glared at her. 'Tell him you're finishing and pack your kit. You're coming home wi' me. I've brought a barrow.'

Lucy could see it, standing a few feet behind him. He had borrowed it from a hawker and there were still some rotted cabbage leaves on it. 'Leave? I've got to leave? No.' She could not take it in, could not believe this was happening to her.

Josh insisted, 'Aye! She needs looking after and there's nobody else to do it.'

It finally sank in. She was to give up her job, the little room that was hers alone now – leave the house and everything she had worked for.

There was nobody else to care for her mother, so Lucy explained to Devereaux why she was leaving without giving notice and packed her belongings in her chest. The picture of the Buchanan house that Andrew had painted went on the bottom, carefully wrapped in brown paper. Sykes hauled the chest down the narrow back stairs for her and Josh dumped it on the barrow. Lucy bade farewell to the others in the kitchen and there were some tears and many good wishes. Lucy stayed dry eyed. She would weep later.

They set off, Josh pushing the barrow and Lucy walking

alongside. When they had gone just a few yards, enough to be out of earshot of anyone coming to the kitchen door – though that was not Josh's intention – he growled at her, 'I saw you and that lodger walking up Church Street the other day. And he was out here, wasn't he? He brought them flowers back from here.'

Lucy answered, 'He only came to tell me he was going to be away for a bit.'

'Never mind what he told you. Listen to what I say: you have nothing to do wi' him. You give him his meals and that's the end of it. I'll have no scandal in my house.'

'We were just talking—'

'*D'ye hear what I say?*' Josh let go of one of the shafts, ready to give the back-handed blow.

Lucy said dully, 'Yes, Dad.' It was useless to argue with him.

She turned to look back as they passed through the gates on to the road. The sky had clouded over, and it looked like they would have rain before they got home. There was no sunlight, but still the house looked warm and welcoming. Lucy had no illusions as to what awaited her. She would have to take on her mother's burdens and care for Amy as well. She was saying farewell to the house for ever. And to all of those she had worked with and for. And Nick. And Murdoch . . .

Chapter Six

Lucy made herself smile brightly and said, 'I've come home to look after you till you get better, Mam.' She was shocked by her mother's appearance. In a matter of only weeks Amy had collapsed as if the life had been drained out of her. Her face was gaunt and white as the sheet that covered her skeletal body.

Amy asked weakly, worried, 'What about your job at the house?'

Lucy lied, 'They've promised to keep that open for me,' although there had been no such promise. Lucy had not asked for one because she knew she would not be going back.

However, the white lie calmed Amy and she relaxed against the pillow. 'That's all right, then.'

Lucy cooked a meal that evening, but inevitably it was late. Rose grumbled, 'Isn't it ready?' when she came in from her work, and so did Tommy.

Elsie said, 'He would grumble anyway.' She was a skinny, leggy twelve-year-old now with a mane of red hair falling down her back. She stood before the mirror hanging over the mantelpiece and practised piling her hair on top of her head, preparing for the day when she would finish school and 'put it up' – and also exchange her schoolgirl mid-calf skirts for the long ones of a young lady.

Tommy demanded, 'What are you talking about?'

Elsie went on, 'He's always moaning about working in that barber shop.'

Tommy denied, 'No, I'm not!'

'Yes, you are! He says he'll never get anywhere. I don't think he will, either. You listen to him. He says himself he's always being told off for making mistakes. He'll get the sack if he goes on like that.'

Tommy warned, 'You'll get a clip on the ear!'

Lucy stepped between them. 'You leave her alone, Tommy. And Elsie, you keep your opinions to yourself.'

They were silenced for a moment, then Elsie repeated the question asked by the others: 'Is Mam going to get better? Dad says she will, but she looks very poorly.'

Lucy avoided a direct answer. 'Well, Dad should know,' but she doubted if he did and said quickly, 'Now, come and sit down.' And she served up the meal.

Lucy took her mother's food to her, but Amy ate nothing, though Lucy sat by the bed and tried to feed her. When she gave up in despair and took the cold food back to the kitchen she found there was nothing left for her, but she didn't feel hungry and decided to have something later. The table was filled with the dirty dishes.

Lucy asked, 'Where's Rose?'

Billy looked up from where he sat on the cracket by the fire, immersed in a comic. 'She went out right after me dad.'

Tommy sat in his father's chair, sullenly prodding at the small fire with the poker.

Lucy asked, 'And what about Elsie?'

Tommy shrugged. 'Out in the street, I suppose.'

Lucy looked into the coal bucket standing in the hearth and found it empty. 'One of you take that down to the coalhouse and fill it.'

Tommy said, 'Billy can do it. I've been at work all day.'

'Do it yourself,' replied Billy. 'You do bugger all.'

'*Shut up!*' Lucy hissed. 'Your mother's lying very ill next door, so I don't want a row. Now, Billy, you fetch Elsie. Tell her she gets up here or her father will belt her. Tommy, fetch the coal.'

She had shamed them into obedience for the moment and they went, albeit sulkily. Lucy stood a kettle of water on the fire to boil for washing up.

When Billy returned with Elsie, Lucy charged her, 'You didn't tell me you were going out.'

Elsie pouted. 'Don't have to. Dad doesn't mind. I'm always back before him, anyway.'

Lucy, out on the landing with her hands in a bowl of hot water with the dishes, said, 'Get the tea towel and wipe these, then put them away.' She heard her mother coughing in the front room, and told Elsie, 'Finish these,' then hurried into the bedroom, wiping her hands on her apron.

Amy had rolled over on to her side and was half out of bed as the coughing racked her, drawing great whooping breaths. Lucy held her, settled her down and gave her water to sip. The coughing ceased but Amy panted for breath.

Lucy ran back to the kitchen and snapped at Tommy, 'Go and fetch the doctor!'

Lucy was sitting with her mother when the doctor came. Lucy heard the clopping of his pony's hooves in the street as his trap arrived, and then he ran up the stairs two at a time. He was a young man and explained, 'I'm Dr Franklin. Dr Galloway is on holiday.' He took Lucy's place on the bed and examined her mother while she looked on.

Dr Franklin delivered his verdict out on the landing. 'I saw your mother only yesterday and told your father how ill she was. Is he here?' When Lucy shook her head dumbly, he went on, 'I see. Well, she's — very ill.' He glanced back through the open door and saw Amy was sleeping, exhausted. He turned to Lucy again. 'You are the eldest daughter, the one in service at the Buchanan house?'

'Yes, Doctor. Lucy.'

'Are you living here now?' When she nodded: 'That's good. I think someone should sit with her tonight. I can't do anything for her, I'm afraid.'

Lucy asked, 'What ails her?'

'It's her heart and—' he could have added, 'And a lot of things,' but he said simply, 'She's just worn out.' Dr Franklin saw the girl bite her lip. She was a very pretty girl, a beauty. He marvelled at her, and wondered sadly if she would go the same way as her mother.

Lucy had Tommy help her move one of the battered old armchairs from the kitchen into the bedroom. She left some bedding on the couch in the kitchen for her father, then settled down in the chair by her mother's bed.

Lucy heard Josh Campbell return when all the others were abed, his stumbling step on the stairs, his muttering as he made his bed on the couch. When Lucy crept into the kitchen after midnight to make herself a cup of tea, he was snoring and the room smelt of stale beer.

Despite the tea, Lucy dozed off. She woke with a start, curled up uncomfortably in the old chair, and saw her mother's eyes were open, watching her. Amy's lips moved and Lucy went down on her knees by the bed to hear her. Amy said, 'You've got a look of your father about you.'

'Have I?' Lucy did not believe it, did not want to, but now her mother was shaking her head.

She said, 'Not Josh. He fathered the others, but not you. I sinned bringing you into the world, but Lord! I have paid.'

Lucy whispered, 'You haven't sinned, Mam.'

'Aye, I did.' Amy nodded slowly, just an inclination of her head on the pillow. 'Your father was one o' the gentry, a friend of that Andrew Buchanan but a lot younger. He was good to me, and I hadn't been long married. Josh had badly used me and I was young, on my own, so when this chap was so kind I – gave in to him. It was one night up at the Buchanan house. We loved each other – true love. He was a fine man, a gentle man, but not my husband. I knew it was wrong and I was not long married, but I was tempted and I've paid, I've paid.'

Tears ran down her face. Her hand came out to fasten on Lucy's arm like a claw. 'Think long and hard before you marry. Promise me! Promise!'

Lucy wiped away the tears and told her, 'I promise, Mam. Now don't you fret yourself.' She stroked Amy's hair and her mother's eyes closed and she slipped into sleep again.

Lucy returned to the chair, confused, not sure what she had heard. Her father was a young gentleman? Her mother had been involved in an adulterous affair?

Or had she just listened to the ravings of delirium?

Amy woke, or regained semi-consciousness, twice more as the night wore on. Once she murmured recollections of her life as a young woman in service, later she went back further still to talk of her childhood, but most of the time the mutterings were incomprehensible.

Lucy sat with her all through that long night. It was just before the dawn that she heard her mother sigh and say quite clearly, 'Oh, my love.' Then the breathing stopped and there was only that terrible stillness.

Lucy woke her father and told him. He squinted at her out of bloodshot eyes, groaned and shook his head. He said dolefully, 'I've lost my truest friend.' Then, sinking back on to the couch and pulling the blankets up to his chin, 'I'm not going to work today, but you get the bairns away.'

Lucy gave the others, subdued and tearful, their breakfasts and sent them off to work or school, and Billy to fetch the doctor. With the help of a neighbour who knew what to do, she laid out her mother's body.

Later she got out the tin box that held the family's few documents, birth certificates and so on, and her mother's bible. Lucy set that aside, inspected her own birth certificate and saw that Josh Campbell was shown as her father. That came as no surprise. Amy would not have shown a lover's name if . . .

Lucy wondered and went to stand before the mirror and study her reflection. She did not have Josh Campbell's red hair nor was there any resemblance to him facially. She had something of the look of her mother in her face, but the dark hair and eyes . . . She remembered her mother saying several times over the years as Lucy grew up: 'Lucy takes after my father's side. His brothers were all dark.' Had that been a convenient explanation?

As Lucy stared into the mirror she became convinced that the girl she saw was not fathered by Josh Campbell. So? What difference did it make? She would not advertise the fact that she was a love child. She would still be Lucy Campbell. But now she owed Josh nothing, neither affection nor respect, because he had given neither to her. She felt a sense of freedom, even saw herself smiling in the looking-glass, until she remembered her mother lay dead in the next room.

Lucy returned to the box and searched for the insurance policy on her mother's life. She emptied out the box, but it was not there. She had seen the policy numerous times when the box had been opened to get at the other contents, and she knew what it looked like. The identical policy on Josh's life lay there, but that on her mother's life was not.

Lucy knew what had happened and what she had to do. At first she quailed at the thought, until she remembered this man was not her father, and how he had treated her mother over the years. Lucy had been born because Josh had 'badly used' his young wife. The anger boiled up inside her and Lucy snatched up her shawl, threw it around her shoulders and marched out of the house.

She found Josh Campbell in the Frigate. She entered the little snug where the old women sat to drink their glasses of port and stout. From there she could see through to the bar where Josh was standing with a group of men, a glass in his hand. Lucy asked the barmaid, 'Will you tell Josh Campbell his daughter wants to see him outside, please?'

She saw the girl deliver the message and Josh wave a hand at her. The girl returned. 'He says he'll see you at home later.'

Lucy called in ringing tones that carried through the pub, 'Tell him I'll go in there if he doesn't come out to see me.' She heard the break in the buzz of talk but did not stay to see the girl pass on that message, turned her back and walked out.

Josh met her outside in Dundas Street, slamming out of the door of the pub and standing over her, demanding through his teeth, 'What the hell d'you think you're doing, ordering me to come out here? Are you looking for a bloody good hiding? 'Cause that's what you'll get!'

Lucy could feel his breath on her face, see the red in his eyes, but she held her ground. Her weariness after that long night, her mother's death, her losing her place at the Buchanan house, the years of this man's bullying – rage and outrage gave her courage. 'Give me the insurance money,' she said, and held out her hand.

'What?' Josh gaped, incredulous.

'The insurance money. Give it to me.'

Josh started. 'I haven't—'

Lucy would not listen. 'Yes, you have. Don't lie to me.'

Josh looked around, trying to grin, to summon up sympathy from the passersby, some of whom were pausing to listen. He put a hand on Lucy's arm. 'Come away in and I'll get you a drink. You're all upset—'

Lucy shook off the hand, still held out her own. 'The money.'

'Go to hell.' Josh turned away to go back into the Frigate but now Lucy seized his arm and swung him back to face her. Voice rising she accused him, 'That's the money for my mother's funeral! Without it she'll be buried like a pauper! You're no better than a grave robber! You give it to me or I'll call the pollis and have you charged with thieving!'

'Stop shouting!' Josh snarled at her. 'Or I'll—'

'No, I won't!' Lucy was heedless of threats, her clear voice carrying. 'I'll shame you in front of the street, but I'll have what's right! That money's to bury my mother, your wife, and you won't booze it away and send her to a pauper's grave!'

83

A little crowd was gathering. Josh shoved his hand in his pocket and thrust a handful of coins at her. 'Here! Take it!'

Lucy inspected it then stared up at him. 'All of it. I want all of it.'

'You've got it all.'

'No, I haven't. There's more, I know. Never mind how, but I know.' Lucy lied without shame, knowing the man she was dealing with.

Josh muttered under his breath but brought out more coins and poured them into Lucy's open hands. 'There! That's every penny.' He turned away and this time Lucy let him go. There was a bitterness in his tone that indicated he had kept back very little. He hurried away from the curious eyes, and instead of taking refuge in the Frigate, where he would be the butt of comments, he headed up Church Street to the pub that stood at the top of the bank.

Lucy arranged with the undertaker for the funeral and ordered a wreath from herself and the rest of the family, then she took a tram across the river into the town. She had a black dress which she had worn in service and a black ribbon to sew on to the arm of her coat, but not a black hat. She found a cheap one in the High Street. She decided to walk back across the bridge as it was a fine day, and at Mackie's corner at the end of Fawcett Street she met Nick Buchanan.

'Hello, little Lucy!' He grinned down at her, teasing, but this time Lucy was not annoyed.

'Mr Nick! Did you enjoy yourself in London?' She smiled at first sight of him, but her smile quickly faded.

'We had a wonderful time.' Nick's grin had gone and now he was serious as he said, 'I hear you left in a hurry because your mother was ill.'

'Yes. She died, early this morning.' The tears started to come then.

'Steady on.' Nick put his arm about her shoulders, looked around and said, 'Come along here.' He led her down Bridge

Street and into the foyer of the Palace Hotel. Lucy stopped then, aware that she was in strange territory, but Nick urged her on into the restaurant, sat her down at a table and took a chair beside her.

Lucy whispered, 'Please, Mr Nick, I don't belong in here.'

'Well we can't talk out in the street, it makes my legs tired.' Nick went on softly, 'You'll be the better for some tea, and you can tell me all about it.'

A waitress came bustling then, a girl of Lucy's age, neat in white cap and apron. Lucy thought she looked nervous as Nick ordered. While they waited for the tea he talked of the shows he had seen in London with Helen Whittaker. 'And I talked to some shipping companies. I've got a berth and she sails next week.'

Lucy managed to smile now. 'I'm glad. Do you think you'll like her?'

'She sounds good. And this job may lead to others. They have a lot of ships trading out foreign, China and India and that way. But we'll see. Ah! Thank you.' He grinned up at the waitress as she set out the tea things. Her hands were shaking, and as she picked up the sugar bowl from the tray her sleeve caught the milk jug and overturned it. The contents splashed across the tray and on to Lucy's dress.

The girl squeaked in panic, 'Ooh! I'm sorry, miss!' She tried to seize the jug but only succeeded in knocking the cups from the saucers. Lucy deftly clapped one hand on them to hold them on the tray while fielding the jug with the other. The girl wailed again, 'I'm very sorry, miss,' and looked fearfully over her shoulder.

'Ssh!' Lucy whispered. 'Are you new here?'

'I only started today, on a week's trial.' She gazed at Lucy with frightened eyes.

'Don't worry,' said Lucy, low voiced, 'nobody noticed. And the dress will wash.' She reflected wryly, 'It has before, many a time. Now, let's have the rest of the tea things and you take the jug back and get us some more milk. Tell them I knocked it over.'

As the girl turned away with the jug she said, 'Thank you, miss.'

'Don't call me miss. I'm Lucy. What's your name?'

'Isabel.' She was still nervous and doubtful about this familiarity, but Lucy was smiling, and after a moment Isabel returned it, albeit shakily.

As Isabel went off, Lucy turned back to Nick to find him regarding her with a mixture of amusement and surprise. 'You handled that well. Prevented a catastrophe and saved the girl's job as well.'

Lucy said, 'I know how she felt. I've just lost mine, remember?'

'Tell me about it,' Nick urged her.

Lucy shrugged. 'You know. I had to leave because my mother was taken ill and she died this morning.' Lucy had control of herself now, answered calmly and dry eyed, looking down at her hands folded on the table.

Nick pressed, 'Tell me the rest. There's a lot more to it than that. How are things at home? Is your father bearing up?' Lucy's head jerked back to stare at him, angry, and Nick said, 'Now what does that mean?' He reached out a hand big enough to cover both of hers. 'Tell me.'

So she told him a little of Josh, reluctantly, and Nick led her on with questions from there. He released her to pour the tea when Isabel brought the jug of milk, but then held her hands again, until he had a very clear picture of Josh – and the Campbell household. At the end he stared at her over the empty teapot and cups and said, 'How old are you, Lucy?'

'Seventeen.'

He sucked in a breath. 'You cannot go on like this.'

Lucy answered, 'Yes, I can carry on. I have to. Mam would want me to look after Rose and Tommy and the other two.'

Nick growled, 'But not like this! It's slavery!'

Lucy agreed with his first statement: 'No, not like this.'

'Then what are you going to do? Is there any way I can help?'

He grinned briefly. 'There was a time when you helped me to run away to sea.'

That got a smile from Lucy, but she shook her head. 'There's nothing you can do. It's up to me.' She rose from the table. 'I have to go now. The longer I'm away, the more there is to do. But there's going to be some changes.'

Outside in the street the trams, carts, carriages and motorcars were clanging, rattling and tooting to and fro across the bridge. Most were drawn by horses and there was a mingled smell of manure and exhaust fumes.

Nick said awkwardly, 'We've been friends a long time. I wouldn't like that to end because—' He stopped, not knowing how to put it into words.

Lucy said, 'I know what you mean.' She recalled the Buchanan house and Helen Whittaker, then thought of the three crowded rooms down by the shipyard – and Josh Campbell. She smiled at Nick and left him.

Josh was still out drinking that evening when the family sat down to the meal Lucy had cooked. It was eaten in silence, in the dimness behind closed curtains. Afterwards she asked them, 'Did you like that?' She was well aware that all of them were grief-stricken, but none were more so than herself and this had to be settled now.

They stared at her, Rose already at the door, about to go out. Tommy said, 'I enjoyed it, aye.' The others muttered or nodded agreement.

Lucy eyed them grimly. 'Well, I'm bringing in some new rules. You'll have to follow them if you want to go on eating in this house.' As they looked at each other, puzzled, Rose impatient, Billy grinning, Lucy went on, 'First off: you two girls can do the washing up, so Rose, you can get back in here and roll up your sleeves.' Billy laughed and Lucy told him, 'Get the coal bucket and fill it. That's your job from now on. Don't let me find it empty, ever. And Tommy, you sweep the yard whenever it's our turn.'

There was a moment of shocked silence before they erupted in a chorus of complaint and defiance. Rose spoke for all of them: 'I'm not taking orders from you,' and with a toss of her head she turned away. 'I'm going out.'

'*Don't bother coming back!*' Lucy's voice cracked like a whip.

It stopped Rose in her tracks. She turned again and asked, 'What d'you mean?'

'I mean you follow the rules or you find another place. And that goes for the lot of you.' She stared them down, implacable. 'Now, get on with it or get out.' Lucy pointed at the dirty dishes and Rose retraced her steps to gather them up from the table, her lip trembling from anger and fright. Elsie silently followed her lead with a sideways glance at Lucy. She saw no weakening there. Billy picked up the coal bucket and Tommy went down to the yard and began sweeping it.

Later, with the washing-up done and Tommy up from his sweeping, Lucy said, 'Don't think that's the end of it. There'll be more jobs to be done around this place, and those who don't work, don't eat.' And to Rose, sulkily silent and ready again to go out, 'You be in by nine o'clock.'

'*Nine!*' Rose protested. 'I never come in before ten. Mam let me—'

Lucy cut her off. 'Because she probably got tired of arguing with you. I'm not arguing. I lock the door at nine.'

Rose flung out of the room and clattered down the stairs.

That night Lucy lay in the bed she shared with the two girls. They slept peacefully while she lay awake. She had made a start, but that was all. She had told Nick Buchanan she would carry on, although that was easier said than done. She would have to start again tomorrow.

There were all the tomorrows.

Chapter Seven

'She was a good wife to me, a fine woman.' Josh Campbell was still coherent, but becoming increasingly maudlin. He had drunk steadily from a flat bottle of rum before the funeral. At the grave-side he had wept with his other four children while Lucy stood dry eyed and raging inside. Afterwards he had nipped at the bottle again as they drove back from the cemetery in the undertaker's cab.

Now he was addressing the few neighbours who mourned Amy. Lucy had bought the food to regale them, the bread, ham, pickles and the rest. She had made the tea, as she had organised and paid for the funeral, ordered the simple wooden cross for the head of the grave – the insurance money would not run to a stone. Now she moved quietly among them, asking, 'A drop more tea, Mrs Charlesworth? Another piece of cake, Mrs Harris?' And all the while Josh Campbell bemoaned the loss of his wife, shook his head, and drank.

At last the flat bottle was empty and Josh got up from his seat before the fire. 'I'm going to get a breath o' fresh air. It might help me to sleep tonight.'

He did not return until after midnight, long after the mourners were gone and all in the house were asleep – except Lucy. She still lay awake, grieving for her mother and wondering and worrying about the future. She heard Josh stagger up the stairs and collapse on the bed he had shared with Amy Campbell in the room that was his alone now.

Next morning, bleary eyed and nursing his head, he told Lucy, 'I'm not going in to Buchanan's. I've got another job.'

'What job is that?'

Josh only growled at her, 'None o' your business.' He left after eating his breakfast, wearing what had been his best suit before he bought another for the funeral. He did not return until midnight again, and followed that pattern for the next few weeks. He did not tell Lucy where he was working or what he was doing. She wondered what job he could have that he would wear his suit. He paid Lucy little and grudgingly. It sickened her that he should be out drinking when the rest of them were still mourning Amy.

One Friday evening Josh returned as the family sat at their meal. He was cheerily drunk, waved a hand holding a cigar at the circle of faces, and greeted Lucy, 'Hello, lass! This is Charlie Garvey. He's a lad you want to be nice to.'

Garvey was of an age with Josh, in his early forties, podgy in checked tweeds and carrying a walking cane in one hand. In the other was his lavender bowler hat. His hair was oiled and carefully quiffed. He smirked at Lucy and spoke round a cigar clamped between brown teeth. 'How d'ye do.' His double chin wobbled.

Josh elaborated, 'Garvey is a bookie. He used to help a bookie around the racetracks but learned the trade and now he's worth a bob or two — or a quid or two come to that.' He guffawed.

Lucy looked through Garvey. 'I want nothing to do with your boozing mates.'

Josh started, 'Now look here—'

'Never mind, Josh.' Garvey's smirk had become a scowl. 'You get dressed and I'll see you in the Frigate.' He turned to the door and called back to Josh from the head of the stairs, 'Don't be too long. We're meeting them at eight o'clock.'

'Right y'are, Charlie,' Josh answered, and went across the landing into his bedroom, pausing only to tell Lucy, 'It's Garvey

I'm working for now, and better money than I ever got going to sea or at Buchanan's.'

Lucy sat on at the table, silent, while the others speculated in whispers as to what their father was up to. She waited for him, her heart thumping. When he emerged a few minutes later he was wearing the new navy blue suit he had bought from the insurance money to attend Amy's funeral, with a stiff stand-up collar and a tie. Lucy challenged him, 'What are you doing for Garvey, working in his office?'

Josh sniggered. 'He hasn't got an office!'

Lucy nodded. 'That's what I thought. He's a street bookie and you're taking bets for him, his runner.'

'What's wrong wi' that?' Josh shrugged and passed her to reach the fire. There he relit his cigar from a paper spill.

Lucy pushed back her chair and stood up. 'What if the pollis catches you?'

'No fear o' that. We keep a good watch out.' Josh made to push past her.

Lucy stood in his way. 'What's on the table is the last of the food in this house and today is Friday.'

Josh met her gaze truculently. 'What about it?'

'It's payday and I want my housekeeping money.' Now her anger was overlying her fear again.

'Get out o' my way!' Josh lifted his hand to strike her but Lucy slipped away from the blow and seized the poker where it lay in the hearth. She ran to stand in the doorway, the poker raised. Voice high, she warned, 'Lay a hand on me and you'll be sorry!'

Josh hesitated. He saw her rage and determination as she faced him, flushed but ready to carry out her fearsome threat. He could not see the fear she hid behind that façade. He fumbled in his waistcoat pocket and threw a handful of silver on to the table. 'There y'are. If you'd asked properly you'd ha' got it sooner.' He stepped forward and Lucy moved aside to let him go, still holding the poker ready. His eye on it, he sidled round her then descended the stairs, shouting a threat of his own: 'You'll regret this afore long!' Then he was gone.

Lucy was regretting it already. She felt sick and her hands were beginning to shake so that the poker rattled as she put it down, but the others were watching her, silent, so she tried to keep her face calm, her voice steady as she said, 'Make a cup o' tea, Elsie, please.'

The four obeyed her orders now, albeit reluctantly and grumbling. They looked at her warily, their resentment tinged with caution — enemies still.

Lucy counted the money and put it in her purse. There was just over a pound. It would have to do. Tomorrow she would cross the river on the ferry to the market in the East End and do her shopping there where the food was cheaper. But she was going to need more money.

And what had Josh Campbell meant by his threat — or was that just braggadocio?

Josh did not come home that night, nor the next.

On Monday Lucy set out early in the morning to walk to the Buchanan house. As she walked on the path leading to the rear of the house she peeped between the trees, looking for Nick — and Murdoch — but she saw neither.

Arriving in the servants' hall, with its long table where the servants ate, she was met by Jinny Unwin, who exclaimed, 'Why Lucy! What brings you here?' Then replying to Lucy's question, 'There's only Mr Andrew here. Mrs Jarman and Mr Nick are out for the day.' She added with a pout, 'And that Murdoch has gone touring and we don't know when he'll be back.'

Lucy felt a twinge of disappointment, told herself she was being silly, but hoped she was not to have another. 'Will you ask Mr Andrew if he'll see me?'

Andrew saw her in the drawing room. He laid down his *Times* when Jinny announced her. 'Ah! The only person who appreciates my painting.' He smiled at her. 'What did you want to see me about?'

Lucy bobbed a curtsy. 'I was hoping Mrs Jarman might have some work for me, sir.'

'Oh!' Andrew thought back, then said slowly, 'She didn't say anything to me about wanting anyone . . .' His eyes on her face, he saw the flicker of disappointment, and remembered this girl was a favourite of Nell Jarman's. He went on, 'But we have a dinner party tonight and doubtless Mrs Yates could use some extra help in the kitchen. Tell Devereaux you're to have a day's work there.'

'Thank you, sir.' Lucy hesitated.

Andrew, *The Times* half-raised again, paused to ask, 'Was there something else?'

Lucy worked in the kitchen under Mrs Yates, the cook, all that day. For that length of time she was able to forget her worries, but as she walked home they crowded in on her again. The few shillings she had earned that day would help her to make ends meet, but she knew she could not hope for regular work at the Buchanan house. She suspected she had been given this day wholly or partly out of kindness.

A barrow stood outside her front door when she returned home. It looked very like that which Josh Campbell had borrowed to bring her chest home from the Buchanan house, and it held two of the kitchen chairs. Lucy ran along the passage and up the stairs. She was just in time to meet Josh at the kitchen door, his arms loaded with pots and pans. Lucy caught him unprepared and knocked them from his grasp so that they clanged and rattled across the kitchen floor.

'Bloody hell! You—' Josh started.

Lucy shouted, 'What are you doing?'

'I'm taking what's mine!' Josh stooped to pick up a pan and Lucy kicked it away from him.

'None of it's yours!' Lucy saw Tommy and Billy standing by the table, Rose and Elsie behind them. She shouted to them, 'Pick up this lot and put it back. Take no notice of him.' She pointed a quivering finger at Josh. 'He's off to his fancy woman!' She saw the jerk of Josh's head and knew she had got it right. So did the others and they began collecting the scattered pans. Lucy encouraged them: 'But he's not taking anything of our mother's with him. Billy! Run and fetch a pollis!'

Billy sidled round his father, ducked away from his grasping hand and ran down the stairs.

Josh bawled, 'Billy! You come back here!'

Billy checked in his flight for a moment, ingrained habit holding him, until Lucy called, 'If you come back here he'll belt you! You know that!' Billy did, and ran on.

While Lucy addressed her siblings, her words were meant for Josh: 'This time I'm turning him in. They'll find him with his pockets full o' bets and it'll be Durham jail for him!' She saw from Josh's face that she had guessed right again, and his hand instinctively went to his waistcoat pocket.

He hesitated for long seconds, fists clenched and mouth working, but then he growled, 'Aw! Bugger it! I've had enough o' you lot and this place, all o' you. You can keep this rubbish. With the money I'm making now I can get some new. I'm off and you can all go to hell.' He turned on Lucy: 'That lodger feller you were snuggling up to will be back soon. Your mother thought he was the blue-eyed boy but I know different! You can jump into bed wi' him and that's all you're good for!' His glare shifted to Tommy and the two girls. 'It'll be the workhouse or the orphanage for the rest o' you!' He spat the words at them then hurried down the stairs.

Lucy followed him at a distance and saw him trotting off up the street, shoving the barrow with the two chairs wobbling on top of it.

As he disappeared round one corner of the street, Billy came around the other. He saw Lucy standing at the front door and ran to her, panting, 'I couldn't find a pollis that way. I'll try in Church Street.'

Lucy said wearily, 'Never mind. He's gone. But thanks, you're a good lad.'

She led the way upstairs and found Tommy and the girls in a whispering group. Billy joined them, grinning now, remembering only the excitement. Then, as Rose muttered to him, Lucy saw his face change. 'What's the matter?' Lucy asked them.

They looked at each other, then Tommy ventured, 'It was what he said at the finish.'

Lucy felt the blood rising into her face. 'What about it?' she challenged.

Elsie, lip quivering, burst out, 'He said it would be the work-house or the orphanage for us!'

'Oh, *that!*' Lucy had thought they were talking of Josh's refer-ence to her and Clem, the lodger. She dismissed the threat: 'Don't take any notice of that. It won't happen while I'm here.' She sat down at the table because her legs were shaking now, and they gathered round her.

Rose asked, 'Do you want anything done towards getting the dinner ready?'

And Elsie said, 'I'll make a pot o' tea.'

Lucy smiled at them wanly. 'I could do with a cup.' She had told Nick Buchanan there would be some changes, and now, at last, they were coming about. She opened her bag, took out the envelope Andrew had given her in response to her plea and handed it to Tommy. 'That's a letter from Mr Buchanan. You take it down to the yard tomorrow and they'll start you.'

'A job in Buchanan's yard!' Tommy stared down at the enve-lope delightedly.

Lucy turned to Rose. 'There's some evening classes in short-hand and typing starting at the technical college next week. Go over there tonight and sign on.'

Rose said blankly, 'What for?'

'Mam told me how you were a good scholar, and got top

marks at writing and English. You need to build on that.'

Rose said doubtfully, 'Do you think I could?'

'I'm certain.' Lucy was sure Rose would work at it. 'You don't know what you can do till you try.'

Rose said dreamily, 'I could get a job in an office, couldn't I?' Lucy knew she was thinking of the men she would meet every day there, but Rose would learn more than just shorthand and typing as she grew up.

After the tea was drunk, the meal cooked and eaten, the others went about their affairs. Lucy sat by the fire alone with her thoughts, and they were bleak. She had secured a day's work at the Buchanan house but did not know when there would be another. The only money coming into the house would be the wages of Tommy and Rose, both small because of their youth.

Something would have to be done.

The next day Lucy put on her good black dress and her coat with the mourning ribbon. She walked across the bridge into Sunderland town, seeing the river crowded with shipping, the shipyards on both banks busy with a constant din of hammering and the gulls wheeling and shrieking above. She smiled. Young Tommy would be down in Buchanan's yard and working now, happy at last.

Lucy presented herself at the back entrance of the Palace Hotel and asked the scullery maid who opened the door to her, 'Is there a lass called Isabel working here today, please?'

'Oh, aye. Wait there, hinny, and I'll tell her you're here.'

Isabel came hurrying a few minutes later. Her first expression was one of surprise, but then she smiled. 'Lucy, isn't it, miss? I remember. I didn't expect to see you.' That was as much question as statement.

Lucy answered it, 'I was wondering if there was a job going here, because I need one.'

'Oh!' Isabel was surprised again. 'A job? I didn't think – I mean, when I saw you with your young man, I thought . . .' Her voice trailed away, embarrassed.

'My young man?' Lucy burst out laughing at the idea. 'He's not my young man! I used to work for his uncle, that's Mr Buchanan who owns the shipyard. When I met Mr Nick that day I was upset because I'd just lost my mother and he kindly brought me in here and gave me a cup of tea. I'm not a young lady, let alone his.' She was serious again now. 'I need a job.'

Isabel bit her lip and shook her head. 'There's nothing here. There was a lass here earlier and they turned her down flat. I'd love to help you out after what you did for me, but you see how it is.'

Lucy smiled wrily. 'Aye, I know. It's hard. Never mind, don't you feel badly, because it's no fault of yours.'

She started to turn away but Isabel called, 'Where do you live? If anything comes up I'll let you know straight away and put in a word for you.'

'Thanks, Isabel, that's good of you.' Lucy told her the address, then managed a bright smile and went on her way.

She told herself that the Palace had been a long shot, and anyway, there were plenty of other places, although she tried to forget that there were lots of other girls looking for work, a fact that was rubbed in over the course of the morning. She tramped the streets of Sunderland looking for work, and met with nothing but a shake of the head and, 'Sorry, lass, we're not wanting anybody at present.'

So it went on, all that day and week after week. Occasionally she got a few days work for a pittance but mostly she searched for employment.

One mid day Lucy made her way back over the bridge, heading home for a meal. She would try again later, but she was in despair. The strain of her mother's death, becoming a dull distant pain now, the confrontations with Josh Campbell, the responsibility for her siblings, had all worn her down. She was still just seventeen and felt she carried the world on her shoulders, had no one to turn to. Her brothers and sisters had now moved from being enemies, but only to become dependants.

It was a daily battle to keep the family's head above water, to put food on the table, a fire in the grate and a little away for the rent. Tommy's and Rose's pay would only mitigate, not solve the problem. Her own small savings were dwindling despite desperate economies. And when they were gone? When the rent was paid and there was not enough money left to feed them? They would have to apply to the Poor Law Guardians for relief, and behind them loomed the orphanage and the workhouse – as Josh had sneeringly threatened. Lucy had said steadfastly, 'Not while I'm here.' Brave words, but could she back them up?

The money paid by a lodger would have bridged the gap, but that avenue was closed to her after Josh's accusations: 'You can jump into bed wi' that lodger you were snuggling up to!' The neighbours on both sides and below would have heard his bawling. Lucy could not take a lodger now; she would see in their faces what they were thinking every time she entered or left the house. They would regard her as no better than a whore. His other remark, about Clem being a blue-eyed boy but Josh 'knew different', she dismissed as spite on his part.

She was close to tears as she passed through the front door. She was not surprised that it was not shut because it was usually left open during the day except in bad weather. She walked along the passage and climbed the stairs – and found the kitchen door stood wide. That was not usual. Lucy had locked the doors of bedrooms and kitchen that opened on to the little landing before she left that morning. She assumed one of the children had come home from school early, and she called, 'Is that you, Billy?'

'No, it's me.' Clem Nolan stood up from the armchair by the fire, smoothed a hand over his yellow hair and apologised, smiling, 'Sorry if I shouldn't have come in, but your mam showed me where to find the key and she said she would keep me place for me. I just got back this morning. We're all finished at Hartlepool and I start at Buchanan's again tomorrow.'

Lucy saw his cheap cardboard suitcase stood by the chair. She said, 'O' course I don't mind,' and smiled at him. 'It's good to see you again.' Her heart had lifted at the sight of him. 'I'll make you a cup of tea and get you a bite to eat. Though it'll only be a sandwich because I've still got to go to the shops. Sit yourself down.'

Clem sank back into the chair. Lucy bustled about and his eyes followed her as he said, 'I was expecting to see your mam here. Is this your day off?'

'No, I've left the Buchanan place. Mam died while you were away, Clem.' Lucy told him about that and how Josh Campbell had walked out. And all the time she wondered how to break it to him that she could not take him in again. He heard her out in silence, with only a sorrowful click of the tongue and shake of the head. She poured out his tea, standing at the table with her back to him. She decided that now was the time to grasp the nettle and turned round to hand him the cup. She found him on his feet and facing her.

Clem's face was solemn as he said, 'It's mebbe not a good time to ask, then, but I've got ready to say it and I've been thinking about it all the time I was away. I didn't expect to see you here, didn't think you would be living here and on your own, like, with just the young 'uns. So I couldn't stay here, the way I feel about you, it wouldn't be right and it would look bad for you. I was going to ask you later on if you'd have me, but as things are now, I've got to get out. But I will ask you if you'll have me.'

Lucy stared at him, open mouthed. 'You mean, marry you?'

'Aye, that's right. I'm no catch but I'll do my best to make you happy. I'm not rich but I can work, and I'd work like a horse for you. I love you, Lucy.'

'Oh, Clem.' Lucy set down the tea, put her arms around his neck and kissed him.

His arms wrapped around her. 'Does that mean you will?'

'Yes, it does.' Now Lucy shed the tears she had fought against all the morning. She was not alone. Here was a man who loved her enough to marry her. Who would care for her, she was sure of that. She felt as if a weight had been lifted from her shoulders. 'Oh, yes, Clem!'

'When?'

Lucy laughed up at him through her tears. 'Whenever you like.'

'As soon as we can, then.' Grinning apologetically, he went on, 'I can't give you an engagement ring like some fellers put on their girls' fingers.'

'We don't need one.' Lucy suddenly put a hand to her mouth in horror.

Clem asked, 'What is it?'

Lucy whispered, 'We'll need Josh's permission for me to marry.' She was under twenty-one and Josh was recorded as her father. 'He'll never give it. I don't even know where he is.'

Clem reassured her, 'I'll find him. You say he works for a bookie called Charlie Garvey?'

Clem asked around at Buchanan's yard, shouting above the din of the hammering, 'D'you know a bookie called Charlie Garvey?' And after a day or two he found a plater who told him Garvey lived and worked on the other side of the river. The 'fancy woman' Josh had gone to when he had deserted his family had soon spent what money he had and thrown him out. He now shared in Garvey's rooms.

Clem followed up that information and ran Garvey to earth in a pub near the Garrison Field. Garvey's lavender bowler hat was on the back of his head and Josh Campbell was with him. They sat at a table facing the door. A pall of blue tobacco smoke hung below the low ceiling. A naked gas jet burned on one wall for any customer to light his pipe or cigarette. Clem shouldered his way through the crowd until he stood on the sawdust strewn floor before them.

Josh looked up and asked, 'What do you want?'

Clem grinned at him. 'I've come to make you happy. What'll

you have?' He brought the beer for the three of them and they talked in friendly fashion. Finally Clem laid two sovereigns on the table. 'So you'll let me marry your daughter?'

'Aye.' Josh laughed and swept up the coins. 'But there's something else I want.'

Clem scowled. 'You've been paid.'

Josh ignored that. 'I walked out o' Buchanan's yard, but Garvey here reckons I ought to get back in. He thinks I could do a lot o' business in there, taking bets for him.'

Clem grimaced, 'I'm warning you as one mate to another. It's no skin off my nose, but old Andrew Buchanan doesn't like that. Not only because it's illegal. He's a bit of a Holy Joe, won't stand for a feller taking bets in his yard.'

Josh dismissed that. 'He won't know about it! Now, can you put a word in for me, get me a job?'

Clem sucked in a breath and shook his head. 'That won't be easy.' However, Josh, despite his many faults, was known to be a good worker. Clem knew there was a foreman in charge of a gang working on the quay who would take a backhander – and who wanted two men. 'I'll try . . .'

Josh sniggered. 'If you want our lass you'll have to do better than try.'

Clem drank up then set down his empty glass. 'Aye.'

Clem departed, cheerful, leaving Josh confident and calling for another round for Garvey and himself.

Later Josh told Garvey, 'He'll fix me up with a job at Buchanan's. He's mad on that lass o' mine.'

Josh was right. A week later he started work on the quay at Buchanan's yard. He grumbled because he would have preferred a job in one of the sheds, while work on the quay in all weathers could be cold, wet and windy, but Garvey said he was to go, so he grumbled but went anyway.

A grinning Clem told a surprised but delighted Lucy, 'He's agreed.'

Lucy clapped her hands. 'You can move in again now. If we

let folks know we're going to be married soon, that will keep it respectable.'

Clem had found lodgings in the next street, but now he returned to sleep on the couch in the kitchen. On the Saturday night he came home from the pub, explaining, 'Celebratin' our engagement.' The words were slurred. Lucy had waited up for him and when she kissed him he fondled her breast. She stepped back quickly, taken by surprise. For a second he glared at her, then his smile came again and he said, 'Sorry! I didn't mean that.'

Lucy returned his smile, but shakily, and went to her bed. She lay awake for a long time, uneasy. This was a side of Clem she had not seen before. But then she told herself it was no more than a lover's eagerness. It had to be, because this was the man she was to marry.

On the following Sunday they sat together in St Peter's church and heard the banns read for the first time. In the evenings they would sit around the fire and discuss the arrangements for the wedding. Lucy decided she would wear the lace embroidered blouse and long skirt in cream serge she had worn when walking out from the Buchanan house on her days off. Clem's navy blue suit with its narrow trousers and buttoning close to the neck was barely a year old and had only been worn on Sundays.

Later that week Lucy was passing Mackie's corner when she heard her name called. 'Hello! Little Lucy!' She turned her head, and saw the tall figure of Nick Buchanan threading his way through the High Street traffic of trams, horse-drawn carts and steam lorries. He caught up with her and asked, 'How are you now?'

Lucy smiled easily. 'I'm fine.'

'We've both been shopping, I see.' Nick nodded at the bag Lucy was carrying.

She blushed and answered, 'Yes.' It was the week before the wedding, and she had searched the stores in the High Street for a nightdress and finally found what she wanted at three shillings and sixpence.

'I've just been ordering some kit at Caslaw's.' Nick indicated a shop across the street with a jerk of his dark head. 'I've got a ship and I'll be sailing next week. Now, how are things at home?'

'They're fine, too.' Lucy told him how Tommy and the others had come round after Josh Campbell left, and then burst out with the big news: 'And I'm going to be married.' She told him about it, the words running together, and finishing, '. . . Rose and Elsie are going to be bridesmaids.'

Nick laughed. 'It sounds as though it's all organised. Where is it and when?'

'St Peter's, next Saturday at eleven.'

'That's a bit of luck. We don't sail out of the Tyne till six that night so I can come and throw some confetti.' And then as the thought struck him, 'If your father has run off, who is going to give you away?'

Lucy stared at him blankly. 'I don't know. I hadn't thought of that.'

'What about me?'

Lucy eyed him uncertainly. This was one of the people she had worked for, nephew of Andrew Buchanan. Was he teasing her again? She asked, 'Seriously?'

'Yes.' Nick was grinning but he meant what he said. 'For old times' sake. If you'll let me.'

They both laughed and so it was agreed.

Lucy and Clem walked to their wedding at St Peter's church with the rest of their party. The best man was a distant cousin of Clem, Fred Smart, who had come from Newcastle. He had leered at Lucy when they were introduced, nudged Clem in the ribs and said coarsely, 'You've got a ripe bit o' stuff there.' They both laughed and Lucy was embarrassed.

The priest asked, 'Who giveth this woman to be married to this man?'

Nick, in his uniform of navy blue reefer jacket with gleaming brass buttons, answered deeply, 'I do,' although he felt a qualm of uneasiness. The bride and groom made a fine picture in the ancient church with the sun lancing in through the stained glass windows, but Nick was not sure about Clem. He told himself he had only met the man for the first time this day, and then only exchanged a few words, while Lucy had known Clem for months. But still . . .

Nick left at the end of the ceremony to take a train through to the Tyne and join his ship. Lucy came to thank him and Nick looked down at her with his teasing grin and warned, 'There's a condition attached: you have to invite me to the other weddings.' He waved a hand at her siblings and the boys grinned awkwardly and shuffled their feet, Rose and Elsie giggled. Nick stooped to kiss Lucy and said gently, 'Here's wishing you all the best in life, little Lucy.'

'Don't you dare call me that!' Lucy called after him, but he was already striding away up Church Street, laughing.

Lucy's joy and excitement carried her through the first hour after the ceremony as the reception was held in the kitchen, toasts were drunk and sandwiches and cake eaten. Several neighbours were present and a crowd of men who worked with Clem at Buchanan's yard. Clem said to her, off-handedly as he made for the door, 'I'm taking the lads down the street for a drink.'

Lucy followed him down the stairs to the street door to see him off. She lifted her face to kiss him and he bruised her mouth with his, laughed at her expression of hurt, before swaggering away with his cronies.

Lucy stood at the door until he had rounded the corner and gone from her sight. She dabbed at her mouth with her handkerchief, inexplicably frightened. A small, wiry man was walking along the street from the other direction. He stopped to speak to a neighbour a few doors away and she pointed towards Lucy. The little man came on, halted in front of Lucy and said, 'Excuse me, miss, but I'm looking for a Lucy Campbell.'

She smiled at him, puzzled, but answered, 'I'm Lucy Campbell,' she was about to add, 'Lucy Nolan now', but he was quicker.

'Ah!' Now he took off his cap, showing thinning grey hair. Lucy guessed he was close to sixty. He said, 'I'm Joe Huckeridge, Clem Nolan's uncle. Has he mentioned me?'

'No, Mr Huckeridge. He—'

'No, I wouldn't think he would. I'd ha' come sooner but I only found out about the wedding last night. A pal o' mine heard Fred Smart shouting how he was going to be best man and the young lass was a Lucy Campbell, living alongside Buchanan's yard.' He stopped then and fiddled with his cap.

Lucy said, 'I'm pleased to meet you, Mr Huckeridge. Won't you come in?'

Joe said heavily, 'I don't know about you being pleased.' He took a breath and asked, 'What d'you know about Clem and his family?'

Lucy's smile slipped away. 'I know they were cruel to him.'

Huckeridge nodded his greying head and sighed. 'He's still telling that tale. It's rubbish. My sister and her husband did all they could for him and he broke their hearts. He got two lasses into trouble – that we know of. For years he stole from his mother's purse and his father's pocket. They couldn't put a copper down in their own house. At the finish he hit his father in the head and went off with every penny they had. I wanted them to tell the pollis but they wouldn't.' He stopped and nodded at Lucy. 'That's what I came to tell you. He's evil.'

Lucy said shakily, 'I don't believe you.' This could not be true of Clem, the man she had married.

'Well, I'm not a liar,' said Huckeridge patiently. 'And I didn't want this job. I'd ha' stayed home and minded my own business but my wife said, "There's some young lass walking into this with her eyes shut. You get the train to Monkwearmouth and tell her."' He put on his cap, then finished, 'So I've done it. I've told you about him. You should forget about the wedding next week and give him back his ring. Ta-ra, bonny lass.' And he marched off up the street, heading towards Monkwearmouth station.

Lucy stood at the door, staring unseeingly out at the street where the groups of children played with hoops, whips and tops, or chalked hopscotch squares on the pavements. Eventually Rose came down and asked, 'What are you standing here for?' She peered into Lucy's face. 'Is something wrong?'

Lucy answered, 'No.' How could she tell them? And was it true? Joe Huckeridge had been given the wrong day for the wedding and come too late. Lucy wondered if it would have been better if he had not come at all. She recalled Josh's warning, and how Clem had fondled her drunkenly when he had come back from the pub. Had she made a terrible mistake? She said, 'No, there's nothing wrong. I'm coming up now.'

Rose complained, 'I'd ha' thought Clem would have been back by now.'

The afternoon passed and the evening closed in. One by one the neighbours left. Lucy sat on by the small fire, lit because there was a chill in the air now the sun was down. She made bright conversation with the four children until ten, when she sent them to bed and waited alone.

Clem returned just before midnight. He smirked at her, loose lipped, as he entered the kitchen, showing his teeth. Lucy went to him, anxious and relieved at the same time – and afraid to ask what she had to. 'I was worried about you.'

'We went the rounds, had a few here, a few there. You needn't have worried about whether I'd come home tonight.' Clem reached out a hand to fondle her. 'I thought you'd be in bed, ready for me.' His hand moved to fasten on her arm and he led her to the bedroom. 'I've been looking forward to this for a long time.'

Lucy had to know. She said fearfully, 'There was a man came to see me. Joe Huckeridge. He said—'

Clem swung her round to face him, his fingers digging into her arm so that she cried out. He thrust his face close to hers and hissed, '*Shut up!*' He paused for a moment, breathing heavily, then, 'That pious little bugger! Shoving his nose in! Well, never mind what he said or what I did. I gave Josh a couple o' sovereigns for you and we're married now. That's all I wanted. A place o' my own and you between the sheets. Get in there.' He shoved her on to the bed.

Lucy was still awake when the sky turned grey. Bruised in body and mind, she remembered her mother saying, 'Think long and hard before you marry.' Amy had said she had paid. Lucy knew she would, too. The horror of her wedding night would be with her for the rest of her life.

She whispered, '*Oh, Mother!*'

Chapter Eight

'Frankly, I'm glad to see the back of him.' Billy's headmaster frowned over his spectacles at Lucy. She had gone to see him because Billy was thirteen now and old enough to leave school. The Head went on, 'He's a bright lad, a good scholar, but always fighting. I had to give him a caning just the other day for half-killing another lad.'

Lucy was quick to defend Billy: 'He must have had a reason.'

'No doubt,' the Head replied drily, 'but he would not tell me what it was and neither would his victim. I only know I caught him in the act.'

Lucy forced a smile. 'Well, he's finished with school now. And he's got a job.'

'Has he?' The Head raised his eyebrows.

'Yes, he starts next week.' And put that in your pipe and smoke it, Lucy said to herself as she left.

Once home she confronted Billy and demanded, 'Why did you knock that other lad about?'

Billy stood in the middle of the kitchen, but his gaze avoided Lucy's and was fixed on the window. He smiled disarmingly and played for time. 'What other lad?'

'The one your headmaster caned you for just a week ago.'

Billy shrugged. 'That was Len Walker. He should ha' kept his trap shut.'

'Why? What had he said?' And when Billy did not speak or meet her eye Lucy seized his shoulders and shook him. 'What did he say! I stuck up for you with that headmaster, but you've got to play fair by me and tell me the truth. Did this Len Walker start it?'

'Aye,' Billy admitted stubbornly.

'So what did he *say?*'

Billy, his eyes on the floor, muttered, 'He said you had to get married to Clem because you were expecting a baby. So I gave him a good hiding.'

Lucy put a hand under his chin and tilted his face up to look at her. 'What he said isn't true. And if you meet him again you can laugh and tell him so and that he got a hiding for nothing.'

'You mean you're not going to have a baby?'

Lucy nodded firmly. 'That's right.' She shuddered inside at the thought.

Billy grinned at her. 'I'm going to enjoy telling Len.'

Lucy told him severely, 'You just keep away from him.' However, when he had gone she smiled fondly. She smiled rarely now.

On Monday, just over a week later, when she had been married barely a month, she warned, 'Now you two be careful.' She was seeing Clem and Tommy off to work at Buchanan's yard, carrying their packets of sandwiches wrapped in red and white spotted handkerchieves, their cans holding dry tea, sugar and spoonfuls of condensed milk, to be wetted down for their midday break. 'There's men gets killed or injured every day in those shipyards.'

'Stop your nagging!' Clem answered from the stairs. 'I don't need you to tell me what to do!' Tommy waved a hand, pulled a face at Clem's back then smiled encouragingly at Lucy, then they were out of the front door and setting off towards the river.

Lucy needed all the encouragement she could get. She had partly recovered from the initial shock at the change in Clem as soon as they were married. She tried to bring up her family and to live a seemingly normal life with this man to whom she had entrusted her heart and her body, but he abused both. He continually derided and criticised her, taunted her with, 'You're like your mother! Your father was the only one around here I could get on with. I told him, "Your Lucy thinks I'm Sir Galahad." Didn't we laugh!'

Clem was far worse than Josh, because he also vented his lust on her. Once, hurt beyond bearing, Lucy whispered, 'Why do you treat me like this?'

He grinned at her, showing his teeth. 'Because I *like* it! And because you're like a lady. I like to see that hurt look on your face.' And there was the key: Clem had not changed, just previously acted a part to gain his ends. Lucy recalled Joe Huckeridge saying of Clem, simply, 'He's evil.' She believed him now. And she was bound to Clem for the rest of her life.

Lucy turned back into the kitchen where Billy and Rose were eating hurried breakfasts. They would be next to leave, Rose off to the shop in Dundas Street, Billy across the bridge to the other side of the river and a gents' haberdasher just off Fawcett Street. He had found the job himself, tipped off by a former school-friend who worked there already, a youth who sported high, stiff collars and gaudy ties, bought cheaply from the shop. That – and the girls that worked there – attracted Billy. Elsie had mocked, 'You'll look like him, a proper little masher.' Lucy had smiled to herself at the thought of young Billy as a dandy, but he took the remark as a compliment. She had her doubts as to whether the job was suitable, but he was eager to take it and it was a miracle he had got it, so Lucy gave her blessing.

Rose had lost her first enthusiasm for her evening classes in shorthand and typing and would have given up, but Lucy kept her at it, telling her, 'If you want that job in an office, you've got to learn.'

Now as Lucy saw them out of the door she urged Billy, 'Mind you stick in.' And to Rose, 'Don't be late home tonight. You've got your lessons to go to.'

She got a resigned, 'Aye, all right,' from Rose and a cheerful, 'I'll do that, never fear,' from Billy.

There remained only Elsie, who came yawning out of the bedroom and sat down at the table. Lucy set a steaming plate of porridge before her. 'Eat up and then get away. You don't want to be late for school,' although she knew Elsie would derive little benefit from her lessons. She was as poor a scholar as Billy had been a good one. Her arithmetic was weak and her spelling appalling, her writing meandered over the page and was often indecipherable. Lucy could see only one gleam of hope for Elsie and asked her now, 'I've got the meat for a stew tomorrow. Will you cook it tonight?'

Elsie stared at her over the spoon. 'On my own? I've only done it once before with you. Mam never let us do any cooking.'

Lucy considered that had been her mother's mistake, doubtless born out of years of weariness – 'It's easier to do it myself' – but it would not be repeated by her. She said with feigned confidence, 'You'll manage.'

Elsie said doubtfully, 'I'm not sure,' but she was more cheerful as she left for school. Lucy was determined to persevere with her. Next would come a lesson in baking bread, and then . . .

As soon as Elsie had gone Lucy was able to turn to her own work. She had already lit the fire under the copper in the washhouse in the back yard – this was washing day. First she scrubbed and whitened the front doorstep, and only then went to the washhouse to begin the scrubbing and possing and passing the clothes through the big mangle. She groaned when she saw the first raindrops pattering down into the back yard, and in seconds they became a deluge. There would be no drying the clothes outside today.

*

Down by the river Clem was walking along the deck of the ship with a length of timber over his shoulder. As he sidestepped to pass a sack of rivets his foot slipped on the steel plating of the deck made greasy by the pouring rain. His legs went from under him, and tilted off-balance by the load he carried, he almost fell on to the stocks below. He saved himself just in time by dropping the timber on to the deck and grabbing at the sack.

The boy heating rivets on a brazier close by called, 'Watch what you're doing, Clem! You nearly went ower, then.'

'Mind your own bloody business!' Clem bawled at him. He skirted the sack and retrieved his piece of timber and went on, but picking his way carefully now.

The boy's eyes followed him, resentful, and an older man passing by said, 'He's a nasty bit o' work.'

'Don't we all know it,' muttered the youngster.

By mid-morning Lucy was ready to hang up her washing to dry. As she ran across the yard through the rain with the basket of damp clothes, a voice cried, 'Lucy!' She looked up and saw Brenda Tucker, her neighbour in the upstairs rooms next door, standing at her open window. Despite the time of day she was not dressed, wearing only a coat thrown over her nightgown. That did not surprise Lucy. Brenda was a blowzy young woman, married to a seaman who was often away for months on end. Brenda had a roving eye and was no better than she should be.

Sheltered in the passage, Lucy put out her head to ask, 'Aye, Brenda?'

'Have you got any rain coming in?'

'I don't know.'

Brenda wailed, 'You'd better have a look. It's pouring into my kitchen.'

Lucy hurried upstairs and toured through the kitchen and two bedrooms then heaved a sigh of relief. Nothing was dripping through the ceiling. She put her head out of the kitchen window to call, 'Our place is dry. You must have lost a slate off the roof.'

'Aye.' Her neighbour was disconsolate. 'I'll have to get some-body in to mend it.'

Lucy set up the big clothes horse and hung the washing round the fire to dry. She was able to iron all of it that afternoon, heating the iron on the fire, among the pots and pans containing the dinner. Ironing and dinner were both done when her brood came home and she looked out wryly at the bright sunshine come too late.

As she peered out of the window she heard Clem say behind her, 'I've got plenty of time for you an' all!' Lucy spun on her heel and saw a frightened Rose, trying feebly to pull away from Clem's arm wrapped tightly around her waist. Lucy was frozen in disbe-lieving shock, then she saw Rose's eyes pleading with her for help.

Lucy yanked the girl away from Clem, babbling, 'Come and give me a hand to serve up.' Oh, God! What am I to do? she wondered, and kept on chattering in the face of Clem's glare, trying to pass off the moment, to pretend it had not happened. 'I got all the washing done and ironed this afternoon. Did any of you get wet when all that rain came down? That Brenda next door, she's got a leak in her kitchen where a tile's come off but ours is all right . . .' And so on and on.

They sat down to the meal. Rose ate little and kept her eyes on her plate. Lucy picked at the food, but Elsie had been busy at the oven and the two boys had been washing on the landing, so they had seen nothing, and ate heartily while Clem wolfed down his dinner.

Clem pushed back his plate and wiped the back of his hand over his mouth. 'I'll put some slates on for Brenda, if they can be reached from a ladder.'

Lucy stared at him. 'You're a carpenter, not a tiler.'

Clem scoffed, 'Anybody can put a slate or two on if they've got a ladder. I've got some down in the yard and I can borrow the ladder from two doors down.'

Lucy was washing up when she heard his whistle. She hurried

to the kitchen window, drying her hands, but Clem was in the yard next door, grinning up at Brenda as she leaned out of her window. He called, 'Them slates you've lost were near the edge of the roof. I can see where they were. I've borrowed a ladder and I'm going to put some on for you.' He held them up.

'Ooh!' Brenda pushed at her hair coquettishly. 'Thanks, Clem.'

He settled the ladder against the guttering and started up, the slates under one arm. 'You can give me a cup o' tea.'

Brenda giggled, 'I'll put the kettle on.'

'I'll be there in a minute or two.' Clem turned his head and saw Lucy, only feet away as he climbed, and laughed in her face.

Lucy turned away, ashamed for them both. She sat down by the fire and began patching Tommy's overalls where hot rivets had burned holes in them, but she had to stop to wipe her eyes.

Her head jerked up when she heard the shriek, followed by the scraping of the ladder. Lucy watched it grate past the kitchen window, Clem's legs on the topmost rungs, and realised it had slid sideways and Clem was falling. She fled to the window, hearing the clatter as the ladder smashed into the yard below. She peered out fearfully, and saw the broken ladder – and Clem's prostrate body.

'*Clem!*' Lucy screamed as she ran down the stairs then fell on her knees at his side. He was unconscious, blood running from a scalp wound to mat his hair, his body limp. His wickedness and ill treatment of her were forgotten. This was an injured man and she felt for him. 'Oh, Clem!'

Clem was taken to the hospital in Roker Avenue at the top of Church Street. The doctors told her, 'His back is broken and he's paralysed from the waist down. There's nothing more we can do.'

Lucy went to see Clem and his eyes blazed at her with hatred. He hissed, 'Damn you to hell! You wished this on me! I believe you pushed the bloody ladder!'

Lucy protested her innocence, denied any guilt, pleaded through her tears for him to listen to her. He would not cease from his snarled allegations and cursing. At the end she went away weeping, with his voice following her: 'That's right, get out o' here! You've done enough damage, damn your eyes!'

When Lucy had gone, one doctor asked the other, 'How will that girl manage?'

He received a weary shake of the head in reply. 'God knows. I don't.'

As Lucy crossed the road a girl ran from the tram stop to touch her arm. 'Lucy! I've just been down to your house, looking for you. I'm sorry to hear about your trouble.' Lucy stared dully at Isabel, who went on, 'I left a message with your sister – Rose, isn't it? Two of our girls have left the Palace and we're rushed off our feet.' Isabel stopped. She could see now that Lucy had been crying; the tears were still wet on her cheeks. She said softly, 'Is it bad news, Lucy?'

'Clem, my husband, won't walk again. He's broken his back.'

Isabel breathed, 'Oh, my God!' Then, 'You won't be interested now. I'm sorry I bothered you—'

Lucy cut in, 'Yes. Yes, I'm glad you remembered me. When do they want me to start?'

'Well –' Isabel was taken aback. 'As soon as you can.'

'I'll just go home and change. I've got a black dress.'

Clem would have to be looked after, and they would not have his wage any longer – though he had given up precious little of it. They needed every penny Lucy could earn.

An hour later she started work as a waitress at the Palace Hotel.

Chapter Nine

'What are you doing here?' Lucy halted, breathless from her run up the stairs. The question was levelled at Billy where he sat by the fire. Lucy was on the flying visit she paid every day just before the lunchtime trade started at the Palace hotel. She liked to look in on Clem, make sure he had his lunch and see to his wants. There were always several and the list was interspersed with complaints. Every day, therefore, Lucy had to run to be back at her work before twelve, waiting on in the restaurant at the Palace.

All the others, Rose, Tommy and Elsie, were at work or school – and so should Billy be. She demanded again as she hurried over to Clem, 'Why aren't you at work, Billy?'

Clem jeered, 'He hasn't got a bloody job, that's why.' He sat in his wheelchair, pulled up to the bench set under the window. The parts of a photograph frame that he had made were spread out before him. Some weeks after Lucy had brought him home from the hospital she had seen a frame in a photographer's shop window. It was an oval set on a spindle on a stand. The photograph was slid into the oval and this could be tilted to various angles. Lucy had bought it and asked Clem, 'Could you make some of these?'

He shouted at her, 'Wi' me as I am now? Are you trying to

torment me? Haven't you done enough to me already?'

In fact Lucy was attempting to ease his days with an occupation for his hands. When he had done bemoaning his lot and vilifying her, he examined the frame and said contemptuously, 'I can do a better job than that.' He did, too, being skilled at his trade, and the photographer bought them, and now Clem was busy for a few hours each day making frames or crackets or similar small items that sold for a few pence. It wasn't much and Lucy saw nothing of the money, because he spent it on beer, sending Tommy or Billy down to the pub with a jug.

Now Lucy turned on Billy. 'Is that right?'

She whipped off her coat, worn over her uniform of black dress and white apron, and began setting out Clem's lunch of bread and cheese and tea. 'Now then, Billy, let's hear from you.'

Billy muttered, 'I got the sack.'

Lucy sucked in a breath. '*What!* Why?'

'We were having a bit of a lark and this feller Clancy – he's the one over us – he told us to cut it out, and when we didn't straight away he told the old man. We got a ticking off and when we came out of the office Clancy was laughing so I belted him. One o' the girls started screaming and the old man came out and said I wasn't suited to shop work and sacked me.'

Lucy was silent for a moment. She could picture the series of events, had heard of Clancy and met him when visiting the shop where Billy had worked. She had thought him supercilious and ingratiating in turn, could picture him telling tales and sniggering, but . . . she pointed the bread knife at Billy. 'You'll have to learn not to start punching people every time you think you've been slighted or you'll wind up in jail.' When Billy stared morosely into the fire, she went on. '*Do you hear me?*'

Billy jerked as if struck and answered quickly, 'Aye, I heard you, Lucy.'

'That job was your idea. You were dead set on having it. Now what are you going to do?'

Billy admitted, 'I don't know.'

'I do. There's a bicycle shop in Charles Street. I passed it just a few minutes ago and there's a card in the window saying they want a lad. Get over there.'

Billy protested, 'I don't know owt about bikes.'

'You don't know much about anything, but I know you're not going to sit idle around here. Off you go.'

Billy objected again, 'I haven't had anything to eat. What if they take me on?'

'No chance o' that,' mocked Clem.

Lucy shoved Billy towards the door. 'If you're not back in half an hour Elsie will bring you something on her way back to school.'

Billy left, followed by Clem's raucous laughter. Lucy pleaded with him, 'I wish you wouldn't tease the bairns so much.'

'Tease them? Can't I have a joke wi' them?' Clem glared in outrage. 'You don't know what it's like, sitting in here all day wi' never a breath of fresh air except when you feel like pushing me out in this damned chair!'

Lucy could not manoeuvre him in his chair down the stairs without the aid of the boys, and she started to say, 'I do it as often as I can—'

Clem shouted her down: 'It's all right for you, off out gallivanting! I sit here wondering what you're up to out there without my eye on you!'

Lucy was used to this charge now and said wearily, 'I just go to work.' She looked up at the clock on the mantelpiece. 'I've got to get back now. Elsie will be in soon. Don't ask her to go down to the pub for you because she doesn't like going.' Besides, Clem had been drinking already; she could smell it, and concluded Billy had brought him some beer. The jug was probably hidden under the table close by his chair.

Clem snarled, 'Aw, to hell with you.' As Lucy descended the stairs, he shouted, 'Get away and give me some bloody peace!'

As she walked rapidly back across the bridge into the town Lucy wished she could find some ground-floor rooms where it would be easier for Clem to get out in his chair, though she would get no thanks for her pains. Clem's accident and his dependence on her had not softened his treatment of her. While his legs were useless, his upper body strength was enhanced, and the livid bruises on Lucy's arms, where he gripped her, were evidence of that. In fact his behaviour had worsened, and he blamed Lucy for his condition, though the true guilty party, apart from Clem himself, had been Brenda Tucker. Brenda had been reunited with her seaman husband just a week after the accident and moved away. Rose had muttered, 'Good riddance!' Lucy had silently agreed.

She could only be thankful she was saved from the nightly assault on her body. Clem cursed her for that as well, holding her responsible for his impotence. Lucy had gone back to sleeping with the girls, and Clem had the double bed and a room to himself. Lucy tried to feel sympathy for him and knew he received it from others outside the family, to whom he showed a different face of brave suffering. And always there was the knowledge that she had married him 'for better, for worse'.

Lucy also worried about Billy. His sacking had not taken her wholly by surprise. It had been obvious for a while that he had become disenchanted with the haberdasher's, had frequently grumbled enviously after listening to Tommy's tales of life at Buchanan's yard: 'I wish I could get taken on in one o' the yards.' Lucy remembered how she had asked Andrew Buchanan to give Tommy a job.

Billy got the job at the bicycle shop but was unenthusiastic. All day long he could hear the din of the riveting hammers in the yards. Lucy knew he would not stay long at the shop, and on a Sunday when she did not have to work, she walked out early in the morning, heading for the Buchanan house.

It was cold, but as she left the shipyards silent and still behind her and stepped out on the road outside the town, she found the air fresh and invigorating. The frost had still not melted on the road, but a pale winter sun was shedding some brightness and

Lucy hummed softly to herself as she walked. She felt as if she had been set free, as indeed she had, from Clem's abuse and denigration – for a while.

She paused at the big wrought-iron gates. The Buchanan house was basking in the sunlight, the wide spread of grass before it and the trees around glistening as the light sparked on the rime turned to dew. She looked at the house longingly, this place of her dreams.

Fred Wilson, who had been working in the garden behind his gatekeeper's lodge, now appeared from around the corner and greeted her cheerfully, but told her with a shake of the head, 'Mr Andrew isn't home, nor Mrs Jarman, and I don't know when they'll be back. Gone for the day, I reckon. There's an old friend of his come to stay for a few days: Captain Hawkins, naval officer just come home from the China Station. Him and Mr Andrew were in the Navy together.'

The name of her natural father meant nothing to Lucy. She had walked all this way for nothing. She started to retrace her steps, slowly, but she had only walked a minute or so, until the gatekeeper's lodge was hidden from sight around a bend behind her, when she saw Nick Buchanan step out from a lane ahead of her. He did not see her, his head turned to look back the way he had come. He wore corduroy trousers and an old navy blue jersey. His dark hair was tousled and he was smiling that mischievous smile Lucy always remembered and that so annoyed her when he looked down at her and called her 'little Lucy'.

She stopped in her tracks. Something stirred inside her, a strange emotion not felt before. Standing in that cold sunlight of a winter morning she knew a sudden joy and excitement – that was as quickly gone when she recalled the reality of her situation. In that bleak moment of heartbreak she knew she should walk away, but she could not and stayed very still, her eyes on Nick.

She saw that he was not alone as she had originally thought. Helen Whittaker, looking very pretty in a walking costume of waisted jacket and skirt some six inches from the ground, now came out of the lane. Helen and Nick exchanged a few short words that Lucy could not hear. He held out his hand to take Helen's, and they both laughed. They turned together and started to walk towards Lucy.

They saw her at once and Nick said, predictably, 'Why, it's little Lucy.' This time she was not irritated nor amused, only bereft.

Helen Whittaker smiled at her. 'Hello, Lucy.'

'Good morning, miss,' replied Lucy, and returned the smile, but weakly.

Nick went on, grinning down at her, 'Have you been up to the house? Uncle's away with Mrs Jarman.'

Lucy said, 'Yes, I know.'

Nick asked, 'Were you hoping to see one of them? Was there something you wanted to ask?'

Lucy thought she should say no and walk away, but there was Billy to think of. As she hesitated, Helen said quickly, 'I'll go on to the house, Nick.'

'Fine. I'll catch you up.' As Helen walked on, his gaze returned to Lucy. 'So?'

Lucy explained about Billy. 'I don't want to seem like I'm always pleading, but if Mr Buchanan could see his way to giving a job to Billy, I'd be grateful.'

Nick nodded. 'I can't promise anything but I'll mention it to him tonight when he gets back.' Then he asked, 'And how is married life?'

Lucy answered, straight faced, 'I'm very happy.'

Nick was not smiling now. 'You don't sound happy at all.'

Lucy evaded the point with a half-truth and told him how Clem was now paralysed. Nick was shocked. 'I'm very sorry for the pair of you. If there is anything I can do . . .'

Lucy shook her head. The less she was involved with Nick, the better. She smiled again. 'We're managing quite well, really.' Because that was what you said. Never mind that you had to spend each penny carefully, that it was a continuing worry how to put food on the table week after week, that the man you had married reviled you no matter how hard you tried. She said, 'I'd better be getting back home now.'

Nick stepped aside to let her pass. 'Remember, if there's any way I can help, you know where to find me. I'm sailing next week but I expect to be home again in a month or two. Meanwhile, why not have a word with Uncle Andrew at the yard? I'm sure he remembers you.'

Lucy murmured her thanks and walked on. There was no spring in her step now, no sense of freedom, only of loss. Nick had been in the background of her life so long, from being a childhood friend. But not part of her life; he inhabited another world. She had never thought of him as – as she did now. There had been comradeship, some affection, respect – but this was different. This emotion must have grown inside, unsuspected, over the years. And that was where it would have to remain. She was wedded to Clem Nolan till death. Nick would marry Helen Whittaker, pretty and monied. Lucy told herself she was being foolish, dreaming dreams that could never come true, that she had to face reality. She fought to cast off the mood, and by the time she reached her home she had her thoughts and emotions under control.

Next morning Lucy stood at the gates of the Buchanan yard, her shawl held tight around her head against the bitterly cold wind driving in off the sea. She watched Andrew Buchanan arrive in the rear of the chauffeur-driven Rolls-Royce Silver Ghost. He had bought it only months before, and now used it instead of the carriage with its two grey horses. The Rolls was open to the sky and Andrew was bulky in a heavy motoring coat, a cap pulled down on his head. He saw the girl, white faced in the cold, and thought he recognised her. Then the Rolls swept past and left her behind.

Lucy waited still, trying to screw up her courage. She had seen Andrew Buchanan daily when she had been in service at his house, talked with him – when he addressed her. He had been as a god to Lucy when she first went there to work, and the years between had not reduced that impression. It was one thing to approach him in the Buchanan house, familiar territory to her, and ask him to employ Tommy in his shipyard, but the yard was a male preserve in which Andrew was king. As a child she had seen him arrive there, driving down her street in his carriage, its iron-shod wheels striking sparks from the cobblestones. Seeking another favour from him at the yard was a daunting prospect, but Billy needed the job for his future, his present pride – and the family's economy.

Lucy drew a deep breath and marched in through the open gates, deafened by the din and staring awed at the towering mass of the partly built ship on the stocks swarming with men.

Some ten minutes later, when Andrew Buchanan was settled behind his desk, his secretary entered his office. He was a man as old as Andrew and a servant of the yard for more than forty years. 'Excuse me, Mr Buchanan, but there's a lass outside asking to speak to you. She says she used to work at your house, a Mrs Nolan.'

Andrew nodded, prepared, expecting the visit, following a conversation with Nick the previous evening. He wished he had good news for her, but . . . 'Show her in, please.' When Lucy entered nervously, he greeted her. 'Mrs Nolan. Sit down, please.'

'Thank you, sir.' Lucy chose a straight-backed chair, her own back as rigid as she faced Andrew across the big desk. It was a large room, holding big, heavy furniture. A coal fire burned in the grate.

Andrew had seen Lucy every day for four years but had taken little notice of her because servants were Nell Jarman's affair, although he remembered her now because of the painting – and because of a similar visit she had paid him. He said, 'I understand you want the yard to take on your younger brother.'

'Yes, sir. It's Billy. He's a good boy—' Lucy hoped he would be.

Andrew stopped her with a raised hand. 'His brother works here. I'm told he is a hard worker.'

'Oh, yes, sir. That's Tommy.'

Andrew sighed. 'I'm also advised by my manager that we don't need another lad in the yard at present.' Peters, the manager, had been definite on that point, saying, 'We're carrying extra hands at the moment.'

'Oh!' Lucy flinched but held up her head. 'I see. Well, could you keep him in mind for when you do need a boy, please?'

Andrew was silent for a time, watching her and thinking that the girl was . . . unusual. He noticed no resemblance to his old friend Lucien Hawkins – bearded for the last twenty years. He thought she was a beauty, but it wasn't only that. There was an intelligence and a determination about her – she obviously knew men moved up or moved on. And she had pride, she was not pleading, though he could guess how important it was that she got this job for her brother. Nick had said the husband was an invalid and she was bringing up two sisters and two brothers. Andrew realised that if the boy – Billy? – had anything of the qualities of his sister sitting here now . . . And Nell Jarman thought highly of her, had said so to Andrew, and often.

When Lucy came home from waiting on at the Palace Hotel that evening, she ran along the passage and up the stairs. Billy stood on the landing, having just washed in the bowl in the cupboard, and was towelling his face. Lucy told him, 'You've got a job at Buchanan's starting as soon as you've worked your notice at the bicycle shop.'

Billy whooped and kissed her. 'Thanks, Lucy! You're a marvel!'

'You've more than me to thank,' Lucy said drily. She was sure Nick had 'put in a word' for Billy, and now she was reminded of standing on that frosted road in the pale sunlight and feeling heartache. It was an effort to smile when Billy hugged her delightedly.

Chapter Ten

SUMMER 1910

'There's a good-looking feller just sat down at one o' your tables,' said Isabel. She had covered for Lucy in the restaurant of the Palace Hotel while she was away for her midday break.

'Aye?' Lucy grinned, pretending an interest she did not feel. 'Not one of our regulars, then.' She was still flushed and panting from hurrying across the bridge after seeing if Clem Nolan needed anything and giving him his lunch.

Isabel shook her head, 'No, I've not seen this one before.'

Lucy hung up her coat, smoothed down her apron and pinned on her little white cap. 'Let's have a look at him, then.'

She whisked through the kitchen, pushed through the swing doors lined with green baize, and so entered the restaurant of the Palace Hotel. She took in the group of tables at which she waited in one swift glance, taking in who did and did not need serving now, mentally drawing up a list of priorities. Suddenly she faltered in her stride. There was the 'good-looking young feller', and her heart faltered, too.

Murdoch Buchanan looked up from the menu, saw her and smiled. Lucy had again mistaken him for Nick, with similar dark hair and features, but there was only a similarity. Nick was bigger, with a hardness about him, and not so 'good looking'. Murdoch was more handsome. She walked on towards him, hoping her disappointment had not shown in her face, because she liked this new, adult Murdoch with his easy charm. She could admit to herself that she had been smitten when she had worked at the Buchanan house, but that had been two years ago when she had been very young. And before she had looked at Nick with new eyes . . .

Murdoch welcomed her with, 'Well, this is a pleasant surprise. How long have you been at the Palace?'

'Getting on for two years now,' replied Lucy. For a moment she wondered if that was right, because the days had flown by so quickly, they were so full. How had she managed to carry her burden for so long? And for how much longer could she do so? She spent most of each day at the Palace, hurrying between tables with heavy trays, then returned to the upstairs rooms to wash, clean, cook and encourage and scold her wrangling family.

It had been two years of constant struggle, financially in that it was a weekly battle to make ends meet, physically because of the need to lift Clem down the stairs every time he wanted to go out of the house, then carry him up again later. He demanded to go out often and inevitably there were times when he had to wait for the others to come home. Then he would curse her, a stream of foul abuse, even while she laboured to move him. And all the time she suffered his accusations. The boys helped and so did the girls but Lucy bore the brunt, and Clem still blamed her for his fall. At the end of each day she was exhausted – and bruised. Her dress hid the weals but they showed when she pushed up the sleeves to wash up. Isabel and the others at the Palace had noticed but kept silent.

Now Murdoch asked, 'And how is life treating you?' His eyes flicked to the gold band on her finger. 'I heard you were married.'

'Oh, we're getting on very well,' Lucy lied and smiled. Murdoch talked to her as she took his order, again when she served it, and while he was eating he watched for when she was not attending to another diner, when he called her over to stand by his table so they could talk. He was a sympathetic listener and Lucy warmed to him, and by the end of the meal he had a fairly accurate picture of her life.

Murdoch detected her main preoccupation. 'I can share your feelings about looking for a place to live. I want somewhere in town to save me travelling in from the Buchanan house but I haven't had any luck so far. Is it so difficult to get ground-floor rooms?'

Lucy nodded wearily. 'All these houses have two rooms and a passage on the ground floor and three rooms upstairs, one of them over the passage. With the two girls and the two boys we can't manage with less than three rooms, and you don't get three rooms downstairs. But we need to be downstairs so Clem can get in and out more easily. As it is, he's trapped at the top of the stairs.' That was not strictly true. There were bigger houses with the rooms she needed, but the rent was twice what she could afford.

Murdoch guessed at this but said nothing, except, 'I hope affairs improve for you, because you deserve better,' and he discreetly left her a large tip.

Lucy suspected charity and whispered to herself, 'He shouldn't have given me all that,' but she was grateful.

After she finished the lunchtime shift, she sought out Mrs Wilberforce. A French chef was nominal head of the kitchen, but the kitchen staff all knew Mrs Wilberforce really ran it. She was a large, cheerful woman in her forties. She listened to Lucy's request and agreed, 'Aye, we can do that.' Lucy was always ready to help on the cooking side in an emergency and never complained without good cause.

Lucy then hurried to Elsie's school, and talked to the head-master against a background of distantly chanted multiplication tables. He said, 'Elsie isn't a problem like Billy, but she's learning little, if anything, now.' He sighed, against a faint chorus of 'Seven times seven are forty-nine!' Finally he agreed, 'Very well.'

That evening Lucy showed Elsie the knack of making 'oven shelf cake', the round, flat bread. Her young sister, who would be fourteen in November, rolled out the dough on the board on the kitchen table. The oven alongside the fire was hot with the coals pushed underneath. Elsie slid her hands under the foot-wide circle of dough, turned to the open oven door and flipped the dough on to the shelf so it lay flat without a wrinkle.

'That's good!' Lucy praised her.

Elsie pulled a face. 'But that was my third try. The other two were all crumpled up and had to be rolled out again.'

'Never mind!' Lucy assured her. 'You've got the hang of it now.'

'You can eat the bloody stuff.' Clem poured beer from jug to glass. 'I won't.' He held out the jug to Elsie. 'Take that down to the Pear Tree and get it filled up.'

Lucy intervened and took the jug. 'I told you before not to send her down to the pub. Here, Billy, you go.'

Clem shouted, 'Why can't she go? Billy's working now and she does nowt!'

They all knew Clem did not care about Billy, was only looking for a row, a chance to upset Lucy. She said, 'Elsie is working now. She starts in the kitchen at the Palace tomorrow, learning how to be a cook under Mrs Wilberforce.'

Clem glared, outfaced and furious, but Elsie was both delighted and worried. 'What about school?'

'I got them to let you finish early.' Lucy did not say it was because Elsie was not learning. 'Pleased?'

'Oh, Lucy!' Elsie threw her arms around Lucy and hugged her, leaving floury handprints on the back of her dress.

Murdoch lunched at the Palace almost every day for the next month or more. Helen Whittaker usually ate there on a Thursday. When she saw Murdoch she returned his smile with a nod – and sat at a separate table. Lucy wondered at that, but not for long: waitresses were too busy.

One day when Lucy hurried in for the lunchtime shift Isabel

said laughingly, 'That friend of yours, the gent, he's very chummy.'

Lucy shook her head. 'He's nice but he's not a friend. I told you—'

'Yes, I know,' said Isabel, 'you worked for the family. I only meant that he has a chat with me any time you aren't here.'

Lucy knew Isabel gossiped with everyone, and smiled at her, but agreed, 'I can't get over how he's changed.' When Isabel looked at her questioningly, she explained, 'I hated him when he was a boy.'

Isabel giggled. 'I couldn't hate him now. In fact . . .'

They parted to go about their separate duties, laughing. But Lucy knew she found this new Murdoch attractive, as she had when she worked at the Buchanan house.

While Murdoch remembered her from her time in the house – and still lusted after her.

It was on a Thursday several weeks after their first meeting that Murdoch beckoned Lucy to his table and told her, 'I have a suggestion to make that might be beneficial to both of us. I've been wanting a place in town for some time to save me travelling in from the Buchanan house. I've got one now, a house halfway along Park Place, by Mowbray Park. I need a housekeeper, and I remember how good you were when you worked for the family. There are three ground-floor rooms you can have. Come and look at them,' he said, as Lucy stared at him open mouthed.

They made arrangements, Lucy excited at the chance to realise her ambition to be a housekeeper, if not exactly as she had intended – this would not be a big establishment. Nevertheless, it would be infinitely better than waiting on at the Palace. Murdoch smiled, amused at her obvious delight.

Half an hour after Murdoch left, Helen Whittaker came in, looking very attractive in an ankle-length muslin dress with a sailor collar and straw hat. Helen said happily, 'I just want a quick bite, today. I'm meeting Nick off the train. He's home for a few days because his ship is in the dockyard in the Thames. He sent a telegram to Andrew asking him to send the Rolls in to pick him up, and I said I'd go along.' Then she became more serious, asking, 'Are things all right at home, Lucy?'

'Yes. Why?' The denial was instinctive, but Lucy's flushed face told a different story.

Helen was also embarrassed now. 'I'm sorry. It's just that I heard – I wondered if I could help in any way . . .'

Lucy guessed Helen had been talking with Isabel. She sighed, and because she saw that Helen was genuinely concerned, Lucy admitted, 'It's not very good, but there's nothing you can do.' Now she busied herself with pad and pencil, indicating she waited for Helen's order, and changed the subject: 'Mr Murdoch has just left a few minutes ago.'

Helen looked up from the menu, smiled, but said coolly, 'Oh?'

'Yes.' Lucy explained, 'I'm meeting him later when I finish here. He's taken a house in the town, halfway along Park Place. He wants a housekeeper and there are three rooms – on the ground floor – that go with the job.' She explained why the ground floor rooms were needed.

Helen said again, 'Oh. Good luck.'

'Thank you.' Lucy went off on flying feet and a whisk of skirts.

Helen was as good as her word, ate a light salad and went on her way.

When Lucy left the back door of the Palace at the end of her working day she found Murdoch waiting with a cab, the horse wearing its nosebag, its driver standing at its head. As Murdoch handed in a flustered Lucy, the cabbie took off the nosebag and the horse blew at him gratefully. The cabbie climbed into his seat and Murdoch settled beside Lucy, telling her, 'We're only five minutes away.'

*

At the station the chauffeur stowed Nick's case in the Rolls but Nick stood with one foot on the running board, frowning at Helen. She said unhappily, 'I talked with one of the waitresses at the Palace the other day. She works with Lucy and said that husband of hers ill-treats her. This girl has often seen bruises on Lucy's arms. And she said Lucy's sister has started in the kitchen and she let slip that this . . . Clem, I think is his name . . . behaves abominably to Lucy. I asked her about it and she half-admitted it, so it must be pretty bad. You know Lucy.'

Nick said softly, 'Damn!'

Helen went on, 'And Murdoch has taken a house.'

'He's done what?'

She repeated, 'Bought a house in the middle of Park Place.' She added, 'Lucy said he's taken her on as housekeeper and when she finished work she'd be going up to see the rooms she's having. She said she needs ground-floor rooms so this Clem can get out.' Helen hesitated, then said reluctantly, 'I'm afraid I don't trust Murdoch. A week or two ago he made an approach to me that I didn't like.' She flushed now at the memory. When they had been briefly alone in the drawing-room of the Buchanan house, Murdoch had run his hands over her body. She had recoiled in shock and revulsion – and ran.

Nick stood with his head turned to stare in the direction of Park Place, nearly a mile away. He muttered, 'I wonder what he's up to?'

'Here we are.' Murdoch pointed out the house to Lucy. It stood in a street of tall houses near the park. There were long gardens in front and trees spaced out along the wide pavements. Lucy could see the windows of three floors. Murdoch handed Lucy down and paid the cabbie, took Lucy's arm, then led her up to the front door and let them in with a key.

Standing in the hall, he gestured right and left. 'I'll use the drawing room and dining room, but those behind are yours.' At the rear of the house there were two sitting rooms and a bedroom, besides the kitchen, and they looked out on another garden. Lucy thought that all three rooms could be used as bedrooms, and the kitchen was big enough to serve also as living room.

Murdoch asked, 'So what d'you think? I'll pay you whatever you were getting at the Palace and the rooms will be rent free.'

'It's – it's perfect!' Lucy could not believe her luck. With tears in her eyes she stood on tiptoe to kiss his cheek.

Murdoch laughed. 'Good! Now, while you're here you may as well see the rest of the place. Come on.'

Lucy went with him, climbing the wide stairs to see the other rooms, until finally he said, 'This is my bedroom.' Murdoch waved a hand as he ushered her in, his other hand in the small of her back.

Lucy took in the big bed, wardrobe and washstand, but her gaze was drawn to the window overlooking the park. 'It's beautiful.'

Murdoch's arm went around her. 'You'll be happy here, I'll see to that.' He pulled her to him.

Lucy tried to resist, tried to push him away with her hands on his chest, not believing this was happening to her. 'Please! I'm a married woman!'

Murdoch tightened his grip. 'Only in name. I talked to your friend Isabel the other day, and she said you never complained but it was obvious that husband of yours makes your life a misery. And he can give you nothing. You need a man.' His hand was forcing between hers to get at the neck of her dress. For a moment they strained, body to body, then Lucy raised her boot and stamped its high heel down on his foot. Murdoch yelled with pain, threw her away from him and hopped on one leg to clutch at the wall for support, cursing.

Lucy yanked the door open and ran down the stairs. A second later she heard the thudding of Murdoch's boots on the carpeted treads with their brass carpet rails. He was close behind her when she reached the front door, but she was able to pull it open and slip through, pulling it shut behind her. She heard him slam up against it and shout, 'Come back, you little bitch!'

His muffled curses rang in her ears as she ran on, down the path through the long front garden then out through the gate. There she was halted as she ran into a broad chest in a blue serge jacket. She clung to it to save herself from falling and a voice said over her, 'Good Lord, Lucy! What's wrong?'

Lucy threw back her head and saw she was holding on to Nick Buchanan. She pushed away from him and beat at his hands when he tried to hold her, so that he let her go. 'Lucy! What is it?'

'Don't touch me! Leave me alone!' Lucy backed away from him. She was still in shock, trying to come to terms with what had happened to her, could not trust him, or any man. 'Keep away from me!'

'I will. I'll stand here. Just tell me what's wrong.' Nick's gaze went past her to the house from which she had come, and his expression changed from concern to anger. 'Was it Murdoch? Helen Whittaker told me about his offering you rooms and you coming here now to see them. I came along because I wanted to know what he was up to. What did he do?' But Lucy would only shake her head.

Nick muttered under his breath and strode past her, heading for the house, but Lucy reached out to him to tug at his sleeve. 'No! Please, don't leave me. I can't bear you to – touch me. But don't leave me. And don't go in there. I can look after myself. I don't want you fighting my battles.' Her pride was making her defiant now, yet she needed him. 'Please don't go away.'

Nick hesitated, then turned back to her, though not without one last look at the house which hid Murdoch. He said, voice low and rough, 'I'll see you home.'

He walked alongside her, back down Fawcett Street and across the bridge, then down to the streets by the river. Lucy halted on the corner of Church Street. It was late, the streetlamps lit, but dozens of children ran and played in Lucy's street, and women stood at their doors to gossip. Though this was summer, the evening was chill with a cold wind off the sea, and the women pulled their shawls more tightly around them.

Lucy said, 'I'll be all right now. It was my own fault. I should have had more sense. But I thought he had changed. I need the rooms and I only thought how lucky I was. It seemed like a dream come true.' She shook her head bitterly, then took a breath and smiled up at Nick, a fragile smile that just lifted the corners of her mouth. 'But no harm done. And no need for you to worry. Thank you for bringing me back here, Mr Nick, but now you forget about it. Goodnight.'

'Goodnight.' Nick put a finger to the peak of his cap in salute and set off up Church Street. Lucy had asked him to 'forget about it', but he had not agreed.

She watched his broad back going away from her, then walked on to her home.

As she climbed the stairs Clem's voice hailed her, 'Where the hell have you been till this time? I'm wanting to be pushed down to the Pear Tree for a drink! I've never been out o' this bloody prison all day!'

Lucy could have wept.

Nick hammered on the door of the house by Mowbray Park, but it was dark and silent. No one answered. He searched through the haunts in Sunderland which he knew Murdoch frequented, without success, and finally ran him to earth at the Buchanan house. As Nick stepped into the hall he saw through the open door into the drawing room. Andrew and Nell Jarman sat on a big chesterfield on one side of the fireplace, Murdoch in an armchair on the other.

Nick stood in the doorway and said, voice rasping, 'Murdoch! Outside!'

Murdoch raised his eyebrows. 'Why?'

'You know damned well why. Because of what you were up to this evening.'

Nell started, 'What on earth—'

Andrew was on his feet. 'What's going on, Nick?'

'I'll explain later, when I've finished with him,' replied Nick. He took a pace into the room and demanded of Murdoch, 'Are you coming or must I drag you out by the scruff of your neck?'

Murdoch stood up, keeping his distance from Nick. 'Try it!' He put up his fists. Murdoch had wept all those years ago when he had been a boy and Lucy had bitten him, but he had grown out of that. Now he was a bully and a lecher but not a coward. He had plenty of brute courage and was ready to fight.

Nick started for him, but Andrew was in the way. He held a hand flat against the chest of each of them and ordered harshly, 'Not in my house! Now, I want an explanation. Murdoch?'

'Me?' Murdoch glanced at him then pointed at Nick. 'Why don't you ask him?'

'Because I want to hear it from you! What have you been up to that you can't tell me about it?'

Murdoch shrugged. 'It was nothing much. Just a woman.'

Nick snapped, 'It was a girl.' He glanced at Andrew. 'I told you about her a year ago and I think she came to see you at the yard to ask for a job for her brother. She was Lucy Campbell when she worked here, but her name is Nolan now. She's married to a man who is crippled for the rest of his life, and she's trying to bring up her sisters and brothers.' He stopped then as Andrew held up his hand.

Andrew's shoulders slumped. 'I remember her.' He asked grimly of Murdoch, 'What is the rest of it?'

'I've taken a place in town. I need a housekeeper so I offered her the job. She threw a fit and ran off.'

Andrew asked, 'Is that the truth?'

'No, it isn't,' said Nick.

Murdoch snapped, 'What do you know about it? I take it she complained to you. I seem to remember you two were chummy when you were little. Do you think she's your property?'

Andrew staggered as Nick shoved forward and he shouted,

'*Stop it!*' He glared at the two young men. 'I've heard enough.' He looked at Murdoch and said heavily, 'I think you should leave us.'

'You mean you believe him and that trollop rather than your own son?' Murdoch scowled sullenly. 'And how do you think you can judge me? What about you and Mrs Jarman here?' He indicated Nell with a jerk of his head.

For a moment it seemed Andrew would strike him. His fist was clenched and raised for the blow, but then he relaxed his fingers and lowered his hand. He glanced at Nell Jarman and said, 'I apologise for my son.' Then to Murdoch, 'Get out.' It was said with loathing and contempt, shame and bitterness.

That reached Murdoch, and he obeyed, at first in silence, rounding Andrew and Nick at a distance as he made for the door. He paused there, but only to throw back at them, 'I'll get out, right out of this house. I'll find a hotel for tonight and tomorrow I'm off to London.' He slammed the door behind him.

Andrew passed a shaking hand over his eyes. He muttered, 'Oh, dear God! He is the son of his mother. I thought he had changed.'

Nell said softly, 'So did we all. Don't blame yourself.'

Andrew sighed. 'Sit down, Nick.' Nick sank into a big armchair. 'Has the girl been harmed?'

Nick replied harshly, his temper still simmering, 'Frightened and insulted, but not physically hurt.'

Nell Jarman said, 'She is a very good type of girl.'

Nick nodded his agreement. 'But I gather she's having a hell of a struggle to survive.' He told them what he knew: of the crippled, savage husband, the desperate need for a ground-floor home.

Nell Jarman shook her head unhappily. 'We can't solve that problem here. I will give her some work when I can, but taking in a family . . .'

Later, when Nell had gone to bed and the two men sat over a nightcap, Andrew asked, 'What is this girl to you?'

'Lucy?' Nick frowned, puzzled because he had not considered

this before. He answered with his customary honesty, 'Not just a servant. Not a friend exactly, as Helen is a friend, but we played together as children.' He grinned at Andrew. 'I have no romantic attachments.' But then seriously again, 'I think she is a decent girl who would make some man a wife to be proud of – a man with any sense, that is.' He shook his head in regret. 'But not the one she's married to. And I gave her away, thought I was helping her! If only I'd known!'

Andrew said, 'But you didn't, so don't blame yourself.'

At the end of his few days at home, Nick walked into the Palace Hotel restaurant with Helen on his arm. They sat at one of Lucy's tables, and when she came to them Helen said, 'We have a little more time today. Nick's train leaves in just over an hour.'

Lucy stood with pencil poised and addressed Nick: 'I'm grateful for your help the other evening. I'd been very silly.'

Nick shook his head. 'No, you weren't. You believed Murdoch was a gentleman. It's a mistake anyone might make if they didn't know him.' He assured her, 'Don't worry about him now. He's gone to London, and it will be a long time before he comes up here again, if ever.' He grinned. 'You'll probably have Aunt Adelaide coming in here instead.'

'Who?' queried Helen, mystified.

'Aunt Adelaide Pearce, Uncle Andrew's sister.' Nick explained, 'She got Murdoch his job in India and later told Uncle she regretted it! Anyway, she's a widow and she's coming home. She wants to start a finishing school for young ladies – Andrew says he's damned if he knows why, because she's over sixty and rolling in money – and she wants him to find a house that will do.' Nick switched his attention from the laughing Helen to Lucy, waiting patiently. 'And I expect she'll be coming in here. Watch out for her, she's a terror.'

Lucy feigned horror, rolling up her eyes. 'Gawd help us!' Then, remembering her place and that she had other customers, she asked, 'Would you like to order now, sir?'

Nick laughed. 'I would. I'm starving.'

Later Lucy watched them leave on their way to the station and Nick's train. Helen, slender and fashionably dressed in an ankle-length frock that cost twice Lucy's weekly wage, smiled up at the tall ship's officer in his uniform of dark blue and gold. They passed through the swing doors of the restaurant, with their stained-glass panels and polished brass handles, and were lost to sight.

Lucy went on with her work and tried to forget Nick. Now that he had gone back to sea she could go to the Buchanan house seeking extra work without fear of meeting him. She would go on her next free day.

That came four days later. Lucy rose early and gave final instructions to Rose and the others before leaving: 'Don't forget, now, Elsie will cook the dinner and get your tea ready but you've got to help her. Billy, if Clem wants beer from the Pear Tree, you go for it.' And putting her head around the door of Clem's bedroom she called, 'I'm off now.'

He peered at her, bleary eyed, and growled, 'What did you wake me for? Gerrout!'

The pain of that farewell was left behind her as she walked, and the sight of the Buchanan house lifted her spirits as always, but by then she was excited anyway, having another reason for being there.

Lucy presented herself at the back door to be told by Jinny, 'They're still having breakfast, but I'll tell Mrs Jarman you're here.' She returned a few minutes later to say, 'She says will you do a day's washing?'

Lucy said gratefully, 'I will, thanks,' then, 'Will you ask if I can see Mr Buchanan before he goes to the yard?'

Jinny blinked, startled. 'Ooh! I don't know. I'll ask Chesterton.'

Chesterton, the Buchanans' chauffeur, was in the kitchen, drinking a mug of tea he had cajoled from Mrs Yates, the cook. He had overheard the exchange and called, 'The boss doesn't want the car for another half-hour, Jinny. Go and ask him if he'll see her.'

So Jinny went off again, and returned with a message from Andrew. 'He said to take you up in ten minutes, so you might as well come in.'

When Lucy stepped into the kitchen she found Mrs Yates and the rest of the indoor staff there, except Devereaux the butler. She knew he would be serving breakfast to Andrew and Mrs Jarman, but the others also had duties and she wondered why they were there.

Lucy found out when Jinny asked eagerly, 'What d'you know about the row the other night? I'd just been round making up the fires when I heard Mr Nick and Mr Murdoch shouting at each other. I couldn't hear what they were saying, but I thought your name was mentioned.'

'I don't know.' Lucy could not meet their eyes.

Jinny saw it. 'Go on! You know summat but you don't want to let on. You can trust us, though.'

Lucy shook her head. Trust them with that story? She had heard too much gossip in the servants' hall to believe that. Her account would be picked over and there would be sniggers and suggestions: 'O' course, that's what she *says*, but there's two sides and no smoke without fire. She must have led him on to think . . .'

Devereaux saved her by entering. He stared around the crowded kitchen, irate and incredulous, and demanded, 'What are you lot doing in here at this time? You've got work to do!' As they scattered he saw Lucy. 'Ah! there you are. Mr Andrew will see you now. Come along.'

As Lucy passed her, Jinny whispered, 'There *was* something, wasn't there?' Lucy ignored her and walked on.

Devereaux ushered Lucy into the breakfast room, announcing, 'Mrs Nolan, sir.'

Andrew Buchanan set aside his newspaper and sat back in his chair. Nell Jarman sat opposite him, and she had a smile for Lucy. Not for the first time Lucy wondered at the relationship between these two. Nell shared Andrew Buchanan's bed and showed no shame, but Lucy could not think of her as the archetypal scarlet woman. Andrew was a churchgoer, who bedded his housekeeper regularly, but Lucy could not regard him as immoral. He banned gambling in his yard because he believed it was bad for his workers, yet attended Newcastle races and betted there. Lucy still did not think he was a hypocrite. However, what concerned her now was not Andrew's relationship with Nell, but how she could obtain from him what she wanted. She stood with heart thumping, tense.

Andrew did not smile, but prompted, 'You wished to see me?' He wondered if the girl was seeking a job for another of her family. He was sympathetic but becoming impatient with the repeated requests. But there was that disgraceful business with Murdoch. It seemed clear he had tried to seduce the girl. Andrew said harshly, resenting the shame that was none of his fault, 'I understand I may owe you an apology on behalf of my son. Did you think I owed you anything else?'

He caught an angry glance from Nell Jarman and recalled the girl was well thought of by Nell.

Lucy had thought Murdoch might come into it but the question still came like a slap in the face and she winced, but answered shakily, 'You don't owe me anything, sir. Not that I wasn't upset – because I hadn't encouraged him, if that's what you think.' She saw Andrew blink at that, her guessing at what he was thinking. She went on. 'But I'm not here today because of him.' She took a breath and plunged in. 'I heard your sister was coming home from India, sir, to start a school.'

Andrew nodded. 'I don't know how you heard, but it's no secret.' He was sure the girl was being honest with him and he was impressed – but still on his guard. 'So?'

Lucy sensed that caution, but kept on: 'I thought, maybe she'll need a housekeeper, sir, if she's going to have some young ladies to look after. I'd like to apply for the place. I'm working at the Palace at present but I'd like to better myself.'

Andrew was taken aback. He had not considered the question of staff for his sister's school, but staff would certainly be needed. Adelaide was a competent lady and he was sure she would run a good school, but she would not make beds or empty slops. He glanced at Nell Jarman and asked, 'What staff d'you think Adelaide will need?'

Nell had obviously thought about that, because she had her answer ready, and it came crisp with disapproval of him: 'A footman for the heavy work, two housemaids, kitchen and scullery maids – and a cook, of course.'

Lucy put in quickly, 'Begging your pardon, ma'am, but I can cook. I learned a lot from Mrs Yates when I was kitchenmaid here.'

Nell nodded and glanced at Andrew. 'Mrs Yates told me Lucy picked up things very quickly.'

Andrew was watching her, and saw Nell nod fractionally. The girl certainly *might* be pushy, but was that determination and desperation? He saw the tension in her as she stood very straight, head up. And Nell was in favour, but . . . He asked, 'How old are you?'

Lucy was expecting the question because this was a senior post. She replied, 'Nearly twenty, sir.' Well, she was turned nineteen – just.

Andrew guessed nineteen and a few days. He asked, 'Why do you want the job? I know you said to better yourself, but how? Money? Or do you want to order people about?'

A red tide of anger rose in Lucy's cheeks, her tension snapped and she flared, 'I need to be able to afford three ground-floor rooms! My husband's in a wheelchair and can't get out of the house because of the stairs!'

Andrew remembered Nick telling him this girl was supporting a bad lot of a husband while bringing up her brothers and sisters. He decided she was not pushy but determined. He was silent for a long minute and Lucy thought sickly, You've wrecked it!

Andrew was aware of Nell's chilly stare and thinking that he had made an unholy mess of this interview. He had jumped to the conclusion that this girl was using Murdoch's advances as a bargaining counter — and he had been wrong. He had snapped questions at her when a moment's thought would have given him the answers. He recalled the times he had met this girl — been *aware* of her, rather than as a servant — and always she had impressed him. From the time she had admired his painting . . . He shifted through the memories.

Eventually Andrew said, 'I've found a house in Ashbrooke. There are three rooms on the ground floor at the rear which will serve for you and your family. I'll let you have a key so you can go and look them over at your convenience. There'll be a wage of a pound a week, and, of course, your food and accommodation. However, if your family are accommodated, they will have to earn their keep because they will be occupying rooms I'd earmarked for staff.'

A pound a week! That was twice what Lucy was paid as a waitress. She swallowed her excitement and nervousness.

Andrew asked drily, 'Can I take it you will accept the post if the rooms are suitable?'

Lucy breathed, 'Yes. Oh, yes!'

Chapter Eleven

'The cart's here!' Billy shouted from the front door, his voice rising above the ringing of the Sunday morning church bells. He ran back along the passage, boots hammering on the bare boards. As he took the stairs two at a time he called again, 'The cart's come!'

'I heard you.' Lucy answered him, laughing. 'We're all ready for him.' They were, thanks to her organisation, though she reflected wrily that their poverty helped. When you have next to nothing, it is easy to move. The beds were already dismantled, the faded curtains and worn linoleum packed or rolled, and the single rug – made from canvas and old clothes cut up into clippings – taken up from its place by the fire. What coal they had left in the coalhouse had been shovelled into sacks. In little more than an hour it was all stacked on the cart and the driver took his seat.

'Ta-ra hinny! I hope you settle in all right!' called one of the neighbours, to be echoed by the other women standing at their doors. Lucy bade them a tearful farewell and climbed up on the cart to join Tommy and Billy. She would have to be present at its unloading to tell the boys where everything had to go. Rose and Elsie were already pushing a grumbling, cursing Clem, in his wheelchair, towards the corner. Predictably, he had fought against moving, raging, spouting oaths, abusing. Lucy had the bruises to show for it. But she was even more determined that the family was going – and Clem with it.

The cart rolled away down Church Street, then up Charles Street and on to the bridge over the river. There were few people and little traffic about this early on a Sunday morning, just a rattling tram or two, occasional cabs and carriages. The shipyards were silent, with only a fine wisp of smoke from a few chimneys where fires had been banked up for the weekend. Only the gulls mewed and wheeled in their usual numbers.

Sunday had been chosen because it was the only day when no member of the family was at work or school, and even more importantly, the cart was not being used for its normal purpose of selling coal. It had been swept, but Lucy was resigned to the fact that she would have some washing to do. However, she was closer to happiness than she had been since her marriage. She knew that Clem would still be complaining at having to move, blaming her for his condition, and the girls would be less than patient with him, had run out of patience, but Lucy would cope with him when she saw him. Now she smiled into the sunlight.

The house in Ashbrooke had been renamed Poona House – the paint on the sign was fresh – by Andrew Buchanan, acting on the written orders of his sister. Like Murdoch's rooms of shuddering memory, it had a big kitchen that would serve as a living room for all of them. The girls and Lucy would have a room of their own and so would the boys. They would no longer share one room with a dividing curtain.

It was a large, rambling house on three floors, and Lucy made clear from the start, 'This is a palace compared to where we used to live, but it takes a lot of work and you're going to have to help.'

Lucy had a staff of housemaid and kitchenmaid, who would not live in and would start the following week. Their numbers had been reduced due to Lucy's agreement with Andrew Buchanan that her family would work for their accommodation. The boys would do any heavy work in their spare time while Rose and Elsie would help Lucy in the kitchen and about the house. With a dozen girls to be taught, some of whom would board, there was work enough.

Lucy's siblings looked at their new surroundings, in appreciation. They knew Lucy now, and also knew their responsibilities. 'Aye, we'll help.'

A week later Lucy answered the *rat-tat!* of the polished brass knocker on the front door and was confronted by a woman a head taller than herself, wearing a twill raincoat that hung down to her ankles and a feathered round hat slightly askew. A dangerous looking pin held the hat fast on greying hair, tendrils of which escaped wildly. She measured Lucy with a quick up and down glance from cold blue eyes and demanded, 'Aren't you going to let me in?'

Lucy stood her ground. 'Who did madam wish to see?'

'My housekeeper, for a start. I'm Adelaide Pearce and I live here, or I will just as soon as I get in.'

'I'm sorry, ma'am.' Lucy hurriedly stepped aside, opening the door wide. 'Please come in. I wasn't expecting you. Mr Buchanan said you would not be arriving until next week.' She peered past her employer.

So this was Aunt Adelaide, who had found a job for Murdoch in India – and later regretted it. Lucy had first heard of her five years ago when Nick came home from abroad and was talking with Andrew, his uncle.

Adelaide told her, 'Don't bother looking for a cab. It was a fine day so I left my bag at the station, asked my way and walked. Would have walked anyway, fine day or not. Fed up with sitting on my behind in that damned train. Fed up with London, too, so I came up a week early. Now, where's the housekeeper? Tell her I'm here and let me have some tea. I could drink a bucketful.' She stood very erect and held her head back, looking down her nose as she took in her surroundings.

Lucy said quickly, 'The drawing room is here, ma'am. And I'm the housekeeper, ma'am. Lucy Nolan.'

'You?' Adelaide fished inside her coat and took out a pince-nez that hung from a silk ribbon around her neck. She perched this on her nose and inspected Lucy again. 'Good God! How old are you, child?'

Lucy tried hopefully, 'I'll be twenty next year, ma'am.'

Like her brother, Adelaide was not misled. 'That means you're nineteen.' She said again, 'Good God. And you don't even look that.'

Lucy said unhappily, seeing this first meeting as a disaster, 'That's because I'm not very big, ma'am.'

'No, you're not, little Lucy.' Adelaide agreed.

Lucy blinked. No one but Nick had called her 'little Lucy', and it came as an unwelcome reminder, but she replied, 'I'm sure I'll be able to cope, ma'am.'

Adelaide laughed softly, not the horsy whinny Lucy expected. She let her pince-nez fall to the length of its ribbon and patted Lucy's arm. 'I expect you will. My brother thinks so, and he's usually right. He used to be a scruffy little bugger when he was a boy, though. Just goes to show you can't prejudge people. Now, where's that tea?'

'I'll fetch it straight away, ma'am, if you'll let me have your coat.'

When Lucy brought the tray with the tea Adelaide pointed to a chair with a long finger. 'Sit there.' Lucy was startled. She was not used to an employer telling her to be seated. She had always stood. That was the normal master/servant relationship. And describing Andrew Buchanan as a scruffy little—! When Lucy had perched on the straight backed chair Adelaide went on, 'Now tell me about yourself and I'll tell you what I want.'

In the next hour Adelaide learned a lot about Lucy, and Lucy a little about Adelaide: that the blunt, tart woman could be gentle and tactful, had a strong moral sense but was compassionate.

Over the next months Lucy learned a great deal more of a

number of subjects. The school was fully subscribed, and Adelaide, dressed precisely at every moment of the day, lectured her charges on dress and deportment, etiquette and the ways of the world and of men, in a refined accent but practical terms. For thirty years she had run large households, at first in Europe and then India; her late husband had been in the Foreign Service and then the Indian Civil. She had organised balls and dinners for hundreds, involving complex rules of protocol, without ever putting a foot wrong.

Lucy was at first taken aback by Adelaide's frank, terse speaking, then impressed by her capability and knowledge, finally became fond of her for her genuine kindness. Lucy also learned along with the girls, though not so regularly. She overheard what was being taught, and often she had a private tutorial, off the cuff but comprehensive, when she reported to her employer at the beginning and end of each day. In the morning it was as Adelaide returned from riding. She rode every morning, dressed in a black habit and mounted side-saddle, on a tall hunter brought by the groom from a livery stable.

Lucy came to see that there was a great deal more to being a housekeeper than she had thought. She learned how to organise her staff of Annie and Phoebe, housemaid and kitchenmaid respectively, plus assistance from her siblings. She saw that their duties were divided fairly and performed efficiently and the whole house ran like clockwork. More than that, she took in Adelaide's lectures to the girls on deportment and manners and practised them herself. She soaked up the knowledge and looked for more.

When she had been in the post some six months Adelaide told her brother Andrew, 'That Lucy Nolan is an excellent house-keeper and conducts herself like a lady. She is a damn good sort. Not like that man of hers. He should have been strangled at birth.' On the one occasion she had met Clem Nolan he had played the part of the bravely suffering invalid. However, Adelaide knew him to be a hypocrite, having also heard his voice coming distantly but clearly from the back of the house, when he was cursing Lucy.

Clem only ate and slept at Poona House. Now, living in ground-floor rooms, he could easily get out and was absent all day and every day. After a while Lucy found out how he spent those days.

Tommy and Billy were now members of the same riveting gang, and on a cold windy March day they were working on the ship currently on the stocks. Up on the staging they felt the bitter bite of the wind from the river running black and cold only forty yards away, and the gulls wheeled and screamed about them. Tommy, as a 'heater', heated the rivets on a brazier until red hot, then passed them to Billy, the 'catcher', on the staging above him. Another member of the gang shoved the glowing rivet through the hole in the plate to be secured to the hull of the ship and the riveter flattened the end with his pneumatic hammer. The din was deafening, but as the hammers were briefly still a voice called, 'Hey! Tommy! Billy!'

They looked around and saw Josh Campbell standing below. He shouted up, 'I hear you've moved to a big house in Ashbrooke!'

The boys exchanged glances and Tommy challenged, 'Who says so?'

'A little bird – on wheels!' Josh guffawed at his joke.

Billy probed, 'So Clem is takin' bets an' all?' He knew Josh took betting slips and money from men in the yard, knew also that if a foreman caught Josh at that business he would be sacked.

So did Josh, and he bawled, 'You keep your trap shut!'

The boys eyed their father with hostility for a moment, then the riveter bawled, 'What're you standing about for? Come on!' And they turned back to their work.

Later they told Lucy that Clem was taking bets for Garvey. She knew that could not mean anything good for her, except that she would spend most of her days in peace. She gave thanks for that.

✲

It was about that time, the spring of 1911, that Lucy entered Blacketts, the department store, and found Jinny Unwin making a purchase. A silk gown was being carefully folded by one assistant as another made out the bill. As Lucy came up, Jinny was saying, 'Deliver it and charge it, please.'

Lucy said, 'Hello, Jinny.'

The full-bodied young woman was startled to see Lucy, but quickly recovered. 'Good morning.'

Jinny was well dressed, and already wore a silk gown, under a cape of boxcloth with a fox-fur collar that must have cost four or five pounds and would be unseasonably warm in the spring weather.

The assistant asked, 'The name and address, madam?'

Jinny would not look at Lucy. 'Mr Murdoch Buchanan.' She went on to give the address of Murdoch's house in Park Place.

'Thank you, madam.'

Jinny turned away, and Lucy went with her until they were out of earshot of the assistants. Then she asked, 'Are you keeping house for Murdoch?'

'What if I am?' Jinny was defiant. 'It's nothing to do wi' you.'

Lucy warned her, 'You're making a terrible mistake.'

Jinny charged, 'You're jealous.'

'No! Jinny, he asked me to take on the job and I thought it would be above board but – he tried to bed me.'

Jinny looked away. 'What's wrong with that? I've known worse fellers. It's no worse than Nell Jarman, and she's doing well for herself.'

Lucy pleaded, 'No! It's not the same. There's love there, and Murdoch isn't like Mr Buchanan.'

Jinny shrugged. 'Well, I've had enough of working all hours and being at everybody's beck and call, while young lasses like that Helen Whittaker have nowt to do but enjoy themselves. I know where my bread's buttered and I'll thank you to keep your nose out of my business.' With that, she sniffed and walked away.

Lucy sighed and carried on with her shopping. She hoped Jinny would find happiness, but doubted if any good would come from the affair.

A week later Adelaide returned from riding accompanied by a tall young man walking beside her hunter. Lucy opened the front door to her as Adelaide slid to the ground and tossed the reins to the groom from the livery stable. Nick grinned and said, 'Good morning, little Lucy.'

She felt a prickle of annoyance at that 'little Lucy' but found herself smiling back at him. In her confusion, heart thumping, she found it hard to maintain her decorum and reply, 'Good morning, Mr Buchanan. It's nice to see you again.'

'You'll be seeing a lot of me.' Nick followed Adelaide into the house and said in passing, 'I'm captain now. Only of a collier running up and down the coast, but she is a command and all *mine!* So I'll be home for a day or two every week.'

'Oh! That's lovely.' It was easy for Lucy to smile. She knew she could never have Nick, because of the gulf between them and because she was wedded, and knew she would be hurt as a consequence, but for now it was sufficient that he was there.

Nick was as good as his word and was a frequent visitor at Poona House, often accompanied by Helen.

As spring turned into summer Lucy told herself she had a lot to be thankful for. She had a good job. Rose had obtained her diplomas in shorthand and typing and was now working in a bank. Both boys were settled in Buchanan's yard and there were good reports of Elsie's progress from Mrs Wilberforce in the kitchen of the Palace Hotel. Lucy was even saving money, and while Clem's moods were as brutal and vicious as ever, he was rarely there to vent his spite on her. And she had avoided the fate of Jinny Unwin. She wished the girl well, but knew Jinny would regret trusting Murdoch.

Lucy enjoyed something approaching happiness and wondered uneasily if everything was going too well.

Chapter Twelve

SUMMER 1911

'Get out o' my way!' Clem Nolan thrust his wheelchair through the legs of the others in the kitchen, regardless of what damage he did to them.

'Ow!' Elsie yelped as a wheel ran over her foot.

'Steady on!' Tommy protested as the wheelchair scraped his shin.

Clem made no apology. 'You'll shift yourselves a bit quicker next time.' He opened the back door, gripped the stencils in his strong hands then yanked the chair over the low step that was the only bar between him and the outside world. The door closed behind him.

Lucy called after him, as always, 'Mind how you go!' but Clem did not respond.

'He gets worse every day,' Billy complained. This was Saturday evening and he was dressed to go out. He stood before the small mirror over the fireplace, tweaked at the knot of his tie and eyed his reflection for the twentieth time.

'You take longer to get ready than our Rose.' Elsie shoved her elbow into his ribs. 'Move over and let me have a look.'

Lucy said drily, 'He's not the only one that takes some time getting ready.' Elsie was pinning on her hat, a straw boater, and had been dressing for the past hour.

'I've been ready for ages.' Rose sat primly on a kitchen chair. Her hat, this time a cartwheel, was already secured.

Elsie replied pertly, 'Because you started ages earlier.'

Lucy stamped on the argument before it went further: 'That's enough, you two. Get that hat on, Elsie, then we're away, or we're going to be late.' Lucy and the girls were going to the Empire Theatre, while the dandified Billy was headed for Crowtree Road where the young men and girls of the town promenaded, seeking a 'click'.

Tommy paused at the door. He was smart in his first suit, painfully saved for, with a stiff shirt collar and his red hair watered down and carefully parted. 'I'll see you when you get back tonight, then.' Tommy had already 'clicked' with a girl, Daisy Marsden, who worked in a shop in the High Street.

Lucy asked, 'Where are you and Daisy off to?'

'I expect we'll go for a walk along the seafront.'

Elsie giggled. 'There's a lot o' courting couples wander along there. You should see what some o' them get up to!'

Tommy, red faced, started towards her with revenge in mind, but Lucy turned him around and pushed him out of the back door, warning him, 'You're going to be late,' which was enough to set Tommy hurrying away, Billy following him.

Elsie called, 'Hurry up, Billy! All those lasses will be waiting for you.'

Billy only grinned at her and replied, 'A few o' them will, anyway.'

Lucy said, 'You'll not get a rise out of Billy. Now come *on*, Elsie! We'll miss the start!' And she ushered the two girls out ahead of her.

As they sat on the tram rattling down into the town, Lucy wondered uneasily about Clem. His absence was a relief, but she worried that somehow he was going to hurt her again, and not just with the relative pinpricks of cursing and insults when he was in the house for an hour or so and not sleeping drunkenly.

As the tram rolled up to their stop the first rain splashed in huge drops against the window. The entrance to the Empire was close by and they ran to it through the deluge, holding on to their hats. As they stopped in the shelter of the foyer, laughing and wiping at their wet faces with handkerchiefs, Elsie said, 'I hope Tommy and Daisy don't get wet.'

Lucy shook her head. 'They won't have got to the seafront yet. They're probably still in the town and in shelter.'

Inside, the lights of the house were lowered and the curtain rising. They stumbled over umbrellas and legs to reach their seats and settled down.

Lucy was right. Tommy and Daisy stood in a shop doorway near Mackie's clock and looked out at the rain. He said gloomily, 'There's no point in going down to the front in this.'

'No,' agreed Daisy. 'We'd get soaked. What a shame.' She was just turned twenty-one, nearly four years older than Tommy, a shy, gentle, affectionate girl with soft brown hair and eyes. She hesitated then said, 'I'd ask you back to our house but you know what Mam is like.'

'Aye.' Tommy knew. On the only occasion he had met her, Daisy's mother had made it plain that she intended something better for her only child than marriage to a rivet heater. Mr Marsden, Daisy's father, was a floor walker in a department store. He wore a morning suit to work and ruled the girls under him with a rod of iron — as his wife ruled him.

'No,' said Tommy, 'I don't fancy that. Tell you what, though, we could go to our house.'

'Will Lucy mind?' Daisy asked doubtfully. 'She isn't expecting us.'

'Lucy won't mind. Come on.' Tommy took her arm.

'Wait a minute.' Daisy struggled with her umbrella and snapped it open. She laughed up at Tommy, 'We can both keep dry under this!' He had to put his arm around her waist, of course, but neither minded that.

Despite the umbrella, they were damp about their lower legs when they burst into the kitchen, still laughing. Daisy shook the rain from her umbrella and stood it up to dry. She dabbed the worst from her damp skirt with her handkerchief then joined Tommy where he patted the sofa beside him. Dusk had come early, with the sun hidden behind low, leaden clouds. The rain spattered against the windows, but the little summertime fire burned brightly. Its heat warmed them and the glow lit their faces, Daisy's smiling and flushed, eyes shining, Tommy's wondering and awed.

Daisy said, 'This is nice.'

'You're lovely,' Tommy breathed, and tentatively put his arm around her. Then he kissed her. And again. Then again.

'Tommy . . . Tommy . . . *Oh, Tommy!*'

When the lights went up for the intermission, Lucy sighed delightedly and looked around her. The house was full but she had a good view from her seat even though it was at the back of the stalls. Her gaze drifted from the curtained stage to scan the rest of the house, and movement caught her eye. In one of the boxes which lined each side of the theatre, a tall young man had risen to his feet. He wore a dinner jacket and his lean features were weatherbeaten so they looked dark against his starched white shirt. It was Nick Buchanan.

Lucy had seen him frequently over the past months. He was home for a day or two every weekend, his ship usually sailing on a Monday to London with coal, then returning to port on the Friday night or Saturday. Lucy had had practice in hiding her emotions, but controlling them was another matter.

Now Elsie said, 'Here! Look! There's that Nick Buchanan!'

'Don't point!' Lucy hissed, and pulled down the excited girl's arm.

Elsie insisted, 'It is! There! In the box! See?'

'Yes! Now be still!'

Elsie kept her hands in her lap but said, 'He's with that girl —
what's her name? Helen Thingummy.'

'Whittaker,' Lucy supplied automatically. Nick was smiling
down at Helen, who was laughing — at something he'd said?

Elsie asked, 'Who are the other couple with them?' The young
man was also in a dinner jacket, not so tall as Nick nor so dark,
but handsome. The girl was an attractive brunette. The young
man was talking to her but her eyes were on Nick.

Lucy replied, 'I don't know.' The girls were dressed in silk and
wore jewellery that glittered in the light. Nick and his party were
some fifty feet away from Lucy, but she knew the gap was far, far
wider than that. These girls whiled away their time at tennis
parties, their evenings often spent in the theatre. This was a rare
treat for Lucy, and her work waited for her next day.

Rose said from the other side of Lucy, 'They're off to the bar.'
Nick had turned his broad back to them, and he and the other
man followed the two young ladies out of the box. Now Elsie
turned her gaze on Lucy, but she had buried her face in her
programme.

Lucy kept it there through the intermission, until after the
warning bell had rung and the lights began to dim again. She
looked up then, and saw that the others were seated but Nick still
stood tall in the box, his eyes on Lucy. She caught her breath as
he smiled and lifted a hand in salute.

Elsie said excitedly, 'Here! He's waving to us!' She flagged
frantically with her arm.

'Stop it!' Lucy hissed at her again, but Nick's eyes were on her,
and courtesy demanded at least an acknowledgment. She
waved and smiled, then the darkness descended on them and the
curtain rose.

The lights went on again at the end of the show, and the audi-
ence rose with them to stand for the National Anthem. The men
standing in front of Lucy now restricted her view and she saw no
more of the party in the box — nor they of her. They travelled
home by tram, but while her sisters enthused over the show, Lucy

merely stared out of the window at the passing lights and smiled.

At Poona House they found the fire glowing brightly. Lucy was mildly surprised, had thought it would have burnt low, but thought nothing of it. She made a pot of tea and the three of them sat around the fire drinking it, steam wisping from the damp hems of their skirts. As Elsie flicked at hers she stooped and asked, 'Has anyone lost a button?' She held it out, a white pearl button such as might have fallen from a lady's blouse.

Lucy and Rose checked their own dresses and shook their heads. 'Not one of mine,' said Rose.

Lucy took the button from Elsie and put it on the mantelpiece. 'I'll probably find out where it's from when I'm ironing.'

The two boys arrived almost together. Billy was first, glancing up at the clock on the mantelpiece, and Elsie crowed, 'You're late!'

Billy panted, 'Only five minutes. I ran all the way from Chester Road.' He went on quickly, trying to change the subject, 'Was it a good show?'

Lucy refused to be sidetracked, but was in a generous, gentle mood this evening. 'You know the rule. You should have been in before this time. Don't do it again.'

Billy promised, 'I won't.'

Elsie giggled, 'He was walking a girl home. Chester Road! He must be keen.'

Billy grinned at her bashfully, then glanced round as Tommy entered. He took off his cap and shook it outside before closing the door. Rose said incredulously, 'You've never been walking along the seafront in this weather!'

'No.' Tommy's eyes were on his boots as he wiped them on the doormat. 'We just sat in a café.'

Elsie pulled a face. 'That must ha' taken all your pocket money.'

'No. We just had the one cup of tea each and made it last.'

Lucy offered, gesturing towards the teapot under its cosy, 'Do you want one now?'

'No, thanks.' Tommy sidled towards his bedroom door. 'I think I'll go to bed.'

'I think it's time we were all in bed.' Lucy was wondering if Clem might come home early. She did not want to face him.

A half-hour later, Billy, Elsie and Rose slept peacefully. Tommy lay in the bed he shared with Billy, eyes wide open and staring at the ceiling, unable to sleep.

Lucy's eyes were closed, but she was seeing the crowded theatre ablaze with lights and Nick smiling down at her. She told herself she was being foolish and admitted guiltily that she was a married woman, bitter mockery though that marriage might be. She meant nothing to Nick Buchanan. She was only a friend of sorts, not a friend like Helen Whittaker, but a servant girl he had played with as a boy. Yet she was still smiling when she fell asleep.

Clem Nolan sat in a kitchen down by the river, one of two rooms rented by Garvey, the bookmaker. The oilcloth-covered table held a number of bottles of beer, three of them half-empty, and three glasses. There were also piles of coins in neat rows: pennies, threepenny pieces, sixpences and shillings. The hearth was littered with crumpled scraps of paper – betting slips, each signed with a code name so the gambler could not be traced if the police got hold of the slip.

Garvey, his bulk overhanging a creaking, straight-backed chair, cigar clamped in brown teeth, pushed a column of silver towards Josh Campbell. 'There y'are, Josh: ten bob. Not bad for a day's work, eh?'

Josh grinned as he scooped up the money. 'A hell of a sight better than I'm getting at Buchanan's for sweating my guts out!'

Garvey pointed the cigar. 'Ah! But look at the bets you take there!' Then he warned, 'Mind you don't get caught at it.'

Josh shrugged, carelessly confident. 'I'll watch it.'

Garvey slid another pile of coins across the oilcloth. 'That's for you, Clem. Ten bob an' all, same as Josh.'

'Ta.' Clem pocketed the money. He had been taking bets for Garvey for several months, since meeting Josh in a pub soon after moving to Poona House and gaining his newfound freedom.

Garvey asked, 'The bobbies aren't looking at you at all, are they?'

'Naw!' Clem said with derision. 'When they came round today I was alongside the Salvation Army. They were standing in a ring, praying for me and my affliction and there was the pollis watching – and me with me pockets full o' bets!' All three of them sniggered.

Josh asked, 'Here! Has that daughter o' mine twigged what you're up to?'

'No chance!' Clem sneered. 'She's just glad I'm not around the place. I sometimes think I'll get out for good. Her and those kids o' yours, Josh, looking at me like I was Jack the Ripper – it makes me bloody mad!'

Garvey shrugged. 'There's room for you here if you want to get out o' that place.'

This brought a growl and a glare from Clem: 'I'll get out o' there when *I'm* ready, not when they want me out. And when I do, I'll still be her husband and I won't let Lucy forget it. She's got nowt, but in her job she's always working beside money, and you never know when we might want some.'

'I'm getting out of it.' Jinny Unwin was fashionably dressed in a narrow, ankle-length skirt, bolero jacket and a blouse with a froth of lace at her throat, all topped by a cartwheel hat. She carried a parasol and a porter walked behind with her suitcases and hatboxes piled on his barrow. She and Lucy had met by chance outside the station, Lucy passing by as Jinny got down from her cab.

Lucy did not probe, only waited.

Jinny told the porter, 'I'm getting the London train. Wait for me on the platform.' As he trundled the barrow away, she went on, 'Murdoch left. He sold up the house and went out to France or Italy. He talked about both but never said which. Gave me a few pounds and got on a train.' She stared at Lucy, daring her to say, 'I warned you.'

Lucy would not. 'I'm sorry, Jinny.'

Jinny shrugged. 'I should ha' known. He was always a hard-hearted bugger.'

Lucy offered, 'Have you got a job in London? If you were staying here I could put a word in for you.'

Jinny shook her head and the ostrich feathers on her hat bobbed. 'Oh, no! It's London for me. I'm not going back into service. I can't, not after living the way I have. He had some friends staying a few months back. One o' them fancied me.' She smirked triumphantly. 'He had me an' all, one night when Murdoch was drunk and asleep. He's in London and I'm going down there to look him up.' She eyed Lucy with her shopping bag. 'What are you doing?'

'I'm housekeeper for a lady who runs a finishing school,' Lucy said with pride.

Jinny grimaced. 'Better you than me. Anyway, I've got to catch my train. Ta-ra!'

Lucy watched her sway across the yard into the station, tapping on high heels, assured. However, Lucy had seen the fear in Jinny's eyes and was certain she was heading for trouble.

Chapter Thirteen

'You'll have nothing but trouble with him,' Lucy warned. She lifted the big clothes horse, laden with damp washing, from where it stood around the fire. The kitchen of Poona House was already shadowy, on this day of wind and rain. There was no question of drying the washing outside.

'I love him,' said Rose, lifting her chin and looking down her nose. She had come home for a late lunch and was about to go back to work at the bank.

Lucy took up the poker and prodded the coals in the fire so they crackled, hissed and settled in the grate. The ash worked through to the box below and the live coals that were left glowed brighter. She pointed the poker at Rose, who was sulkily pulling on her gloves. 'Love him! You loved the last one and all the others before him!' Over the years Rose had brought home a succession of undesirables. 'When are you going to learn? He's all show — oily hair and fancy clothes his mother buys him. She goes out cleaning to make ends meet and he never keeps a job longer than a week!' She banged down the poker and snatched up the coal-rake.

Rose, stung, retorted, 'You're a fine one to criticise me, after marrying that Clem.'

Lucy winced and bit her lip as she used the rake to drag coal down on to the fire from the shelf at the chimney back. She said grimly, 'It means I know what I'm talking about. Our mother told me before she died: "Think long and hard before you marry."'

Rose sniffed scornfully, 'Well, did you?'

Lucy dropped the rake. 'No.' She lifted the horse and stood it round the fire again, hiding the glow, then she dusted her hands and looked at Rose. 'And what sort of life have I got? Would you change places with me?'

That silenced Rose. From being a rebellious adolescent she became an uncertain young girl, wiping at tears of disappointment with the heel of her hand.

Lucy put an arm around her and said gently, 'I don't want to be hard, but I don't want you making a big mistake, either. Why don't you tell him you can't see him for a couple of weeks, say you've got a lot of work? Then see how you feel after that – and see how he feels.'

Rose sniffed and fumbled her handkerchief from her bag. 'If you think so . . .'

'Just try it.' Lucy kissed her and Rose went off to work. Lucy watched her go with a wan smile and a sigh. It was hard being strong for all of them – and usually thankless.

Before the two weeks were out Rose reported she had seen the boy with another girl. 'She's welcome to him.' She added indifferently, 'I'd had enough of him.'

Lucy breathed a sigh of relief.

The winter closed in around them with short dark days and cold nights. That did not keep Clem at home. He still went out in the morning each day and did not return until close to midnight, when the house was asleep. Lucy was content in her work and she and her siblings were looking forward to Christmas, though the two boys were only working short time because of a scarcity of work for Buchanan's yard, and had little money left after paying for their board. But it was a cosy time, of evenings spent sitting around the fire, the boys reading, Lucy and the girls sewing or working on dresses, all of them talking. Only Tommy had little to say.

Lucy could look around them happily. Rose, blonde like her mother, was quieter now, more mature. The procession of boys had stopped; she had not been 'walking out' with a young man for months now. Of the other three, with their father's red hair, Elsie was doing well in the kitchen of the Palace Hotel and the cook, Mrs Wilberforce, said, 'She's a good little lass and she'll get on.' Billy, the younger boy, still wore his wide grin and was ready for a fight but did not seek one nowadays. And while Tommy had become very quiet, Lucy put that down to his maturing, emerging from adolescence. She was well-pleased with them.

It was on one such evening that Billy said, 'Was that a knock on the door?' Conversation stopped as they looked at him and listened. Then they all heard the soft tapping and Billy got up from his chair. 'I'll see who it is.' He opened the door and Lucy looked past him and saw the girl outside in the yard, standing in the light spilling out from the kitchen.

'It's Daisy.' Lucy set aside her sewing and called, 'Come in, Daisy!'

But as she said it she had a foreboding that her cosy little world was about to be shattered yet again. There was something about Daisy's sudden appearance and the lateness of the hour.

The girl did not move. 'Can I speak to Tommy, please?' Her face was pale in the gaslight and she looked like she had been crying.

Tommy was already out of his chair and on his way to the door. 'I'm here.'

Lucy followed him. 'You can't leave the girl outside in the cold. Come on in, both of you.' Now she was close enough to see that Daisy's face was indeed tear-stained, her trembling mouth drawn down at the corners. As Lucy took her arm she felt the girl shaking.

Daisy came reluctantly into the room, frightened, eyes flicking over the others then resting fearfully, pleading, on Tommy.

Lucy said, 'Give me your coat and sit down.'

Daisy shook her head. 'I can't.' She clutched the coat around her and whispered, 'I'm not — decent underneath.' Her eyes fell before their stares and now Lucy could see Daisy wore only damp slippers on her feet.

Lucy said quickly, 'I want to talk to Daisy on her own.' Rose, Elsie and Billy silently left the room, and Lucy heard the whispering start as the door closed behind them. They would find it chilly sitting in their bedrooms, but that could not be helped. Tommy had remained, looking mulishly stubborn and worried at the same time. Daisy reached out a hand to seize his.

'Come on over to the fire.' Lucy seated them there, then prompted, 'Now . . .'

Daisy said, haltingly, stumbling over the words, 'When I got home I told Dad I didn't feel well and I was going to bed. And I'd got undressed when Mam came in. She said a neighbour had seen me coming out of the doctor's and asked Mam if I was all right. I hadn't told Mam about going to the doctor and she looked at me and knew straight away what he'd said. And she said, she said —' Daisy stopped, her eyes cast down, her fingers twisting and turning in Tommy's. 'I — I put on my coat and ran.'

Lucy said, 'You're expecting.'

A whisper: 'Aye.'

'And Tommy is the father.'

'Aye.'

Lucy looked at Tommy, and he met her gaze for a moment before turning back to Daisy. He put his free arm about her and said, 'Daisy told me she thought she was. I thought she should see the doctor.' And with another brief glance at Lucy, 'We want to get married.'

Lucy asked, 'Is that right, Daisy?'

Daisy nodded. 'I thought about it a long time, before I knew about — this. I was hoping he would ask me.'

'I was going to,' Tommy insisted. 'I just wanted to save up for a ring first, but we can get married now.'

Lucy thought, Just like that. Aloud, she said practically, 'Well, you can't go out again in a coat and slippers, Daisy. I expect we can find you some clothes between Rose and myself—'

Daisy burst out, 'I can't go home! Mam turned me out! She said I'd disgraced them and she never wanted to see me again.'

Lucy tried to reassure her. 'Naturally, she'd be upset. You're an only child, aren't you? I'm sure she'll come round.' The tears were springing again and Daisy was shaking all over, so Lucy went on quickly, 'You'd better sleep with the girls tonight. Come on, now.'

There were bran bags, small cushions stuffed with bran for bedwarmers, already heating in the oven. Lucy took one out and led Daisy to the girls' room, then sent Rose and Elsie back to the kitchen and put Daisy to bed. The girl cried then, great wrenching sobs of heartache, and Lucy dried her tears, sat with her until she slept at last from exhaustion.

Billy and the girls had to have an explanation, and Lucy gave it to them, matter-of-factly.

The next day Lucy called on Daisy's mother. Lucy felt some sympathy for her before the meeting. Hadn't she, Lucy, worried that Rose would 'go wrong', and fought to prevent it? But Tommy was not like the ne'er-do-wells Rose had collected.

The Marsdens lived in one of a terraced row of cottages. There was no sharing of a house here, and the Marsdens occupied the whole cottage. Nor did the front door open on to the street: there was a strip of garden a yard wide stretching across the front of the single bay window with its lace curtains. Mrs Marsden was thin, narrow faced and vinegary. She stood at her front door with its polished brass knocker and asked, 'Yes?'

Lucy smiled. 'Hello, Mrs Marsden. I'm Lucy Nolan, Tommy Campbell's sister.'

'*Him!*' That—' Her mouth clamped shut and she glared quickly up and down the street, saw no neighbours listening but still decided to be sure. 'Come in.' She opened the door a few more inches so Lucy could slip through the gap.

The hall smelt of polish and disinfectant. There was just room to edge through between the wall on one side and an ornate, mirrored hatstand on the other. Lucy followed Mrs Marsden into the parlour, the room at the front with a bay window. It was crowded with a three-piece suite, sideboard and piano. A spindle-legged table holding an aspidistra took up half the space between the close-drawn, heavy curtains. It was bitterly cold because a fire was only lit on Sundays.

Mrs Marsden did not take a seat nor offer one. She stood on the rug before the empty fireplace with its screen and charged, 'He's made a harlot out of my daughter!'

Lucy flinched in the face of this attack but held her ground. 'Daisy isn't a harlot. She's a sweet girl. I know her and Tommy did wrong, but they love each other and they're going to be married.'

That did not soothe Daisy's mother. 'Married? To *him?*' She sneered, 'He's nothing! A rivet heater! Not much better than a labourer! A common workman! Daisy could have married one of the young gentlemen that works with Mr Marsden, that has a position and comes home in a suit and not mucky overalls! I could sit down and cry my eyes out to think what she's thrown away. Her life is ruined!' She wiped at her eyes, although there were no signs of tears.

Lucy had listened with anger boiling up inside her, but she tried to suppress it now. 'Tommy is a good boy. He did well at school and he likes his work. His pay isn't much, but others manage to live on it, and he and Daisy will. And when he's twenty-one and gets the tools out—'

'Gets what?' Mrs Marsden was disconcerted for a moment, baffled.

Lucy explained, 'When he's finished his apprenticeship and becomes a riveter, then his pay will be better.'

'Money!' Mrs Marsden sniffed, contemptuous. 'That's all you

people can think of. It's not just money, it's *class*! *Breeding*! You can't make a silk purse out of a sow's ear.'

Lucy was silent for a moment, waiting for the rage to subside, and Daisy's mother said triumphantly, 'That's put you in your place, my girl!'

That was too much. Lucy asked the only question that remained: 'I take it you will not oppose the marriage? You'll allow my brother to make an honest woman out of your daughter?'

The irony was wasted on Mrs Marsden, who took the second request in all seriousness: 'I haven't any choice! I'll tell you this, though: *we*'ll not pay for any wedding.'

'And you said *I* only thought about money!' Lucy laughed. 'You can keep yours. We want nothing off you.' She turned, walked back to the front door and yanked it open herself. Then she turned to address Mrs Marsden, following behind, mouth agape. 'And as for putting me in my place, I wouldn't be in yours. You're mean and spiteful, rejecting your own daughter *and* your grandchild, and you'll end your days lonely. God help you, because no one else will!' She slammed the door behind her so that its brass knocker rattled, and marched away up the street.

As her temper cooled and her pace slowed, Lucy told herself wrily that the interview had been a disaster. She had hoped to make a friend and instead was left with an enemy. And a wedding to pay for. Over the past year she had accumulated some small savings, but she could see them disappearing now. What else could she have done, though? She had no answer to that. She would take nothing back, had no regrets. Having made her bed, she would lie on it.

Lucy plunged into preparations for the wedding – and afterwards. The happy couple would need somewhere to live and she tramped the streets for days until she found two rooms to let in Monkwearmouth. They would be close to Tommy's work at Buchanan's yard and not far from the shops in Dundas Street

— Daisy would appreciate that. They needed cleaning and furnishing, of course: Lucy recruited her family to deal with the first, and dipped into her savings to provide the other. All of it was secondhand or older, but Tommy and Daisy would start their married life with crockery, linoleum on the floor, table, chairs, a bed — and no debt.

Lucy returned, weary, to Poona House one Saturday evening and found Rose and the others grouped around the fire — with a new young man, whom Rose introduced as George Fenwick.

Lucy eyed him critically. George was older — Lucy learned later that he was twenty-three — and an inch or two taller than Rose in her cuban heels, and was broad shouldered and barrel chested. His suit was ill fitting and not new. Lucy judged he had bought it from a pawnshop. However, he had a square, pleasing, fresh face and looked back at Lucy with a tentative smile but some surprise.

Rose said nervously, seeing Lucy's inspection, 'George is a carpenter, but he doesn't work for anybody. He's on his own.'

George spoke up for himself, mild but firm. 'I'm not working for anybody, but I've got work to do.'

Lucy liked him, and said as she took off her coat, 'You're welcome. I could do with a cup of tea. Elsie, will you make a pot for us, please?' And to George, 'She's our cook.'

Elsie giggled, 'Go on!' But she was flattered and set the kettle on the fire, bustled about with teapot and crockery.

Lucy smiled at George. 'How long have you known Rose?'

'Only a week or so to speak to.' He grinned sheepishly. 'I noticed her a while back but never said anything. I didn't have any money to take a girl out, so I didn't ask her. I see her every week when I bank my takings, but I can't touch them. That money is to pay the rent on my little yard and to buy timber.'

Lucy questioned, 'Your yard? What do you do there?'

'I make ladders for the ships. I get contracts from Buchanan's, Ballantyne's, Thompson's. I used to work at Ballantyne's, but then I thought I'd more chance of getting on by working for myself.

So I gave notice a year ago to try it. I spent all my savings –' he pulled a face and Lucy could sympathise with him there – 'and had to borrow, but I'm just about in the clear now.'

Lucy regarded him thoughtfully. He had spoken simply, neither boasting or whining. Lucy could see past the brief, bald statements to the story of hard work, pinching and scraping and eventual success. She decided Rose had finally found a good man and smiled at her.

George had called to take Rose out, and Rose explained, 'We're going to the pictures.' The cinema had become very popular, with its jerky, black and white images.

Lucy saw them off, and as Rose went to get her coat, had a private word with George. She apologised. 'I'm sorry if I was a bit slow to welcome you when I first came in. I was tired and not expecting anyone.'

George turned his cap around in his big, broad hands and said shyly, 'That's all right. I was a bit surprised myself. I mean, I was expecting somebody older. See, Rose and the others, they said you were more like their mother than their sister.'

Lucy managed to laugh. 'You don't need to be frightened of me, George.'

He grinned. 'I know that now.'

Tommy sought out his father and found him in a pub down by the South Dock. Tommy asked, 'I want your permission to get married.'

Josh was drunk and peered at him owlishly. 'How old are you?'

'Seventeen.' Tommy eyed him with disgust.

Josh shook his head in disbelief. 'What d'ye want to wed for? You're making a mistake, I'll tell you. I know. I've tried it.'

Tommy repeated patiently, 'I want to get married.'

Josh leered, 'Got her in the family way, haven't you?' He saw Tommy's face turn red and laughed hoarsely. 'I know.' In fact, he had only guessed wildly. He poked a finger at Tommy: 'What was she like, eh?'

Tommy stared for a second, shocked, then he grabbed the poking finger and twisted. Josh yelled and the other drinkers looked round at them, curious. Face contorted with pain, Josh pleaded, 'Let go! You're breaking me finger!'

Tommy twisted it further. Furious, he warned, 'You're my father, but if you talk like that again I'll break your bloody neck! D'ye hear?'

'Aye! All right. Let go.' Tommy pushed him away and Josh massaged his finger, wincing. He muttered, 'So you want my permission to wed?'

Tommy told him, 'I'm going to have it, one way or another.'

Josh read the warning message and conceded, 'Right.' Then with a hint of his previous bravado, 'But it'll cost you a couple o' quid, same as I charged for Lucy.'

Tommy dug in his pocket and tossed two sovereigns on to the table. 'There y'are.'

Josh blinked. 'You came prepared, then.'

'Aye.' Lucy had warned a disbelieving Tommy that his father would want paying, and had told him to take two sovereigns.

Tommy and Daisy were married in the Registry Office. Billy was best man and George gave the bride away. The only guests were George and the groom's family. After the wedding they all walked back to Poona House and a reception held in the kitchen, sitting down to ham, salad and pickles. Toasts were drunk in beer, sherry or lemonade.

Adelaide Pearce appeared at the door leading to the main rooms of the house. She accepted a glass of sherry, wished the couple well and presented them with an envelope that proved to contain five sovereigns. In the evening bride and groom left to go to their rooms in Monkwearmouth while the others sat up late, talking.

It was close to midnight when a tired but happy Lucy sought her bed. She had taken her mother's Bible to the ceremony and now when she went to set it on the chest of drawers it fell to the floor. Lucy retrieved it quickly and carefully. It had fallen open and now she saw a white edging against the black binding. A card of some sort had been slipped into a slit in the binding. She could not grip it with her fingers, but using a needle from her workbox was able to slide it out a fraction of an inch then hold it and pull it out.

She held in her hand a photograph showing two young men. They wore Norfolk jackets and deerstalker hats, breeches, woollen stockings and heavy boots. They were obviously walkers or climbers. The photograph was old, in sepia tones and no bigger than a postcard, but she recognised one of the men at once. This was Andrew Buchanan, much younger but unmistakably he. The other man was tall, and a stranger to her.

Lucy's knees gave under her and she sank down to sit on her bed with a bump. She stared at the old picture of the two young men. Her mother had kept it hidden all these years. She had said there had been a young man and a night at the Buchanan house. Lucy knew she was looking at her father.

A week after the wedding, life had returned to normal and Lucy was rapidly cleaning through the downstairs rooms when the doorbell rang. Annie, the housemaid, ran to open it and Lucy heard Nick Buchanan's voice and then that of Helen Whittaker. Lucy glanced out of the window and saw a shining black Humber parked outside the front door, the chauffeur standing by its door. She recognised it as the Whittakers' motor car. She cast off apron and duster, put a hand to her hair then hurried out to the hall.

Nick was smiling down at Annie but now looked around. 'Hello! I looked in to say goodbye to Aunt Adelaide. We're on our way to the station.'

Helen stood by his side, smiling. 'Andrew is away with his car, so I'm acting as Nick's cabbie.'

Adelaide Pearce appeared, her young pupils at her heels, all with a rustle of skirts. She announced brusquely, 'Can't stop for long. These girls will chatter all day if I let them.' They tittered and swarmed around Nick. Adelaide 'tut-tutted' and held out her hand. 'Goodbye and good luck, Nick. Where did you say you were off to?'

'Hong Kong, Shanghai, Singapore, Borneo . . .' He waved a large, long-fingered hand. 'All around there. I'm only second mate, but this is a much bigger ship than the collier I've been commanding. I could be captain by the time I come back, though, in three or four years' time.'

Lucy swallowed. She stood patiently with a fixed smile, hands behind her, fingers twisting. She listened as they went on talking about Nick's job, his passage out through the Mediterranean and the Suez canal.

Adelaide said wistfully, 'I miss India. My God! How I miss it!'

Helen looked at the tiny gold watch on her wrist and said, 'It's time we were going if you want to catch that train, old boy.'

Nick followed her out of the door then turned on the steps. His eyes sought out Lucy behind Adelaide and her girls and he chided, 'I nearly forgot. Aunt Adelaide told me about the wedding. You promised to invite me to all of them.' But his grin belied his reproof. He glanced at Adelaide. 'Lucy is like a sister to me. We grew up together.'

Adelaide said drily, 'Then she's turned out very well, considering that handicap.'

Lucy smiled with confused emotions.

Nick laughed and said, 'Don't forget me next time. Whose wedding will it be? Elsie? Rose?'

'Rose, I expect,' replied Lucy. 'Elsie is too young. But I will send you an invitation – to Borneo.' Nick laughed, and went on down the steps, and Lucy gave up forcing the smile.

Nick turned once more before getting into the back of the Humber beside Helen. 'Goodbye!' he called. 'Goodbye, little Lucy!'

Lucy waved with the others and watched him driven away.

'Little Lucy.' Her siblings thought of her as their mother, and he regarded her as a sister.

Three or four years. Oh, God!

Nick sat back in the Humber, taking away with him that last memory of the little group on the steps of the house, Aunt Adelaide and the others, all smiling. Except for one face, the eyes huge, mouth drooping at the corners. His own smile slipped away.

He wondered, Now why had the girl looked like that?

And too late, at sea, the answer came to him.

Chapter Fourteen

It was to prove a crowded year. Lucy thought of it later, with sad humour, as the mating time. But on a fine afternoon, as she set a tray with tea things, she thought only of Rose's wedding, planned for July. Billy and Elsie were unattached and, she believed, unlikely to marry for years; Billy was eighteen and Elsie a year younger. There she was wrong. Their lives were to change, rapidly and for a terrible reason.

She had no inkling of this as she carried the tray through Poona House to the drawing room. As she entered, Nell Jarman sighed, 'Murdoch doesn't write.' She sat with Adelaide Pearce and Helen Whittaker. The occasional visits of Helen and Nell had coincided this time. All three ladies were in afternoon gowns of embroidered cotton or taffeta.

Lucy, in her grey serge dress that was her uniform, put the tray down on the table near the fire and Adelaide said absently, 'Thank you, Lucy. Will you serve, please.' And going on, speaking now to Nell with asperity, 'That boy has always been a burden on his father. Andrew is hurt, no doubt.'

Nell nodded. 'I'm sure he is. He never mentions it, but Andrew's first to look through the post when it arrives, and he's always disappointed, that's clear. Mind you, Nick's letters help to make up for it. He's been in the Far East nearly three years now, but he still writes sometimes to Andrew. I believe you hear from him, Helen?'

Helen replied, smiling, 'At irregular intervals. I gather he takes pen in hand when his ship is in port and he has time.' The cups rattled on the saucers as Lucy set them out. Helen went on, 'He sounds to be full of life and enjoying himself.'

Adelaide said longingly, 'I bet he is. There's disease and sunstroke, but the countries! I do miss India.'

Helen said softly, 'I'm sure you do. You've spent more of your life abroad than in England.'

Adelaide visibly shook herself. 'Never mind me! Tell us about Nick.'

Helen laughed. 'He's working hard, too. He'd only been out there a year when he was promoted to first mate and six months ago they made him captain.'

'I always knew he'd get on,' said Adelaide tersely. 'His father would have done well, too, but the cholera got him and his wife when Nick was very young.' She turned to Nell again. 'Harking back to Murdoch: where is he? Do you know?'

Nell shrugged. 'About a month ago Andrew met some people who had just returned from the South of France and they'd seen Murdoch there. He'd told them he'd be coming back to London for the summer season. That's all we've heard.'

Lucy asked, 'Will that be all, ma'am?'

'Yes, thank you.' Adelaide smiled dismissal and Lucy retired to the kitchen.

Lucy looked at the clock. Elsie would be finishing work at the Palace Hotel early today – in an hour or so – and was going to meet Rose as she finished at the bank. Then they were going to visit Daisy and Tommy. It was the second birthday of their little daughter, Violet, and the girls had presents for her. As had Lucy, who would be calling on Daisy later.

She went on with preparing the evening meal for Adelaide and her boarding pupils with the assistance of the kitchenmaid. Later she collected the tea things from the drawing room and saw the ladies leave. When next she looked at the clock she saw that Rose would have finished work fifteen minutes before. Lucy hoped Elsie would be there on time and not still be dawdling at the shops. She was just eighteen now and an excellent cook, but a notorious window shopper.

Elsie had already been waiting outside the bank for twenty minutes and looked up at the clock above the door for the fourth or fifth time. Was it slow? Where was Rose? Ten minutes later she was still fretting impatiently over the latter question. A stream of young men and girls had left the bank, all of them more or less in uniform — dark lounge suits and high collars for the men, crisp white blouses and ankle-length skirts for the girls. Elsie saw enviously that the girls, like Rose, were smart and very pretty.

The young man who came out on his own, after the rest, was boyish and thin faced, neat and slender in his charcoal-grey suit of worsted. He saw Elsie at once, an auburn-haired girl with wide blue eyes, but still hesitated, looking to see if any other girl was waiting. When he had confirmed she was the only one, and the one he wanted, he descended the steps and asked, 'Excuse me, but are you Elsie Campbell?' He was her senior by a year or two but looked no older and stood eye to eye with Elsie in her high heels.

She answered, startled, 'Yes. I'm waiting for my sister.'

'Ah! Rose asked —' He stumbled over the words, shy, face reddening. 'She asked me to tell you — she'll be late. She's been given some work by the manager and has to finish it before she leaves.'

'Oh!' Elsie looked past him blankly but saw only the empty windows of the building and the clock. What now?

The young man said, 'Would you like a cup of tea while you're waiting?' Elsie half-turned her head so she looked at him out of the corner of her eye, wary. He went on quickly, 'I work with Rose. I'm Stephen Kennedy, but I don't suppose she's mentioned me.' And then, scarlet faced but persisting, 'There's a place just across the street.'

It was a tea room with small tables behind lace curtains. Elsie thought it looked respectable, and there were other women in there so it seemed safe. 'Well, all right.'

Together they crossed the street and Stephen held open the door for Elsie to pass through. He found a table, helped her shrug off her coat then pulled back her chair and slid it under her. He ordered tea for two. There was an awkward pause before he fought his shyness to make conversation and tried very hard not to stare at her too often. Elsie did not mind him staring but wished she did not keep blushing when he did. Two grand-mothers at another table looked at them then winked at each other.

'Oh, I forgot,' Stephen said untruthfully after some time, 'Rose said you were to go on to Daisy's and she would see you there.'

'Did she?' Elsie did not look at her watch nor the clock above the cake counter, but said brightly, 'Well, there's plenty of time.'

When Elsie eventually walked into Daisy's kitchen, Rose demanded, 'Where have you been?'

Elsie smiled down at little Violet where she sat on a rug before the fire. 'I stopped to have some tea with Stephen Kennedy and we got to talking.'

'Until this time? What were you talking *about?*'

'Oh, things,' said Elsie vaguely. 'I can't remember now.'

Lucy, seated on the rug with Violet, looked up sharply.

Rose shook her head in bewilderment. 'It beats me. That Stephen never has much to say to anybody.' Rose had missed the point, but then, she had a lot on her mind, and went on, 'So we've seen the vicar. We'll have my birthday party at our place — and the reception. It'll be a bit crowded but we'll manage . . .'

Rose would celebrate her birthday in July and would be

married a week later. 'I won't ask my father for permission. When I'm twenty-one I won't need it, and that's when I'll get married.'

Lucy listened as Rose recited her plans, and put in a word here and there, cautioning or encouraging, while playing with Violet. She kept an eye on the dreaming Elsie, thinking, I must have a word with Rose about this Stephen Kennedy.

It was on a Saturday evening in that spring, in the kitchen of Poona House, that Billy said over-casually as he brushed down his suit, 'I'm off to the dance with Florence.'

Elsie was half out of the door, on her way to meet Stephen, but she spun on her heel to ask, 'Florence?'

'That's right.' Billy hung up the brush.

'Florence who?'

'Florence Irvine.'

'And you're going *with* her? You always meet the girls *inside*. That's what you said.'

Billy saw he had mishandled his announcement but yielded with a grin, 'That's right.'

Elsie pressed, 'So why are you paying for this Florence?'

He explained simply, 'She said if I wanted to take her out I'd have to take her in.'

'Ooh!' said Elsie. 'You must have got a tartar this time!'

'Get out!' And Billy chased her.

Lucy finished ironing and sat down by the fire alone. Rose had already gone to meet George Fenwick. His business was doing well now. He worked long hours but was always ready to escort Rose. Tommy and Daisy usually visited on a Sunday afternoon, bringing little Violet. They were living frugally, but managing, with a little discreet help from Lucy, on Tommy's wage of twenty-four shillings a week. Sometimes there was overtime to add a few shillings, but there were other weeks when bad weather stopped the men from working and their pay packets were thin. However, Violet was thriving and they were happy.

Lucy was content, told herself there was no sense in crying for the moon. She had a lot to look forward to, with Rose's birthday and wedding. She approved of Stephen, and had a feeling he and Elsie would not wait too long to marry. And now there was Billy and this Florence. She would have to tell Billy to bring the girl to tea.

That opportunity came a week later. All the family, with George and Stephen, were gathered in the kitchen when Billy poked his head around the door, and said bashfully, 'Here we are.'

Lucy got up from her chair. 'Come on in, then.'

Billy held the door open and ushered the girl in. 'This is Florence.' She looked nervous, as well she might, with all eyes on her. Her fluffy blonde head barely reached Billy's shoulder.

'I'm Lucy.' She went quickly to take the girl's hand. 'I'm pleased to meet you.'

Elsie stage-whispered boldly, 'Is this the tartar?'

Lucy snapped, 'Elsie!'

Florence was unperturbed, however. Her china-blue eyes were wide as she stared at Elsie and said, 'Ooh! Is that what he calls me?'

'No, it isn't.' Lucy and Billy spoke in chorus and he pointed a finger, 'Look here, Elsie, I'll—'

'Never mind,' said Lucy.

'He told me about you, Elsie,' Florence said with a grin, and mimicked deeply, ' "She's a right cheeky monkey." ' It was Billy to the life and they all laughed.

Lucy heaved a sigh of relief. 'Come and sit down.'

They learned that Florence had been orphaned at sixteen and lived on her own in one room in Millfield, south of the river. She worked behind the counter in Binns, the big department store — and gave an uproarious impersonation of her floorwalker.

Later that evening, after tea had been eaten and the talking round the fire was done, Lucy sat alone. She summed up Florence as pretty, honest and bubbling with life. She would be good for Billy.

These were happy times – except for Clem Nolan, the dark background to her life, rarely seen but always there, never far from her thoughts. Sometimes she took the photograph from its hiding place in her mother's Bible, looked at the smiling young man with Andrew Buchanan and wondered who and where he was. Andrew could have answered her questions, but she could never ask him. She had no proof of paternity other than her mother's half-delirious ramblings. The young man would be middle-aged now and doubtless with a wife and children. He would not welcome Lucy turning up like a ghost from his past and claiming kinship. It would be better to leave things as they were.

Lucien Hawkins, now commodore, met his old friend Andrew Buchanan in London and they dined at Andrew's club. Hawkins said, in reply to Andrew's commiserations, 'I miss her. It's five years since she died of the fever in China but I still miss her.'

'And your boys?' asked Andrew.

'Both in the service. Jeremy's ship is on the West Indian Station and William's is in the Med, so I'll be seeing something of him. I'm off to join the Mediterranean Fleet at the end of the month. And Murdoch?'

'That's why I wanted to talk to you.' Andrew hesitated, then went on reluctantly, 'I want you to be executor of my will. I'd put Murdoch's name in, but now . . . The estate goes to him, of course, as next in the male line, and I can't alter that. But I've made a number of bequests to friends, servants and so on, and I want to be sure they will be honoured. Will you do this for me?'

Lucien saw only too well the pain his friend was hiding. To doubt that your own son . . . ! He said gently, 'Of course,' then determinedly changed the subject to avoid any more embarrassment for Andrew. 'I'm going to be very busy. There's always trouble in the Balkans, of course, Serbia and the rest . . .'

Chapter Fifteen

'You'll all be out on the street!' Clem Nolan jeered. His wheel-chair was drawn up to the fire in the kitchen of Poona House. Until he had arrived on this fine, sunny morning, Lucy and Elsie had been singing as they worked. Elsie was not due to start at the Palace Hotel until midday, and Lucy had sent the kitchenmaid to town on an errand. Clem had kicked open the door and wheeled his chair between them, scraping their legs. The sun glinted on his yellow hair like a halo and now he grinned triumphantly. 'She's selling the place over your heads. You'll be out of a home and out of a job.'

Elsie was white with shock. She stared at him then turned on Lucy. 'It's not true – is it?'

Lucy felt as if a cold hand gripped her stomach. 'I don't know.' The cosy little world she had built up at Poona House – was it to be shattered? Clem's statement had caught her unprepared and unsuspecting. 'I've heard nothing.'

Elsie pleaded, 'He's making it up. Or he's got it wrong.'

Lucy did not think so. There was an awful certainty about Clem, which he confirmed: 'I'm right and I'm not making it up. I *know*, don't ask me how, but I do.' In fact, a crony of Garvey's was the caretaker in a solicitor's office. He had glimpsed the papers on a clerk's desk while he was making up the fires with coal, and Garvey had passed the information to Clem.

Elsie snapped bitterly, 'If it is true, then I don't know why you're laughing. You'll be hit as hard as the rest of us.'

Clem's grin did not falter. 'No, I won't. I've got another place to go to and I won't have you lot hanging round my neck.' He spun the chair around and propelled it towards the door but in passing reached out and seized Lucy's arm. His fingers gripped her flesh like teeth, she cried out and he laughed. 'But you'll never be rid of me! Wherever I am or you are, you'll still be mine and always will be.' He shoved her away and wheeled on to the door. 'Right! I'm off. I just thought I'd come in and give you the news, wish you luck. You're going to need it!' The door slamming shut behind him cut off his mocking laughter.

Lucy rubbed at her arm. She was numb with shock. It took time to sink in that her husband for nearly six years had left her – though in fact she had never been as a wife to him, rather just a chattel, something he owned. Lucy thought numbly that she should feel sorrow, and there was – but only for the waste of those years, not for the breaking of the marriage. She was not relieved nor exultant, either. Clem had said she would never be rid of him. This was not freedom, only a kind of parole that could be withdrawn at his whim.

The sun still shone outside but there was gloom in the kitchen. Elsie, tears in her eyes, blinked at Lucy. 'What are we going to do?'

Lucy took off her apron and breathed deeply before saying shakily, 'I'll go and see Mrs Pearce about it.' And with a glance at the clock, 'She'll be wanting her coffee in a minute.'

Adelaide was taking a break between classes and Lucy found her in the drawing-room. She was seated at a table set in the bay window and reading through a sheaf of apparently legal documents, stiff paper that crackled as she turned the pages. 'Ah! There you are, Lucy.'

Lucy set the tray, with its coffee pot and crockery, on the table. 'May I ask a question, ma'am?'

Adelaide Pearce smiled at her. 'Of course. Fire away.'

The smile vanished as Lucy asked, 'Is it true you're selling up, ma'am?' and held her breath.

It was a question many an employer would have answered with, 'That's none of your business,' but Adelaide said, 'Damn!' Her brows came together in a frown. 'How did you hear of that?'

'It's true, then.'

Adelaide sighed. 'Obviously someone has been talking.' She reached out a hand to pull out another chair at the table and patted its seat. 'Sit down, my dear. I have to say that, yes, I'm closing the school. I'm going back to India.' She gave a bark of ironic laughter. 'For thirty-odd years I looked forward to coming home, and now I am and I can't settle. So Poona House is up for sale and I think I have a buyer. I'll be writing to the girls' parents today, telling them the school will close at the end of the month, three weeks from now.'

Three weeks, Lucy thought. Twenty-one days in which to start to build her life again. She made to rise but Adelaide's hand pressed her back into her seat.

'Wait a minute, girl. I can see this has come as a nasty shock. I wouldn't have had this happen for the world. I intended to break the news to you myself in a civilised manner, not for you to hear it from some third party. Now, normally you would be entitled to a month's notice but I'm going to pay you for three. Once the girls have gone at the end of the month you'll be able to concentrate on your own affairs. I shall sell off my furniture and move in with my brother Andrew until I sail for India. The school will be closed but the house won't be sold until the end of June and you can stay here until then. Now, are you more cheerful?'

Lucy was relieved. Three months! 'Oh, yes, ma'am. That's good of you.'

'No more than you deserve.'

Then Lucy asked, 'What about Annie and Phoebe, ma'am?'

Adelaide thought, She always thinks of others. And she replied, 'I'll give each of them a month's notice.'

Lucy said, 'They'll be grateful.'

Adelaide eyed her thoughtfully. 'To tell you the truth, when I first came here I had grave doubts about you. I thought you far too young and inexperienced. And with that husband like a millstone hung around your neck . . . Well, I didn't think you could cope, but you've done damned well. You never have to be told twice and you've become expert at your job.' She went on drily, 'And I've seen you learning with the other girls. You know as much as they do about comporting yourself as a lady.' Adelaide paused, amused at Lucy's obvious surprise, then finished, 'You're a treasure.'

'Thank you, ma'am.' Lucy blushed at the praise as she made her way back to the kitchen, but did not believe it.

She reported to Elsie the terms of her notice, to Elsie's relief.

'Three months!' Elsie clapped her hands. 'We'll be able to find another place to live in that time.'

Lucy agreed, 'I'm sure we will,' although that was only to cheer Elsie. She doubted they would find another house like this, and she was unsure about her own prospects of finding a job. But then her customary determination asserted itself. She would find work and make a home for the family. Rose's wedding and birthday celebrations would go ahead.

Lucy told the maids the news, and that they were to have a month's notice.

Annie said, 'Ooh! I've never had a month before.'

And Phoebe agreed, 'Sometimes I've not even had a week. It's been a couple o' shillings and "Get your coat on, my girl", and that's all.'

Then Lucy turned to and worked furiously for the rest of that morning. After she had served lunch, she left the washing-up to Phoebe, the kitchenmaid, hung up her apron behind the door and took down her coat and hat. 'Can you manage for the rest of the afternoon?'

''Course I can,' replied Phoebe.

Lucy explained, 'I'm off to find another job.' She jammed the hat on her piled hair and set out.

Phoebe called, 'Good luck!' She and Annie, the housemaid, were confident they would find new positions in a week or two, but Lucy did not want to go back to being a kitchenmaid.

Lucy worried at the problem as she rode down into town on the tram. She knew vacancies for housekeepers in large houses were scarce, but she had heard that there had been changes at the Palace Hotel. Elsie had said, 'Chrissie Carter has handed in her notice. She was on reception but she did a lot of other things: secretarial work, keeping the books and so on.' Now Lucy wondered if there might be an opening for her there, although she had never done that kind of work before and it was not what she wanted.

Lucy got up from her seat as the tram passed the junction of High Street and Fawcett Street. She glanced out of the window and saw painters working on the front of the old Railway Hotel, and remembered Elsie had also said, 'Chrissie's going to work for Lance Morgan. He's bought the Railway and closed it while they do it all up.'

So Lucy pushed through the revolving doors of the Palace Hotel and crossed the foyer to the reception desk. The pretty, smartly dressed girl who sat behind it had dark eyes and dark hair with a hint of copper in it. Lucy asked, 'Are you Miss Carter, please?'

'I'm Chrissie Carter.' The girl smiled at her. 'Can I help you, ma'am?'

'I'm not ma'am,' Lucy stumbled. 'I mean, I'm not a guest. I'm looking for a job,' and added quickly, 'Not here, but I heard you and Lance Morgan were doing up the Railway Hotel and I thought you might be wanting a housekeeper.'

Chrissie blinked but her smile did not falter. 'You're getting in early. We don't plan to open until the first of August.'

'I won't be free for another three weeks. In fact I've been given three months' notice but I only need to work to the end of the month.'

'Three months!' That was highly unusual and Chrissie's brows lifted.

Lucy explained, 'I'm housekeeper to Mrs Pearce at Poona House, the finishing school, and she's going back to India.'

'Ah! Mrs Pearce.' Chrissie knew the lady and nodded. She had also heard reports of how Poona House was run and now she said, 'We can't talk here and now.' As if to make the point, a guest came striding across the foyer to the desk. Chrissie said quickly, 'Lance Morgan keeps The Bells, and I'll be in there with Lance at eight tonight. Will you come?'

'Yes.'

Lucy knew the pub in Monkwearmouth, and that night she emerged from The Bells and smiled up at a starlit sky. She had secured the position of housekeeper at the Railway Hotel, to commence her duties the first week in July. Lucy hesitated for a time. She was tired and wanted to go to Poona House to give the others the good news, but as she was on the north side of the river she decided to visit an old friend. Mrs Harris, now close to eighty years old, still lived in the same rooms and not far away.

Lucy walked down Charles Street, across Nelson Square and up Church Street. The front door of the house where Mrs Harris lived was closed but only latched. Lucy thumbed it open and closed it behind her. She tap-tapped along the passage, climbed the stairs and knocked on the kitchen door.

'Come in!' came the quavering voice of Mrs Harris. Lucy entered and found the old lady seated in an armchair before the fire, her head turned. She exclaimed, 'Why, Lucy hinny, it's lovely to see you!'

Lucy sat down beside her and talked for an hour, bringing her up to date with the doings of Tommy, Rose and the others. Then Lucy told of her new job and added, 'I've still got to find some rooms.'

'Aye?' Mrs Harris looked at her questioningly. 'Where? When?'

Lucy answered wrily, 'Anywhere, because I can't pick and choose. And I've got to be out of Poona House by the end of June.'

'Ah!' Mrs Harris nodded and laid a hand, all skin and bone, on Lucy's. 'Now, I've not told anybody around here because I don't want people knocking at my door and asking me to speak for them, but I'm leaving next month, the middle o' May. My daughter, that's the eldest that's married to the coalman, she wants me to move in with them. She has done for the past year, she's a canny lass and I get on all right with him, only I didn't want to give up my independence, d'ye see?' Lucy nodded and Mrs Harris patted her hand and went on, 'But I can't manage these stairs any more. Every time I want to go to the lav or I want a bucket o' coal it's down the stairs and up again. So! Will I give your name to the rent man and tell him you're moving in?'

They were three good rooms – Lucy had been in them many a time since childhood – similar to those she had left to go to Poona House and big enough for Rose, Elsie, Billy and herself. She had no pressing need for ground-floor rooms since Clem had left her, and whilst the rooms were not exactly what she had been hoping for, for now she was happy.

As she sat in the tram, returning to Poona House, Lucy looked back contentedly on a day which had started with seeming catastrophe. Now, at the end, she was well pleased. She had a new job she was looking forward to, and had taken a step nearer her goal of being a housekeeper in a big establishment like the Buchanan house. She and her brood would also have a home once Poona House was sold.

They moved in the middle of May, and Lucy was reunited with her old neighbours, who welcomed her: 'Hello, bonny lass! By, it's grand to see you back again!' They were frankly sympathetic when they learned Clem had left her. They had known him and the life he led her. 'You're better off without him, lass!' There was relief in his absence. Her own family did not regret his going and with the passing of the months were open about it. Elsie summed it up: 'It's like a load lifted off all of us.' For Lucy there was a comforting familiarity in returning to the street where she was born and raised, close to the yards and the clamour of the riveting hammers, the blaring sirens of ships in the river and the bull bawling of the hooters in the yards calling the men to work – and sometimes the deep drone of the foghorn when the thick grey mist curled in from the sea.

Lucy started work as the housekeeper at the Railway Hotel at the beginning of July, and Rose celebrated her twenty-first birthday shortly after. The kitchen was crowded with family, friends and neighbours, the window pushed up to let in the breeze and let out the noise. There was a lot of laughter, a concertina played and everyone sang the old favourites: 'Blaydon Races', 'Keep Your Feet Still, Geordie Hinny' and 'The Lambton Worm'.

Lucy told Rose and George, 'I've got another present for you.' She handed them a key. 'Two rooms in Victor Street – if you want them.' It was only two streets away. Rose fell on Lucy in delight and George beamed happily.

Rose said, 'We looked everywhere and couldn't find a place.'

Lucy recalled the long hours tramping the streets as she searched for rooms for Rose and George. She had considered herself lucky to find these two. She would never have found three rooms for her family, if she had not visited old Mrs Harris because of fond memories . . .

It was in the following week that Elsie put her arm around Lucy and said, 'I'm joining you at the Railway.' When Lucy stared, she explained, 'Chrissie Carter has given Mrs Wilberforce the job of cook there and she is taking me with her. It's a move up as well, because I'll be getting another five shillings a week.'

'That's marvellous,' said Lucy, and hugged her. 'I've been

thinking. There's not much room at home for Rose's reception . . .'

Lucy and Elsie approached Chrissie and asked if they could hire a room at the Railway Hotel. Chrissie was eager to fill her diary with bookings and accepted on the spot. 'I think I know where I can get a band for you,' she offered.

The wedding was held at St Peter's church, late on a Saturday afternoon. Lucy took the place of the bride's mother and Tommy gave Rose away. The room at the Railway was not one of the biggest, but a smaller one at the rear. However, it was ample for the reception and Lucy had obtained it at a discounted rate. There was a good dance floor and a buffet prepared by Lucy, Elsie, Daisy, Rose and Florence. Lucy had spent all her savings painfully acquired by living carefully during the good years and in the bad ones breakfasting on bread and dripping, of conjuring up a broth to feed the family out of a six penny ham shank and what vegetables she could get cheap — and making it last two days. Having only one pair of shoes and those letting in water — and never a new dress, always second hand or handed down. That was how you paid the rent each week and still saved a penny here, a halfpenny there. Now she thought it had been worthwhile. She kissed Rose and whispered, 'Happy?'

'Um!' Rose nodded, then asked, 'And you?'

'Very.' Lucy believed she was.

Rose added, 'You've got Clem off your back now, anyway.'

Lucy knew she would never be rid of Clem Nolan, however: she was married to him and there was no changing that. It was a life sentence. Divorce was long-winded, legal and expensive, she could not afford it and would not seek it. She had made her vows.

After the meal was eaten, the toasts drunk and the cake cut, the tables were pushed back against the walls. This time there was not just a concertina but a five-piece band to play waltzes and some of the new ragtime tunes. George Fenwick and Rose led off the dancing, circling the floor to applause. As others joined in, Lucy sat on a straight-backed chair against the wall, smiling and watching Rose and George go by, looking into each other's eyes. They were soon followed by Elsie and Stephen, and Billy and Florence, with her head thrown back, eyelashes fluttering, every movement exaggerated and clowning. Even Tommy and Daisy danced by, little Violet held between them.

Suddenly, through a gap in the whirling dancers, Lucy saw the swing doors pushed open and Nick Buchanan strode in. The gap closed, like a curtain twitched across. Lucy sat still, her heart in her throat. Had she been mistaken? She had thought Nick on the other side of the world.

The gap opened again, and he stood there, looking around him with a quizzical grin, eyes searching. His face was very brown, his dark hair tousled as always. He wore a suit of white linen that Lucy concluded he must have bought while abroad. The dancers hid him again, and Lucy thought absently, ridiculously, that the brief glimpses of him were like a magic lantern show. But then that he was nothing to her, she was nothing to him. Lucy knew he thought of her as a sister he'd never had. Helen Whittaker would be somewhere around. Or another girl just like her. Not like Lucy Nolan.

The dancers parted again and Lucy stood up. That movement caught his eye and now he saw her. She saw the smile wiped from his face. He was no longer amused, nor teasing. He was serious. He had never looked at her like that before.

Nick had never forgotten his last sight of Lucy, her miserable pale face as she waved farewell. He had wondered and then realised why she was so stricken. He had thought about her ever since, found he could remember every second they had spent together but he had not written because she was married – albeit unhappily. But he had made up his mind, knew what was in his heart and he would have to tell her to her face, not scribble it in a letter. Now . . . this was the girl become woman in the three years he had been away, and this woman caught at his breath.

The music stopped and the dancers strolled off the floor. Nick edged through them, his eyes fixed on Lucy, until he stood before her, over her. He was bigger. Lucy had to tilt back her head to look up at him. His shoulders were broader, heavier, his face stronger.

His voice was deep when he said, 'I got home just in time to see Aunt Adelaide before she left for India. She told me about the wedding. You promised you'd invite me.' Lucy said nothing, did not need to, she knew that. Because of the heat and the dancing, the men were discarding their jackets. Nick shrugged off his own, hung it on the back of a chair and rolled up his shirtsleeves.

The leader of the band announced a waltz. A chord was struck and then they launched into a Strauss. Nick took Lucy in his arms and they moved out on to the floor. His head was bent above her and Lucy looked up into his eyes. They circled and spun and he tightened his grip on her, held her closer and closer still. Body welded to body they swept around the floor to the pulse of the music. Lucy hungered for him, as, she was certain, he did for her. This was excitement she had never known, this was happiness.

Then the music stopped.

Lucy came back to earth, to reality. She saw Rose with her young husband, and remembered her own. '*Please!*' A shuddering whisper. Lucy made herself pull out of Nick's arms.

Nick followed her as she walked, heels clicking rapidly, back to her chair — but she passed it and went on, almost running now. Nick snatched up his jacket and followed her out through the swing doors and across the foyer of the hotel and into the night.

Outside, the trams were *clang-clanging!* up and down Fawcett Street and across the bridge, and the pavements were crowded with evening strollers.

Long striding, Nick soon caught up with Lucy, and paced alongside her, one hand wrapped around her arm. Together they weaved through the crowds and he asked, 'Lucy! What is it?'

She did not halt until she came to the bridge and fetched up against its parapet. She leaned on her arms against it and he stooped over her, set his arm about her. He demanded again, 'What's wrong, Lucy?'

She did not answer for some time. The shipyards were shut and silent. The ships crowded into the river lay to their buoys or their moorings against the quays, their lights reflected in the sliding, glassy black current.

At last Lucy asked in a small voice, 'What about Helen?'

'Helen Whittaker?' He stared at her. 'What about her?'

Lucy, confused and torn apart by her emotions, stumbled, 'You and Helen were always – I thought you were . . .'

'No!' Nick shook his head. 'We're friends and that's all. I courted her for a while when we were young, but then we agreed to go on as just friends. I even remember when that was! You came to the house looking for a job for your brother and we met on the road outside. That was years ago.'

'Oh!' Lucy remembered very well. She had fallen in love with him then as she stood on the icy road, but . . . She said, voice barely above a whisper, 'I'm a married woman. I can't— What we did, dancing . . .' She shook her head helplessly then looked up at him. 'I'm tied to another man. For life. Just go away again and leave me in peace.'

Nick could see her shivering in the cool of the evening and he put his jacket around her. 'That's not how you feel. It's not what you want.'

'It is,' Lucy insisted.

'No, it isn't, and it's not how I feel, what I want. All these years I've known you and I've never thought – But now I've come ten thousand miles, walked in through that door and found you.'

'Stop it, Nick!' Lucy pleaded.

'I can't. I love you!'

'Nick! *Please!*' Her face was turned up to him, desolate, and he saw her cheeks were wet. She begged him, 'Leave me alone. You're hurting me.'

He could not resist that appeal and stood away. Lucy pulled off his jacket and thrust it into his hands, then she walked past him and back through the crowds, letting the tears run. Nick followed until he saw her enter the Railway Hotel and disappear from his sight.

But not out of his life. He swore that. He would not give her up. Tomorrow he would seek her out. Tomorrow they would both be calmer, not torn by passion as they were this night. He would take her to some place where they could talk quietly, sensibly. He knew she was a virtual prisoner in her marriage, but he would find a way out for her. If she would not seek a divorce – and he feared she would not, having made her vows – then he would find another way. There had to be one, he was determined on that. He would never give up.

On the morrow Nick ripped open the buff envelope and read the telegram inside. He was summoned to duty in the Royal Naval Reserve. His country would soon be at war.

Chapter Sixteen

'Mrs Nolan!' The boy came running to Lucy, where she was issuing linen from the cupboard on the first floor.

She pushed a neat pile of sheets into the arms of a chambermaid and turned to meet the newcomer. 'Yes?' He was one of the young pages employed in the hotel to help the doorman and porter and to carry messages. He was smart in his uniform of short jacket with double row of gleaming brass buttons up to his neck, and pillbox hat tilted at a rakish angle.

He panted, 'There's a gent, a Navy officer, asking for you at the desk.'

'I'll come,' Lucy answered calmly. The summons was not a surprise: she had suspected Nick would not be sent away as easily as that.

She had wept her heart out the night before, but had put on a cheerful face all through the wedding celebrations, right to the bitter end. Lucy had been last to leave, after ensuring that all was as it should be: the band paid, the staff tipped, every guest bade farewell. Only when she was hidden from curious eyes, alone in her bed in the darkness, did she let go.

Lucy had slept little and rose early, washed her face in cold water to mend her eyes and to hide the signs of her tears. She had gone to work in a calm, almost cold mood of acceptance of her situation. The tangled emotions had been washed away and she saw right and wrong very clearly. And she had been sure Nick would come.

As she descended the stairs she saw him pacing back and forth across the foyer, his cap in one hand. His navy blue reefer jacket bore the two gold rings of a Royal Naval Reserve lieutenant on its sleeves. The staff and the few loungers in the foyer watched him excitedly. Lucy had seen that almost feverish anxiety mixed with patriotic fervour in the crowds thronging the streets as she walked to work. They all had the same question for each other: will we go to war?

Lucy saw Nick glance down at the watch on his wrist, frowning, then he looked up and saw her, turned in his pacing and strode to meet her. He was smiling now. Lucy was not. She deliberately stopped before reaching the foot of the stairs so that she could face him eye to eye – and maintain a distance.

Nick looked about him and asked, 'Where can we talk?'

'Here.'

He glanced back at the foyer, seeing the staff on reception, guests coming and going. He saw through the open doors of the restaurant that it was almost empty and began, 'It's quieter in there. We—'

'No, Nick. Here.'

He glanced again at his watch then set his foot on the first step and reached out to her. 'Lucy, I—'

'That's close enough, Nick.' Lucy held up her hand, took a pace back. 'No closer. Don't touch me.' She knew she would weaken.

He said desperately, 'For God's sake, Lucy!'

She told him flatly, 'It's no good, Nick.'

'You don't know what I'm going to say.' He was not smiling now.

Lucy shook her head. 'I don't need to. I know what you want.' What she herself had wanted for a long time, but she dared not tell him that. This parting would be difficult enough. 'I gave my vows for better or worse, without reservation. I'm married and I can't change that.'

Nick said quietly, 'He's an evil man, Lucy.'

'I know that as well as you do,' she said bitterly, and thought, More so.

Nick said, 'You could divorce him. If it's a question of money—'

'No!' Lucy cut him off. 'I won't do it. I married for better or worse.'

Nick had expected that. He sighed, then went on, 'I haven't got long. I have to join a ship lying in the Tyne and she's under sailing orders. I can't say now all that I have to say, but I'll write—'

'No!' Lucy's cold calm was deserting her again. She had been right to hold this meeting in the open, to keep him at a distance. It would be so easy to give in. 'Don't write letters. I won't read them. I'll send them back. Letters will only make it harder for me. I'm going to try to forget you, Nick, because there's no future for us together.' The phrases came glibly, with no need to hunt for words, because she had reached her decision in the night and rehearsed it before she slept at last. Nick heard her decision, and saw her determination. 'Please Nick, if you love me, leave me alone.'

He cast one last look at his watch. There was just time because he was almost done. There was another function in the equation that he had ignored up to now, but it had to be faced: he might not return. There was no point in raising that now, but it had to be borne in mind. He could not, in all fairness, bind this girl to him, but when – if – he did return . . .

'Very well,' he agreed quietly. 'The last thing I want is for you to be hurt. I won't write, but I won't give you up, either. One day I'll come for you.' He retreated a pace, lifted his cap in salute and turned away.

'Goodbye, Nick.' Lucy found the words hard to say.

Nick paused and turned his head to say, 'Just till we meet

again,' then he clapped his cap on his head and marched out of the hotel.

That was the worst, but only the first of many partings for Lucy's family. Two days later, the country was at war.

Lucy returned home that evening and as she climbed the stairs, she heard the sleepy voice of Violet. As she entered the kitchen and saw Daisy seated by the fire, she asked, 'It's late to have Violet out. Is something wrong?' Daisy's face crumpled, and Lucy ran to kneel at her side, put an arm around her. Violet, sitting on Daisy's knee, looked up worriedly. Lucy asked, 'What's wrong?' She looked round for Tommy but saw only Elsie sitting opposite with Stephen at her side.

Daisy choked out, 'He's joined up.'

'Tommy?'

Daisy nodded. 'He's signed on in the Navy for the duration.'

'Oh, Daisy! Where is he?' Lucy pushed a handkerchief into Daisy's grasp.

'Gone with Billy.' Daisy dabbed at her eyes.

'Billy! Where—'

Elsie put in, 'They've gone to see their father. Billy's signed on with Tommy and he wants Dad's permission to marry before he goes.'

Lucy thought, Oh, dear God! Both of them in the Navy. Billy wanting to be married and Tommy with a child of two years. Billy was only just nineteen.

Elsie said soothingly, 'Don't worry, Daisy. I expect he'll be all right. It'll probably be all over by Christmas.'

Daisy wailed, 'How do you know he'll be all right? He could be dead by Christmas! It's all right for you because your feller's not going!'

Elsie flinched and reached out to grip Stephen's hand. He stayed silent, his gaze cast down, but Elsie defended him, 'He can't! It's against his religious beliefs, that's why. Don't try to shift blame on to him. It's not his fault if Tommy joins up.'

'Ssh!' Lucy held up a hand. 'You're frightening the bairn.' Violet sensed the sudden, crackling tension and her mouth was quivering. Lucy told Daisy, 'Don't upset yourself.'

'It's easy for you, as well,' Daisy charged. 'You haven't got anybody going, either.'

'Yes, I have.' Nick had already gone, and might be killed. Lucy had thought of that already, felt sick as she thought of it now. The others stared at her questioningly. 'Yes, I have. Tommy and Billy.' And a gentle reminder, softened by a smile and a hug, 'I was caring about them and for them a long time before you came along, Daisy love.'

'I know, I'm sorry.' Daisy clung to her. 'You've been like a mother to me an' all, like you were to them. I'm sorry, Elsie. Sorry, Stephen. It was a daft thing to say, but I'm that worried about Tommy.'

'Never mind, Daisy, I know you must feel badly about Tommy.' Stephen looked up now. 'You're not the first, anyway.'

Lucy asked, 'What do you mean?'

He shrugged. 'People say, "When are you going to join up?" I say I'm not going to, and they ask, "Aren't you fit?" and look sorry for me. Then I tell them, "I'm fit, but it's against my principles." Then they call me names.'

Lucy said, 'Oh, Stephen.' She saw Elsie nodding, tears in her eyes, angry. Lucy had known that Stephen was more religious than the rest of them. It sat easily on him. He was a regular chapel-goer but he did not preach, least of all to the family. He was good company, always ready to tell a joke or laugh at one. She had never considered how his religious beliefs might affect his life, least of all like this.

Now he explained, 'I'm not going to take up arms against anyone. I think it's wrong. The commandment says, "Thou shalt not kill", and I follow it.' There was a quiet determination in his words.

Lucy remembered another commandment, 'Thou shalt not

commit adultery'. She had sent Nick Buchanan away rather than break that. She and Stephen had something in common.

When Tommy and Billy returned she met them downstairs at the front door. They were excited and laughing as they sauntered along the street, but sobered when they saw her awaiting them.

Lucy asked, 'Well?'

Billy answered, 'No bother. We found our dad in the pub. He'd had a few—'

Tommy put in disgustedly, 'A few over the eight. He was well away. We told him we'd signed on for the Navy and Billy wanted to get married before he went off to sea. When he heard that, he started slobbering over us and shouting about his two lads joining up.' Tommy grimaced. 'Bloody hypocrite.'

'Anyway,' said Billy, 'it's fixed. I didn't have to pay him or punch him. He'll give his permission, and me and Flo are getting married before the Navy sends for me.'

Lucy warned him, 'She'll be as upset about you going as Daisy is about Tommy. She's been crying, Tommy, breaking her heart. You'd better get upstairs and comfort her and the bairn.' Then as she turned to lead the way she issued another warning to both of them: 'I'll not have you making remarks about Stephen, either.'

Tommy asked, 'What sort of remarks?'

'Criticising him because he's not joined up. I won't have it.'

Billy asked, 'Why hasn't he?'

'It's his duty, isn't it?' said Tommy.

Lucy stopped and faced them. 'Is that how you see it, the pair of you?'

Billy said, 'Aye. It's like my duty to my country.'

Lucy nodded. 'Well, Stephen sees it as his duty to God not to shoot anyone. So leave him alone.'

They followed her up the stairs, pondering that, and Billy said sheepishly, 'I can't see me shooting anybody, anyway.'

Lucy could not imagine either of her brothers doing that.

It seemed George Fenwick would, however. He came into the

house a week later with a weeping Rose and announced stolidly, 'I've volunteered for the artillery.'

The next few weeks were busy ones for Lucy. All the younger men working at the Railway Hotel had joined up, and one by one they left. The porter, a reservist in the Northumberland Fusiliers, was the first to go, recalled to the colours. This meant that their work had to be done by the remaining members of the staff until they could be replaced. So Lucy had her share — and more — of extra work.

Then there was Billy's wedding to arrange, and a lot of that fell on Lucy's shoulders. Florence's only relative was an elderly uncle living in Dorset. His wife wrote sending their good wishes and a wedding present of a hand-embroidered tablecloth — a lovely thing they all exclaimed over — but said he was too unwell to travel.

The ceremony was a simple one, held on a Saturday morning at the Registry Office, but there was a reception afterwards. Lucy, Elsie and the other girls prepared that, laying out the spread on the sideboard and the kitchen table. It was a subdued but some-times shrill affair. George Fenwick was not there, already called to his regimental depot at Woolwich, and Billy and Tommy were leaving on Monday morning, headed for the naval barracks at Portsmouth.

It was into the evening when a number of neighbours looked in to wish the happy couple well. One of them, a walrus-mous-tached man in his fifties, buttonholed Stephen, slapped him on the back and asked with drunken joviality, 'When are you off, then? Show that bloody Kaiser Bill a thing or two, eh?'

The room was crowded, but Lucy heard the remark, and moved quickly with Elsie to intervene. They both stopped when Stephen answered politely, 'I'm not sure yet. They said they'd probably have a travel warrant when I report again on Thursday.'

Elsie's eyes were big with shock, and Lucy was quick to reach her side.

The neighbour said, 'Are you goin' in the navy an' all?'

'No,' replied Stephen, 'the Medical Corps.'

'Ah!' Then vaguely, 'You're doin' your bit, anyway.'

He lurched away and Elsie took his place before Stephen. 'You didn't tell me.'

He smiled at her apologetically. 'I didn't want to spoil the party for you. I was going to tell you later.'

'Why?' Elsie pleaded, and now fear crept into her voice. '*Why?* I thought, Thank God, he won't be blown up or drowned. He'll be staying here with me, not leaving me here to worry. You said you wouldn't go against your beliefs! And now—'

Stephen pulled her to him, held her as sobs racked her body. He stroked her hair and looked over her shoulder at Lucy. She saw his pain as he said, 'I didn't want to hurt her.' And then to Elsie, 'I've not gone against my beliefs. Men are going to get hurt and they'll need looking after. That's something I can do. I see that as a Christian duty.' He put a hand under her chin and lifted it so she looked into his eyes. He joked, trying to reassure her, 'I'll probably spend all my time fetching bedpans and come to no more harm than getting flat feet from running up and down the wards.'

Elsie sniffed and asked hopefully, 'You won't be in the front line, then?'

'Not me! Tending to wounded? What do I know about that? I'll be in some hospital doing the sort of job any chap could do.'

Elsie fumbled for a handkerchief. 'And you were going to tell me later? Not leave it till the last minute?'

'There were a couple o' things I wanted to talk about after this.' He waved his hand at the party crowded into the kitchen. 'That was one of them.' He saw Lucy relax then start to move away and he reached out a hand to stay her. 'I might as well ask your consent while you are here, Lucy,' and to Elsie, 'The other thing is: I've got a ring in my pocket.'

Lucy went to the station with Billy and Tommy, Florence and Daisy. She held little Violet while the girls embraced their men and bade them tearful farewells. The train was packed with men in civilian clothes on their way to serve in one or other of the armed forces. People sang 'Goodbye, Dolly Gray', and scarves, handkerchiefs and flags were waved as the train pulled out. Elsie was there, too, in tears like the other girls and the women lining the platform. Lucy wept to see her children going from her. She had already gone through the ordeal with George and Rose.

A week later they did it again as Elsie, married at short notice by Common Licence, watched the train take Stephen away on the long journey to Aldershot. It was now that Lucy thought of that year as the mating time. She reflected sadly that at the start of it she had believed Billy and Elsie would not marry for years. She had not foreseen the war that had propelled them into marriage – like so many others.

By the end of September they had all gone: Tommy, Billy, Stephen, George – and Nick.

Nick stood on the bridge of the *Ada Barr*, an armed merchant cruiser, a former tramp now armed with two six-inch guns and steaming south across the Bay of Biscay, bound for the Mediterranean. He balanced easily, legs set apart and acting like springs as the ship rolled and pitched under him. His binoculars hung from their strap around his neck and rested against his chest. He wore his blue reefer jacket over a thick, white jersey. This was his ship to command: she was not big and therefore only warranted a lieutenant to command her. She was a new ship to Nick and to her crew. This was their first, 'shakedown' cruise together. He knew he had a lot to learn about his crew, as they had to learn about him, but believed they would not let each other down.

His ship and his men filled most of his waking thoughts, but in the quiet of a nightwatch, or lying in his bunk and staring up at the rusty deckhead, he could see again the slender, dark-haired girl. She was there then gone, lost then seen again through the gaps between the dancers. It was a memory he would carry with him for ever, because that was when the world had changed for him. And he had given her away! He had stood in church, smiling fondly, and handed her over to a monster. The thought tormented him.

Chapter Seventeen

'There's a Mr Buchanan downstairs wants to see you, Mrs Nolan.' The page in his brass-buttoned uniform had sought out Lucy on the third floor of the Railway Hotel. She was making a swift inspection of the rooms there to see they were all as they should be. She put a hand to her head. The last time this boy had brought such a message she had found Nick waiting for her, but now he went on, 'He's an old feller. Would he be the one that owns the shipyard?'

Who else? Lucy let out her breath. 'I expect so. I'll come.' As she descended the stairs, running light-footed, she smiled to herself. 'Old feller' indeed! She would like to see Andrew Buchanan's face if he heard that! He was getting on, of course, would be into his sixties by now, but old?

Lucy checked in her stride halfway down the last flight of stairs. It was Christmas Eve, the foyer was garlanded and there was a tree in its centre. However, Lucy could see past this and over the heads of the people passing, to where Andrew Buchanan stood by the reception desk. He was stooped and leaned heavily on a walking-stick. The last time Lucy had seen him, admittedly six months ago, was before she left Poona House. He was then hale and hearty, striding out vigorously and straight in the back. Not now. He looked his sixty-odd years and more, a frail old man. She was shocked at the change in him.

She went on more slowly now and crossed the foyer reluctantly, already sensing that only calamity could have brought about this sudden ageing. 'Good morning, Mr Buchanan. You asked to see me.'

He summoned up a smile at sight of her but his voice quavered. 'Ah! Lucy. You're looking very well, very pretty.'

'Thank you. Can I be of help, sir?'

Andrew peered about him vaguely. 'I hope so. Do you think we could sit down and talk?'

'Of course, sir.' Lucy pointed to two armchairs at an occasional table set in an alcove. Andrew gestured to her to lead the way and followed, shuffling, his walking-stick tapping on the parquet then thumping dully on the carpeted floor.

When they were settled in the chairs, Andrew slumped, Lucy primly upright, he said, 'I have some bad news. You heard about the shelling, of course.'

'Oh, yes.' Only a few days before two German cruisers had appeared off the coast and hurled huge shells into Hartlepool, Whitby and Scarborough. The newspapers had been enraged, demanding, 'Where is the Navy?'

Andrew's head was shaking as he went on, 'Nell was there. In Scarborough. She was visiting some friends, was supposed to come home that day. I was expecting her and instead—' Lucy saw the tears in his eyes. He fumbled a white handkerchief from his sleeve and wiped his eyes. 'They said she wouldn't have known anything about it, felt no pain. It was instantaneous.'

Lucy whispered, 'I'm so sorry.'

After a time, Andrew lowered the handkerchief and looked at Lucy out of sad eyes, but he had regained his composure and now came to the purpose of his visit. He had reasoned his way to it through his grief. He had sought a housekeeper before, not so long ago – for his sister Adelaide – and found a good one. Adelaide had given this Nolan girl a glowing testimonial. And he had known Lucy from childhood, had grown to know her more over the years – not as well as had Nell because servants were not his business – but enough. Nell had always had a lot of respect for Lucy and they had met almost every day for four years when Lucy worked at the Buchanan house. Finally, he had come to respect her, both as an employee and as a person.

He could advertise for someone to fill the post and might find a woman even more efficient, though he doubted it, and with more references. But she would be a stranger. He did not want a stranger.

That had been his train of thought. Now he tried to explain: 'I have no family. Oh, there's a distant relative, two or three times removed, in Argentina. I've never seen him. There's no one else, except Adelaide and she's in India and wouldn't like to leave again. I've lived a private life for over twenty years. I had Nell and my work and wanted for nothing more. But now . . . There have been so many changes at the house. Devereaux went into the Army. He needn't have done because he's well over forty but he would go. A lot of the people you knew, that *she* knew, have left.' Lucy recalled Jinny Unwin leaving years ago. Andrew was going on, 'You are one of the few people left who spent some time with her and she always spoke highly of you. So will you come to the funeral?'

'Yes, I'll come.' Lucy did not hesitate.

Andrew had not finished. 'And afterwards – you would need to give notice, of course – will you come to the house and take her place? I mean as housekeeper, not—' He was becoming confused in his embarrassment, stopped and looked at Lucy, appealed for understanding: 'Not like a wife. Nell was that to me. Always. I know how people talked, but . . . You see, my real wife ran off with another man a long time ago, left me with Murdoch as a baby, left him motherless. And then I learned that man was not the first by a long chalk. He was just the latest in a long line. And I'd loved her. So I swore I would never marry again and I kept that promise.'

Lucy listened patiently, sympathetically, to his stumbling

explanation. She realised he was talking like this to her, a former servant, because he was desolate from the loss of Nell Jarman. He was reaching out in his loneliness to someone he remembered from happier times, who would themselves recall those times and understand. He stared bleakly out into the foyer at the shifting pattern of staff and guests, hurrying or strolling, then he said quietly, 'Now I know I was wrong. I think I did it because I was afraid if I married again, that would happen again and I would lose Nell. It was cowardice of a sort. It hurt her, I'm sure, though she never complained and I think she understood. Now it's too late to put that right – ever.'

Lucy could find no way of consoling him, knew she could never free him from that guilt, but she said softly, 'I'll be your housekeeper, Mr Buchanan.' She did not hesitate. 'I'll hand in my notice today and join you when I've worked it.'

'Thank you.' Andrew levered himself up on the walking-stick. 'You're very kind.'

Lucy walked with him as far as the swing doors and watched him shuffle away with his grief, his chauffeur helping him up into the Rolls.

Lucy attended the funeral, as did Fred Wilson and the rest of the staff at the Buchanan house. Even Devereaux was there; the Army had granted him seventy-two hours compassionate leave, but it was Lucy who stood by Andrew's side, at his request, her arm he leaned on, she who helped him away from the graveside. Chrissie Carter had granted her some time off, not only for the funeral but to help with the arrangements. It was due to Lucy that the ceremony was carried out with dignity and without a hitch or any jarring note. As Andrew had said, there was no family, and Helen Whittaker had taken her two aunts to the South Coast a week before and would not return until the New Year. However, she caught sight of significant glances between some of the ladies of local society, and guessed the message they exchanged: 'So this is

Andrew's new bit of stuff. He did not wait long.' Lucy had expected it from the moment he had asked her to be his house-keeper. She had known they would talk about her as they had gossiped about Nell Jarman. And as she had thought of Jinny Unwin.

It hurt, as she guessed Nell Jarman had been hurt, but that did not deter her. They could think what they liked, but she saw her duty clearly. Andrew needed her. Not to share his bed, she would never have gone to him for that, but because he was old, lonely and had to be looked after. She would always be in his debt for past kindnesses, help when she needed it. That help had cost him little or nothing, but had been important to her.

Did she take the post because of the house? She had to admit that the house attracted her, and she was finally achieving her ambition to be housekeeper at the Buchanan house. However, even that was only a bonus, not the main cause. Because Andrew was Nick's uncle and Nick would want him cared for? Lucy thrust that reason aside.

At the end of January 1915, when Lucy left the Railway Hotel to take up her duties at the Buchanan house Andrew, sent the Rolls to fetch her. Her belongings were packed in the big chest she had from her mother when she first went into service at the Buchanan house. Chesterton, the chauffeur, loaded it into the Rolls and Lucy sat in the leather-cushioned rear. It was an open car and she tied a scarf around her head to hold her hat and hair in place. As Chesterton swung the big car in at the gates of the house Lucy called, 'Can we stop here a moment, please, Mr Chesterton?'

'Right y'are, Lucy.' He braked the Rolls and waited.

Lucy leaned over the door of the car to see past him to the house. It spread its red-brick arms warm and wide to welcome her. She had left it six long years ago. The pale winter sun reflected from its windows, almost blinding her, and made her eyes water. She touched Chesterton on the shoulder. 'Thank you.' He steered the Rolls to head up the gravelled drive, and

Lucy called, 'No! Round to the servants' hall, please!'

'Mr Buchanan's orders. He said to bring you up to the front door.'

So Lucy walked up the wide steps she had washed so often, to enter by the front door. Andrew was waiting in the hall to greet her. 'Chesterton will take your things up to your room.' He explained, 'Both the footmen have gone off to the war, and he's off shortly, but I have his promise he will teach you how to drive the Rolls before he goes.'

'Me?' Lucy stared at him open mouthed. Women, particularly young women, were learning to drive now, but they were always the wives or daughters of the wealthy. However, Andrew pointed out reasonably, 'Someone will have to drive it so we can get about, and I'm too old to learn.'

So Lucy, in addition to running the house with a much depleted staff, also learned to take on the chauffeur's job.

There were several empty servants' rooms because of staff leaving, men to go into the Army, girls to take work in the factories springing up everywhere to feed the war machine. Lucy took one of those rooms, not Nell Jarman's. This she quietly changed, later, to just another spare bedroom and Andrew agreed, heavily: 'It's best not to dwell on these sadnesses.'

Lucy was not the only one to learn to drive. Early in the New Year the Whittakers' gleaming black Humber rolled up the drive with Helen at the wheel. Lucy saw the car from the drawing-room window as she was about to draw the heavy curtains against the early dusk. Helen handled the car well, and the young man at her side was not the Whittaker chauffeur but a stranger.

Lucy opened the door to them and Helen said cheerfully, stripping off her gloves, 'This is Will Ogilvie. He's just learned to fly, but my driving terrifies him.' Will was tall, with toffee-coloured curly hair and a reckless grin, and Lucy warmed to him. He wore the 'maternity jacket' of the Royal Flying Corps.

Lucy showed them into the drawing room, where Andrew sat by the fire with *The Times*, reading the war news. He rose to greet them, tossing the paper aside and stretching out his hand, smiling. In the weeks since Lucy had come to the house, his condition had hugely improved. Physically he was still aged and frail, nothing could reverse that now, but he had recovered from the worst of his grief, though sometimes he still sat and stared blankly into space. Mentally he was alert and decisive again, almost his old self, and he had taken to going to the yard again to work there through the mornings.

All this was due to Lucy's nurturing him. She had sat with him and listened as he poured out his grief, cheered him when he was lonely, talked to him when he could not concentrate on reading, persuaded him to leave the fireside and go walking around the grounds with his arm through hers for support. He had admitted to her only a week before, 'You've brought me to life again. Thank you, Lucy.'

His doctor, Fairfax, a contemporary of his, called weekly. On his last visit he had told Andrew genially, 'You're in fine fettle these days, old boy.' He took Lucy aside and told her, 'You've done wonders for him. He's much more alive and cheerful. But we have to watch him. He has a very weak heart.'

Now Lucy went off to fetch tea. Mrs Yates, the cook, was still in office, for which Lucy had already given thanks. She made the tea but Lucy served it. There was now only one maid; the others had joined the women's services or gone into war work.

As Lucy entered with the tray, Will Ogilvie was saying, 'So when the machine stalls like that we say we've got the wind up.'

Andrew was nodding, smiling. 'And what is this uniform you're wearing, young lady?'

Helen wore a tunic with patch pockets and an ankle-length skirt. She laughed, looked down at herself and smoothed the skirt. 'I'm a VAD now, that's Voluntary Aid Detachment. I'm just wearing the uniform for swank at the moment, because I haven't done anything. They said they'd have a job for me somewhere after Christmas and I'm expecting to hear any day now. We have to help in hospitals, sweeping and cleaning and things like that.'

Andrew stared. 'Good Lord! A young lady like you doing that sort of work? You can't!'

'Well, I'll have to. I've taken it on now.' Helen was both defiant and unsure. She went on, smiling, 'Actually, I think it will be a bit of an adventure. And we've all got to help, do our bit. Talking of doing our bit . . .' She fumbled in the patch pocket of her tunic and took out a letter in its envelope. 'I've had another letter from Nick.' She glanced at Will. 'I told you about Nick, didn't I?' He nodded placidly. Helen went on, unfolding the letter, 'He doesn't say where he is – not supposed to, you know – but I reckon he's in the Mediterranean. He says his ship is fine and he's pleased with his crew. But here you are.' She passed the letter to Andrew to read.

Lucy, having set out the tea things, made her exit. So Nick had written to Helen, and more than once. That was under-standable, since they were friends and Lucy had sent him away, told him not to write and that there could be nothing between them.

A week later she drove into Sunderland in the Rolls, taking Andrew to Buchanan's yard where the old man planned to work until noon. Lucy shopped busily through the morning then returned to the yard to meet him. He climbed into the rear, and as Lucy tucked the rug around his legs Andrew said, 'I'd rather like to lunch at the Palace today. Let's go there.' So Lucy drove to the Palace Hotel and as Andrew got down from the car he said, 'Come on, then, let's have lunch.'

Lucy demurred. 'It's not my place to go in there, sir.'

Andrew chuckled, 'Nonsense! You've eaten with me every day for weeks.' That was true. He had requested it, and she had acceded, because he did not want to eat alone, staring at the empty chair where Nell Jarman used to sit. On that first occasion Lucy had felt uneasy and out of place, sitting at one end of the table with Andrew at the other and being served by the maid. But she knew very well how to comport herself, had watched the 'gentry' when she had been a maid there herself, and at the Palace Hotel.

She had learned even more from Adelaide. So Lucy soon relaxed and, after a time, became used to the situation. But now . . .

'That was in the house, sir, and this is in a public place.' Lucy knew they would be seen and there would be gossip, she had no doubt of that – 'There's Andrew Buchanan lunching with his new housekeeper'.

Andrew nodded. 'I know there's a difference. But Adelaide told me you were as much a lady as any of her pupils, and I've found that to be true. If I employed some gentleman's daughter as my housekeeper, I could take her to lunch at the Palace. I don't see why I shouldn't take yourself. And it would please me.'

Lucy gave in for his sake and walked into the restaurant where once she had served. She had been there as a customer only once before, with Nick Buchanan, another reason why she had not wanted to lunch there. The memory came back to her painfully clear, as she had known it would, and as she took her seat she pictured Nick smiling at her across the table. The moment passed, and Lucy managed to thrust the memory behind her. She listened attentively to Andrew and answered appropriately, even joked to make him laugh.

At the end of the meal, as they left the restaurant to go back to the Rolls and then to his club, Andrew said, 'I enjoyed that.' He was silent for a second or two as he shuffled across the foyer, but as he came to the swing doors he said, 'I've never heard from Murdoch, you know. Not a word. I don't know where he is nor what he's doing.'

Lucy tried to reassure him. 'I'm sure he will be safe and well. No news is good news.' Bad news came in buff envelopes, brought by the telegraph boys. They were always busy, racing on their bicycles, after a disaster at sea or an action fought in Flanders.

Andrew said no more at the time, except to smile at her and say, 'You always cheer me.'

Lucy spent the afternoon in Monkwearmouth. She left the Rolls parked in the town, because its huge opulence would be incongruous and would attract attention in the streets of terraced houses down by the river. She did not want her old neighbours to see her getting down from it. Instead she walked across the bridge where trams rattled and clanged and a train chuffed over the railway bridge that ran alongside, trailing its plume of smoke, which joined with the pall hanging over the shipyards. The smoke rose up from them, a visible sign of activity, to match the din from hammering. All the yards were working at full blast now that several ships were being sunk daily and replacements were demanded.

Lucy tapped on the kitchen door. 'Come in!' called Daisy. She rose from sweeping the dust from the coal fire out of the hearth and smiled at Lucy as she entered. Violet sat before the fire on a mat made from rag clippings. She crowed in delight as Daisy said, 'Here's Auntie Lucy. I'll put the kettle on for a cup of tea.'

With Tommy and Billy gone into the Navy and Rose with her own place, only Lucy and Elsie were left. When Lucy moved into the Buchanan house, Elsie moved in with Daisy – while Florence joined Rose – for company and to share expenses. They all congregated in Daisy's kitchen when work was over for the day. There was a determination to be cheerful, bolstered by relief that they all had recent evidence, in the form of letters, that their men were safe. Underlying that, however, was the fear that one day there might be a buff envelope.

Rose had more cause for celebration than the others, having won a promotion. 'More like an extra burden,' she joked wrily. 'So many of the chaps have gone into the Army, and us girls are being given their jobs to do.'

Elsie was quieter than the others and stared into the fire, only now and then shooting unhappy glances at Lucy. Lucy finally asked, 'Is something the matter, Elsie?'

Elsie sniffed. 'I got in a row over you today.'

'Me?' Lucy blinked at her, bewildered. 'Why?'

'Why d'you think? Because one o' the waitresses came back after this afternoon and had a dig at me!' Elsie mimicked, voice rising in a ridiculous falsetto, '"I've just been talking to my friend that works waiting on at the Palace. She said she saw your sister eating out wi' that old Mr Buchanan."' Elsie glared. 'I said, "What about it? She's his housekeeper." So she laughed and said, "More like an old man's darling." I hit her over the head wi' my ladle and that took the grin off her face!'

'Ooh! Elsie!' Daisy was round eyed. 'You didn't!'

'I did.' Elsie said it with satisfaction, but it was short lived. She muttered, 'It's embarrassing when people make remarks like that.'

Rose agreed unhappily. 'I didn't want to say, but I've heard talk from customers. These women waiting to be served and gossiping among themselves as if we didn't have ears. All going on about this Mrs Nolan that's got the job of housekeeper with old Mr Buchanan.' She put on a plummy voice: '"We all know what that means, don't we?" They haven't said anything to me, because they don't connect Mrs Fenwick with Mrs Nolan. I just hope they don't.'

Lucy looked from one to the other, her face burning, and asked, 'What do *you* think?'

They exchanged glances and Rose replied, 'What can we think? It's how it looks, you taking that Mrs Jarman's place.'

'That's not *true*,' Lucy burst out. 'It's not like that! He loved her and wished he'd married her. To him I'm just his housekeeper, and I look after him because we owe him a lot and he's a lonely old man. That's *all*! I'm doing what I think is right, and I'm not going to stop because of tattling old women!' That silenced her sisters. She looked round at all of them. 'I'm a married woman.' She paused. No, she would not bewail the tragedy of her marriage, would not fish for sympathy that way. 'Married! So do you know what you are accusing me of? Adultery! Do you think I could be guilty of that?' Her voice weakened then, because she knew she had once gone perilously close.

They heard that tremor and thought it signified pain. Elsie was quick to kneel at her side and tell her, 'No, I don't believe it.'

Rose joined in from the other side, 'I'll tell them so if they start on me.'

Lucy was trying hard not to cry, was determined not to. She wanted to be out of this, away from the eyes all round her and watching her every expression.

Her prayer for deliverance was answered. In their absorption they had not heard the tread in the passage, but now there came a tapping at the door. Florence was nearest and bounced out of her chair to open it. She squealed, 'Eeh! Look who's here!' and swung the door wide. Turning, they saw Stephen standing in the doorway.

Elsie flew into his arms and a laughing Rose dragged the pair of them in. Florence snatched off Stephen's cap and Daisy pushed him into the best armchair, previously used by the absent Tommy. He looked taller and heavier because of the uniform and the thick-soled, heavy ammunition boots. The khaki serge was rough and ill fitting but he looked well, had lost the bank clerk's pallor, and was fresh faced from exercise in the open air.

Lucy looked on, still shaken, as they questioned him. He replied, smiling, 'They've kept us busy, taught us an awful lot. Our instructor says the Army usually takes a year to drum into recruits all they've crammed into us.'

Elsie asked the inevitable question: 'How much leave have you got?'

'Two weeks.'

She clapped her hands delightedly. 'That's marvellous!'

Rose said with a tinge of jealousy, 'You're lucky to get leave so early. George can't get any and says there's no sign of it.'

Stephen said, concerned, 'I'm sorry. I hope—' He stopped and amended, 'Maybe you'll hear some good news from him soon.'

Lucy had noticed that change and guessed at the reason for it. When Andrew Buchanan read his copy of *The Times*, he discussed the war news with her. His service in the Navy and a continuing interest had given him an insight into service administration and Lucy had picked up some pearls of wisdom from him. She had wanted to use Stephen's arrival as an excuse to escape, had intended to say she had to meet Andrew from his club, though in truth she was not due to do so for another hour, but now she decided to stay because Elsie would be in need of comfort when she learned the reason why Stephen had been given two weeks leave so soon, why he had not hoped for the same for George. Stephen was on embarkation leave before going to Flanders on active service.

So it proved. When Elsie learned the truth she kissed Stephen and gripped his hand, but wept on her knees with her head in Lucy's lap.

Chapter Eighteen

MARCH 1915

'I have to go to the Admiralty in London. They want to talk to me about those destroyers we're to build.' Andrew Buchanan looked up from the letter he was reading to address Lucy across the breakfast table. He was going through his mail after his usual quick scan of the envelopes to see if there was a letter from Murdoch. Lucy had watched him and heard the small sigh as his search proved fruitless.

'When will you go? I'll get your ticket. If you'll let me know what clothes you will need, I'll pack your case.'

Andrew murmured, thinking, 'I have to go on Monday.' That was two days hence. He consulted the letter again. 'It looks as though I'll be there for the week. I'll want lounge suit and evening suit.'

'I'll see to it.'

Andrew set the letter aside with a smile. 'Bless you.'

Lucy drove him into town and down to Buchanan's yard on the river and left the Rolls there. She reminded him tactfully, 'I'll be back at twelve if that's all right, sir.'

'Of course, Lucy. I'll manage from here perfectly well.' Andrew tottered away to his office, leaning on his stick. As always, the sight of the busy yard and the ship growing on the stocks, put a little fresh life in him.

Lucy walked from the yard to the ranked streets close by where many of the workers lived – and her family. She knew the others would be at work, but she would probably find Daisy at home with little Violet.

She walked along the passage and found the kitchen door unlocked. She pushed it open and George Fenwick said, 'Hello! Here's Lucy.'

She checked in the doorway, startled, then the cold hand that had gripped her when Stephen went away seized on her heart again. Daisy was looking anxious, Violet on her knee. Rose was not at work, but sitting in the armchair, George perched on the arm with a big hand on her shoulder. His khaki fitted his broad, solid body better than had Stephen's. He wore the lanyard on his shoulder of the artilleryman. George was smiling, but Rose stared into the fire with red eyes. Lucy knew George was going overseas.

Rose confirmed it, voice husky from crying. 'I came round to Daisy's for a bit o' company. I've taken the day off. He's got two weeks' embarkation leave.'

Lucy passed the morning in an atmosphere of nervous tension. Rose was alternately artificially bright or verging on breaking into tears.

Lucy found it hard to present a cheerful face as she drove Andrew back to the Buchanan house in the middle of the day.

The house was now without a maid and Mrs Yates was complaining loudly. In the early afternoon Lucy interviewed three girls who had just left school and were looking for positions. She dismissed two as only seeking a stop gap until they found a job in the town. The third was the daughter of a farmer, and Lucy thought she might stay so took her on in desperation. Then she spent the rest of the afternoon in a frenzy of housework – the Buchanan house was an enormous task for one woman to keep clean. Lucy worked hard because she was proud of it, but she knew she would have to admit defeat and tell Andrew. The house could not be run without staff, and because of the war, staff were unobtainable. She was determined to solve the problem somehow, though.

It was early evening when the Whittakers' Humber drifted to a halt in the drive with a crunching of gravel and Lucy opened the front door to let in Helen in her VAD uniform. She had whipped off the grubby apron worn when cleaning, but the polish and cloth she had used in the hall still lay, only half-hidden, behind the umbrella stand.

Helen saw this and laughed. 'Hello, Lucy.' She nodded at the polish. 'I know something about that now. And scrubbing. *And* changing soiled sheets.' She grimaced. 'Plus a lot more.' The grimace became a smile. 'It's a bit of a lark, though. I feel I'm being some use and I'm moving up. They're going to let me train as a *nurse!* I don't start until Tuesday, so I decided to dash over here for a visit. Is Mr Buchanan in?'

'He's working in his study, miss.' Lucy announced her then went to fetch tea.

When she took it into the study, Helen was saying, 'And here's another one. He writes about once a month, roughly. It depends on how busy he is, I suppose.' She was handing a letter to Andrew, and several more already lay open on the table before him.

Andrew chuckled as he took the one she held out to him. 'He dashes off a letter to me about once a month, too. That's extraordinary for Nick. He was never one for writing letters. I just wish —' He stopped and shook his head, the smile gone.

Helen prompted, 'Yes?'

'Nothing,' Andrew replied. 'Now, what does he say here?' And he lifted the letter.

Lucy knew Andrew had been about to say that he wished he had a letter from his son, Murdoch. He glanced up at her. 'Will you serve, Lucy, please.'

As Lucy poured and distributed cups, Helen said, 'And this

one – no! That's from Will Ogilvie. You remember Will? He was here a while back. He's in the Flying Corps, in France.' She did not pass that letter to Andrew.

Andrew murmured, reading, 'I'm glad you came today. I'm off to London on Monday.'

'You are?' Helen laughed. 'So am I! I have my ticket. Shall we travel together?'

So on Monday Lucy drove first to the Whittaker house, where Helen joined Andrew in the back of the Rolls. As it pulled away Helen's elderly maiden aunts, Teddie and Binkie, waved and cried, 'Goodbye! Good luck!' the tears running down their faces.

Helen said chokingly, 'The poor dears. They're so upset,' but she recovered her spirits on the drive, looking forward to the adventure awaiting her.

Lucy took them to the central station in Sunderland and waved from the platform as the train pulled away. Her last glimpse of them was of Helen leaning out of the window, laughing and excited.

Lucy returned to the Buchanan house and an interview with Mrs Yates. The cook said, 'Begging your pardon, Mrs Nolan, but I'm due some time off, as you well know.'

Lucy did, because Mrs Yates repeatedly reminded her. 'Yes?'

'Well, with Mr Buchanan away I thought I'd go and have a few days' rest at my brother's place. Him and his wife live at Byker. I don't get on that well with her, but I can put up with her for that long and it'll be a change from this kitchen. I tell you straight, I just can't cope with this place no more. Trying to run the kitchen wi' no help and me turned sixty, nearly sixty-five. So I don't want to complain . . .' However, she did, again and again.

Lucy listened patiently to it all once more, then agreed, 'I think it will be convenient for you to go for a few days. I hope you enjoy yourself.'

The next morning Mrs Yates went off to her brother and Lucy was left alone in the house. The new girl was not due to start until the following Monday, so Lucy told herself determinedly that this would be an opportunity to catch up with some of the work of the house. She laboured through the rest of the day and most of the next, only finally calling a halt in the early afternoon.

Lucy luxuriated in a hot bath and put on the good dress she had bought new for Rose's wedding. She had worn it when she danced with Nick – but she tried to put that out of her mind.

She was descending the stairs when the front doorbell rang. She went to answer it, wondering who it might be, and saw through the side window a khaki-clad back. A soldier, then. She opened the door as a cab wheeled away down the drive behind a trotting horse. The khaki was not the rough serge worn by George and Stephen, but the fine barathea of an officer's service dress, crossed by a gleaming Sam Browne belt. Its wearer turned around and Murdoch Buchanan grinned at her. 'Well, well, *well!* And what are you doing here?'

Lucy realised she was staring at him, disbelievingly. She tried to recover her poise and replied, 'I am Mr Buchanan's house-keeper, sir.' She automatically held the door open for him.

Murdoch snapped thick fingers. 'Of course. I heard about Mrs Jarman.' He stepped into the hall, dropped the valise he had carried in one hand, and tossed his cap on to the hall stand. His face was fleshier but still darkly handsome, tanned from an outdoor life. On his sleeve were the three stars of a captain. He looked Lucy up and down. She felt the blood rising from her neck to flood her face, cursed it but could not prevent it. Murdoch grinned. 'You were a fetching little filly and you've grown into a handsome woman.' He glanced past her and asked, 'Where is he? Down at the yard?'

Lucy answered, 'Mr Buchanan is away in London for the week.'

'Good,' Murdoch said with satisfaction. 'I'm only staying through tomorrow and going off on Friday morning.'

Lucy ventured, 'He would like to see you.'

Murdoch shrugged. 'I didn't come to see him. There are a few of my things here that I want – a fishing rod and a gun. I'm expecting to go overseas soon and I'm hoping to get some sport.'

Lucy said, 'He wants to hear from you. Every day he looks for a letter from you.'

'He'll be disappointed, then.'

Lucy persisted, though she knew she was inviting a rebuff. 'He's your father and he cares very much about you.' She added, 'Mrs Jarman's death hurt him greatly. He's – not very strong now.'

Murdoch was watching her, and now he laughed unpleasantly. 'And you are looking after him, the faithful retainer,' he said with contempt. 'You're fond of him, aren't you?'

'Yes, sir, I –'

'Wouldn't hurt him for the world?'

'No, sir.'

'No. And you'd suffer anything to keep him from being hurt.'

Lucy tried once more, 'He cares for you, sir. If you would only—'

Murdoch's black brows came down. '*I* don't care about *him!* I'm his son. This estate descends to the next in the male line, and that's me. He can't do anything about that and I'm tired of his moralising, had enough of it years ago. And I've had enough of your mealy-mouthed pleading for him. I am the son of the house, you are the housekeeper, and you'll do as you're told or get out. Is that understood, Mrs Nolan?' He glared at her.

It was very clear. He had stated their relative positions as master and servant, brutally, as if he had laid a lash across her back. The blood had drained from Lucy's face now. She whispered, choking with anger, 'Yes, sir.'

'Good. I'm going to have a bath and then a good dinner. Tell Mrs Yates I am here and I want a beef steak, rare and tender.'

'Mrs Yates is away on a few days' holiday.'

'Damn! Well, whoever cooks it, tell them I want it rare and tender.' Murdoch climbed the stairs two at a time, whistling, leaving his valise in the hall.

Lucy stood still, biting her lip, swallowing her anger. She thought of Andrew, how eagerly he scanned the post each morning. It was unlucky and unfair that he should be away when his son finally came home. She glanced at the telephone which stood on the hall table – but suppose Murdoch came out of his room and overheard her? Lucy ran for her coat and then out of the house.

At the wheel of the Rolls she drove into town and stopped at the General Post Office. It was still open, and she took a telegram form and addressed it to Andrew Buchanan at the hotel where he was staying. She hesitated for a few seconds, framing the message in her mind, then she printed, HOME FOR FEW DAYS WISH TO SEE YOU PLEASE COME. She signed it, MURDOCH.

Back at the Buchanan house she entered by the servants' door and busied herself in the kitchen. The meal was almost ready when Murdoch shoved open the door that led to the main house and strode in. He wore a dinner jacket, starched white shirt and bow tie. He glowered at Lucy and demanded, 'Where the hell is everybody? I had to come down and carry my valise upstairs myself! Then dig out this dinner suit! I can't find a bloody soul in the place!'

'I'm sorry, sir,' Lucy replied equably. 'Nearly all the staff have left to join one or other of the services or to do war work. It's difficult to find replacements and at present there are only Mrs Yates and myself. But I've cooked your steak and I'm almost ready to serve it. Also, I took the liberty of taking a bottle of wine from the cellar and putting it on the table. I'm sure it is what your father would have wished.'

Murdoch's brows lifted. 'Ah! Well, I'll have an aperitif first. Scotch?'

'In the drawing room, sir.' Lucy did not offer to get it for him. 'I will call you when dinner is served, sir.'

She served it to him where he sat alone at the head of the long table in the dining room. He sprawled in his father's chair, watching her every move. Having demolished the steak and emptied the bottle of wine, he pushed back his chair. As Lucy came to clear away the dishes he told her curtly, 'I'll take coffee in the drawing room. And a brandy. Fetch them.'

He walked past her, only inches away, but did not touch her. She followed him with the coffee pot on a tray and set it down on a small table.

Murdoch stood before the fire and ordered, 'Pour. One spoonful of sugar, no cream. And the brandy. Two fingers.' Lucy measured the spirit, the decanter clinking on the rim of the balloon glass as her hand shook.

Lucy set the decanter down and mouthed the servant's request for dismissal: 'Will that be all, sir?' She was quivering as much from anger as from humiliation. She knew he was toying with her, aware that she could only submit or leave, and he had guessed, correctly, that she would never leave, because Andrew would be puzzled and deeply hurt, feel abandoned if she did.

Murdoch's mocking smile confirmed all this. 'No, it isn't. I suppose you've done well, according to your lights. I seem to remember you always liked this house. I take it you're now sharing my father's bed and keeping it warm for him while he's away. Will you be passed on with the rest of the estate?'

Lucy walked away from him, slamming the door behind her, which muffled his jeering laughter but did not cut it off completely. It followed her faintly as she ran up the stairs and into her room on the top floor.

She wept then, lying on her bed, but after a time she wiped her eyes as cold anger replaced hurt. She told herself she would not be beaten by him. Now she would try to sleep. There was only the next day to get through, and then she would be rid of him.

Lucy locked her door, for the first time in that house, and began to undress. She had just pulled the frock over her head when she heard his tread on the landing, coming clearly in the silence of the empty house. He stopped at her door and she saw the handle turn as he twisted it. Lucy clutched her frock in front of her, breath held, then let it out in a shuddering sigh as he retreated. However, he only did so for two paces, then the door shook as he ran at it and kicked at the lock. It sprang and the door crashed back against the wall.

Lucy screamed, although she knew no one would hear her. Murdoch lunged for her, arms outstretched, and she spun away from his clutching fingers. They caught hold of the frock, and as he yanked at it she threw it at him. It flailed across his face, blinding him, and she ran round him and out of the door. He was after her flying figure at once, casting the frock aside, leaping down the stairs.

He caught her on the next landing. Lucy screamed again as he seized her arm and swung her around, laughing, but as he swung her away from the stairs, his own momentum carried him on. His foot slipped from the edge of the topmost stair and trod on air. He released Lucy to try to claw for a hold on the banisters, but his hooked fingers missed and he fell backwards down the stairs.

Lucy watched, her hands to her face, her eyes huge with shock. She jerked as if struck at every impact as his body rolled down in a tangle of arms and legs. He stopped only at the foot of the stairs, spreadeagled limply and still.

In the sudden silence Lucy heard her own rapid, shallow breathing. She retreated, shaking, and climbed the stairs back to her room on legs that wobbled. She saw the dress there and pulled it on, then sat down on the bed, her legs giving way.

As her breathing returned to normal, her heart ceased its pounding, and she began to think straight again. After a time she went down to see to Murdoch. He lay face down, his head turned so she could see his eyes were closed. He was breathing. She could not see any blood but did not know what damage had been done to him and had an idea she should not move him. She went to the telephone on the hall table, but it was dead. A pair of scissors lay on the table, and she saw the line had been cut. Murdoch must have done that – to make sure she did not call for help? Lucy shuddered.

She left the house and drove into the town in the Rolls. Old Dr Fairfax was relaxed and urbane. Besides always tending Andrew Buchanan, he had looked after Murdoch as a boy. He listened to her story: 'I heard a cry and a crashing noise and found him lying in the hall. I think he must have slipped on the stairs.' Fairfax accompanied her back to the house, following the Rolls in his Vauxhall. They found Murdoch sitting in a chair in the drawing room with a glass of whisky in his hand. He was red eyed and the glare he shot at Lucy was murderous.

Fairfax was jovial. 'Now then, Murdoch, what have you been up to? Mrs Nolan heard a crash and found you in the hall. She thinks you must have fallen down the stairs.'

Murdoch gulped whisky. 'I crawled in here. Bloody leg won't hold me.'

Fairfax took the whisky from him. 'That's enough of that. It may be why you fell.'

Murdoch growled, 'What the hell d'you think you're doing?'

'I'm going to take your temperature in a minute.' Fairfax was unruffled. 'But in any case, as you were unconscious, you may be concussed, so no spirits for you.'

Fairfax ignored Murdoch's grumbles and took his pulse and temperature. He examined his head and injured leg before delivering his verdict. 'Just a sprain, I think, though a bad one. Keep your weight off it.' He glanced at Lucy doubtfully. 'Can you look after him here?'

Lucy shook her head definitely. 'I'm alone in the house. I couldn't help him to get about.'

Fairfax nodded understandingly then beamed at Murdoch. 'So it's the hospital for you.'

Murdoch snapped, 'To hell with that. I'm not going.'

Lucy said, 'I'm sorry, sir, but I can't accept responsibility for you and risk a repeat of –' She paused, then finished, 'Of what happened tonight. If you insist on staying here, then I will leave with the doctor – and go to the hospital myself.' She met him eye to eye, and with one hand rubbed her arm where he had seized it.

Murdoch was silent for some seconds but took the point: Lucy would seek treatment from the doctor for her bruises and scrapes, and Fairfax would ask questions . . . Murdoch ground out, 'Very well.'

Fairfax looked from one to the other, puzzled, then shrugged, fetched a walking-stick for Murdoch from his car and helped him out to the Vauxhall. Murdoch never opened his mouth but his glare told Lucy he was cursing her.

The doctor told Lucy, 'I'm putting him in the hospital in Roker Avenue for the night, and will keep him there for a day or two – see how he gets on.' Lucy's last sight of Murdoch was his face peering out from inside the Vauxhall, glowering with hatred.

Before Lucy went to bed she locked all the doors and saw that all the windows were fastened. The door of her own room, smashed open by Murdoch, would not lock, but she wedged a chair against it. She lay awake for a long time before she slept, and when she closed her eyes she saw Murdoch's face looming over her, hating and threatening.

She woke several times in the night, dazed from exhausted slumber but in a panic of terror that he was pursuing her again.

The morning cheered her. Sunshine flooded in through her window and banished memories of the night. She set about her work happily.

The telegram arrived just after breakfast. LEAVING FIRST TRAIN ARRIVING TWELVE NOON BUCHANAN. Lucy smiled, then bit her lip. Andrew was coming as fast as he could to see this son of his, and Murdoch was in hospital. She sighed and did what had to be done about the house then drove the Rolls into Monkwearmouth.

Lucy was just in time. As she entered the hospital in Roker Avenue she saw Murdoch pushing aside the nurse and rasping, 'Get out of my way, girl! I don't give a damn what Fairfax said,

I'm getting out of here!' He was hobbling but still had the walking-stick to help him and was managing better than he had the night before. He only stopped when he saw Lucy confronting him. He demanded, 'And what the hell do you want?'

Lucy answered coolly, 'I came to tell you your father will be arriving soon, Mr Buchanan. I've got the motor car outside and now I can take you to meet him.' She turned and led the way to the car. Murdoch muttered a curse under his breath and followed her.

As Lucy drove, he lounged on the leather upholstery in the rear and asked, 'What brought him home so early?'

Her eyes on the road, Lucy answered, 'Your telegram.'

Murdoch stared. 'I didn't send any telegram. Did you?'

'I said you were here for a few days and wanted to see him. I signed it with your name.'

Murdoch said softly, 'You insolent little *bitch!*'

'I did it for your father. I want you to be kind to him, make him happy.'

Murdoch laughed. 'You can wish as much as you like, but you won't see it!'

Now Lucy gambled: 'If you refuse I will tell how you attacked me in his house.'

He jeered, 'You won't. He wouldn't believe you and it would only hurt him.'

Lucy shook her head. 'I wouldn't tell him. I'd tell your regiment, your clubs, your cronies. And Jinny Unwin would back me up.'

'*Jinny!*' Murdoch snapped upright at the name. 'Is that harlot up here again?' Lucy only smiled. 'It would still only be your word against mine.' However, there would be two accusers – and those who would believe them. When dirt flew, a lot of it stuck. He would be barred from his clubs, asked to leave his proud regiment, not welcomed at any decent house. He laughed contemptuously, 'If that's all you want I'll jolly the old boy along – and in exchange you keep your mouth shut.'

Lucy agreed, her hands on the wheel, tight with anger. 'I promise.'

Murdoch kept his word. When Andrew stepped down from the train he was welcomed by his son, smiling and with hand outstretched. Murdoch made light of his sprained ankle: 'Just a minor accident. I slipped on the stairs. Anyway, with both of us using walking-sticks we can keep each other company.'

Together they limped around the grounds of the house and chatted pleasantly through the dinner Lucy cooked and served. When she sat down with them – as Andrew expected – Murdoch glared. But then Andrew explained, 'Lucy and I always eat together. With only the two of us it would be damned silly to have separate tables.' Murdoch grunted agreement, but Andrew did not see the malevolent glare he shot at Lucy. Afterwards Lucy excused herself and retired to her room while the men talked on over coffee and brandies, sitting in big chairs before the fire in the drawing room.

Murdoch stayed through the following day but left the next morning. Lucy drove him and his father to the station, and Murdoch contrived to see her alone as they waited on the platform. He asked, smiling ironically, 'Satisfied?'

Lucy admitted, 'He's much happier for your visit.' It was difficult to say, but she mouthed the words for Andrew's sake: 'Thank you.'

'Don't thank me.' Murdoch was not smiling now. 'I did it because you promised to hold your tongue. I won't forget this and one of these days I'll settle with you.' He left her with that threat.

Lucy forced a smile as she held open the door of the Rolls for Andrew. He said wistfully, 'I wish he could have stayed longer, but he has to join his regiment.' Lucy doubted the truth of that, but kept the smile in place. Andrew was happy and sat in contented silence as she drove him back to the Buchanan house. He had seen his son and they had passed some pleasurable hours together. As Lucy swung the Rolls into the drive Andrew said, 'I have some memories to hold on to now.'

Lucy had some she wished to put behind her. To change the subject she asked, 'Did you complete your business, sir?'

'Oh, yes.' Andrew chuckled. 'It's remarkable how quickly you can reach decisions when you want to go home very badly, but, yes — it was done. I had thought to stay on and rest for a day, potter in Hyde Park and see the first signs of spring, but it was much better to come home to Murdoch.'

As they entered the hall, Lucy asked, 'May I have your advice on some matters concerning the house, sir?'

'Come into the drawing room,' Andrew invited her. He sat in one armchair and pointed to another. Lucy obediently sat rigid on the edge of it. She told him of her problems, trying to run the house without staff and how Mrs Yates was complaining, albeit with cause. Andrew listened, concerned, and admitted, 'I hadn't realised.' He added worriedly, 'You aren't going to give notice, are you?'

'No, sir.' Leave this house? She hoped she never would. 'But may I make a suggestion, please?'

Andrew nodded. 'Fire away.'

'I've read in the newspapers how many big houses like this have been lent to the Army to use as hospitals. In the south they deal with wounded coming from France, but further north they take convalescent cases. I wondered if you would consider this?' Lucy went on quickly as she saw a worried look on his face, 'It's only a suggestion.'

Andrew said doubtfully, 'Give up my home? The Buchanans have lived here for over a hundred years.'

Lucy reassured him: 'You wouldn't give it up. It would still be the Buchanan house and you would keep a suite of rooms for yourself, quite private. The Army would just use the rest.'

Now Andrew looked thoughtful. 'It would solve the problem of staff. How many rooms d'you think we'd need to keep?' He grinned. 'We do rattle about in this place now, just the two of us.'

Lucy reminded him, 'And Mrs Yates.'

Andrew shook his grey head. 'No, I think I'll retire Mrs Yates and give her the pension she's earned. She's nearly sixty-five, you know.' Lucy did know, and that Mrs Yates would be delighted to take her pension. Andrew went on, 'But how do you feel about cooking?'

Lucy answered quickly, eager that nothing should stand in the way of this solution to her difficulties, 'I could manage that. It's trying to keep this big house in order on my own that's the trouble.'

They talked it over, Andrew enthusiastic after his conversion. They settled that they would retain two bedrooms and, at Andrew's insistence, just one sitting-cum-dining room for the pair of them: 'I'm sure we'll get on all right, and the fewer rooms you have to care for, the better.' He slapped the arm of his chair. 'Right! I'll make enquiries of the Army on Monday.'

Murdoch spent the rest of his leave in London, at shows, in clubs, with women. On his last night he strolled down the Strand, an overcoat hung on his shoulders over his dinner jacket, a silver-topped cane swinging from one hand. His ankle had fully recovered. He was on his way to attend a show, and afterwards was taking an actress to supper – and her bed.

'*You swine!*' The words came thickly, scratchily, across the width of the pavement. 'You – Murdoch!' He saw her standing in a shop doorway, hat tilted drunkenly on one side, hair hanging in wisps and rats' tails beneath it. The costume she wore was bedraggled, with mud spattered on the hem and on her buttoned boots. At first Murdoch did not recognise the gaunt, haggard features of the old woman, until she stepped out of the doorway into the harsh glare of the gaslights – the blackouts had not yet been enforced. It was Jinny Unwin. She swayed and staggered as she hurried to stand in his way. Facing him she shouted, 'You! You brought me to this!'

Murdoch snarled, 'Shut up! Here!' He fumbled a sovereign out of his pocket and tried to hand it to her but she knocked his hand aside with a blow from her own and the coin skittered away into the road and the horse droppings.

Jinny shrieked, 'Don't want your money! Damn you to hell for what you did to me! You put me on the streets!'

Murdoch reached out, gripped her shoulder and threw her out of his way. Jinny's legs tangled and she fell in the gutter. Murdoch seized his chance and hurried away.

Jinny lay where she had fallen, weeping, and only called after him once: 'I can see you hanging on the wire!'

Murdoch heard the prophecy but ignored it in his rage. He stalked on to meet his latest conquest – and his fate.

Chapter Nineteen

DECEMBER 1915

Murdoch lay in the mud, head pressed into it, rigidly still. His eyes were slitted against the light from the flare that had burst above him and was slowly sinking. It revealed a landscape as bare and empty almost as the moon. There was no building, no tree nor bush, only the gluey plain of mud. Before him and scarcely a dozen yards away, the German barbed wire was strung. Beyond the wire lay the German trenches and the enemy. Murdoch waited for the flare to go out. When it was finally extinguished and darkness rushed in again he waited for his night vision to return.

He was on a night raid and its objective was to bring back prisoners. He had been chosen because he had made a reputation for himself as a man of brute courage who always brought back a German prisoner when you wanted one. He had also established a reputation for a savage temper and cruelty, but he always led from the front and almost always brought his men back intact, so they respected him for that. For the rest, they hated him.

His sergeant and a dozen men were lying behind him now. Before the flare had gone up, he had seen the party of German soldiers on his side of their wire, working to repair it, rigging fresh strands where shellfire had cut gaps. They had dived for cover as the light flooded down on them, but they were still there. Murdoch could hear lowered voices, sergeants giving orders no doubt. Once his eyes could pierce the night again, he saw them, cut deeper black than the night around them, standing but stooped over their task again. He thought there were — five? No, six of them. One was standing beyond the others, inside the wire, keeping a lookout. Let him. He would not save them, would probably run when the fighting started.

Murdoch carried his pistol in a holster on his belt but had no intention of using it. In his right hand he held a short, thick length of rubber hose which he would use as a club, since it was quieter and gave off no flash to blind its user. He fixed his gaze on one man a foot or so closer than the others. He was Murdoch's target, the man he would take back. *Now!*

He pushed up, running like a sprinter from his mark, though this was no running track. He slipped and slid in the mud as he had expected, cursing under his breath, but was quickly across the few yards of open ground, his men floundering after him. Murdoch was almost on the man he had picked. His arm went up and then brought down the hose. A voice yelled in front of him. The lookout? The man struck by the hose had sunk to his knees, was sliding on to his face. Murdoch snapped, 'Take him!' There were other shadows milling, panicking, behind the man's body. Murdoch stepped over him, lashed out with the hose and felt it connect, again and again.

The voice of his sergeant reported from behind him, hoarsely, 'Got him, sir.'

The shadows before Murdoch had melted away, all except one, staggering with a hand to his head, reeling back through a gap in the wire. Two prisoners are better than one, Murdoch thought exultantly. He went after the man, was up to the wire when the flame licked out in front of him. He felt as if he had been kicked in the chest, his legs folded under him and he fell on to the wire. The lookout. The man had stood his ground and fired at pointblank range as Murdoch came to the wire.

He hung there, suspended from the barbs hooked in his clothing. He felt cold now and the world was slipping from him.

It was then that he remembered Jinny Unwin's curse: 'I can see you hanging on the wire!'

'Here y'are, Mrs Nolan. Put that up an' all.' The soldier in loose-fitting 'hospital blues', the light blue uniform worn by the wounded under treatment, handed up the sprig of mistletoe.

Lucy, perched at the top of the stepladder to hang up the ward decorations, laughed and warned him, 'All right, but you behave yourself.' He grinned up at her, balanced on his crutches.

Lucy had become an unofficial mother, elder sister and general assistant to the patients since the Buchanan house had been turned into a hospital in the summer. Andrew and Lucy had kept a small suite of three rooms but the other fourteen had been turned into hospital wards and others built in the grounds. A doctor, Major Faraday RAMC commanded with another two doctors, RAMC captains, assisting. There were a score of nurses and VAD orderlies and a matron headed them. She soon, gratefully, confined herself to the nursing side and left the administration of the building to Lucy. They worked very well together. She pushed wheelchairs around the grounds, sat with the miserable, helped to write letters for those disabled, was always ready to help hard-pressed nurses with cleaning work or bedmaking. And she always managed to smile, even when her heart ached for the broken bodies of the men brought back from the war. Now it was almost Christmas she had taken on the task of decorating the wards with paper streamers, holly and trees. The job was done and she was just applying the finishing touches now when the mistletoe was proffered.

It was time to collect Andrew from Buchanan's yard and she drove into town in the Rolls. Traffic stopped her at the Wheatsheaf corner, and as she waited to ease the Rolls through a gap a voice called, 'Lucy!' She looked around her and saw the caller stood on the platform of a tram.

It was Florence, Billy's wife. She had thrown up her job in a shop in June when the tram company had said it would be recruiting women conductors. Florence had been one of the first to be accepted and now as she waved to Lucy her ticket punch swung from its straps over her shoulders. Florence was laughing, but with more reason than usual. 'Billy is home! Got in late last night!' she called, and as the tram started to move and the gap between them widened, 'Tommy came with him!' Finally her shouting fading away: 'They're home over Christmas! I'll see you tonight . . .'

Her brothers home! Rose had invited Lucy to tea that evening in the two rooms in Victor Street where Florence also lived and the boys would be there! Lucy went on her way, smiling.

When she reached the yard the men were pouring out for their midday break and she had to edge the Rolls in against the human tide that was running against her. She stopped the Rolls when she reached the office, left a message there that she was waiting in the car and then returned to sit behind the wheel. The tide had slowed and thinned to a trickle. There were only a few men strolling out now, not hurrying home to eat, but on their way to a local pub for a pint of beer to drink as they ate the sandwiches they had brought, wrapped in red bandannas.

She saw Josh Campbell before he saw her. He walked up from the ship part-built on the stocks with a little group of men about him. They looked to be furtively passing things to him in closed fists, and he continually thrust these into his pocket – betting slips. When the last had made the surreptitious transfer and turned away, Josh looked up and saw the Rolls with Lucy sitting behind its windscreen.

She flinched with shock. On taking up the duty of driving Andrew to the yard, she had assumed she would meet her father. However, as the weeks and months had gone by, she had concluded that he had left Buchanan's and so she never expected to see him.

Now she realised she had been wrong. He had simply been hidden among the 10,000 men working in the shipyards. Those yards were working flat out all through the four years of war. The river turned out 200 merchantmen in that time to make up for those ships sunk by U-boats. And they built destroyers for the Navy as well.

Lucy tried to remain calm, and sat without moving though she was trembling inside. She stared out through the screen, not looking at Josh as he strolled up to the car and leaned on the door beside her.

He said, leering, 'I heard you'd started working for the auld man again.' The news had only recently reached him. The gossip about 'Andrew Buchanan's new housekeeper' had initially been exchanged between the censorious ladies in the big houses, and it had taken a long time to filter down to the dockside pubs. Josh continued, 'Is this one o' the things you do for him?' He stroked the glistening coachwork with one hand. When she did not answer he went on, 'And what do you do for him as his housekeeper? It can cover a lot.' Lucy remained silent and now Josh began to lose his temper. 'Don't come on your high horse wi' me! You might be living in the big house but I'm still your father, remember.'

Lucy recalled the photograph she had found in her mother's Bible, the story her mother had told on her deathbed, that Josh was not Lucy's father. This evil man was a stranger and nothing to her. She would not tell him what Amy had told her because he would only use it to abuse her mother's name. However, anger made her blurt out, 'You're not my father.' As he gaped at the charge, Lucy continued, 'A father cares for his children, gives them love and guidance, sees them fed and clothed, brings them up in cleanliness and decency. You've done none of those things. I don't regard you as my father, don't regard you as *anything*! You'll get just as much affection and respect from me as you showed to your bairns – damn all!'

Josh was stunned for a moment by this attack, then his fingers curled into a fist and too late Lucy recalled his violence in times past. He lifted the fist to strike and Lucy warned, voice shrill, 'You don't know who might be watching!'

She was bluffing, could see no one, but Josh, glowering past her, saw Andrew Buchanan limping across from the office to the Rolls. Josh pushed away from the car. Voice lowered but venomous, he hissed, 'You'll regret that! One o' these days you'll wish to God you never said that to me!'

Lucy drove back to the Buchanan house. She tried to listen attentively as Andrew talked to her from his seat in the rear, but the meeting with Josh Campbell and his parting threat had shaken her.

At the house they entered through the front door. Andrew had retained a small suite in one wing, just two bedrooms, a sitting room, bathroom and kitchen. A green-baize-covered door separated this suite from the rest of the house, but to reach it they had to pass through the hall. The drawing room was now used as a common room by the doctors. Its door stood open and they glimpsed one doctor seated before the fire reading a newspaper.

In their own rooms Lucy served the lunch she had set to cook earlier that day. Soon after moving into the rooms Andrew had said, 'I see no sense in you serving me then sitting down to your own meal later,' so they ate together. There were just the two of them now. Mrs Yates had happily taken her pension and retired, while the girl who had come to train as a maid had left within a month to work in the town.

Andrew still dressed for dinner, and Lucy, unbidden, would put on an evening gown that had come secondhand from Helen Whittaker, and which Lucy had altered herself. Lunch was a more informal affair, however, and Lucy soon found herself relaxing. Josh's threat receded and was forgotten, for the time being at least. The melancholy discussion of the daily casualty lists had taken place at breakfast and was behind them. Andrew was looking forward to an afternoon spent reading or painting; Lucy to helping in the wards.

The electric bell was an innovation installed when they had

moved into the self-contained suite. When it rang Lucy went to the door connecting to the rest of the house and found one of the nurses there. She was a pretty girl of Lucy's age, usually cheerful but grave faced now. 'A telegraph boy brought this. It's for Mr Buchanan.' She held out a buff envelope.

Lucy's heart plummeted. 'Thank you.' She took the envelope and closed the door as the nurse walked away. Lucy stood with her back to the door for some seconds, a hand to her mouth and staring down at the buff envelope that trembled in her hand. Was it . . . ?

Andrew Buchanan looked up from stirring his coffee, then saw the envelope. His spoon rattled as he replaced it in the saucer, then held out his hand for the telegram. He ripped open the envelope and pulled out the form inside, read its message then handed it to Lucy and put a hand over his eyes. Lucy glanced at the form, and read that Murdoch had been killed in action. Her first feeling was one of relief, that the telegram had not brought news of Nick. Then she felt guilty because of that first reaction – and then came the pity for Andrew, who had lost his only son.

She comforted Andrew as best she could. He slumped in his chair by the fire and called for his medicine – Fairfax had prescribed it when diagnosing Andrew's weak heart – but refused to call the doctor. Lucy sat with him, holding his hand, talking quietly.

Late in the afternoon Andrew said, 'You're going to see your family for tea, aren't you?'

Lucy had asked a week earlier for leave to do this when Rose and the other girls had invited her. Now she answered, 'No, it's not important.'

Andrew insisted, 'No, you must go. I will be all right now. I'll just sit here by the fire.'

So Lucy left him reluctantly and walked into Monkwearmouth and to Rose's rooms. 'Hello, Lucy!' First Tommy, then Billy took her by the shoulders and stooped to kiss her. They both seemed bigger and older in their uniforms. They sat down to a knife and fork tea of meat and potato pie.

The men were full of talk of their life at sea in a destroyer. 'We're based at Rosyth. It's our boats that provide the destroyer screen for Beatty's battlecruisers,' Tommy explained. The girls listened avidly, then reported the home news in their turn.

Rose and Elsie brought out the letters from George and Stephen. 'George says the food is good but the cooks spoil it. He's with a good lot of chaps and they all get on well. He doesn't mention the war, except he says he's writing this last letter in a nice quiet billet. So it sounds as though he's not in the fighting.'

Elsie put in, nervously eager for reassurance, 'That's like Stephen. He says the country well behind the line is quite pretty. I suppose "well behind the line" means he's safe.' Under the bright chatter flowed an undercurrent of fear.

Lucy remembered the talk in August 1914, of a war that would be over by Christmas. Now, eighteen months later the slaughter still went on and showed no sign of ceasing. So Rose and Elsie feared for their men in France, and Daisy and Florence for Tommy and Billy, both of them here now but soon to return to the war at sea.

Each of them could cherish, or worry about, the one they cared for, trying to ignore the fear that seemed to sit like a spectre in the corner of the room. Except Lucy. She sat alone, seemingly outside it all. But in her silence she worried over Nick.

It was Billy who finally asked, 'And how are things with you, Lucy? Still liking it up at the Buchanan place? I hear it's a hospital now.'

'That's right. It keeps me busy, but that's a good thing nowa-days.' She would not mention Murdoch's death in front of Rose and Elsie, because that sort of reminder would bring the spectre out of the corner and into the feast. 'The boys we have are all convalescent and good company.'

It was Rose, when they had a quiet moment just to the two of them, who said to Lucy, 'You're lucky you haven't got anyone away. I never get a proper night's sleep with worrying about George.'

Lucy could not answer that. She had hoped that she would forget Nick Buchanan in time, but thinking back to August 1914 had reminded her that she had not seen him since then. She could see him clearly now, looking down at her with that teasing grin.

She said, 'Yes, I suppose I'm lucky.'

Lucy left early, saying, 'I have to get back. I have one or two things to see to and it's a good walk out there.' As she stepped out on the road to the Buchanan house she thought of Nick. She told herself that he could be nothing to her and nothing had changed, but still she wondered where he was and whether he was safe.

Nick was on the bridge of the *Ada Barr*, bound for Alexandria, when the torpedoes struck. The night was dark and the old ship was blacked out. The first torpedo blasted into the engine-room amidships. Nick's cabin was directly above it, and if he had been there he would have been killed instantly. As it was he was hurled across the bridge. As he clawed at a stanchion to haul himself to his feet, the second torpedo struck home just aft of the first. The combined explosions broke the back of the *Ada Barr*. Bow and stern lifted together to make a huge V and the sea rushed into her. She sank in minutes.

Nick's first thought was for his men but there was little he could do for them. He fought desperately to get a boat away but there was no time. The ship went down taking the boat with her, leaving Nick and a scant dozen men splashing about on the surface. He swam about among the wreckage that littered the sea, fumbling in the dark for anything that would float and keep a man from drowning. He collected a pair of oars, a grating and the dozen survivors. They clung to the wreckage and he made them keep swimming and talking. But hard though he tried, one by one slipped away. When the dawn came and a destroyer found them, there were only three holding on with Nick. One of them, a boy just turned seventeen, Nick had shoved out of the sea on to the grating and held him there.

The destroyer took them to Alexandria and a hospital. All were ill from exhaustion, delirious for a day and a night but then quickly recovered.

When Nick was discharged from the hospital he sought out the nurse who had cared for him. 'I've come to thank you.' He grinned at her apologetically. 'The doctor tells me I was raving for a while. I hope I wasn't a nuisance.'

The girl laughed up at him. 'Not at all.' When he had gone she wondered, Who was Lucy? He had called for no one else.

Chapter Twenty

Lucy had thought she was safe. She had not seen Josh Campbell for six months. She drove the Rolls into Buchanan's yard at noon on a summer's day. The sun glinted from the surface of the river and the children in the streets around the yard ran barefoot. She was early, the clock above the timekeeper's office showing five minutes to twelve. The din in the yard was easing as men put down their tools. Those living near the yard made ready to trudge home for their dinners, eaten at midday. They began to collect in little groups which drifted towards the gates.

'How's your Tommy?' shouted one of the men in a passing group, all of them too old for the Army or Navy.

Another called, 'Aye, and what about your Billy?' They had come to know her as the sister of the two boys.

'They're fine!' Lucy replied with a smile. 'We had letters from both o' them just a week back.' The smile lingered as she thought of Tommy and Billy. They were safe.

A week ago their destroyer had taken part in the Battle of Jutland, which had involved two huge fleets and resulted in thousands of casualties. Lucy and the girls could only hope and pray. They turned to her in their fear and Lucy tried to cheer them: 'No news is good news.' Bad news came with the telegraph boy. Then the letters came, proof positive that the boys had survived the bloody action. The girls had wept and Lucy with them.

Lucy's smile froze on her face when she saw Josh Campbell burst out of a shed, throwing the door wide, then stride up the yard towards her. His face was dark with fury and his eyes glared. Behind him came a stocky man, in an old suit and a battered trilby hat set square on his head, marking him out as a foreman. Although he scowled, there was a triumphant look about the foreman.

Josh glanced at Lucy, but did not stop because the foreman was close on his heels. One man shouted at him, 'Where are you off to, Josh? I've got something for you.'

Josh shouted back, 'I've got the bloody sack!'

'What for?'

Josh did not answer that, but the foreman did: 'Takin' bets when he was getting paid to work.' He followed Josh into the office.

Lucy relaxed with a shudder. Now that Josh Campbell had been sacked from the Buchanan yard, she could go there without fear of meeting him. That was a relief. Surely now she could hope that he had gone out of her life for ever.

The hooter blew to signal noon and the dinner hour, a sonorous blast that was taken up by the other yards and engineering shops on both sides of the river. Minutes later Andrew Buchanan came shuffling across to the Rolls, leaning on his walking-stick. As he climbed into the rear of the open car, he said, 'I've made a change of plan. Young Helen Whittaker called in this morning. I said we'd lunch at the Palace with her.'

Lucy drove to the Palace Hotel, reflecting that the casserole she had prepared for their lunch could be eaten for dinner instead.

Helen was already in the restaurant and they joined her at the table. She was flushed and lively, full of her news. 'I'm going to France! I'll be nursing in one of the Army's hospitals there. It's a bit frightening, but they called for volunteers so I put my name down. I've written to Nick and I've told Will Ogilvie. He had a week's leave in London and I went up to see him.' She laughed and blushed. 'It's possible I might see him in France when I get over there.'

Glancing mischievously at Lucy, Helen said, 'I hear you're breaking hearts at the Buchanan house.' As Lucy stared open mouthed, she explained, 'I called in there this morning and talked shop with the nurses for a while. They were full of praise for the way you run the place and help them out. And the boys are all in love with you.'

Now it was Lucy's turn to blush. 'They are a nice bunch of lads.' A lot of the patients were still in their teens and she was aware of their worshipping looks.

'That's what Will says, too,' put in Helen, 'that he's with a good crowd. He's flying a lot and it's hard work but they are all grand chaps. He doesn't say so, but I think it is quite dangerous. I just hope he's all right.' The smile wavered, but she went on brightly, 'And Nick has been involved in some excitement. His ship was torpedoed and sunk.'

The room swayed before Lucy's eyes and she mouthed, 'Oh, really?'

'Yes. He said he wasn't hurt but he's awfully bitter, says he lost a lot of men who were working below. I thought he might have been sent home, but they've appointed him to another ship and he's staying over there.'

The room had steadied.

Andrew said, 'I'm glad they're both all right, very glad. If you'll excuse me a minute, there's a chap over there I would like to talk to.' He got out of his chair and shuffled across the room to shake hands with a man as elderly as himself.

Helen sighed and said softly, 'He's looking very old, but I didn't think he would survive very long after Nell died. I'm sure that's due to you.'

'I owe him a lot,' Lucy explained.

Helen said drily, 'You may have owed him a lot. I think he owes you a great deal more now.' Lucy did not answer that and Helen continued, 'My guardians have aged these last two years.

It's understandable because they're both well into their seventies, but until the war started they were pretty active. Now Binkie is almost housebound and she and Teddie venture into the town just once a month, and only then if the weather is fine. This war is hard on everyone.'

Lucy could attest to that. Tommy and Billy, George and Stephen, were never far from her thoughts. And Nick . . .

Helen grinned lopsidedly. 'I suggested lunching here today because I wanted to visit one of my old haunts again. I'm glad you came with Andrew. There aren't many of the old faces left. When I think of the boys who have gone –' She broke off then, bit her lip and shook her blonde head, the bobbed curls dancing. Lucy reached out to grasp her hand and Helen clung to it and whispered, 'I get so frightened for Will. And Nick.'

Lucy said, 'I think you're very brave.'

'I'm not, you know.' Another shake of the head. 'It scares me just thinking about France. Not getting hurt, though I'm afraid of that, but of not being able to do the job, of letting the side down.'

'You won't,' Lucy assured her. 'I'm sure you won't.'

Helen blinked at her, then said, surprised, 'I believe you. What would we do without you, Lucy? We had some good times as children, didn't we?'

Lucy nodded. 'We did.'

Helen saw Andrew returning and she sat up straight and wiped her eyes.

Garvey kicked the front door shut behind him and stamped along the passage to the two rooms he rented. He shoved open the door to the kitchen to find Clem Nolan with his wheelchair drawn up to the oil-cloth-covered table, smoothing out the betting slips he had collected, scraps of paper of varying shapes and sizes, the bets written in a bookies' code and signed with cover names like

Esto, Able and so on, in case they fell into the hands of the police. There were only a few slips.

Clem looked up from his task and growled, 'I'm in trouble.'

'You? How?' Garvey questioned.

'I had to pack it in.' Clem slapped the last opened slip on the table. 'A feller tipped me off that the pollis had heard about me takin' bets and was looking for me. This is all I got before I had to give up.' He poked morosely at the stakes, the small pile of coins that had come with the slips.

Garvey muttered, 'Somebody's been talking, because you're not the only one. A pollis walked out o' the back lane today and caught me at it. I was standing there with the slips and money in my hand! I'll be lucky if I don't get a bloody big fine this time.'

Garvey was right in his suspicion that someone had been talking. Two weeks before, he had been approached by an old man wanting to put threepence, all he had, on a rank outsider. Garvey had taken a pocketful of money already and rejected the bet: 'I can't be bothered wi' threepence! Get away wi' ye!' The outsider had won at 15 to 1. The old man knew about Josh and Clem, as well as Garvey. He had brooded – and then sidled up to a policeman on his beat.

Now Garvey cast his eye over the coins on the table and muttered, 'That lot won't last us long.'

Clem agreed. 'If the whole lot are losers, that won't take us past the weekend. We'll see how Josh got on when he comes in tonight.' Then he told Garvey brusquely, 'We might as well eat now. What's in the cupboard?'

Clem was now the unspoken leader, the strongest personality of the three, and Garvey obeyed. He brought out of the cupboard a half-loaf of stale bread, a hunk of cheese and some pickles. In the bottom of the cupboard were a few bottles of beer. He and Clem began to make a meal from these.

There was the banging of booted feet in the passage then the kitchen door swung back to slam against the wall and Josh marched in. Clem demanded through a full mouth, 'What are you doin' here?'

'I got the sack, the bloody sack!' Josh hurled his tea-can across the room so that it bounced off the dusty old sideboard.

'What for?' asked Clem.

'The foreman caught me takin' bets. He must ha' been hidin' and watching me. The first I knew about it was when he grabbed me.'

Garvey and Clem exchanged glances and the bookie said gloomily, 'See? I told you somebody has been talking.' He explained to Josh how he and Clem had become targets for the police.

Josh muttered, subdued, 'So we're all in it. I tell you this: I'll not get another job around here. Wherever I go, they'll know why I was sacked.'

He sat down and joined in the glum meal. They chewed over their misfortune and pondered how they could improve their circumstances. Once Garvey said to Clem, 'You could always go to that lass o' yours for a few bob.'

'Lucy?' Clem sneered. 'That's right. She'll be my sheet anchor as long as she's alive. But you were right when you said "a few bob". I don't reckon she has much money or will part wi' more than a shilling or two and she could easily complain to auld Buchanan. So we'll leave her 'till we're desperate.' The only conclusion they came to was that they would not make any money from betting, at least for a while.

Matters did not improve. Two weeks later Garvey had spent the capital he needed to cover bets, and a magistrate fined him five pounds and warned him that, if arrested again for the same offence, he would go to jail.

Clem said, 'I know how we can make a few quid for ourselves.' He told them, and Josh was uneasy, Garvey frightened, not through any sense of morality, but because of the possible conse-quences. Clem mocked their fears, described the poverty that lay ahead of them if they did not act, and dangled before them the tempting thought of the rewards of his proposed action.

So late one Saturday night they broke into a public house and made off with the takings. Clem kept watch outside in his wheel-chair, Josh forced a window and Garvey helped him up and through it. No one heard them. They returned to Garvey's dirty rooms and found they had just over twenty pounds. They roared with laughter – for Josh and Garvey, mostly a release of tension – slapped each others' backs and opened bottles.

Later, after the euphoria was spent, Clem warned, 'It won't always be that easy. And we can't muck on our own door-step. We've got to pick out places in other neighbourhoods, pubs takin' a lot o' money, and look at them beforehand, see how we can get in and where the money's kept.'

His accomplices agreed, nodding, and Garvey suggested, 'I'll hold the money. I've got a savings bank account. We'll put it in there and draw so much a week to live on. Otherwise you two will booze it away. And this place is mine, I'm paying the rent.'

Clem glared at this challenge to his authority and Josh jeered, 'This isn't the flaming Palace Hotel!' However, after a time they admitted there was some sense in Garvey's proposal and agreed.

Helen had left for France. Lucy drove her to the station, picking her up from the Whittaker house. Helen's two maiden aunts stood on the front door steps, two white-haired and frail old ladies, heavily corseted in voluminous black dresses. They used their handkerchiefs alternately to wipe their tears and wave goodbye.

Helen hugged Lucy before boarding the train and called as it pulled out, 'Bye, bye! You're a brick, Lucy! Bless you!' And Lucy knew that familiar sense of loss again, as another longtime friend passed out of her life. For how long?

The war went on and on and a year dragged by. Helen wrote several times and once came home on leave, in the summer of 1917. She was thinner and looked tired, but after a week at home was almost her old self. She told Lucy, 'I'm in a hospital not far behind the lines and we're kept busy. Gosh! There's plenty of work! But I really feel I'm doing some good. *You* know what I mean. The nurses here tell me you make this place run like a clock!'

Lucy had been told that by Major Faraday, the doctor in charge, and she flushed, embarrassed. She sought to change the subject, but Helen did it for her: 'I've seen Will Ogilvie two or three times, but only for a few hours. It's so difficult for both of us to get leave at the same time.' She finished wistfully, 'That would be lovely.'

Helen returned to France and her subsequent letters became fewer and shorter. Lucy concluded that was due to the pressure of her duties, but in the New Year of 1918 she received a single sheet scrawled in joy and haste: 'Will and I have finally got forty-eight hours' leave together and we're spending it in Paris . . .' Helen's happiness leapt out of the page at Lucy and she smiled. She had hoped there might be news of Nick, because Helen's letters sometimes contained a paragraph detailing his doings as he had reported them to Helen, but this time Lucy was disappointed. She told herself she only wanted to know that he was well. She prayed that he was.

She prayed again, this time for Stephen Kennedy when Elsie came to her bearing the telegram. She held it out to Lucy, face drawn with misery. 'They say he's wounded but not what's happened to him! He might be half dead!'

Lucy folded her young sister in her arms and encouraged her, 'He's *not* dead! Just wait and keep your spirits up. You might hear good news soon.'

Stephen's name appeared in the *Echo*, reporting that he had been wounded – and again, two days later, when it was announced that he had been decorated for bringing in wounded under fire.

A week later, at the end of March, Elsie had a letter from him and she came running to Lucy with that, too. This time she was tearful but proud. 'He doesn't say *anything* about a medal, only that he's not hurt badly and I'm not to worry. But I do!' Lucy comforted her again and sent her away more cheerful.

Then a letter came for Lucy.

Chapter Twenty-One

Lucy sensed the letter held bad news. It came early in the month, on a day left over from March, with a bitterly cold wind driving in from the sea bringing spatters of fine rain. Lucy was touring the wards in the Buchanan house, helping nurses make beds, talking to men in need of company and gentle sympathy, ensuring all the mundane chores of running a big house were performed well and in due season. She was passing through the hall when the postwoman — who had taken over the job for the duration of the war — delivered the pile of letters. Lucy sorted through them on the little table in the hall, found a dozen addressed to Andrew and one bearing her own name.

The writing was not familiar and was wavering and erratic. She turned it over and saw the name of the sender written there: Helen Whittaker. The address was a field hospital in France. Lucy examined the handwriting again and decided it could be that of Helen, but a Helen weak and ill — or in the grip of some terrible emotion. Lucy shuddered. Had Helen learned something of Nick Buchanan?

She took the letters upstairs and handed the thick wad of them to Andrew. He sat by the fire with a rug around his legs. He had not been to the yard for over a week. He had suffered a bad attack of pneumonia before Christmas and the doctor had warned Lucy,

'He isn't very strong now, catches infections easily and takes a long time to throw them off. He needs watching over very carefully.' So when Andrew caught a cold just a week ago Lucy had persuaded him to stay at home.

He looked out of the window now as rain rattled on the pane and he chuckled, 'I'm glad I stayed home today.'

Lucy smiled stiffly and tucked the rug around him, handed him his paperknife and he began to open his letters. Lucy sat in the chair opposite him and thumbed through the flap of her own, her fingers not working properly, and unfolded the sheet within. Lucy glanced at the shaky signature and saw it was indeed that of Helen.

Lucy thought she could hear the girl's voice, her heart broken, in her words: 'I didn't want to write to Andrew because he has already suffered enough from the death of Murdoch, but I have to tell someone. I have said nothing in the hospital because I'm afraid if they find out they might send me home and I don't want that. I have to stay here and keep busy. If I came home and people fussed and I had nothing to do I would go mad.'

Lucy turned the page with shaking fingers, wondering what was wrong? Nick?

Helen went on, 'I saw Will less than a week ago and today I heard he had been killed. One of his friends from the squadron came to see me and brought me some of his things that they thought I would want. His aeroplane was shot down.'

Lucy realised she had sighed with relief and was ashamed. A young man was dead and she was relieved that it was not Nick Buchanan. She remembered Will Ogilvie, had seen him in the theatre and met him when he was with Helen. She did not know him at all, but he had been young, tall, good looking, with his life before him and now it was snuffed out. Now Lucy felt sorrow.

She read on, 'I've written to you, dearest Lucy, because you're one of us from the old days, before this awful war. And because I always felt I could tell you about things that troubled me, as if you were my nanny.'

Andrew asked, 'Are you feeling cold? I thought I saw you shiver.'

Lucy got up quickly and made an excuse to turn her face away. 'I am a bit. I'll make a cup of tea for us, sir.'

'Good idea.' Andrew went back to his correspondence and Lucy set about making the tea. Now she could dab at her eyes with her handkerchief.

She wrote to Helen in the evening, sitting in her own room when Andrew had retired to bed and the house was quiet around her. Lucy said how sorry she was. 'Please let me know if there is anything I can do to help.' Afterwards she wondered bleakly why so many of the brave men were dying, while others stayed at home and made money. Josh Campbell came to mind . . .

That night Josh stood outside a public house called the Three Bells. The street was silent and dark, all its residents long abed. The rain of earlier had passed over and the wind had died down, and now, at one in the morning, the sky was moonless but clear and pricked with stars. Josh looked from Garvey to Clem where he sat in his wheelchair close against the wall, and whispered, 'Ready?'

Clem nodded impatiently. 'It's time we got on wi' it.'

Garvey flapped a fat hand, signalling silence, then whispered in his turn, 'I thought I heard something, somebody moving inside.'

They all held their breaths for long seconds then Clem hissed, 'You're imagining things. Now *get* on! We need the money.'

That was true, but Josh asked, 'Give me another mouthful.' He took the flat bottle from Clem and sucked at it until Clem snatched it from him.

'You've had enough o' that already.' Clem stowed the bottle in his wheelchair and then demanded of Josh, 'Give me that an' all.'

Josh had brought a club along, insisting, 'The feller that runs this place, Pascoe, used to be a wrestler and he's known for knocking people about if they cross him.' Now he protested, 'What if the feller inside wakes up and comes down?'

'We'll run for it, same as we always have. But you're more likely to wake him if you try to climb in while you're carrying that thing!' Clem wrested the club from him. 'Now get in there, the pair o' you!'

Garvey and Josh led the way into a narrow alley which ran down the side of the Three Bells, Clem coming behind them. They stopped by the back gate of the pub and Garvey cupped his hands for Josh to stand in and so climb over the wall. He dropped down into the yard, eased back the bolts on the gate and pushed it open to admit Garvey. Clem sat there by the open gate as the other two tiptoed across the dark yard to where a window reflected the starlight darkly. Josh used a knife to force the catch and shoved up the window. They froze as it squeaked, but no other noise followed and after a moment they drew breath again and carried on.

Josh slid in over the windowsill and Garvey waited by the window. Inside, Josh made for the bar. The till stood against the wall behind the bar, but he passed that. Their observation had told the three that Pascoe, the landlord, regularly emptied his till and transferred the money to a locked cash box. Josh found it in the cupboard where he expected it to be and grinned, success and whisky lending him confidence.

Suddenly the beam of an electric torch sliced through the darkness of the bar from behind Josh. It lit him up and a voice bellowed, 'Got you, you bastard!'

Josh ran. The open window beckoned and he rolled through it to fall into the yard. Garvey, stationed there to deal with such an emergency, tried to slam the window shut but Pascoe was too close behind Josh. The wrestler was broad and heavy but quick on his feet. His outstretched hand grabbed at Garvey and seized a handful of his jacket. Garvey squealed as he found Pascoe's arm was holding the window open and that he was held. He let go of the window and pulled away in a panic. He could not break Pascoe's grip, but the pocket flap which Pascoe held came away with a tearing of stitches and Garvey was free.

Garvey ran across the yard and out into the lane. He was just in time to see the flying shadow that was Josh turn the corner into the street.

Clem propelled his wheelchair in Josh's wake, and yelled as Garvey ran past him, 'Wait for me!' He cursed as Garvey lumbered on without pause.

As Garvey swung out of the lane he heard the hammer of Pascoe's feet behind him, his panting and cursing. A light came on in the pub, and the glow lit Garvey as he passed in front of it. Startled, he checked in his stride for a moment then ran on.

Clem cursed the other two for leaving him, then he stopped his chair just around the corner of the alley. The club lay in his lap and he seized it. As Pascoe emerged, running, from the alley, the torch in his hand casting a wavering beam about the street, Clem thrust the club between Pascoe's legs. Pascoe sprawled his length and Clem steered his wheelchair round the fallen man. As he did so, Pascoe tried to rise and Clem hit him over the head with the club. Pascoe lay still and Clem hurried away, spinning the wheels of his chair furiously. He could see nothing of the other two.

Josh had turned right when coming out of the alley, away from the pub. He ran until he was gasping for breath and only then slowed to a walk. He headed for Garvey's rooms and arrived there without seeing another soul. Garvey turned up a few minutes later, followed by Clem, who shouted, 'You left me to clear up your mess!'

All three of them were sweating, Josh and Garvey shaken, Clem furious. He went on, 'If it hadn't been for me, he would ha' caught one o' you two!'

Garvey asked, 'How d'ye mean?'

'I stopped him, that's how! Tripped him wi' Josh's club and then put him out wi' it.'

'Did he see you?'

'He never got the chance!' Clem was contemptuous now. 'I just did what you two should ha' done when he showed up.'

Josh said defensively, 'Well, I got the money.' He produced the box and Clem took it. He forced it with a screwdriver and peered inside then finally grinned at the others. 'That'll keep us going for a month or two – or more. And nobody saw us.'

Josh said, 'Not too bad a night after all, then. What about a drop o' rum to celebrate?' And they sat down around the table, laughing, as the fear ran out of them and the alcohol took hold.

Olive Barnes was twenty-two years old. Her fiancé was the same age and she had not seen him for two years because he was serving in France with the Durham Light Infantry. She feared for him daily, and nightly she prayed for his safe return. She did not sleep well, worrying about him.

The room she shared with her younger sister faced the Three Bells, and that evening, after lying awake and hearing the distant church clock chiming the hours, she had despaired on the stroke of one, crawled out from under the tangled covers and went to stand at the window.

By pushing aside the curtains and then the lace curtains she could see out into the street. It lay below her, a dark chasm peopled only by shadows. The front of the Three Bells showed only the glassy, sightless stare of unlit windows. She stood there for some minutes, reluctant to go back to tossing and turning and staring wide eyed at the ceiling, but the night was chill – there was never the money for a fire in the bedroom – and she began to shiver, clutching her nightgown about her.

She was about to let the curtains fall back into place and climb into her bed again when she heard, faintly, a voice raised – down there in the street? Or in the Three Bells? She was not sure, could not make out any words. A light danced inside the pub opposite, like the beam from a torch, and Olive waited, curious. She wondered what Pascoe was doing, wandering about in the night with a torch. Its beam disappeared, but she could still hear a commotion from across the way.

A shadow burst out from the alley next to the pub. She could see it was a man, and he turned to his right and made off. A second man trotted out of the alley, but this one swung to his left and ran across the front of the Three Bells.

Just at that moment a light bloomed in the bar. Olive saw Pascoe's wife through the window, swathed in a dressing-gown and with her hair in curlers. She had lit the gaslamp in the bar and its yellow glow fell on the man running past the window. He checked in his stride as the light fell on him, his head turned as he sought escape, and Olive saw him quite clearly. He was fat, moon faced with pendulous jowls, a button nose and small mouth. His hair was oiled and set in a quiff. Then he ran on and became just a shadow once more.

Olive scurried to wake her sister and her parents. 'There's summat happened at the Three Bells!'

By the time they all stood at the window Mrs Pascoe was out in the street and shrieking for a doctor: 'They've killed him!' They had not, but Pascoe was taken to the hospital suffering from concussion.

Olive told the policeman, 'I saw a fat man, bald, and he didn't have any whiskers.'

'Did you recognise him?'

Olive shook her head. 'I never saw him before.'

The policeman reflected gloomily that there were plenty of fat, bald men in the town. And anyway, there was no guarantee the feller was from the town. He sighed and put away his notebook.

Lucy read the account of the burglary and assault in the *Sunderland Daily Echo* but took little note of it, unaware of the involvement of Clem and Josh. Besides, Andrew Buchanan's announcement drove everything else from her mind. He looked up from a letter he was reading and waved it at Lucy. 'From Nick. He says he may be seeing me soon. It sounds like his ship is coming back to home waters. Good news, eh?'

It was easy for Lucy to smile excitedly and reply, 'Oh, yes!' although later she wondered if this was good news. Did it signal only temptation and unhappiness?

Chapter Twenty-Two

APRIL 1918

'Hello, Lucy!' The man's voice came from the open door leading to one of the wards.

Lucy was hurrying down the stairs, on her way to bring the Rolls to the front door because she was driving Andrew to the station this morning to catch his train. He had been called to a meeting of shipbuilders in Hull and he would be staying there overnight and returning the next day. He was much better and Lucy had thought the change and the outing would do him good. She had sent and received telegrams booking his room, emphasising his fragility, so she knew he would be cared for. But now she halted her progress in response to that greeting, her heart leaping, and spun in a swish of skirts to see who had called her name, already guessing – wildly, since Andrew had received Nick's letter only the day before.

The young man rising from where he sat on his bed, one of six in the ward, was Stephen Kennedy, but Lucy's disappointment was swamped by surprise and delight. She ran to throw her arms around him and kiss him.

'Stephen! When did you get here? The last we heard, that *Elsie* heard, was a letter from you written in France. That was just two days ago.' She held him at arm's length and saw he was leaner, both in face and body, and the 'hospital blues', the woollen uniform issued to the wounded while in hospital, hung on him. But he was a good colour, fresh faced, and was smiling cheerfully.

'They put me on the train the day before yesterday. Right out of the blue. "We're sending you home," they said, and I got here late last night.'

'Does Elsie know?'

'Not yet.' Stephen pulled a face. 'I'm not allowed outside the grounds for the time being. Do you know how I can get word to her?'

'I'll tell her. I'll tell a lot of people who keep asking after you.' Lucy cocked her head on one side, smiling. 'You're quite famous, you know. It was all in the *Echo*.'

Stephen said shyly, 'Oh, that.'

'Yes, "that",' and Lucy hurried on, recalling now that she was to drive Andrew to the station, 'I have to go, but I'll tell Elsie.'

She pulled him to her to kiss him again, and there was a grumbling chorus from the rest of the ward: 'You never kiss us like that!'

Lucy laughed, blushed, and said, 'Well, you aren't married to my sister.'

'Have you any more sisters?' came the chorus.

After settling Andrew into his seat on the train she told him, 'Your case is in the guard's van, Mr Buchanan. I've told him you will want a porter and I've tipped him already.'

'There's no need for you to fuss like that, Lucy,' said Andrew testily.

Lucy knew there was, recalling what the doctor had said, but she answered soothingly, 'I *know* you're quite capable of doing that yourself, sir, but I thought it would be one less job for you.'

He reached out of the window of the first class carriage to pat her cheek. 'You're very good to me.'

'Enjoy yourself, sir.' Lucy squeezed the hand then let it go and stepped back as the train pulled away.

From the station she drove to the Railway Hotel. Lucy entered by the front door and passed through the restaurant, greeted with smiles and nods by the waitresses. Some of them remembered when she had been the housekeeper at the hotel, but she was also known there now as a guest. She and Andrew had lunched or dined there as often as they did at the Palace.

Lucy found her sister in the kitchen. 'Elsie!' she called, and gave her the news.

Elsie put her hands to her face, then lowered them to stare around her in delight and shock. 'Stephen? He's out at your place?'

Lucy amended, 'At Mr Buchanan's place. He's convalescent, not allowed out of the grounds at present.' And teasing, 'But if you wanted to see him I suppose it would be all right for you to visit.'

'*If?*' Elsie squeaked. '*If* I want to see him? There's no if about it!' Then she saw Lucy grinning and laughed herself. 'You're having me on. But –' she stopped and gestured wordlessly at the busy kitchen – 'I can't just walk out.'

'Yes, you can.' Motherly Mrs Wilberforce, the cook, plump and rosy from the heat of the kitchen, broke in, 'We can manage. If you look in for dinner tonight we can sort out then what we're doing tomorrow.'

Elsie looked around, saw them all nodding at her and whipped off her apron. As she shrugged into her coat, Mrs Wilberforce said, 'I'll tell the manager. Don't worry about him. Just get yourself away, lass.'

'Thanks! Thanks everybody!' Elsie gave a final wave of her hand and skipped out of the kitchen after Lucy.

Lucy drove her out to the Buchanan house, only making one early stop at Elsie's insistence, where she ran into the bank where Rose worked and panted, 'Stephen's home, at the Buchanan place, convalescent. Will you tell Daisy and Flo?'

'I will! I will!' Rose promised excitedly.

Lucy saw Stephen as she turned the Rolls in at the gates of the house. He was strolling on the lawn before the house among another dozen or so soldiers, wearing his cap and his khaki greatcoat over his 'blues'. She stopped the car and said softly, 'There he is.'

'Where?' asked Elsie, peering, and then, following Lucy's pointing finger, 'Oh! He's lost weight. Oh, Stephen!' Then she was out of the car and running. He had seen the car, saw her coming and opened his arms. Elsie ran into them. 'My bonny lad! What have they done to you?'

When she had ceased to smother him in kisses, and had paused to draw breath, he answered, 'I'm just about better. Another couple of weeks and they'll send me off on leave.' He stopped there, did not follow the progression he knew well: after convalescence came leave, and after leave you went back to duty.

'But they said you were wounded.'

'Shrapnel, but they dug it all out. Honestly, I'm nearly as good as new.' He tucked her arm through his and said determinedly, 'Let's go for a walk. There are too many people around here.' He led her off along the path that curled into the trees.

Lucy watched them go, smiling, but faintly now. She looked around and realised that the Rolls was stopped just about where she had stood all those years ago to watch Andrew sitting at his easel. That painting now hung in her room, and she always found pleasure in looking at it, as she did in drinking in this view of the house. Lucy reflected that she and Andrew would never have dreamed that they would see the place as it was now, a hospital for wounded soldiers.

That reminded her that she had work to do, so she put the Rolls away in the garage that had been one of the old coachhouses, and set to. First she saw to the rooms occupied by herself and Andrew, then she went on her tour of the wards.

The day passed quickly. She saw Elsie and Stephen later, when Elsie came in with him to eat lunch with the rest of the patients. They were quieter now, and afterwards sat in the dayroom and talked.

After tea, Lucy got out the Rolls again and drove Elsie back to the Railway Hotel. Elsie asked at one point, 'You won't get into trouble if old Buchanan finds out about you bringing me out to the house and taking me back again, will you?'

Lucy assured her, 'He knows already. When I drove him to the station this morning, I asked if it would be all right.'

Apart from that Elsie sat smiling and silent.

As Lucy eased the Rolls into the garage for the night the first raindrops fell, big and slow, but as she walked round to the front of the house they came thicker and faster. She ran, taking the steps up to the door two at a time. As she entered, a motor taxicab trundled in at the gates. Lucy paused just inside the door to shake the rain from her skirts. She had worn a hat, held on by a scarf, in the open driving seat of the Rolls, and now she took them off and shook them, too, put a hand to her hair.

Stephen came to stand before her. 'Thank you for bringing Elsie to see me.'

'I'm just glad I could. It was lovely to see the pair of you together.' That picture of them had stayed in her mind all day.

She heard the front door open and saw Stephen's gaze drift from her face to focus on something behind her. She turned and came face to face with Nick Buchanan.

She had forgotten him. For just this day her mind had been full of Stephen, Elsie and Andrew. In the jumble of her thoughts she recalled Andrew saying that Nick might be coming home, and here he was. His reefer jacket with its two gold rings on the sleeves was worn and salt stained, as was the cap he carried in his hand. His black hair was as unruly as ever and a thin scar ran down the right side of his face. Had that happened when his ship was torpedoed? Lucy wondered.

He said, 'Hello, little Lucy.' He wore that same teasing grin, his teeth white against the tan from years in the Mediterranean sun, but it did not reach his eyes, now dark and serious.

Lucy did not take up the challenge, only answered, 'Hello.' It came out in a whisper. Her eyes were locked with his.

Stephen said, 'If you'll excuse me . . .'

Lucy turned to him quickly. 'I'm sorry. This is Mr Buchanan.

I mean Lieutenant –' She floundered. 'Nick. I – wasn't expecting to see him. This is Corporal Kennedy – Stephen. He married my sister, Elsie.'

The two men shook hands, Nick courteously, but with his attention elsewhere, his eyes on Lucy. Stephen saw this and studied the big young man with the unruly black hair. He would know this man again. Now he saw without resentment that his presence was superfluous and excused himself.

Lucy and Nick were left in the hall but not alone. There was a constant traffic of doctors, nurses and patients passing through. Nick glanced around him and asked, 'Is there anywhere we can talk?'

'Yes, of course.' Lucy was trying to regain her calm and failing. 'Mr Buchanan has kept a small suite for his use.' She led the way and he followed. She could sense his gaze on her back and repeated shakily, 'I wasn't expecting you. Mr Buchanan said you'd written that you might be coming home soon, but I didn't think today . . .' Her voice trailed away.

His came from behind her. 'My ship docked in the Tyne. She's only here for a few hours.'

After three years, just a few hours? 'Here we are.' Lucy pushed open the door and led the way into the drawing room.

Nick glanced around the room and asked, 'Where's Andrew?'

'He was called to a conference. In Hull.' Lucy stood in the centre of the room, her hands at her sides, and looked up at him. 'He won't be back till tomorrow.' She became aware that she had left the door to her bedroom open. 'I have to meet him at the station at two in the afternoon.'

'How is he?'

'The doctor says he is very frail. It's his heart. He must be careful. But he has been better these last few days.'

Nick said, 'I will always be in his debt. He was very good to me.' He went on, 'But I came to see you.' He took a pace towards her and she took one backwards. 'You told me not to write but I couldn't stop thinking about you.' He took another pace – and so did Lucy, as if they were in some formal dance. 'I love you.' Yet another. 'I want you.' One more.

This time she did not copy him, because she stood in the open doorway. He was close to her and she could smell the sea-smell and coal smoke on his jacket. 'No, Nick.' But it was only a whisper. He put his arms around her and she strained against him. 'Oh, Nick!' As he pressed his mouth to hers, she tasted the salt on his skin – or was that from her tears?

It was dark and Lucy had drawn the curtains and switched on the light. Nick shrugged into his jacket and combed his hair with his fingers. Lucy pushed at hers that had fallen down. She had pulled on her dress over her nakedness, not caring about modesty now because he was leaving. She wanted to cling to him for a little longer. 'I'll drive you to the station.'

Nick shook his head. 'There's no need. I told the cabbie to come back for me.' Nick glanced again at his watch. 'He'll be here about now. Just time to get me to my train for Newcastle and the ship.'

He looked up and saw the misery on her face and misinterpreted it. 'I don't want to leave you again.' He put a hand on her shoulder, another under her chin to tilt up her face. 'These last three years have been – very bad. We can't stay here, not in this town where we're both known. When this war is over –' He paused there, wondering if this was tempting providence. Was it dangerous to look ahead like this? But he was eager and hungry for this woman and he ploughed on. 'When it's over we can go to the States, or Australia, or anywhere. We can start again, the two of us.'

He stopped then because she was shaking her head. 'No, Nick. When the war is over I will still be married. No matter where I went, I would still be married.'

'You're not tied to him.'

'I tied myself to him – for life. Clem would never divorce me, would hold me to my vows to spite me. I can't divorce him. I can't stand up in court and say what he did to me. I have no witnesses.'

'He deserted you.'

'He would say I drove him out. He's very clever. He would angle for sympathy and play it for all it was worth.' She gently but firmly shifted his hands from her and gave him his cap. 'Your cab will be waiting. You must catch your train. We've had our moment and now we must part, for good.'

'No!'

There was a rap at the door and one of the nurses called, 'There's a cab here for Lieutenant Buchanan.'

'He's just leaving!' Lucy stepped around him quickly to open the door.

They saw the back of the nurse as she walked away, skirts and starched apron rustling. Nick said, 'I'll come back for you one day.' He kissed her again and she let him, but did not, dared not, respond. This had to end now.

Lucy watched him go, his broad back disappearing down the stairs. She felt no remorse. She had been afraid for him for so long, had wanted him so much, and now it was over.

From the window she watched his tall figure stride from the front door across the gravel of the drive and duck into the motor taxi that stood with its engine running. It eased down the drive and out of the gates, out of her sight.

His last words stayed with her, however: 'One day I'll come back for you.' He had said that before, when she had first turned him away in that far-off summer of 1914. Could she refuse him for a third time? It might be he would find another woman. There would be many eager to snap him up.

Chapter Twenty-Three

Nick went looking for Helen Whittaker.

His ship was employed on escort duty in the Channel for some days then berthed in Calais for an estimated seventy-two hours while her engineers carried out some much needed work. There was some grumbling from her crew, who were allowed shore leave in Calais but could not get home. Some of them had got ashore when the ship lay in the Tyne but only for a few hours. There was no time to visit distant homes and most had not seen their families for three years. Commander Beauchamp, their captain said, 'I've pleaded your case and I've got a promise that you will have home leave in a few weeks' time.' They accepted that because they knew their man, and settled for a few drinks in the dockside bars.

Nick dug out the last letter from Helen. He made enquiries of a major in the Royal Army Medical Corps whom he met on the quay, and learned where he could find Helen. He begged a lift in a motor bus, one of a convoy carrying a draft of men up to the front line. They were double-decker buses with the top deck open to the sky, but Nick sat in the cab between the driver and the subaltern commanding the draft. It was a bright spring day of clear blue sky and sunshine that narrowed the eyes and lay warm on the shoulders, but there was no singing among the men,

277

and little talking except for the warning cries of, 'Look out for wire!' Telephone wires were strung along the side of the road on poles, and sometimes they were taken across in a sagging loop. The men had to duck their heads under the wire, but there was no laughter.

'They're very quiet,' Nick said.

The young lieutenant answered curtly, 'They've been up before, got wounded and now they're going back. They don't have much to sing about, really.'

'You too?' The young man nodded.

When he set Nick down at the gates of a château, he joined him to stand in the road. Looking at the house over Nick's shoulder, he said, 'They're very good in there. Wonderful girls. They looked after me before sending me on to Blighty. I would have lost the leg if it hadn't been for them.' He glanced behind him to make sure he could not be overheard by his men and the driver of the bus. The engines of the convoy panted impatiently as they waited for him to climb on board again. He added wrily, 'Now I might lose my bloody head, but that's not the fault of the girls.'

His gaze returned to Nick. 'Sorry to be morbid, old boy, but I've spent a year out here. Came out as a private and got promoted corporal then sergeant and finally commissioned in the field. And stepping into dead men's shoes all the time. I just wonder who's going to step into mine. There's talk of another big push this summer.' Such mass attacks resulted in thousands of casualties, and were led by junior officers such as this subaltern.

Nick watched the convoy trundle away, then started up the drive to the house. It was deeply rutted by the wheels of motor ambulances and he had to thread his way between the puddles that glinted in the sunlight. A number of wooden huts had been built in the grounds, and several young women in nurses' uniform of white apron and cap could be seen entering and leaving these.

He saw Helen before he could ask for her. He stood aside to let a swaying ambulance pass, its wheels sliding in the ruts. It drew up in front of the house and a number of orderlies ran down the steps to take out the stretchered patients carried in the body of the vehicle. One of the nurses with them was Helen.

Nick did not call her and she did not see him. He let her get on with her job, but watched her uneasily. She looked to have lost weight and there were shadows around her eyes. When she went back into the house, stooping over the stretcher of the man she was tending, he followed.

The matron had an office in the hall, and she told him severely, 'We don't encourage this kind of visit, Lieutenant.'

'Miss Whittaker is an old friend,' put in Nick.

'So you've told me. But you might be surprised at how many young men find they have old friends or distant relatives among my girls.' She fixed him with a critical eye. 'However, I will speak to Helen, and if she is agreeable I will arrange for her to have an hour or so off to meet you.'

So later that day Nick walked out with Helen. She was pathetically pleased to see him, clinging to his arm and smiling up into his face. He could not help but remember Lucy sending him out of her life, her mouth drooping. It was a bleak memory of their parting. He tried to put that out of his mind, to concentrate on this girl pressed against his side.

They strolled slowly along a lane behind the house. Wildflowers coloured the grass verges and women worked in the fields. It would have been a peaceful scene, except for the continuous rumble of distant gunfire.

Nick studied the girl. She had always been a beauty and now there was an ethereal quality to her loveliness. He said gently, 'You're not looking too well.'

Helen shrugged. 'I'm not ill. I'm never ill. Did you ever know me to be poorly?'

'No,' Nick admitted. 'But—'

'Well, then. I'm just tired. We're all tired, always tired. The work goes on and on. We live in those huts you saw in the grounds and work in the house. When we get time off we're only too glad to go to sleep. And the food – I don't seem to have any appetite these days, not since—' She stopped there, staring to the north and east where tiny aircraft swooped and circled and anti-aircraft bursts pocked the sky like balls of cotton wool.

Nick prompted, 'Since?'

She told him about Will Ogilvie.

When Nick boarded his ship in the late evening, Sub-Lieutenant Sanderson, the officer of the watch, greeted him with, 'The captain wants to see you.'

Nick asked abstractedly, 'What's it about?'

'Don't know, old cock, but it might be leave. He's unofficially letting some of the chaps go home if they live close to the ports on the other side. I've got a couple of days because my people live just outside of Canterbury. I'm off as soon as I finish this watch.'

Nick said flatly, 'My home is three hundred miles north of the Channel ports.' And who would welcome him there?

When he faced his captain in his austere cabin there was no talk of leave. Beauchamp said, 'There's been a call for officers for a special duty and I've been requested to supply my best man. I can't tell you the nature of the duty, except that it is hazardous. You will have to report aboard *Vindictive* and she's lying in the Thames Estuary. Only volunteers will be taken. What do you say?'

Nick answered, 'I'll go, sir. May I make a request?'

'You may. What is it?'

Nick went to pack his kit, but first wrote a hurried letter and sought out Sanderson, now off watch. 'Will you post this when you get over the other side? It will get there quicker.'

Sanderson grinned. 'If she's pretty I'll deliver it myself.'

Nick said, unsmiling, 'She is very pretty.'

Sanderson stared after him, puzzled at Nick's serious manner. He picked up the letter to slip it into his pocket and saw it was addressed to a Mrs L. Nolan. A married woman? But then he told himself it was none of his business. He was on leave and the sooner he set out the better.

Sanderson got away sooner than he expected. He had only walked a hundred yards along the quay when he came upon a small coaster on the point of casting off her moorings. Her captain stood on her open bridge, an elderly man with a walrus moustache drooping over a stubby pipe and a bowler hat crammed on to his head. Sanderson called up to him, 'Where are you bound?'

'Dover. D'ye want a ride?'

Ten minutes later Sanderson was stretched out on a bunk in a spare cabin, luxuriating in the knowledge that he could sleep for the two hours of the crossing and be home not long after that.

In mid-Channel, however, the little coaster struck a floating mine that blasted her in two. She sank in minutes, taking Sanderson and most of her crew with her.

Nick reported for duty aboard HMS *Vindictive*, lying in the Thames Estuary with a flotilla of other craft. She was an old cruiser, built twenty years before in the nearby Chatham dockyard. He was told he would take the place of an officer injured in an accident, and was briefed on his duties. A few days later, on the night of 22 April, the flotilla sailed.

'Good Lord!' A startled Andrew looked up from the *Sunderland Daily Echo*. 'D'ye know what it says in here?'

Lucy was using the quiet hours between dinner and bed to catch up with mending and was busily sewing. She paused to answer, 'I haven't seen the paper. What is it?' She wondered, with an edge of anxiety, whether another local man had been killed at the front, someone they both knew.

She caught her breath as Andrew waved the paper at her and said, 'It's about Nick. Here, take a look.' As she stared at him in dread he went on, 'He's got married to Helen.' He pushed himself stiffly up out of his chair, laid the paper in her lap and pointed to the relevant paragraph. Lucy tried to hold it still but it shivered in her hands so she could barely read the few sentences:

LOCAL OFFICER WEDS

Lt Nicholas Buchanan RNR and Miss Helen Whittaker VAD were married in France last Thursday. Lt Buchanan is the nephew of Mr Andrew Buchanan of Buchanan's yard. The bride was a popular figure in local society before the war and is now nursing in a field hospital in France. The best man was Commander Beauchamp RNR, captain of the ship in which the groom is at present serving. The bridesmaid was Miss Celia Edwardes, also a VAD.

Andrew chuckled delightedly. 'Well, I'm damned! The sly dog! He never said a word that they were serious. Always good friends – but you know that, of course. It's wonderful to have some cheerful news for a change, eh? I must send them my congratulations and a present.'

He held out his hand to retrieve the paper and Lucy handed it to him but kept her head bent down, pretending to bite off a cotton. She could no longer see the work and put it aside. She rose hastily, pleaded, 'Excuse me,' and almost ran from the room.

She fell on her knees by her bed as if in prayer, her face buried in her hands, and laid on its cover. The sobs shook her. This was a dimension of grief not known to her before. That she had lost Nick was bad enough, but after making passionate love to her, he had gone from her bed to wed another woman. That was a betrayal she could never have believed possible. And the woman was Helen, who had claimed to be a friend, and who, dear God! was mourning the loss of Will Ogilvie.

The tears stopped after a time and she lay still. She recalled Andrew sitting alone, and washed her face in the bowl on the dresser and went back to him. She kept him company through the interminable dragging last hour of the evening, forced herself to reply sensibly when he addressed her, and even instigated one or two items of conversation herself. She was exhausted when they finally retired to their respective rooms for the night.

At Zeebrugge the fog that had shrouded the flotilla and hidden it from the enemy shredded on the wind. That wind also ripped aside the curtain of smoke laid by the motorboats leading the flotilla to cover the ships closing the port. They came under fire from 120 heavy weapons.

Nick crouched on the deck of *Vindictive* as the shells screamed in to burst on the old cruiser, tearing huge holes in her. He wore a steel helmet instead of his cap, and carried a rifle, having refused a pistol as being useless for this kind of fight. His party of blue-jackets crowded behind him, their eyes watching for his signal, because they would never hear an order in the din. It was hard enough to see as darkness was split by flashes of brilliant light and then became black as pitch again. Suddenly a searchlight on the shore lit up *Vindictive* and the incoming fire redoubled.

There were three blockships in the flotilla. These were old ships filled with concrete and fitted with scuttling charges. The objective of the attack was to sink these three in the entrance to the port and so prevent U-boats from entering or leaving. *Vindictive*'s part in the attack was to create a diversion. First she was to draw the fire of the guns, and she had done that. Secondly she had to land parties of seamen and marines on the mole to destroy the guns and machine-guns in emplacements there. Nick led one of those parties.

He rose to his feet as the old cruiser ran alongside the mole, the massive long pier of stone that ran out from the shore. The gangway was being lowered from *Vindictive*'s bow to crash on to the mole, but the parapet stood high above the cruiser's deck and the gangway was angled steeply upward. As the ship surged and sank on the tide, so the gangway soared and plummeted. One second its end was suspended high above the parapet, the next it crashed down on to the concrete and stone with shattering force. Crossing would be perilous, and now it came under small-arms fire from further along the mole.

Nick turned to look back at his men and mouthed, 'Follow me!' He ran at the gangway and pounded across it. He saw the tracer flying close past his head, heard the bumbling whine of ricochets, but then he was over and standing on the wide parapet. The mole itself lay some fifteen feet below him, machine-guns on its landward end, the flames marking their muzzles. These were Nick's objective. He had to silence them. He saw the first of the bluejackets were with him, slung the rifle over his shoulder and lowered himself over the edge of the parapet to the length of his arms, then he dropped down to the mole, seized the rifle and ran towards the guns.

It was a long night for Lucy. She began by telling herself she just had to forget him, that she was not free to marry him. Later she reasoned that she had sent him away and told him he could not hope to win her, that they had to part for ever. Therefore it was her own fault. She could hardly expect him to live like a monk henceforth, and might expect him to marry another. But so soon? Surely she was better off without him?

Lucy's eyes were closed but she could still see him. She knew that he was, and always would be, the only man for her.

And across the cold North Sea, Nick's lifeless body lay among a hundred others on the mole at Zeebrugge.

Chapter Twenty-Four

'Regret to inform you Lieutenant Nicholas Buchanan . . . missing, believed killed.' The words drummed in Lucy's head. She realised the doctor was addressing her and tried to put aside her shock and grief to take in what he said.

'He will have to go to hospital, of course.' Dr Fairfax spoke in low tones, because the door to Andrew's room was still open. He stood in the drawing room with Lucy, packing his Gladstone bag on the table. He snapped the catch on it and glanced across at her. 'He's suffered a total collapse, of course. A massive stroke and his heart is much worse.'

Lucy had returned from a walk in the grounds to find Andrew sprawled behind the door of their suite. She had called for help from the doctors and nurses in the house and they had put the old man to bed and watched over him while she telephoned Dr Fairfax. Only then had she found the telegram that had lain underneath Andrew's body.

Fairfax left to send an ambulance, and Lucy went to sit by Andrew's bedside. He was aware now, though his mouth was twisted at one corner and his speech slurred. Lucy gripped his hand, but it lay loose in hers. He murmured, 'Both gone. Murdoch and Nick. All the young men are dying. I'm so sorry for that girl, Helen. Married barely a week and then to lose him.'

Lucy tried to cheer him, to offer a glimmer of hope. 'The telegram said "missing". He may turn up yet.' But she could not persuade him and did not believe it herself. He lay quiet and still as if life had already deserted him.

Lucy did not write to Helen, now widowed by Nick's death only months after that of Will Ogilvie. She could not find it in her heart to do so. It would have been hypocrisy because her hurt was too deep. Nor did she hear from Helen, who would not have known about Nick and Lucy. She thought Helen's failure to write was strange but did not call for any action on her part. Lucy nursed her wounds and filled each day with work.

When Andrew had been two weeks in hospital, Fairfax spoke to Lucy at the end of her daily visit. He sat her down in his office and said gently, 'I'm afraid there's been no improvement, in fact he's worse.' Lucy nodded. Andrew hardly spoke now, seemed barely conscious of her presence. Sometimes she was sure he did not know her. Fairfax added, 'I don't think he will be going home, and we must look for a nursing home for him.'

Arkenstall, the solicitor, came to see her at the Buchanan house the next day. Lucy broke off from her work with the wounded and took him upstairs. He sat opposite her in the drawing room, accepted a cup of tea and told her, 'There's no surviving family. The only person who might act is the executor of Andrew's will, an old friend of his, but he is serving abroad. I've written to him, but for the present I will deal with matters.'

Lucy needed to know where she stood and asked, 'What do I do now, please? If Mr Buchanan is not coming home again he won't need a housekeeper.'

Arkenstall was quick to reassure her: 'It would be convenient if you could stay on for the time being. I think Mr Buchanan would like that. When we talked in happier times he said how much you liked this house. He would be glad for you to look after it. And I understand you give a great deal of help here.'

Lucy managed to smile at that. 'I have no official position but I do keep busy.'

'Very well, then.'

Lucy returned to her labour of love. A few days later Major Faraday, the doctor who commanded the hospital, met her in the hall and told her, 'We've orders to clear the place out and take some leave. We're taking no new patients and those we have will be discharged or transferred.'

'You're closing the hospital?'

'No. It's just preparation for the summer weather and the campaigning season. We have to be ready to take a lot of casualties.'

Lucy shivered inside. Another big push. And another. She watched the patients leave, Stephen among them, going home for two weeks' leave before returning to his unit in France. Lucy waved to them all and kissed them.

The last of the staff to go was Faraday. He asked her, somewhat concerned, 'Aren't you nervous of staying in this great house on your own?'

Lucy laughed at him. 'No! I've always loved this house. I could never be afraid here. And who would harm me? There's no one for miles.'

That night, in a bar down by the river, Josh Campbell set down his empty glass and wiped his mouth with the back of his hand. 'I've had enough here. Away, we'll have a walk up the road.'

'Aye, righto! Not too far, mind,' Garvey warned, 'they shut in ten minutes.' The public houses now closed at ten in the evening. He paused only long enough to finish his own beer then followed Josh.

As Garvey passed through the door into the street, a girl's voice said clearly, 'Here, Robbie! That's the feller that broke into the Three Bells and knocked down Mr Pascoe.' Olive Barnes, her arm through that of her fiancé, had been passing and now halted.

Robbie, a burly young man in khaki with the buglehorn badge of the Durham Light Infantry in his cap, glared in the direction she pointed. 'The fat one?'

'That's him!' Olive nodded excitedly. 'The one I saw! I'd know him anywhere!'

Garvey tried to run, but the fit young man overtook him in a dozen strides. Robbie grabbed him by the collar and slammed him back against the wall. 'You're coming down to the station wi' me.'

Olive squeaked excitedly, 'Here's a bobby now!' A policeman was pacing steadily towards the little group.

Josh, who had been a dozen yards ahead of Garvey, turned when the voices were raised. He heard Olive's accusation, saw Robbie arrest Garvey, and now saw the policeman. He fled. He arrived panting at Garvey's rooms, where Clem Nolan sat in his wheelchair by the fire, and announced, 'They've got Garvey!' He recited what had happened, breath sobbing, the account interlaced with curses as he ransacked the drawers and cupboards of the meagrely furnished rooms.

'What the hell d'you think you're doing?' Clem demanded.

'Looking for the money. He was keeping it for us. There's a bankbook.' Josh threw the mattress off Garvey's bed.

'You won't find it,' said Clem with contempt. 'He's got the book inside his shirt. He told me: "It never leaves me," he said.'

Josh swore, and whined, 'We've got to get out of here. He'll split, that's certain, tell them everything to save his own skin, and the bobbies will be round here banging on the door.'

Clem snarled, 'I know that! How much money have you got?'

Josh turned out his pockets. 'Ten bob.'

'I've got about the same. We're not going to get far on a pound between us. It would cost a hell of a lot more than that to get to London.'

'I'm not going to London.' Josh picked up an armful of clothes and stuffed them into a small case. 'I've got a brother living up on the Clyde. I haven't seen him in twenty years but he can hide me now.'

'What about me?' Clem demanded.

'Aw! He'll put you up an' all. But we've got to get to him and he'll want paying. That's money again.' He resumed packing. 'We can get to Newcastle, anyway. That will be a start.'

Clem was now busy packing his own case, but he stopped to point at Josh. 'If we're taking the Newcastle road we can call in on your daughter and my wife. Lucy will have a few bob and she'll be glad to give it to us to be rid of us. And the old feller, Buchanan, will have a damn sight more.'

Josh objected, 'The place is full o' wounded, doctors and nurses.'

Clem reminded him, 'You told me you'd heard at the yard that they still had rooms of their own. Once we get into them we'll be out o' the way o' the others, doctors or whatever.'

'Aye.' Josh banged down the lid of his case. 'Let's away!'

It was close to midnight when the electric bell rang, telling Lucy that there was a caller at the front door. She had sat up late, bringing her household accounts up to date. She left the drawing room and walked down through the empty house, wondering who could be calling on a night like this. She switched on the lights in the hall but the rooms on either side were dark. Rain drummed on their windows, hurled by a cold wind. She peeped through the narrow window at the side of the front door and saw Clem Nolan sitting in his wheelchair on the top of the steps. Behind him stood Josh Campbell.

Lucy's heart sank. She knew their presence meant no good to her. 'What do you want?' she called.

Josh answered, face woebegone, 'Can you let us in? Just to shelter for an hour or so till this rain stops. We're walking to Newcastle because I've been promised some work there. I don't care for meself, but Clem here feels the cold awful badly in this chair and he's soaking wet.' That was true enough. Lucy could see the water running down Clem's face from the sodden cap covering his head. Both men looked soaked through and Clem's face was white and haggard in the light from the hall. He was her husband, she could never forget that, and Josh believed himself to be her father. Anyway, could she leave anyone out in this weather?

Lucy set the door wide. 'You'd better come in for a while to dry out.'

'God bless ye,' said Josh piously.

'Aye, thank you, lass,' added Clem as Josh pushed him into the hall.

Lucy closed the door and then started along the hall towards the back of the house. 'You'd better come through to the kitchen. I'll light a fire in there for you.'

'Ah! that's good of ye,' said Josh as they followed. His eyes on Lucy's back, he nudged Clem and pointed to the empty rooms on either side, his eyebrows raised, questioning.

Clem nodded. Aloud he said, 'I was wondering if one o' the doctors here could have a look at me. My chest's terrible bad.' He coughed to add colour to the claim.

Lucy replied over her shoulder, 'There are no doctors. The hospital has been closed for two weeks while the staff go on leave.' She pushed open the door to the kitchen and switched on the light. Clem wheeled himself in after her and grabbed her wrist. He took her by surprise, and with one yank he pulled her to her knees beside him, her arm twisted behind her back. His other hand clamped over her mouth.

Josh had shut the door and stood with his back to it. Clem snapped at him, 'Give me a hand here!' Josh took a hank of clothesline from under his jacket. Lucy struggled, but between them the two men shoved a gag into her mouth and tied her wrists behind her. Clem took a turn of the line about his own wrist and said grimly, 'Now you'll go nowhere without me.'

Clem saw her frightened, bewildered stare and told her, 'Get something into your head. Garvey has been arrested for a burglary when a feller was badly used. He'll go down for a long time. The pollis will be looking for me and Josh, but we're not going to jail. I'll commit murder rather than go inside. You hear what I'm saying?' He jerked on the line and Lucy winced, nodded her head.

Clem said, 'I'm going to ask some questions. If you try to shout when I take the rag out o' your mouth I'll damn soon shut it.' He took out the gag and demanded, 'Where's the old feller – Buchanan?'

Lucy's mouth was dry, her lips bruised. She mumbled, 'He isn't here. He's been in a nursing home for weeks now.'

'So you're here all on your own.' Clem grinned at Josh and got an answering smirk. He went on, 'We need your money. Let's have it.'

Lucy told them where they would find her purse and Josh ran up the stairs. He returned with it a minute later and emptied it on to the kitchen table.

Clem scowled at the coins disgustedly. 'We've got more than that ourselves. Where's the rest of it? You must have saved something!'

'That's all there is. What I've saved is in the bank. What you see is all I need. I've only myself to keep.'

Clem jerked his head at Josh. 'Get upstairs again and see what you can find that we can pawn or sell.' As Josh set out, Clem called after him, 'And don't be all bloody night! We want to be well on our way by morning!'

Lucy thought she saw a way of ending this torture. Could she turn one against the other?

Josh returned after ten minutes carrying a pillowslip filled with a collection of items, from a clock to Andrew's gold cufflinks. He turned them all out for Clem to see. 'We'll get a few pounds for them.'

Lucy whispered, 'You'll never walk to Newcastle by morning if you have to push Clem.'

Clem snapped, 'Shut up!' And to Josh, 'She's trying to split us.'

'I know,' answered Josh, but he did not look at Clem and chewed at his lip. Clem knew he was thinking over what Lucy had said.

Clem grinned. 'We won't be walking, anyway. Your daughter

here, she drove the old man to the yard every day, his regular chauffeur. You saw her. So now she can drive us up into Scotland.'

Josh laughed. 'Aye! In that big motor car. Like proper gents!' He dashed upstairs again and found motoring coats for all of them.

Lucy had to show them to the old coachhouse where the Rolls was kept, Clem beside her holding the rope as if he led her on a leash. The rain had stopped and clouds scudded across a sky filled with stars. He took off the lashing so that she could swing the starting handle. As the engine fired he and Josh cheered ironically.

For a moment Lucy had a yard of space and she broke and ran. Clem cursed and Josh chased after her, but she was going away from him. She ran off the gravel of the drive on to the turf, and slipped on greasy mud, one foot caught behind the other and she fell.

Josh pounced on her and dragged her back to the Rolls and Clem. He slapped her across the face so that her ears rang. 'You won't do that again.'

They bundled her into a motoring coat, Clem snarling, 'Don't say you're too cold to drive!' They pushed her into the driving seat and used the line to lash her to it. Lucy could steer and reach the controls but was unable to lift an inch from the seat. Clem used the strength of his arms to lift himself into the seat beside her while Josh shoved the wheelchair into the back with the pillowcase of stolen goods and climbed in after them.

Clem issued one last warning: 'If we have to stop, you watch what you say. Give us away and I'll swing for you.' He showed her the spanner he had taken from the toolbox, then hid it under the rug covering his knees. Lucy sobbed and drove off into the night. She doubted if there was enough petrol in the tank of the Rolls to carry them to Scotland, but she said nothing.

They passed through Newcastle and were into the Cheviot hills far to the north of the city when the first grey light edged the eastern horizon. At any other time Lucy would have found

the rush of cold, clear air and the beginning of a new day exhila-
rating, but now she was afraid for her life. She did not believe
Clem would let her go free to tell her tale. She had to escape, but
could see no way.

The countryside had been empty and they had passed only an
occasional trundling lorry. The road became a switchback of
steep hills, slow, grinding climbs succeeded by plunging descents
when the Rolls wound up to sixty miles an hour at Clem's urging.
He beat on the dashboard before him with his free hand and
roared, 'Go on!' His other hand still held the spanner. Lucy was
in no haste to reach the end of the journey, but had no choice but
to obey.

The Rolls topped yet another hill and accelerated down the
other side. The road ran straight as a ruled line, but at the foot
of the hill wound a stream crossed by a hump-backed stone
bridge. A church and the houses of a village were clustered on
both banks of the stream. As the Rolls bore down on the village
Lucy saw a farm cart was stopped on the narrow bridge, blocking
it, with a little crowd of people standing around it.

Josh shouted above the windrush of their passage, 'There's a
pollis!' The helmet was unmistakable, lifting above the heads of
the crowd.

Lucy automatically slowed the car, but Clem detected a
reduction in speed and yelled, 'Keep going! Faster! Faster!' He
brandished the spanner.

Lucy obeyed but cried desperately, 'We can't cross the bridge!'

'We're not going to try!' Clem pointed with the spanner.
'There's a turning along here on the right!'

Lucy had seen it already, a road even narrower than the one
they were on, running between drystone walls, but she protested,
'We can't turn at this speed.' The crowd floated up towards her,
pink faces above dark clothing, the knob on the policeman's
helmet glinting in the pale sunlight. The Rolls bore down on
them at thirty yards a second.

Clem shouted, 'Damn you! Turn *here!*' He reached across,

grabbed the wheel and dragged it around. The nose of the Rolls swung into the turn but Lucy felt the seat rising under her, saw the earth canting over and realised the car was falling over on to its side. She held on to the steering wheel with one hand, but flung up the other arm in front of her face to protect herself before she was thrown against the wheel . . .

She became conscious of voices around her, at first a confused jumble: 'The driver's a woman. I think she's coming to.'

Another, deeper voice: 'The other two are finished. Not surprising. I reckon that motor car was making better than fifty miles an hour.'

The lighter voice again: 'Good God! She's tied in!'

'What?'

'Look here, man! She's lashed into her seat wi' a length o' rope!'

The policeman came to see Lucy in the cottage hospital where she was taken. He listened to her story and afterwards said, 'It looks to me as if that rope saved you from breaking your neck or summat near as bad. The two men were tossed right across the road.'

The Rolls was dented and scarred but otherwise intact, and a police driver took it back to the Buchanan house. Physically Lucy had suffered only severe bruising, but there was an inquest into the deaths of Josh and Clem, with Lucy testifying as the principal witness. She broke down while giving evidence and told exactly how it was, including her treatment at the hands of Clem and Josh. At the end the coroner delivered a verdict of death by misadventure and told her, 'You have lost your father and husband in awful circumstances, but you are young. I urge you to put this behind you and make a new life for yourself.' Privately he considered them both evil men, and thought Lucy could count herself fortunate to be quit of them.

Lucy returned to the Buchanan house, which was home to her, and lay alone in its emptiness. Start a new life? How? Where? Immediately after the crash she had known horror and soaring relief, had realised that Nick had been right. She should have put distance between herself and evil, got away from Clem and Josh, gone to the other side of the world if need be. Now she felt no joyous sense of release. She would try to make a new life for herself, but knew it would not be easy. She could not desert Andrew.

It was to become harder still.

Chapter Twenty-Five

AUGUST 1918

'I wonder if you would care to call to discuss a personal matter? It is one which much exercises the minds of my sister and myself and we would be grateful for your assistance. The bearer of this note will wait for a reply.' The copperplate writing was spidery and shaky and at the end abandoned formality: 'Do come if you can, my dear, we are both worried sick.' It was signed, 'E. Whittaker'.

Lucy thought, Teddie. That was short for Edwina. She occasionally saw the two Whittaker sisters, Teddie and Binkie, Helen's aunts and guardians. They would drive past the hospital in their Humber motorcar, the chauffeur at the wheel, and wave to Lucy. They had cared for Helen since she was sixteen and following the death of her father, their brother. Teddie had chaperoned Helen and Nick when they went to London – but that had been a long time ago in the days of peace and the thought hurt Lucy now.

She wiped her brow on her forearm. The sleeves of her dress were rolled up and her hands thick with soap suds and smelling of carbolic. She was helping to scrub out one of the wards. On returning to the house she had thrown herself into whatever work she could find and soon a great deal came her way. The anticipated big push came in Flanders and the enemy launched a massive attack of his own. Some of the doctors and nurses working in the Buchanan house were sent to France. The doctors were not replaced and the new nurses were young, inexperienced and needed all the help they could get.

Lucy was busy every waking hour – and slept little. She had sat up late the previous night with one of the new VAD orderlies, a young girl away from home for the first time. Lucy had cheered her and sent her off to sleep in a happier mood. It was not the first time she had done this.

Now she looked at the bearer of the note, one of the maids from the Whittaker house, almost as old as the ladies themselves. Lucy wondered for a moment what was behind the call. Was one of them ill? But they would have sent for a doctor. There was no point in wasting time in guessing, and she had to go, could not refuse them help if she could give it. However, she was to doubt the wisdom of that decision later. 'Please tell Miss Whittaker that I will call on her and her sister this afternoon at three if that will be convenient.'

'Yes, ma'am.' The maid, almost old enough to be Lucy's grandmother, bobbed in a curtsy and pattered away. Lucy blinked, not used to that treatment.

Major Faraday passed Lucy, overworked himself being now the only doctor as well as having command of the entire staff. He paused to say, smiling, 'You look taken aback, Mrs Nolan.'

Lucy laughed. 'I'm not accustomed to maids curtsying to me.'

'Well, you are the housekeeper here, and a bit more than that.'

'That's my job. I haven't changed.' But now she wondered if she had.

Faraday agreed, 'No, you haven't, but that gesture of respect is like saluting: it's not for what you are but for what you do. And you do a lot around here. We value you.' He went on his way.

Lucy decided it had been kind of him to say what he had, but she had only done the work that came to her hands. She picked up her scrubbing brush and got down on her knees again.

At three that afternoon Lucy presented herself at the Whittaker house. She wore a summery cotton dress with a mid-calf skirt and a wide-brimmed hat to shade her from the afternoon sun. The old ladies received her in a drawing room looking out on the front of the house. Edwina – 'Teddie' – who had written the note, was the younger. Lucy, dredging in her memory for what she had been told about them, guessed Teddie would be seventy-eight at least. Her sister, Binkie – Lucy again wondered briefly what the diminutive stood for – looked older, and had a walking cane propped against her chair. Both were frail in black dresses that brushed the floor, and white lace collars. Teddie wafted a fragrance of lavender water and Binkie was redolent of cologne.

Both greeted her eagerly, seated her and gave her tea, then Teddie explained, 'It's dear Helen . . .'

They showed Lucy the letters. Helen had always written regularly every week, but since March they had been despatched intermittently. The last had been three weeks ago. Until March the letters were two or three pages long, cheerful and newsy. Since then they were briefer, staccato. Lucy recalled that it was about that time that Will Ogilvie was killed. One was livelier than the others. It began: 'My Dears, I'm married!' Lucy read no further. A newspaper cutting of the wedding announcement was pinned to it. Binkie sniffed, 'We were so pleased to hear of the wedding. But then the dreadful news about Nicholas . . .' The tears came again.

Lucy flicked through the rest of the letters. The last was little more than a note promising to write more later.

Binkie mopped at tears with a scrap of lace handkerchief. 'We're sure there's something wrong.'

Lucy suggested, 'Why not write to her commanding officer and ask how she is?'

Teddie shook her head worriedly. 'But that's just it, my dear. She hasn't got a commanding officer now. This came yesterday.' It was a single sheet of paper. Helen said she had left the service and would be writing soon. The address was c/o Mme Dubois in a village in France.

Binkie pleaded, quavering, 'Will you go and see her?'

The idea of going to war-torn France did not alarm Lucy because she knew that, out of gunshot at the lines, she would be as safe there as at home. Patients at the hospital had told her this. And it would be easy enough to look up this house of Mme Dubois. But Lucy recoiled from the idea of seeking out Helen, this woman whom Nick had turned to after he had made passionate love to herself, but she could not voice that reason. When she recovered her breath she explained why she did not think it possible. Searching for reasons, she began with the obvious: Helen was in France.

Teddie replied to that one: 'But that's exactly why we are asking you to go. Binkie and I could not possibly consider such a journey. And dear Andrew always says how competent you are.' Lucy knew that Andrew would want her to go. The two old ladies waited so anxiously for her decision. She could not refuse them and did not look for further excuses. She agreed weakly, 'I'll try.'

They accepted that as a solution to the entire problem, pressed money on her for the journey and a signed letter of authority stating she was acting on their behalf.

Binkie, relieved and smiling through her tears, said, 'We'll be able to sleep at peace now.'

Lucy told Major Faraday of her projected journey and he gave her some advice and a letter to take with her. She got another letter signed by Andrew Buchanan, slightly recovered, attesting that she was his housekeeper and trustworthy, and took from his desk, carefully wrapped, the telegrams advising the death of Murdoch and that Nick was posted missing. She added the newspaper cutting announcing the wedding of Nick and Helen and packed these with a few clothes in a small suitcase.

In London Lucy shuttled between the War Office and the Admiralty, showing her documents and explaining her mission. It was weary, exasperating work, being passed from one official to the other, but Major Faraday's letter gained her a hearing with the Army, and the Navy had heard of Andrew Buchanan's shipyard and were impressed by his interest.

At the end of two days Lucy stood on the deck of a ferry crowded with troops as the ship steamed out of Dover harbour. The day was fine but the hour early and the wind was chill. She hugged her lightweight coat about her and reflected bitterly that she was making this journey to enquire about the wellbeing of the widow of the man she had loved — still loved, for that matter.

That had to be faced: the long hours of furious work, the determined attempt to look forward and forget the past, to start a new life as she had been advised, had failed.

She still woke in the night and started up in bed in fear as she dreamt of Clem and Josh abducting her.

She still loved Nick Buchanan.

Mme Dubois lived in a quiet house in a quiet village a long way behind the line; the gunfire was only a distant murmur. There was a neat, flower-filled garden and a long garden seat from which Mme Dubois rose when Lucy pushed open the gate. Madame was tall and regal in a grey dress that reached her ankles. She spoke passable English and invited Lucy to join her on the seat while she explained her errand. Then she said, 'But Mme Buchanan is in the 'ospital.'

Lucy found the hospital. The elderly French doctor told Lucy, 'I am too old for the army, you see.' He had worked for some years in the United States and spoke very good English indeed. 'Mme Buchanan's baby died at birth.'

Lucy stared at him. A baby? Nick's? But he and Helen were only married four months ago. Suppose that he — *before* he made love to Lucy . . .

'Do you feel faint, madame?'

'No — yes.' Lucy was bewildered, hurt. She prevaricated, 'The atmosphere in the hospital, I think, after the open air . . .'

'Ah! Yes, it affects some people, the smell of the disinfectant.' He nodded sympathetically. 'A glass of water.' He handed it to her and Lucy sipped at it. He waited until she returned the glass, then he asked, 'You are better? Good. Now, I must tell you that madame is very ill. It is, what you call, the consumption.'

Lucy whispered, 'Oh, my God!' Tuberculosis was a killer.

The doctor nodded gloomily, and agreed that Lucy could see Helen, but not for too long. 'Ten minutes, no more. That much will cheer her, I think. A friendly face. More will tire her.'

Helen lay in a small room on her own. Her face was white as the sheet that covered her thin body. Her blonde hair was spread on the pillow, lifeless, and her blue eyes were dull, but she smiled weakly when Lucy came to sit by her bedside. 'Lucy!' and then without preamble, 'I lost the baby. Will's baby. I carried him all the way but at the end I lost him.'

Will's baby? 'Yes, I know.' Lucy did not know at all, but she had to be gentle now. 'And I'm sorry. It wasn't your fault.' She held Helen's hand, kissed her and smoothed back her hair from where it stuck to her brow. 'Just lie quiet until you feel like telling me about it.'

'It's lovely to see you. But why are you here? How did you find me?'

'Your guardians sent me. They were very worried about you. I just asked Madame Dubois and she pointed me this way.'

Helen nodded. 'She's sweet, was very kind when she found I was expecting.' She was silent a moment. 'We were going to be married, but Will wanted to wait until the war was over. Then he got a forty-eight-hour leave and we went to Paris and – I got pregnant. Will never knew. I was going to tell him but then he was killed.'

She cried a little at that, weakly, and Lucy soothed her with soft words. Helen said, 'I didn't know what to do, but I knew I wasn't very well. I thought it might be with me expecting, but it wasn't only that, of course. I didn't want to report sick because it was like letting the side down, you know? Expecting a baby and no husband. And then Nick came to see me, right out of the blue.' She smiled a little at that point. 'I told him all about it and he said he would marry me to make things look right. I promised I would give him a divorce later – I believe it's quite easy in America – because I have quite a lot of money, you know.'

Lucy did know and nodded.

Helen said, 'I asked him, I said, "But have you got a girl you're serious about?" He said there was one but she had turned him down. I was pretty low and I just – let him organise things. He got a licence and we were married by an Army chaplain the very next day. Then he went off right after the wedding. Before he left I asked him again about the girl. He didn't say who she was, only that he hadn't given her up but he had a tricky job to do first. And the next I heard was in a letter from his captain, Commander Beauchamp. He'd been our best man. He said Nick was "missing believed killed".'

The Admiralty telegram had gone to Andrew because he was still officially next of kin. Nick had forgotten to change that, or deliberately left it so in order to save Helen from learning any news from some cold, official buff form.

Lucy stroked the girl's limp hand. 'There now, don't fret.'

Helen shook her head. 'No, I won't. But if I don't get better I want to stay out here, close to Will.'

Lucy thought this would not do at all, and remembering the advice given to her, pleaded, 'You've got to try to put all that behind you. You're young and you have all the rest of your life ahead of you. You must look forward.' She could see the doctor hovering and urged, 'I have to go now, but promise me you'll try, and I'll see you tomorrow.'

Helen smiled. 'You are good to me. I promise, and come tomorrow. It's just like the old days, seeing you.'

Lucy left her, turning to give one last wave as she passed through the doorway, seeing Helen's eyes on her, watching her go.

The doctor said to her, 'She looks better for your visit. It has brightened her a little, I think.'

Lucy went back to Mme Dubois, who gave her a room and a meal. She ate little but soup and bread, and went early to bed. She slept well, the whole night through, for the first time in months. She was not happy, thought she would never be happy again, but had found some peace of mind in the knowledge that Nick had not betrayed her.

The next day dawned fine, with a blue sky, and the guns were quiet. Lucy walked to the hospital in the sunshine, feeling rested and alive. The doctor met her at the door and she knew what he would say when she saw his face.

'Madame, I regret . . .' Helen had died only hours before, in the last of the night.

Lucy telegraphed to the Whittaker sisters, informing them, and then saw to the funeral arrangements. She packed Helen's effects that were still in the room next door to Lucy's at Mme Dubois' house. Among them was a photograph of Helen and Will, laughing in the sunlight. They were sitting at a pavement café and Lucy wondered if it was in Paris.

There was a box full of letters, all but two from Will. The others were from Will's squadron commander and 'J.G. Beauchamp, Cdr RNR', Nick's captain. She read that one. Beauchamp tried to appear full of hope that Nick might yet be found to be alive and a prisoner-of-war, but it came through that he did not believe it. The Zeebrugge action had been over some weeks by the time he wrote the letter. He went on to say that Nick had been like a beloved son, and prayed for his survival. Lucy put the letter back with the others.

The doctor came to the funeral, as did several members of the staff of the hospital where Helen had served. A bugler blew the Last Post, the melancholy notes setting Lucy shuddering. Afterwards she set off for home and sat limply weary in a corner in the French train, with its slatted wooden seats, as it puffed its way down to Calais. She thought back bleakly over the last days and months. She felt sorrow, for Helen and Will, for Nick and herself. There was consolation, to which she clung, because Nick had loved her, he had not given up on her, despite her sending him away.

But she had lost him.

Chapter Twenty-Six

NOVEMBER 1918

'Ah! Mrs Nolan. Let me introduce you to Rear Admiral Hawkins.' Arkenstall waved a hand in a welcoming gesture and Lucy advanced into Arkenstall's office at the lawyer's invitation. Andrew Buchanan had been dead and buried this past week and his executor and old friend and shipmate, Lucien Hawkins, had finally returned from foreign service.

'I'm very pleased to meet you.' Hawkins smiled down at her. Like Arkenstall he had a trimly pointed beard but was younger by ten years, in his fifties, dark and almost as tall as Nick. Lucy had never seen him before. Over the years he had visited his old friend Andrew several times but on those occasions Lucy was not at the Buchanan house. During the four years 1904–08 when she had lived and worked there he had been serving on the China station. She was a little afraid of him, though he was not in his full fig of navy blue and gold braid, but wore comfortable tweeds and highly polished brown brogues. It never entered her head that he might be her natural father and she would have been hard put to it to see a resemblance to the clean-shaven young man in the photograph in her mother's Bible. Hawkins took the hand she held out and shook it once. 'Mr Arkenstall has been telling me about you.'

Lucy smiled nervously. 'Oh, dear.'

Hawkins laughed. 'All good, I assure you. If you are ever seeking a berth as housekeeper, you need look no further than myself.' He meant it, was impressed by the girl. Arkenstall and Andrew Buchanan had both spoken of her in glowing terms. And she was a beauty.

Andrew had been lucky to have a girl like this at his side in the autumn of his days. Lucien could only go back to his big house in Devon, empty but for his servants, none of them like this girl. There was something about her, when she looked up at him and smiled, that tugged at memory. He sought to grasp it but saw she was waiting, beginning to colour under his inspection, so he said, 'Please be seated.' She turned away and the moment was lost.

Hawkins and Arkenstall waited until Lucy had perched on a chair before seating themselves. Unlike the men, Lucy could not relax. She was nervous and shy in front of this tall and distinguished stranger.

Andrew's death had been peaceful and expected, so Lucy mourned him but grieved little. She had laid him to rest alongside Nell Jarman and gone on with her work. It seemed that was all that was left to her now. She was still living in the Buchanan house and helping the staff there, but that might change now this admiral had come home to discharge his duty as executor of Andrew's last will and testament. She waited patiently to hear the details.

The will lay on Arkenstall's desk, and now he picked it up and began to read: 'This is the last . . .'

Lucy listened with a part of her mind but her attention strayed to the scene outside the window. Arkenstall's office was on the top floor of a tall old building at the foot of High Street East, overlooking the river. There were ships in plenty there, in partially built skeletons on the stocks or alongside the fitting-out quays. Others, including two destroyers, lay to their moorings and over all wheeled the swooping, squalling gulls. She could just see Buchanan's yard, where Tommy and Billy had worked. She prayed that they were safe. George and Stephen were in

France and in recent letters had said they were well.

Her gaze drifted back into the room and Hawkins looked up from studying his brogues and grinned at her. She smiled back and decided she liked him.

Arkenstall had droned through the list of bequests to clubs, organisations and charities, and although Lucy had no previous idea what would be in the will, none of these came as any surprise. The lawyer went on, '"To my housekeeper and good friend these recent years, Mrs Lucy Nolan, I bequeath the sum of two hundred pounds and an annuity for her lifetime of two hundred pounds per annum."'

Lucy sat stunned. The bequest would buy her a comfortable little cottage. And it was a well-paid man who was taking home two hundred pounds a year.

'"Moreover, it is my wish that, whoever inherits the estate, Mrs Nolan should be allowed to continue to live in the apartments we occupy at present, or such similar as she should agree, for the term of her life."'

She was to remain in that beautiful house – for the rest of her life if she wanted to. Lucy tried to pay attention to the rest that the lawyer was saying but could not concentrate, could not believe her good fortune.

She finally became aware that Arkenstall had finished and that both men were looking at her. The lawyer said gently, 'Was that last quite clear to you?'

Lucy admitted frankly, 'I'm sorry. When I heard that Mr Buchanan had left me . . . I couldn't take it in.'

Hawkins interposed, 'Putting it simply, the estate passes to a distant relative living in Argentina. From what he has written when replying to Mrs Arkenstall's enquiries it appears he is very wealthy already – he's a cattle rancher, I believe – and will not return to this country. He will sell the house and the rest of the estate, but your position will not be affected. Whoever buys the house will have to honour the provisions of the will. However, none of this can happen and the will cannot be settled until the death of the next in the male line is established. A certain length of time has to pass before a person classed as missing can be certified as dead.'

Lucy felt cold. 'You're talking about Lieutenant Nicholas Buchanan.'

'Yes, I am.' Hawkins explained, 'He would have automatically inherited the estate. This chap in Argentina will have to wait until Lieutenant Buchanan—'

Lucy broke in, 'I can't believe he is dead.'

Hawkins had heard this before from stricken widows and parents of young officers, and whilst he understood their baseless hopes, he also knew the reality. He had served in the Boer War with the naval guns put ashore in South Africa, and been an observer in the Russo–Japanese war, before this present mass slaughter. He knew how many missing were anonymous, uniden-tifiable corpses.

He said gently, 'I think at this stage you must be prepared to face his loss.'

Lucy pleaded miserably, 'If he is just "missing", then surely there is a chance he is alive.'

Hawkins explained, 'The action at Zeebrugge was fought in the harbour and a number of men were lost between ship and shore. It may be some time before they are found – if ever.'

He saw that there were tears in Lucy's eyes, and remained silent for a time. This young woman seemed to be mourning more than just a member of the family which employed her. A scandalous affair? He cast that idea aside, because Nick had been straight as a die, and this girl was not the type, either. Hawkins had only just met her, but he could see that much. Maybe she and Nick had harboured a passion kept secret – and unrequited – because she was a married woman? That was possible. He was suddenly reminded of the girl he had loved all those years ago. He wondered if she had remembered him, or had he slipped from her mind after a day or a week?

Arkenstall and the girl were staring at him and Hawkins

smiled at them. He spoke to Lucy: 'You're right, of course. One mustn't abandon hope.'

Arkenstall chimed in quickly, 'Yes, there's always a possibility of survival.'

Lucy knew they had seen her concern and were trying to cheer her, but all they had done was to hand her Nick's death sentence. They were sure Nick would never come back, that there was no hope.

She went back to the Buchanan house and her work. She had little heart for it now, but that did not matter because the flow of cases arriving for treatment had slowed to a trickle. When the great day came, there were only five patients, one for each nurse. They received the news of the armistice and the end of the war in the early afternoon and there was dancing in the wards. Lucy did not know what her position was with regard to the Rolls, and presumed it would be the property of the heir in Argentina — when Nick was proven dead. She shuddered. In any event, the Rolls was not hers, so she walked into town and found the streets filled with celebrations of peace after four years of war.

'We left the tram where it was!' said Florence, her wide-brimmed hat on one side. 'We couldn't get through the streets so we had to leave it. We'll go back and shift it later on.' They were all in Daisy's kitchen. Rose had come straight from the bank and Elsie from the Railway Hotel, where she had already celebrated with the staff, and now wanted to sing and dance.

Rose said, 'Give over!' But she was laughing.

'Mind the gas!' squeaked Daisy as Elsie gave a high kick that almost reached the light.

Elsie whooped, 'What odds! We're having a party!' Little Violet ran about giggling but bewildered.

Lucy watched them, smiling.

Rose declared, 'We'll have a real party when the men get home!'

*

Stephen climbed the steps slippery with mud and walked out of the deep dugout. The big red cross painted on the roof marked it as an advanced dressing station. Now he trod on the duckboards laid over the mud and heard them squelch under his weight. The most extraordinary thing was the quiet. It took some getting used to. The guns had fallen silent two days before, but the silence was still strange after four years. He paused for a moment to look out at the sea, cold and grey in November. On the other side of that sea was his home and Elsie, and he would see them soon.

He walked on, smiling now and stepping out on to the road that led up to the front line, the pavé ringing under his boots. The lorries of the convoy waited to take him and the rest of the staff of the post further up the line. They would be busy for a few days. He had written and told Elsie so and not to worry that he could not write again for a bit. Suddenly his smile was wiped away as if he had seen a ghost.

'I've called you all together for a few final words.' Major Faraday looked round the little circle of nurses and patients. He nodded at Lucy, who stood at one side, then went on, 'Most of you are going home and a few are being moved to other hospitals. I thank you all and wish you well. However, one of us is staying.' He turned to Lucy, and she saw the others grinning over some secret to which she was not privy.

Faraday went on, 'Mrs Nolan, for the past three years you've been the unofficial, unpaid housekeeper for all of us, and the mother, wife or girlfriend we needed so badly. Early and late you've walked through this place, doing what needed to be done, making beds or cheering people. You've been a treasure. So we've decided to leave you with a small memento.'

He took a brown leather case from his pocket and opened it to show a wristwatch. He grinned, 'So sometimes, when you look at the time, you'll remember the time you spent with us. It's inscribed with our thanks.'

Lucy stood in the doorway and waved as the ambulance and cars trundled away. 'Goodbye!' they shouted. 'Thank you, Lucy!'

She mouthed, 'God bless you!' but no words would come. Then they had gone and she turned back into the empty house.

There was work to be done to bring the place back to its peacetime condition, far more than Lucy could manage on her own, but she made a start, with the help of Fred Wilson, the gate-keeper, the only one of the old staff who was still there. At the end of two days they had made the hall and drawing room presentable so that they looked as they had pre-war. The tempo-rary buildings put up in the grounds would have to be dismantled by workmen in due course. Most of the third day was taken up with packing the furniture and other worldly goods of the Wilsons in the motor pantechnicon that came to collect them. Fred had taken the pension left him by Andrew Buchanan, and he and his wife were retiring to a little house in Darlington, where Fred's younger brother kept a pub.

Fred climbed into the back with the furniture: he would ride in an armchair. Mrs Wilson was seated in front by the driver. Fred leaned over the tailboard to say, 'We've known some times, you and me. It must be over twenty years since you first walked in at these gates wi' your mother. I'm going to miss ye. Give us a kiss.' Lucy kissed him and held him tight for a moment, then stepped away. He flapped his cap with one hand and wiped at his eyes with the other as the pantechnicon lumbered out of the gates and out of sight.

The postman came soon afterwards, bearing a postcard from Daisy, posted that morning, inviting Lucy to a party later that day: 'The lads are back!'

When Lucy walked into Daisy's kitchen she found Tommy, Billy and George Fenwick there with the girls, and all of them charged with a mixture of excitement, joy and relief. The girls had laid a high tea of two hot pies, one of meat, the other apple. There were bread and butter, pickles and cake with pots of tea. A coal fire burned in the grate, making the brass fire-irons glint, and with eight of them crowded round the table they soon discarded tunics and cardigans.

Later in the evening the men had beer and the girls shared a bottle of sherry. The first wild celebrations of the war's ending were behind them but they were still in happy mood and laughed a great deal.

The men were not discharged yet, only on leave, but they talked of demobilisation and how soon it might be. George Fenwick was red faced from wind and weather, his chest straining the buttons on the rough khaki flannel shirt. 'It's a damned shame Stephen can't get here, but he had leave back in April, didn't he? This is my first for two years.' He slapped Elsie's back with a big hand. 'But don't you worry, lass. We'll both be home for good soon. First in, first out, that's the rule.'

'You mean we'll all be home!' Billy chimed in. The war had changed him: he was quieter now, but still ready to have his say.

Lucy smoothed down her skirt. She had put on a daydress she had bought at the end of the previous winter, worn it because it was bright and cheerful with a wide collar. Skirts were shorter now, and this one was mid-calf, showing something of her legs and trim ankles in neat shoes. 'Have you heard from Stephen?' she asked Elsie.

'I had a letter a couple of days ago.' Elsie fished it out of her bag. 'He says they're moving up and will be very busy for a time and not to worry if I don't get a letter. And he'll be home soon.' Elsie stuffed the letter back in her bag. 'The rest of it is about what he plans to do.' She giggled. 'Well, most of it is. He wants to get back into the bank and get on. And how he thinks my idea is a good one.' As they stared at her, she went on, 'I'm going to open a café. Down at the seafront.'

Tommy said, 'That'll do well. But me, I just want to get back to work and come home to Daisy every night.'

'Aye, and that's what we want, an' all,' said Florence. 'The men coming back will be wanting the work at the trams, so I'll give it up and make a home for Billy.'

Rose put in, 'And I'll be leaving the bank and doing the office work for George.'

They chatted on, eagerly discussing the lives opening up ahead of them. Lucy finished her sherry and said, 'Well, I'd better be getting back.'

Tommy protested, 'It's early yet, our Lucy.'

'Aye, but it's a long walk,' Lucy pointed out. She took her tweed winter coat, that had cost her twenty-two shillings at Blackett's, from the hook behind the door and Billy held it while she shrugged into it.

They all walked with her down the passage to the front door to see her off. George asked, 'Will you be all right out there on your own?'

Rose laughed. 'She's used to it!'

Lucy agreed, 'Aye, it doesn't bother me.' Josh and Clem were no more, but in any case, it was not people she feared in that house. She saw Elsie shiver; it was chilly out in the street after sitting in the warm kitchen. A wind coming in off the sea was bringing the first spits of rain. Lucy said, 'Anyway, it's too cold to stand talking out here. It's lovely to see you all, but get away inside now – I'm off.' And she left them with a wave of her hand.

'Goodnight, Lucy! Goodnight, lass!' Their voices followed her until she rounded the corner, when they faded and died.

Lucy walked up Church Street and along Roker Avenue to the Newcastle road. The rain became heavier as she passed the Wheatsheaf corner and the lights of the pub there. As she left the town behind, the road became dark, running between hedges and fields, muddy and pocked by puddles she had to step around, holding up her skirts. There was silence but for the huffing of a distant train, then that ebbed away and the only sounds were the sigh of the wind and the patter of the rain. She had forgotten to bring an umbrella and the little hat she wore was soon saturated, wisps of her hair clinging damply to her brow, but she did not care.

Her inheritance meant she would live in comfort all her days, but for all that, she had nothing because she was alone. Tommy and Billy, Rose and Elsie, she had reared them all, brought them this far, and now they had no need of her. They had their own lives mapped out and they seemed to her like a different generation. She was apart, and the other precious people in her life had gone in this terrible war. She would look to see Nick every time she turned a corner.

She was almost in sight of the house. She had wanted to spend all her days there, but that life was over. She had found the one man in the world she wanted — and lost him. The dreams were dead.

The gatekeeper's lodge loomed ahead of her through the rain, empty now like the Buchanan house itself, which was no longer welcoming but hostile, cold and full of ghosts. She would see it soon, had left a light on in the hall against her return.

She had decided to leave the house: it would not be a home now but a prison. She would go away and look for a post as housekeeper elsewhere. Admiral Hawkins had hinted she would find just such a position at his house in the West Country.

Lucy became aware of the lights that spilled their beams around her, illuminating the pools in the road, and then of the rumble of the engine. She was close to the gates to the house but did not cross the road to them. The motor car came up behind her, and she stood aside to let it pass with one hand held up to shield her eyes against the glare. The car slowed and stopped alongside her with a squeal of brakes.

'*Lucy!* It's me! Nick!' The dark figure jumped down from the driving seat of the car and strode around the bonnet, passing through the headlights' beams, to tower over her. 'I'm real! I'd have sent a telegram, but there have been too many telegrams and all of them bad news. And I have too much to explain to put in a telegram.'

Lucy swayed and he reached out to take her shoulders, a big hand on each, steadying. 'Are you all right?' He peered into her face, dimly seen in the glow from the headlights behind him.

'Yes.' Lucy put her own hand to rest on his broad chest, partly to steady herself again, partly an involuntary gesture to confirm he was really there. 'Yes, it's just the – the shock. They said you were missing, believed killed.'

He grimaced, his shadowed face hanging over her. 'They posted me missing because the Germans couldn't find my body. Some Belgian workmen found me. They'd been brought in to clear up some of the wreckage, saw I was alive – just – and got me out hidden in a cart. They fetched a doctor to me, and when I finally recovered I spent the last few months of the war in hiding. If it hadn't finished, I was going to try to get out through Holland, but then came the armistice. A couple of days later I walked into the British lines and saw Stephen Kennedy.' Nick chuckled. 'He thought he was seeing a ghost!' Then, serious and quiet, 'He told me that Clem was dead – and how.'

Lucy nodded, those scars healed now. Nick said, 'That's why I'm here. But I have so much to explain—'

Lucy broke in, 'I saw Helen just before she died. Her aunts were worried about her and asked me to go to France to see her. She told me all about it.'

Nick stared at her, taken aback. 'Our – arrangement, you mean? But I wrote to you, explaining why I'd – I gave the letter to a chap who was coming home on leave for him to post in England because I thought you would get it sooner.'

Lucy shook her head. 'I had no letter.'

Nick muttered, 'Sanderson wouldn't let me down. I wonder if something happened to him?'

Lucy said, 'It doesn't matter about the letter, Nick.'

'But it explained why I was marrying Helen and about the divorce. I thought it was something I should do, for Helen's sake, and I was sure you'd understand and—'

'And I'd sent you away,' Lucy finished for him. 'I know. I was wrong. I'm sorry, my love.'

His arms were about her now. 'I always said I'd come back for you, one day.'

'I know that, too.'

The engine of the car was still ticking over and Nick felt at the dampness of her coat. 'You're soaking! Come on, let's get inside.' He lifted her into the car, his hands around her waist, and climbed into the driving seat. 'A chap I met on the train lent me this car. He'd been in one of the offshore boats at Zeebrugge. His father was waiting for him at the station with this. They drove back to their place in Ashbrooke then said, "Fetch it back tomorrow."'

He swung the car in at the gates and drove up the drive. The light in the hall glowed out from the windows on either side of the front door, and another glow showed where the fire, made up earlier, still burned in the drawing room at the front of the house.

Nick parked at the foot of the steps. The house now looked warm and welcoming to Lucy. He switched off the ignition and they ran across to the front door together and passed inside. Nick took Lucy's coat and hung it up with his own. She walked into the drawing room and reached up to close the curtains against the world, then went to join him in the firelight's glow.

Lucien Hawkins, advised by a letter from Arkenstall that Nick had survived and would inherit, wondered about Nick and the girl, Lucy. If they were lovers, as he suspected, then he wished them well. He had become fond of the girl, no matter how little he knew her. If he had been blessed with a daughter . . .